*Pra*

**PICTURI**



"A compelling exploration of t
into darkness and destruction
and a page-turning plot, this emotional story is one I
to put down."

—JILL SANTOPOLO, author of *The Light We Lost*

"Weaving together themes of love and loss, seduction and control, this beautifully written novel is a must-read."

—AUDREY INGRAM, author of *The River Runs South*

"Grey is back to break our hearts in the most wonderful way. *Pictures of You* is a knockout. Five stars are simply not enough."

—KERRYN MAYNE, author of *Lenny Marks Gets Away with Murder*

"Whip-smart, punchy, urgent, profoundly affecting, and utterly unforgettable. A masterclass on how to write compelling fiction."

—TESS WOODS, author of *The Venice Hotel*

"The sort of book that blocks out the rest of the world, with Grey's trademark warmth and sparkling insight."

—KATE SOLLY, author of *Tuesday Evenings with the Copeton Craft Resistance*

*Praise for*

**THE LAST LOVE NOTE**

"Relatable, hilarious . . . a book to make you laugh and cry."

—OPRAH DAILY

"Grey's novel will break readers' hearts, taking them on an emotional ride but leaving them feeling hopeful."

—BOOKLIST (starred review)

"What a gorgeous, charming, funny, triumph of a read."

—KATHERINE CENTER, author of *Hello Stranger*

"Beautifully blindsiding . . . a touching page-turner."

—HAZEL HAYES, author of *Out of Love*

# PICTURES OF YOU

A NOVEL

EMMA GREY

Zibby Books
New York

*Pictures of You: A Novel*

 Published in the United States by Zibby Books LLC, New York.



Library of Congress Control Number: 2023946340
Paperback ISBN: 978-1-958506-46-2
Hardcover ISBN: 978-1-958506-47-9
eBook ISBN: 978-1-958506-48-6

Book design by Neuwirth & Associates
Cover design by Graça Tito

www.zibbymedia.com

Printed in the United States of America
10 9 8 7 6 5 4 3 2 1

For seven-year-old Hannah, who told me
not to give up on my dreams

And for twenty-six-year-old Hannah,
who helps me unfold them

*This novel contains sensitive and difficult subject matter. Please read with care. For more, see the Author's Note on page 407.*

# Prologue

My hand fishes surreptitiously through my bag for my phone while a string quartet plays Albinoni's "Adagio" and reduces everyone around me to tears. My throat is aching from the stress. I try to wring moisture out of dry eyes, judgment burning from all corners of the Mary Immaculate Catholic Church in Waverley, and I fight the urge to escape.

I simply cannot be here.

*Shouldn't* be here.

I don't know these people. Not my mother-in-law, Gwendolyn, dabbing her eyes beside me in that careful way that prioritizes the integrity of your mascara over letting go of any real emotion. Not her husband, who hasn't said a kind word to me since I woke up in the hospital a week ago. Not the Gucci suits fidgeting in the pews behind us, glancing at watches and mourning the passing of billable six-minute increments.

And not Oliver Roche. Gloriously good-looking, wildly successful commercial lawyer. Property investor. Philanthropist and taker of extravagant skiing holidays and European shopping trips, according to the "celebration of life" slideshow in which I am currently costarring on the big screen.

*Love of my life, apparently.*

Romantic evidence is blaring in polished, cinematic glory. There I am, growing up at warp speed beside him in the

PowerPoint. He's at his shiny best, all through school and university, on sports fields, at work, socially. I can't help wondering what it would be like if the accident had claimed my life too, and these same people had to scramble together some sort of highlight reel about *me*.

A large teardrop diamond flashes on my left ring finger. Gwendolyn, urging me to wear it, frowning as though she couldn't understand why I wouldn't want to, said it wasn't safe to leave the rings lying around at home. I try to feel grateful for it. For all of this. This luxurious life that Oliver and his family brought me into, even though I can't imagine the steps I must have taken to get tangled up in it.

She looks my way for a second and I strive to squeeze out some sadness. If I concentrate really, really hard and bore the images into my brain of Oliver and me tapping champagne glasses at our engagement party, and the way he looks at me in that wedding photo—like I am *the world* to him—perhaps I'll remember?

But as sunlight streams through stained-glass windows and bounces off the handles of the elaborate mahogany-and-brass coffin, roses trailing up the aisle Royal Wedding–style—every aspect of this showy farewell is another beacon of the kind of excess I loathe—I don't feel anything. Except guilt that I am not the perfect widow.

My heart quickens as I imagine the lavish reception the Roches planned for afterward. It sounds like a Who's Who of Sydney's high society. I'll be expected to make small talk with the kind of people I've only ever known from magazine covers and social pages while I continue, in vain, to search the room for Mum, Dad, and my best friend, Bree, who I desperately wish were here and who I've completely failed to reach. It's as if I am dead too. Or trapped in some fever-induced nightmare from which I'm longing to wake up and can't.

But there's no fever. I'm not sick. And their inexplicable absence is snowballing even more panic—adrenaline coursing, nausea brewing, until I can't take another second of this whole performance. Which brings me to my phone, the Uber I ordered during the Lord's Prayer, and the fact that I am about to cause a major scene as I bolt out of here like some rebellious millennial runaway widow, straight through a throng of paparazzi outside the church. I'm about to hand them the scandal they all seem so breathless for . . .

# 1

***One week earlier***

Last night's party is still throbbing in my head as I scramble awake, a tsunami of remorse crashing over me. Whatever I did that made me feel this horrendous, I will *never* do it again.

The worst part is, I don't even recall having fun. But then, I'm a person who normally spends Saturday nights drinking raspberry tea and debating costuming inaccuracies in period dramas on Facebook. Not loving a wild party isn't far off script.

I make the mistake of inching my head to the right. Pain shoots into my eye sockets and I want to die. *My* poor brain. Is it true that alcohol kills brain cells, or is that an urban myth? I don't actually remember drinking last night. Certainly not enough to make the world feel this heinous.

*Please don't let me have been drugged.*

I wish whoever owns that alarm would switch it off. Scratchy, starched sheets bunch into a ridge under my back. As I wriggle, the plastic mattress beneath me squelches, and the tube that's sticking out of my hand pulls at my skin where the tape is stuck.

My eyes shoot open. Harsh fluorescent lights bounce off stark white walls around me. A tangle of cords and wires and an oxygen mask dangles where my thrifted scarf collection is meant to be draped romantically over the headboard with fairy lights. Where is the framed *Pride and Prejudice* poster of Jennifer Ehle and Colin Firth? Breanna says it is one of the many reasons I will never get a boyfriend. Admittedly, getting a boyfriend seems like the least of my problems right now . . .

I try to sit up. Pain sears across my chest, forcing me back against the bed. My mouth is so dry, I can't even clear my throat as my heart pounds and the beeping from the machine beside me gallops. A blond nurse in blue scrubs and Crocs rushes over, presses buttons to silence it, and looks at me kindly.

"Hello, Evelyn," she says, glancing at her watch. "I'm Liz."

"Where am I?" My voice is groggy, like I've emerged from some sort of swamp. "I want my mum," I squeak out. I sound like a five-year-old, gripped by separation anxiety at kindergarten. Liz places a gentle hand on my shoulder as I try to straighten my spine and act my age, but the pain makes me wince.

"You're in Saint Vincent's Hospital in Sydney. I'm afraid you've been in a car accident."

Oh, God. *Breanna* . . .

Liz checks the tube sticking out of my hand, which trails past purple bruises on my wrist up to a bag of fluid hanging from a metal pole. My gaze travels from the drip and snags on an unfamiliar scar on my hand, just as my hair tumbles across my face. Dark. Is it *colored*?

Who dyed my hair? I must have done it. Drunk. I take back that thing about wanting Mum. She's going to kill me . . .

"Who was I with?" I ask. "In the car?" I can barely get the question out. What if Bree is *dead*? What if I killed her?

Liz signals to a doctor in the corridor, who looks like she belongs on the set of *Days of Our Lives* instead of in a frenzied emergency room. She sweeps into my cubicle, shunts blue papery curtains closed for privacy, then stands at the end of my bed like the grim reaper.

"Evelyn, I'm afraid we have some very difficult news."

I glance at Liz, whose upbeat expression has evaporated in favor of the Bad News Face: kind eyes, serious frown, tilted head.

I feel like I am going to be sick. And I have a phobia of that, which makes my stomach churn and my anxiety skyrocket. *Where is Mum?* I need her whether she's going to kill me or not.

"Your injuries are fairly minor," the doctor explains, even though every part of my body is blaring otherwise. "Sadly, Oliver took the brunt of the impact."

*Who?* Don't tell me I finally got a life and snuck out of the party with some boy?

"The airbags deployed, but they're not always enough. Your husband sustained a very serious head injury."

My *what*?

Everything swims. The room. Her voice. My tenuous grip on reality.

"We did everything we could . . ."

Cartwheels tumble through my mind, gathering speed with every passing phrase. She must have mixed up the hospital records. Walked into the wrong room?

"Evelyn, we're deeply sorry for your loss."

Really, it's perfectly okay, because I have obviously *not* had a loss.

"First, it's Evie," I explain. "And second, I don't have a husband!"

There's an awkward pause. I'd fill it with my views on marriage—that it's an archaic, patriarchal trap that made sense only in Jane Austen's day—but it doesn't seem like the right time. Especially since they are both wearing wedding bands. I sneak a glance at my left hand to double-check for a ring, but it's just the tubing, tape, and that weird scar. How could these people think I'd be crazy enough to get married at my age? It's probably not even legal.

The two of them exchange a pointed glance before Liz scurries off. The doctor settles in on the plastic chair by my bed and smiles at me. It's a smile that says *We're sending for reinforcements.*

She makes polite conversation, avoiding the topic of my deceased imaginary husband, asking things like where I live. *Newcastle.* And what year it is. *2011, obviously.* Did we not watch Will and Kate's wedding just the other week?

"It's expected you'll be a little confused," the doctor says.

I'm not at all confused. They just have their information wrong. Hospital debacles happen all the time on *Grey's Anatomy.*

When nurse Liz returns after about ten years of uncomfortable small talk between the doctor and me, I notice the bags under her eyes, blond tendrils tumbling from messy hair that screams "double shift" and "prone to clinical errors." She's brought with her a man in beige corduroy slacks and a wrinkled off-white shirt, also with a rehearsed smile. These people look like they are on their last legs. No wonder they're making mistakes.

"Hello, Evelyn," the man says, picking up my chart. "I'm Dr. Gordon from psychiatry."

*Psychiatry?*

"How are you feeling?"

"A bit sore, but otherwise normal," I report. Emphasis on *normal.*

"Looking at the notes on your chart, we're a little concerned about your memory."

And I'm a little concerned about him! How can a specialist believe a schoolgirl is married? "There's nothing wrong with my memory." I struggle to sit up straighter, as if they'll take me seriously with better posture. "I can literally remember what I ate for lunch yesterday in the cafeteria. Sausage roll with sauce and a chocolate bar. I eat so much junk, I'm just lucky I have an amazing metabolism. I eat like a horse and I'm still an extra small!" I pat my stomach through the thin sheet as if to demonstrate said overachieving metabolism, and that's when I realize something is wrong. There is . . . *more of me* than there was yesterday. I lift up the sheet to investigate. Yes. Pleasantly curvier hips. A slight rounding to my stomach. I drop the sheet. What has *happened* to me in this car accident? It's like I've been redistributed!

The psychiatrist is studying me closely.

"I'm not extra small," I admit. "How did that happen?"

Liz chuckles and pats my arm.

I envision having been in a coma. Maybe they fed me through a tube and gave me too much sustenance for my activity level. Perhaps the car accident triggered my metabolism to go into shock, and of course, lying around on this bed for weeks or months, I'd be out of shape.

"When exactly was my accident?" I ask. The timing suddenly seems critical, because the only other explanation here is that I've had body dysmorphia all this time and I've finally snapped out of it.

"Yesterday," Liz replies. "You're doing really well."

*Yesterday?* I lift the sheet to inspect myself again, only to be newly baffled by the *boobs*. "That simply cannot be right!" I mutter. I mean, I had boobs yesterday, obviously, but not like *this*. I must be a C cup! "Where have the extra two cups come from overnight?"

All three glance at the plastic tumblers on the bedside table, striving to keep up.

"Evie, how old are you?" the psychiatrist asks.

"Sixteen. But something is very wrong."

He puts his clipboard on the bed and places his hands in the position of prayer, tapping his fingertips against his nose in thought, as if this is the first time in his career that he's encountered someone who has changed shape overnight. "I know this might come as a shock," he divulges after a long pause, "but according to your driver's license and medical records, you're twenty-nine."

*Twenty-nine?* "See, there you go! You've clearly mixed me up with someone else. I don't even have a license, only my learner's permit."

He nods. But not to agree, to placate me—I can tell. "This sort of confusion can be common after a car accident."

He goes on, but I've stopped listening. There is just no way that I am twenty-nine and married. Or whatever it's called when your husband is dead. Widowed.

"I'm opposed to marriage!" I argue. "I am one hundred percent a career girl. I haven't even finished high school. I can't be *twice my age*."

As I shake my head, another wave of hair falls across my face and I sweep it away, then grab it and look at the color more closely. It's definitely not my natural shade. But I've never dyed it, because Mum won't let me. Not even pink for crazy hair day.

"Is there a mirror?"

Liz leaves the room and returns with a compact.

I flick it open and confront the frantic woman—yes, *woman*—staring back at me with shocked blue eyes.

"Fuck!" I say. "Sorry." It's an immediate detention if the teachers catch you swearing.

It's not just the red mark on my neck from the seat belt. Or the dark hair. It's that my freckles have faded, the way Mum always promised they would. And there are tiny creases around my eyes and mouth. They're not full-on wrinkles or anything—in fact, they're sort of hard to see, because everything is slightly blurry. I squint at my reflection and Liz asks if I want my glasses.

"Oh, I don't wear glasses," I brag, just as she passes me a pair of sleek tortoiseshell Prada frames I couldn't possibly afford, which bring everything into perfect focus.

And by "everything," I mean the unbelievable set of facts that I appear to be an adult woman with prescription lenses, fine lines on my face, additional pounds on my frame, and a dead husband I never wanted.

# 2

Half an hour later, my medical team is still parading in and out of my room as I sift through a stylish Gucci tote for my phone. I fling everything onto the bed, producing a stash of luxury makeup, keys to a Jeep, and a small white flip-top case containing a useless set of headphones without cords.

There's a phone, but it can't be mine. It's so big. And there's no ON button! I'm swiping my finger all over the giant screen when it suddenly springs to life and I'm confronted with thirty-eight missed call notifications and a barrage of messages.

"What just happened?" I ask Liz, who's checking my blood pressure. Again.

"It's face ID."

*Like in science fiction?*

"It recognizes your face," she says. "You would have set it up when you first got the phone."

So my phone knows me better than I know myself? I'm madly scrolling through my contacts list now, desperate to call Mum to tell her the bad news: I'm old.

And the good news: I'm awake!

And the other bad news: Her son-in-law is dead.

*Son-in-law!*

My finger hovers over his name in my contacts list. Oliver. Evidence that what they are telling me might be true. If it is, I wonder how many thousands of times I might have dialed this very number and discussed something marital, like what was for dinner or whether he'd remembered to pay the gas bill. Perhaps the screen would light up with his name and my heart would skip a beat like it does for women in novels, because we were the type of couple who direct-debited all our bills and left phone calls purely for romantic exchanges like "Pack a bag, Evie, I'm sweeping you off for the weekend!"

The temptation is too great. I touch the name and hold the phone to my ear. Perhaps it will shift something about this huge cosmic mistake the universe appears to have made and bring him back?

Voicemail clicks in. "You've reached Oliver Roche. Leave a message."

It's a deep, no-nonsense, *manly* voice and I'm horrified to think I was married to it. To *him*. I'm also a tiny bit disappointed that I chose a partner with such an unimaginative recording. My own is an effervescent triumph! I rehearsed it at least seventeen times until it sounded spontaneous. That gives me the idea to listen to my own recording now and check what theatrical feat I pulled off more than a decade later.

"You've reached Evelyn Roche. Leave a message."

*Evelyn?* I never call myself that. And Roche? Not Hudson?

Not to mention the wording is oddly identical to Oliver's bland script. I play it again. "You've reached Evelyn Roche . . ." On its third play, I'm wishing I *could* reach Evelyn Roche and ask her why her voice is so flat and her message so formal. I thought I'd sound more excited by life at twenty-nine.

I go back to my contacts and scroll to *M* for Mum. Just

seeing her name on the screen triggers an avalanche of relief and comfort. I tap the number, fast. Maybe she's already on her way to Sydney from Newcastle. Surely they called my parents as next of kin since my so-called husband is . . . well, I can't even bring myself to say it.

"Evelyn," says an unfamiliar voice as the call connects.

"Hello?"

"You're awake," the woman states.

"Sorry, who is this?" I pull the phone away from my ear quickly to check that I really dialed Mum's number.

"It's Gwendolyn. We're on our way."

The line goes dead and I'm left staring at the screen, which informs me that the conversation took exactly eight seconds. More than adequate time to tumble into an abyss. Who *was* that?

"Who is Gwendolyn?" I ask Liz, hoping she has an intimate knowledge of my family tree, but she's triple-checking my pain relief dosage with the psych. "She's on her way in," I explain, my voice shaking when they look up. "With someone else."

Maybe it's the medication they've got me on, but I'm woozy, and that's before I scroll to find that Dad doesn't appear in the list at all! Instead, the only person at that end of the alphabet other than Cleaner and Car Service Place is someone called Chloe, whom I've never heard of.

Oh, here's Bree! Thank *God.* I touch her name and hit the speaker button. "Your call could not be connected. Please check the number and try again."

Liz, clearly well practiced, notices me signaling for the sick bag in a cardboard dispenser on the wall beside her and passes it to me just in time, making the psychiatrist, still buried in his notebook, look up and flinch.

Everything is wrong here.

*Every single thing.*

No father. An imposter mother. No best friend. Boring voicemail. Even the giant phone is all wrong, as if I've woken up in some horrible, unrecognizable *Freaky Friday* reality that I can't bear!

My shaking finger taps something called Uber by accident and the phone asks, *Where to?*

Liz, who has fetched a warm facecloth, sees the open app, smiles sympathetically, and says, "No, Evie, you can't escape just yet."

"Escape?"

"In an Uber. It's like a private taxi service. You can order cars to pick you up from anywhere and take you wherever you want."

From where I'm lying, this Uber sounds *magical*. I wipe my face and try not to cry about the alarming fact that I seem to have been abandoned in a big, bustling, unfamiliar world where strangers aren't even dangerous anymore and we simply get into cars with them.

"Would they take me to Newcastle?" I ask, my voice small. "The Uber people?"

She smiles. "For a huge fee! Look, I know it's scary. But the chances are your memory will return."

"But what then?" If I'm truly almost thirty and my husband just died, I'll plunge straight from this hellish time warp into an equally horrific black hole of grief.

"Go easy on yourself. You've had a huge shock," Liz reminds me. "You were in a traumatic car accident. You've had a deep loss."

But the shock is not that Oliver died, it's that he existed. And the loss isn't about him—it's about everything else.

"We'll do some more tests," the psychiatrist announces.

"Sometimes, during times of extreme trauma, the brain throws you back to a time in your life when you felt safe."

*Yes.* This part I understand. I do feel safe at sixteen. I have parents who adore me. A best friend who sticks to my side like glue. I have goals and plans and meticulously documented dreams, none of which include waking up thirteen years later with dark hair, posh glasses, and a huge phone, totally isolated from everything in the entire world that ever mattered to me.

"If it's dissociative amnesia," he adds, "the memory loss is almost always temporary. It may just take some time and therapy."

"Amnesia?"

"It can help to surround yourself in familiarity," Liz suggests. "Be around the people who care about you and something might flash back."

What people, though? My husband is dead. The people who loved me aren't even in my phone. Gwendolyn sounded like a cross between Miss Trunchbull and Lady Macbeth.

Then I remember the thirty-eight missed calls. Are they from my friends?

I click on my recent call history. But it's all Oliver Mobile. Oliver Messenger Video. Oliver Messenger Audio.

This is useless. I open my camera roll. At first glance, I seem to have taken about twenty shots of the same autumn leaf. *What's wrong with me?*

I scroll back further, hoping for signs of human life.

There are some pictures of someone's kid. A little girl with blond pigtails. Out-of-focus, crooked selfies she's taken. Photos of her laughing and smiling and pulling faces and poking her tongue out. Wonky pictures she's taken of me, all out of proportion and elongated due to the angles.

"Does she look familiar?" Liz asks.

No.

And nor do I.

I shake my head, zooming in on my face. I'm smiling into the lens at this kid, like I love her. Surely she isn't *mine*?

Oh my God, even worse than not having a mum is the impossible idea that I could *be* one! At the very thought, the bottom seems to drop out of my bed. I grab the guardrails, walls spinning, the concept of having a child giving me vertigo. Maybe she's Bree's. Or the kid of some random friend I've forgotten? Perhaps I'm her nanny—that has to be it. This body hasn't gone through *childbirth*, has it?

I kick the sheet off my legs dramatically. Is this a hot flash? No! I'm not *that* old.

I keep scrolling through more photos, desperate for answers. My heart races as my thumb stops, settling on a picture of a man.

Could this be him? Oliver, the husband? *Crazy hot* husband, if I do say so myself. I pinch the screen and zoom. It must be him. What other man would be gazing into my lens as though he adored me?

My focus ambles over his precision-styled blond hair and across the strong contours of his cheekbones. I admire the sparkle in his blue eyes. A beautiful blue. Startling eyes, really. The kind of intense expression and movie-star jaw that younger me would have absolutely fallen for. It's that boy band perfection I secretly idolized.

*Nicely done, Evie. I mean, if you had to sell out and marry someone.*

And now I imagine for the first time how all of this might have unfolded. If a man like *this* singled out someone like me,

I can see how I might have been swayed. Last I knew, there were precisely zero boys on the scene. Breanna told me it was because I was fixated on the 1800s and on academics, and that I became an anxious wreck the second a boy glanced in my direction. And she was right. My No Romance rule was because I was hugely ambitious. I knew exactly how much love my romantic heart was capable of, and the truth was I was scared. Worried I'd meet a boy so magnetic, so utterly charming and charismatic and fascinating and glorious, that he would make a total mess of me. Of my academic plans. Of my big dreams. Losing myself was always my biggest fear. A fear that has suddenly been realized in the very worst of ways, because here I am, having found that kind of love and lost it, leaving me all at sea in a bewildering reality that makes no sense.

"Breathe, Evie," Liz says soothingly, while the heart monitor charges off.

"I think this is him." I show her the screen. "Oliver."

*The victim.*

She takes my phone, then she glances back at me, probably thinking what I'm thinking. *In what universe did* you *pull off a match this triumphant?*

"I'm so sorry, Evie," she says, mouth grim, eyes welling.

Because it *was* a triumphant match. Past tense.

Knowing the girl I was, there's no explanation for the path I've taken other than this romance must have been *it*. An all-consuming, period-drama-rivaling, personal-rule-breaking love story that teenage me had secretly been pining for all along.

And now I've gone and forgotten every blissful second of it.

# 3

"Anderson and Gwendolyn Roche," a man announces from the doorway, as if he's introducing a couple at a stately ball. Enter Macbeth and Lady Macbeth. I would laugh if I weren't so nervous.

"We're Oliver's parents," Gwendolyn clarifies for the benefit of the staff, unaware that her daughter-in-law also appreciates the intel. She is immaculate in a petite navy shift, her slick silver-gray bob and navy glasses framing an ashen face. Oliver's father—a great bear of a man with the same handsome features as his son—clocks the IV drip and the vitals monitor and takes inventory of all my exposed bruises. I tug the hospital gown across where it gapes at the neck.

"Was it fast?" Gwendolyn says in obvious despair. "Did he suffer, Evelyn?"

The heartbreak in her eyes should be reflected in my own. Instead, I'm still struggling with the fact that this woman—so impeccable compared to my adorably hot mess of a mum—has assumed my mother's spot in my phone. In this moment, I understand that I must triage her grief above my own fear, and my voice cracks as I try to let her down gently. "I'm sorry, I can't remember."

"What do you mean?" Gwendolyn asks.

"It's not just the accident," I charge on. "I've forgotten everything."

They stare at me, mouths agape.

"I don't remember you," I confess. "Or even . . . your son."

She sinks onto the visitor's chair as her husband takes a step toward me, and my body braces hard against the mattress, breath quickening. He's all concealed heat and grief and despair.

He quickly turns to the psychiatrist. "What's going on here? Concussion? Amnesia?"

"We're still evaluating," Dr. Gordon says, but Anderson doesn't seem satisfied with that and looks like he's about to challenge him. Gwendolyn reaches for his arm—a plea for calm in this sea of distress they're both drowning in. People shouldn't outlive their children. I want to throw them a life buoy—*it was instant, I'm sure he didn't even know*—but I don't have one. What was that app again? Uber?

"I'm sorry for your loss," I offer helplessly. My gaze struggles to meet my father-in-law's, skittering instead to the white sheet covering my lower body. Flimsy cotton, hopeless at protecting me from this disastrous situation. Or from him. "Sorry for *our* loss," I clarify.

"Are you?" His voice is grave as he blinks hard, stoic sadness fading as anger jostles for supremacy across his features.

"Darling, please," Gwendolyn whispers. "He's beside himself, Evelyn. Of course you're upset about Oliver."

I suspect my mother-in-law's role is to throw buckets of ice on flames. Live power lines lie hidden beneath the wreckage of this family, and I should be careful where I tread.

"Yes!" I assure them. "I mean, I'm sure I will be, once I

remember. After all, we were married for . . ." I pause, hoping one of them will fill in the chronology.

"Five years," she says, quietly.

Right. So I was twenty-four when I walked down the aisle. Young, but not straight out of high school.

"How long will she be hospitalized? When will she get her memory back?" Anderson starts peppering questions. "People are asking us about the . . . arrangements."

Arrangements? Gwendolyn starts crying and I realize he means the funeral. I hadn't thought this chaos through as far as that. Now I'm imagining a chorus of *Sorry for your loss* while I tiptoe through a social minefield, forced to act the part of grieving widow at twenty-nine going on seventeen.

"Can we keep it small?" I beg them. I'm thinking immediate family only. The funeral equivalent of an elopement. Just a brief, graveside service. Us and the officiant.

"Evelyn, we will want to give our son a proper farewell," Gwendolyn says. This sounds like code for No-Expense-Spared, Scary-Big Send-Off.

*Do I even have to go?* I am a fraud, center stage in this family's nightmare.

"Have you had any calls from the media?" Anderson asks, unexpectedly.

I think of the missed calls I'd assumed were from friends and shrug.

Gwendolyn pulls her chair closer, her expensive fragrance overpowering the smell of hand sanitizer and hospital-strength disinfectant. "We are very private people," she explains, placing a beautifully manicured hand on my arm. "I know you have your little podcast . . ."

This is news to me. I once had a true-crime blog that got

about six hits a month, all from my parents. I was fixated on every iteration of *CSI* and *NCIS*. Fascinated by criminology. I should be forensically investigating crime scenes by now, like Temperance Brennan in *Bones*, according to my Big Life Plan.

"Do I also have a job?"

Gwendolyn's eyes flick to Anderson, who clears his throat.

"You need to focus on your health. Now, Evelyn, we don't do drama," he says, as if he's rattling off a family slogan. "Don't offer comment to the media. Not for any price."

I can't imagine why the media would be remotely intrigued. Gwendolyn must read my surprise. "With all this interest in the accident, it's just a little reminder about discretion."

Sweat beads on my forehead. I wipe it with the back of my hand and try not to panic. I don't understand anything that's going on here. Just that, despite the heat prickling through my body, this room is icy, my in-laws don't trust me, and my voice is getting smaller by the second.

It's two in the morning, three days later, and I'm rifling through every cupboard and drawer in my bedroom in an increasingly frenetic search for myself. I've already exhausted the hunt for my parents, but still *nothing*. Just Mum's dormant Facebook account, a mention of Dad in some charity fundraising walk six years ago, and wide-open, terrifying silence. I'm trying to fill that silence with pep talks that I am an adult now. That almost-thirty-year-old me has got this. That any minute, my memory will return, and I'll remember exactly where I left my life.

I arrived home yesterday to the pristine residence I've evidently curated with Oliver, in the company of a private nurse my in-laws booked. It's unclear to me if she is here for my health or to stop me from going rogue on my podcast, and whether this paranoia relates to my current situation or is just part of who I've become. Either way, Sister Maxwell-Smyth won't let me out of her sight during daylight hours, forcing me into these nocturnal shenanigans.

So now I'm nose-deep in Oliver's business shirts. Apparently, scent is one of the most powerful memory triggers, although all I can detect here is dry-cleaning chemicals. Anderson bragged that Oliver was the youngest partner in his law firm's history, and his expensive-looking wardrobe fits the part. My hand travels along the rail, sifting through his clothes until it lands on a three-piece suit. I imagine the man from the photos wearing these gray trousers and this vest, with one of those crisp white shirts and a tie. No, a cravat. I go a little weak at the knees at the thought. And once I locate his jeans and sweaters and mentally dress him in those, maybe with a knitted scarf if we're in the mountains, I've begun a little crush.

It's a pointless exercise, of course. But there's no denying I seem to be widowed to one of Sydney's hottest young professionals. Hopefully there was more between us than physical attraction. Surely midtwenties me would never have relaxed my No Marriage rule for someone who didn't knock it out of the park in every important category.

Our bedroom is immaculate. No books. No photos. Nothing sentimental. On one of the bedside tables, a pair of black-rimmed Hugo Boss reading glasses lends an academic flair to my imaginary husband fantasy. I try them on, but the room is awash. You're not supposed to wear other people's glasses. Particularly dead people—it's weird. So I put them back exactly as I found them and hope his ghost is not observing my every move and questioning why he married me in the first place.

I creep down the hallway. The first room along this corridor is locked, but I flick on the light in the second, remembering that little girl in my camera reel, praying I won't discover a pink, sparkly child's bedroom crammed with soft toys and princess paraphernalia. Relief washes over when I see a recording studio, padded soundproofing covering the walls. There's a large computer screen and microphone on the desk. I sit in the swivel chair and spin. Perhaps I'll shake some sense into my brain and remember all of this.

Beside the keyboard is a notebook, which I flip open. It's full of handwriting. My own. *So* strange to see this window into thoughts I can't recall having. It's all crime stuff. Podcast titles. Topics. Names of people and dates I've scheduled interviews—the last one several months ago. Cases I've researched. Lists of questions. There's a heavy emphasis on forensic linguistics—always my special fascination. I look down the list and see scattered words and phrases, like *forced confessions*, *lie detection*, *forensic voice comparison*, and *linguistic-phonetic studies*. I'm clearly still a total nerd for this stuff.

I pick up a printed production spreadsheet and blow dust off it. The letters *E* and *O* are initialed down the columns beside *recorded* and *edited*. Did Oliver and I produce this together? One phrase on the notepad stands out, because I've circled it three times, but then crossed it out so hard the words are completely hidden. The pen has pressed through the paper and, if I lift a page or two and shine the desk light at a certain angle, I can read the faintly visible words on the page underneath: *ADJECTIVE ORDER???*

It's such a disappointment. I was hoping for some sort of startling, pre-amnesiac clue that might help me crack the case of who I am now and what possessed me to end up in this lavish, sterile world. But I hug the notebook to my chest. Much-needed proof that I'm still passionate about something other than a man.

I find myself face-planted on top of the quilt on my bed the next morning. Oliver's and my bed, to be precise, although I don't even want to *think* about the activities that have occurred in this very location! All my knowledge about romance comes from books and movies. And whatever I've learned right here, with handsome Oliver in his studious spectacles and dashing suits . . .

"Mrs. Roche is downstairs," Sister Maxwell-Smyth announces, startling me from my X-rated imaginings as she bustles in and pulls back the curtains, bombarding the room with light. I sit bolt upright, contemplating how bad I must look after my nighttime scavenger hunt and hoping she can't read minds.

Minutes later, I find Gwendolyn ensconced on the overstuffed cream sofa, blending into it in layered ivory, flicking through a coffee-table book on art and design from the Smithsonian in Washington, D.C. The décor in this room says "styled for open inspection" and I wonder again how my preferences could have changed so dramatically.

"How are you feeling, Evelyn? You look dreadful."

*Wow.*

"Listen, I won't keep you long. I've come about the funeral."

Last I knew, we were organizing our school formal. The idea of putting me in charge of arranging a proper grown-up, media-attracting funeral for the Lane Cove Roches will only result in utter social catastrophe. I'd likely lace it with a montage of Taylor Swift ballads.

"We'll take care of everything," she says, and I exhale in a rush. "But I wanted to give you the chance to be included. Is there some small idea you'd like to share?"

A school science assignment springs to mind, when I researched the environmental impact of various types of burials and cremation.

"You can get biodegradable cardboard coffins," I venture, perhaps more enthusiastically than I should, but I've been overtaken by a sense of having something useful to contribute, at last. "Maybe we could have an ecological bushland burial?"

I might not remember Oliver, but I know the person I used to be. Surely I married the kind of man who wouldn't want to release several hundred excess kilograms of CO2 into the atmosphere through non-environmentally sound burial choices.

"Goodness, Evelyn, we are *not* burying Oliver in a cardboard box!" She shivers at the concept. "Why don't you plant a memorial tree. We have an estate in the Hunter Valley. A boutique vineyard. Perhaps when you're well, we could put you in touch with our head gardener."

*They own a whole vineyard?* The only wine I remember consuming came out of a cask someone snuck into Milly Donoghue's sixteenth before it was shut down by the police. I try to imagine myself strolling elegantly between the vines, tasting wine straight from barrels and talking about "fruity undertones" or "velvety textures," as if I have any idea what I'm sampling.

"I like native plants," I suggest.

Gwendolyn's face drops, communicating that a memorial tree for their son should not interrupt the Roche family's carefully cultivated horticultural aesthetic. "Is there anything else you need?" she asks, in an obvious attempt to change the subject.

Yes. Despite all my attempts to act twenty-nine, I need an enormous group hug with my parents. The kind where they won't let go until I do. The sort of hug I didn't always make time for, because I was always checking some vacuous thing on my phone or dashing out the door, taking them completely for granted. I need my best friend, the girl who rescued me in Year Seven from friendship oblivion when we were paired together for an assignment. The one who became my person from that moment on and saw me through first periods. First crushes. Picked me up off the floor after that one time I failed a math test. She's meant to be picking me up off the floor *now.*

I'm so upset about Mum and Dad and Bree I can't even say their names, even though I'm longing to ask Gwendolyn about the gaps in my contacts list. Instead, I focus on what's around me—or what's not there. "Where are my books?" I'm shocked that I no longer own my battered copies of *Northanger Abbey* or *Anne of Green Gables.*

"You've come to love audiobooks," she says, trying to pacify me. "You told me once they'd become your friends."

"Do I not have actual friends?"

"You and Oliver entertained a lot. Mainly his business associates and their partners. You'd go to the gym and to champagne brunches . . ."

I stare at her. "Who with? Chloe?" That's one of the few names I remember from my phone.

Gwendolyn checks her watch and picks up her handbag. "No, not with Chloe."

As she moves to stand, I grab her arm. "Did I keep in touch with Bree? Breanna Parkinson?"

She gives a sympathetic grimace. "I'm sorry. I don't know that name."

Surely Bree would have been at our wedding? She would have been my bridesmaid!

"You didn't really want lots of people around you, Evelyn. You had Oliver." She pats my arm as she stands up, conversation over.

"Gwendolyn, I do have one more question—"

"You were so lucky," she says, stepping toward the front door, putting space between herself and the question I'm sure she knows I'm going to ask about my parents. "He adored you enough for everyone."

# 4

***Four days later***

*This is my chance.* While everyone's weaving their way to communion at the funeral Mass, I make my break. Peeling off down the side aisle, I gather speed as I hurry between the pillars, hoping that if anyone notices me, they'll assume a sudden need for the bathroom—perfectly understandable, in the circumstances—before I burst out the back doors into the brilliant sunshine and face a horde of cameras. It's reminiscent of that scene in *Notting Hill* when Julia Roberts is unexpectedly exposed to the British tabloid media.

But it's just me: Evie Hudson. Fish out of water in a dimension where I've signed up for everything in life that I categorically oppose and totally lost track of my own narrative. Hot tears sting my eyes and there's not enough oxygen, no matter how much air I try to gorge into lungs that won't expand nearly enough, breaths coming fast and shallow.

The Uber driver, leaning against a big black car, arms crossed defensively, seems to brace against my approach as I push through the cameras and storm toward him. He looks like one of those humorless undercover cops in a gritty British crime show, all brooding hotness, three-day stubble, and dark, troubled eyes. At first sight, I decide he's the kind of guy you warn your best friend about, but she goes and casts herself as the heroine in his redemption arc anyway, locking you into months of pointless debriefing while she tries to work out what's wrong with her.

Bree would love him, if she were here. It's just not like her to fail to show up to one of my crises, or vice versa, and I'd hoped the well-publicized funeral might smoke her out of whichever hole she's been hiding in. Surely the death of a husband qualifies as a full-scale emotional emergency?

"Hey, can we get out of here fast?" I ask the driver as I brush past him. His arms fall to his sides.

I throw open the back door and tumble in, pushing aside an expensive-looking leather bag and tripod. He's still standing there in his crisp white T-shirt and faded brown leather jacket, raking a hand through dark hair now as he stares at the church, and then at his car, giving me a view through the side window of his denim-clad rear. I'm more into Darcy and Knightley, myself, and while this getup is not breeches and a ruffled shirt, it's also somehow not entirely disappointing. Though, as a newly minted widow literally fleeing my husband's funeral, I am in no place to notice. What *is* disappointing is that the man is demonstrating a complete lack of urgency.

I pound on the glass. "Come on!" I shout. "Drive!"

It's only the movement of the media pack toward his car that motivates him, at last, to climb in, glare at me in the rearview mirror, and shift gears. Of course I've ended up with the rebel of Uberville and not some patient retiree who'd assure me everything is all right and my life hasn't, in fact, been catastrophically derailed.

"Hello to you too," the driver says, occupied with not hitting the camera crews that are swarming around the car, firing flashes through the windows. He performs some precision driving and we exit the driveway, pull into Victoria Street, and head for Centennial Park.

"Sorry! I'm not thinking straight." *Where are my manners?*

"Where are we going?" he asks, frowning at me in the mirror before he overtakes an enormous caravan.

"Airport?" I hear myself confirm. It was the first destination in the saved addresses. I didn't have time to construct a fancy itinerary in the church.

I pull out my phone and search for plane tickets. The nurse had advised me to stick to a normal routine in the hope it will stimulate my memory. According to the very enlightening funeral slideshow I've just witnessed, my normal routine involved a lot of jet-setting. Maybe being in the air will spark something. Medically, I'm sure it's fine. I might have lost a few chapters of my memory, but it's not like I'll be flying the plane.

I let my phone automatically fill out the fields to book a flight home to Newcastle, progress to the payment gateway, and watch the wheel spin until it times out. *Payment failed.*

I try again. *Failed.*

"Everything okay?" the driver asks, after I swear under my breath.

His hands clench over the steering wheel before I catch his eye again in the mirror and shoot him a look that says, *I just absconded from my own husband's funeral. How okay can everything be?*

He returns his focus to the traffic. How am I going to pay him without a credit card? The nurse had said Uber was like a taxi service. I've been in a cab only a couple of times and Bree and I paid with cash. Is this the same? And how is my card not working when I can apparently afford this outfit?

I log into my banking app. The phone has my password saved and a hospital social worker had sat patiently beside me and talked me through the authentication. But there's minus $167 in my account! I scroll through the list of recent transactions, revealing a regular pattern of hefty deposits—monthly—from the account of O. E. Roche. Some sort of allowance? And now it's stopped. He must have done these transfers manually.

"Er, could you pull over somewhere, please? My card isn't working," I admit. He doesn't need to know I'm completely broke. "I can't book a flight."

Is he going to assume I also can't pay him and slam on the brakes in the middle of Southern Cross Drive? Lines crease on his forehead in the mirror, and the muscles in his jaw and neck tighten.

Frantically, I go to the Uber app. Maybe it's linked to another credit card or something? I click on the booking and . . . *oh, God.* There's a photo of the driver. Gray hair. Blue eyes. A balding man in his sixties, driving a red Toyota Camry.

I'm seated in a late-model matte-black Range Rover. My driver is in his early thirties at best. Brown eyes. Dark hair. Not even a hint of a bald patch.

My stomach drops. *Am I being kidnapped?*

No, I masterminded this whole thing. My eyes drop to the gear lying beside me on the back seat. Tripod. Camera bag. The glass of an enormous lens glistening in the sun through the open zippered pocket. I feel sick.

"You're not an Uber driver, are you?"

He looks genuinely surprised at my question. "Photojournalist," he responds, his tone strained.

I've delivered myself straight into the hands of the enemy.

# 5

***Drew***

Definitely should have trusted my gut.

If I had, I wouldn't be stuck with a grieving widow on an arterial road in the lunchtime rush, heading in the opposite direction from where I need to be. I feel bad that I stood up a first date. A Tinder match, Sally. Perfectly nice woman according to our chats. A nurse in neonatal intensive care.

That makes it worse, the nurse thing. She probably worked all night being heroic saving babies. Forced herself out of bed when she should be sleeping, shaved her legs, maybe, only to go to the café in Coogee and wait, while I changed my mind at the eleventh hour and got the guts to face my past. One part of it, anyway.

"Hey, Siri . . ."

"Sorry," my passenger interrupts. "I think you've got me confused . . ."

"I'm sorry, I didn't get that," Siri replies.

"Send a message to Sally Engels . . ."

"Okay, how do I do that?" She's pulling the seat belt loose and leaning forward so she can hear me.

"Could you possibly stop complicating my life for five seconds?" I mutter.

"Could you possibly stop complicating my life for five seconds," Siri answers. "Send message to Sally Engels?"

*Bloody hell!*

"Message sending. You can press the crown on your watch to cancel . . ."

*Shit!* A taxi lurches into my lane and I swerve to the left. "Siri! Cancel! Stop! *Delete!*"

"Message sent."

I think I'm losing the will to live.

"Hey, Siri . . . message Sally Engels . . . Sally comma, profuse apologies, full stop . . . unexpected personal problem, exclamation mark . . . face palm emoji . . . exploding head emoji . . ."

I risk a glance into the back seat and am met with a face like thunder.

"Give me a chance to explain, question mark. Send message."

*Where would I even begin?*

I'd been looking for any excuse not to go into that church, until Evie Roche burst out of it and handed me one. What was I meant to do, pull her back out of the car? Feed her to the media? Worse, hand her back to the Roches?

*Yes, Drew. Any of those options.* Then maybe a big part of the past I've worked so hard to forget wouldn't be ensconced in the back seat, a wrecking ball in my love life yet again, acting like she has no idea we used to be friends.

I glance at her now in the rearview mirror. She looks atrocious, even with a six-hundred-dollar haircut and some sort of high-end blazer and skirt, courtesy no doubt of the platinum credit card she's blown to pieces. For someone so put together, the woman is a mess. Fraught. Fiddling with that chocolate blowout with manicured hands. I know that body language. She needs to calm down before she hyperventilates.

Oh, great—and now she's crying.

"Hey, Versace," I say. Anxious blue eyes meet mine in the mirror and a nanoscopic part of me loses its cool. The rest of me isn't so reckless. "Sorry for your loss."

I'm not sorry Oliver Roche is dead. I just can't say as much to his widow. I've read tabloid reports that she has some kind of amnesia—information leaked by a teenage employee in the hospital cafeteria—but this is pretty intense.

"It's Evie," she replies.

I know who she is. I guess I just arrogantly assumed that, after everything we've been through, the awareness would be mutual, despite the blow to her head.

"And thanks," she adds, delivering the words without a shred of emotion. Maybe she's still in shock from the accident. Maybe she's become emotionless. Either way, I won't waste any more time trying to figure out the kind of woman who'd look at Oliver Roche and see marriage material, while remaining so totally oblivious to—

"Who are you?" she asks, cutting off my train of thought in the most ironic place possible.

I can't believe I have to introduce myself. "I'm Drew."

"Are you going to write about me?"

"What?"

"You said you're a journalist."

"Not the kind you need to worry about."

"You said photojournalist. Please don't take pictures of me."

A mental collage of the hundreds of pictures I've already taken of her flashes through my mind. I read up on amnesia the other night. I'm worried if I stampede into our shared history now it will only damage her. I'm not even sure how I'd position the story, given how things ended.

"I'm just trying to give you a lift," I assure her. The statement isn't untrue. "I'm sorry about the exploding head emoji."

I need to bring this nonsensical encounter to a close. But before I can thrash out a solution, the radio cuts to a news break with a reporter outside the funeral.

"It's like a scene from one of her viral podcasts, as popular true crime commentator Evelyn Roche sensationally vanished today from the funeral of thirty-year-old investment lawyer Oliver Roche, who was killed last week when he lost control of the couple's car on Macquarie Pass and plunged several meters into a ravine. Speculation is rife after Ms. Roche, who survived the accident, was seen rushing from the church in Sydney's eastern suburbs, fleeing in a black Range Rover driven by an unidentified man with whom she is rumored to be romantically involved. It adds fuel to the developing scandal around the accident, with sources claiming—"

I jab at the stereo buttons and curse my decision to show up at that man's funeral.

"I was meant to be a forensic linguist," Evie explains, and she's got that right. But it's a weird part of the news story to unpack. I'd have deconstructed the vastly more problematic insinuation that we've got a thing for each other.

"I can't go home—they'll be looking for me there," she says, as she pulls an elastic band out of her bag and shoves her expensive hairdo up as if she's settling in for a night on the couch watching *The Bachelor.* No, not that. *Bridgerton* would be more her style. Then she strips off her blazer. Unbuttons the cuffs of her blouse, rolls up the sleeves, and pulls the shirttails out of her waistband, fanning herself with the fabric.

I switch the AC to max, swivel the vent, and blast cold air into the back seat before she takes anything else off. I'd drop her at the nearest hotel, but she claims she has no money.

"Is there a friend you could call?" I'm dying not to be the one stuck with her. There was a time when I would have done anything for this woman. When she would have phoned me first, even before Bree. But that was before she made it manifestly clear she didn't want either of us in her life anymore. I refuse to get back on this roller coaster.

"I don't know who to trust," she admits.

Surely she has connections these days. Even one of the many thousands of true crime enthusiasts who hang on her every fascinating revelation about psychopaths and mass murderers.

We're overtaken by a convertible, and I notice the passenger is filming us. Have the paps followed us from the church? I accelerate rapidly, threading through traffic until I lose them, heart pounding. I can't allow myself to be linked to her.

"Don't let them find me," she says, echoing my thoughts. She's rattled as hell, and I know it's because of the family. Not the media.

It's not instinct that tells me that.

It's experience.

We're on the M5 when Coldplay's "Fix You" comes on the radio. The opening bars are enough to fling me straight back to the scene Oliver made at their 2012 concert. I've already got my finger over the button to change the station when she pipes up from the back seat.

"Can you put something else on?"

*Does she remember it too?* She can't possibly. Or she'd remember me being there trying to intervene.

"I don't know what it is about that song," she says, shivering. I dial the AC down a notch.

*It was the soundtrack to your first fight.*

"Is it okay if I charge my phone?" It's a rhetorical question as she passes it over my shoulder. "It's on eight percent."

It always is. I grab it from her and plug it into the charger in the front. The car picks up her playlist and starts blasting Niall Horan's "Arms of a Stranger." She's not still obsessed with him at nearly thirty! I'd rib her about it, except the lyrics are cutting surprisingly close to the bone.

"I don't even know if I can trust you," she admits. I need to get my head together. After all this time, surely I can summon enough long-overdue perspective and keep her safe. That must have been some knock to the head. She's so vague, she's practically two-dimensional. How do you just *forget*?

Maybe it's grief.

No. I know grief. You don't forget details. It's the opposite. Details torment you. They swirl through your mind in a relentless, agonizing loop until you think you'll go mad. The phone call you let go through to voicemail because you were too busy reading a book. The offhandedness of that last text message. The endless, haunting, unchangeable dance of all that was said and unsaid as life pushes you further from the opportunity you lost to make things right.

Evie is not struggling with any of *that*.

"I'm not going to hurt you," I assure her.

Now that she's ditched the airport idea and we've wound up on the motorway, we're heading toward Parramatta. Glimpses of houses and commercial buildings flash between the trees up off-ramps, just as a pair of cars weaves in and out of multiple lanes in a game of cat and mouse around us. My conscious instinct is to roar out of here, but my foot lifts off the accelerator instead, putting extra space between our car and theirs—betraying a leftover protective streak I don't want to think about. *Will I ever get her out of my system?*

Road signs point to Canberra or the Blue Mountains and either option suddenly feels like a massive overcommitment. This is hurtling badly out of control, and I run up an exit ramp at Moorebank Avenue, pull the car into a side street, and cut the engine outside a strip of commercial offices. All I can hear is her ragged breath, and mine. That, and the deafening silence of the gaping void from which a sensible plan needs to materialize, because I'm sure as hell not running away with Oliver's *wife*.

"Where are we?" she asks.

I open the car door and get out, gulping smog and heat. Exhaling history. Shaking my head, as if trying to rattle sense into it. As I hear the click of her door opening, I step away from the car. Away from her.

Away from . . . *me and her.*

"Drew? What are we doing?"

When I turn around, she's standing in front of me, a masterclass in contradiction. Power. Wealth. Fragility. Despair. She's staring at me like I'm her lifeline.

I can't be that. And I have absolutely no idea how to answer her question. All that's clear is that it's not my responsibility to clean up Oliver's mess. Or hers.

Not again.

# 6

***Evie***

The funeral must be over. My phone erupts from the front seat with six calls in a row from my mother-in-law, father-in-law, and their lawyer. It's like I'm being hunted. I fling it into the back seat as if the device is scorching hot and slam the door.

"I shouldn't have ditched the funeral," I admit, my voice quivering. "I've made it worse."

All the scaffolding in my life has crumbled and I'm stranded on a mile-high ledge. Maybe my in-laws should try waking up in a reality they don't even like, grieving the life they had, the years they missed, and the people they've lost. Right now, it's all I can do to focus on my immediate problem. My driver. And the fact that he appears to be having some sort of very inconvenient personal crisis of his own.

This guy has me all wrong.

"I don't wear Versace," I argue. Obviously, I *am* wearing it, but I don't usually. "The last memory I have of shopping for clothes was at a pop-up vendor in an outdoor secondhand market in Newtown." I might have spent time on weekends dressing up as Austen characters at the Regency Reenactment Society, but I didn't *only* wear Empire-waist dresses. "I snagged an amazing pair of burnt-orange seventies hotpants that day!"

His eyes travel critically to where the hotpants used to be, then snap back to my face. "People change," he says.

Maybe I became more like Bree. She was always trendy and stylish beside my retro mishmash, with her jet-black hair and striking feline-like features that stopped people dead in their tracks. We had part-time jobs that summer selling flowers in a stall at Paddy's Markets. A jolt of nostalgia washes over me for simpler times and a life nobody cared about or followed or commented on.

Drew doesn't seem to care about my high school fashion statements, standing here, hands on hips, staring at the pavement while he contemplates his problem. Our problem. *Me*, to be exact. He's definitely that guy you warn your friends about. It's the unreadable gaze. The volatility—acting all tough and distant one minute but charging your phone, playing your music, and making sure the air vents are pointed squarely at you the next. Bree and I would have a field day analyzing his behavior, but I have more than enough problems without my overactive imagination latching on to James Dean here.

"Where do you want to go?" he asks.

I can't tell him. It's way too big a favor to ask.

"Evie?"

This feels like a cross-examination. "I don't know where to go, because I don't know who I am now." Being open with him is probably the shortest way through this conversation. "Listen, Drew, I've been diagnosed with a type of amnesia. I remember everything about my life up until I was sixteen, and nothing after, until I woke up in the hospital last week."

He raises an eyebrow. I knew he wouldn't believe me. "How is this happening?" he mutters.

"The doctors said it can be a response to trauma," I start to explain, as if secondhand medical evidence will convince him.

"No, I understand that bit. I mean, how are we here? You and me?" He's all furrowed brows and irritation.

"You picked me up."

He uncrosses his arms. "You forced yourself into my car."

"I thought you were the Uber driver." I step toward him.

"You're meant to check the license plate and the driver's credentials."

"I've never done this before!" I argue, up close to him now, voice shaking, eyes stinging. "And by 'this' I mean *all of it.* It's like I've arrived in a foreign country and don't understand how anything works. Everything looks the same on the surface, but nothing is exactly like it was."

There's no stopping the wave I've crested. Burning emotion rises to my throat. It's the crash I've been resisting all week since I woke up and found out just how much of a mess my life had become.

"I have to tread carefully back into my memories, they said. So far, I haven't even tiptoed. I'm effectively a sixteen-year-old trapped in a twenty-nine-year-old's body. Like Jennifer Garner in *13 Going on 30* but without the magic-dust explanation, or the cool magazine career, or the long-suffering childhood love interest hovering reluctantly in the wings."

He stares at me as if he can't believe the words exploding out of my mouth, and no wonder.

"And now you want me to tell you where to take me, and it's just piling even more pressure on an already impossible predicament!"

I've never been a delicate crier. I wish I hadn't thrown my phone into the car. I feel the addictive urge to scroll, again, down the contacts list in case the names I need have reappeared. But they won't have. There's not a single person I could reach out to now and fall upon, in my hour of need.

*Years of need?*

It's a quiet voice that pushes that thought to the surface. I don't recognize it. Don't want to dance with it, either. I can sense the way it wants to pull me into a sinkhole.

Empathy flashes across Drew's face. A photojournalist's professional witchcraft, perhaps. He places both hands on the hood of his car and thinks. I hate the fact that I am entirely dependent on this man. No access to money. No ride. No capacity to come up with a workable solution on my own.

"I have nowhere to go," I confess. *When did I become so pathetic?* "I can't go . . ." The word *home* gets stuck in my throat.

He nods as though he agrees. "Let's see your phone. We'll go through it and ring someone."

I barricade the door. Suddenly, I'm ashamed of how short my contacts list has become. I was never the popular girl at school, but I had *friends.* None of whom I appear to have kept.

"Come on, Evie," he says, stepping closer as I push my back harder against his car, heart pounding, mouth dry. For a millisecond, trapped between intense brown eyes and the heat of black metal, I feel sheltered from it all. Until he puts a hand on my shoulder, coaxes me aside, unlatches the door, and reaches into the back seat.

"It's like the list was erased," I admit quickly as he retrieves the phone. "It's mainly my husband's family, and the doctor and dentist and the cleaner and people like that. Oh, and someone called Chloe."

He reemerges from the car, slams the door again, and stares at me. "Maybe you should be careful who you call from your past."

"Calling someone was your idea."

"I know." He shakes his head.

"I need to get home," I blurt. "To Newcastle. I really want to see my parents. I'd go on the train, but—" It's a huge ask, but I'm desperate enough to voice it. I follow up, taking the phone out of his hand, and show him my home screen. It's filled with notifications from podcast followers I've never met tagging me to tell me #runawaywidow is trending. It sounds like a rom-com, but it does *not* feel like one.

"I don't even know if Mum and Dad are alive, but I need to see for myself," I say, trying to keep my voice even. "Why else wouldn't they have been at the funeral?"

Or the hospital. Or in any of the social media posts I've curated over the last several years. They should have been my next of kin, instead of the in-laws I don't remember. They should be in my phone. My inbox. *My life*.

"If my parents can't come to me, I have to at least try to go to them. I've lost everyone that ever mattered to me, Drew. I need to figure out what happened. I know none of this is your problem, and I'm grateful you even brought me this far . . ." I trail off, my desperation hanging in the air between us in a way that I hate.

"I'll take you," he says, simply. *Off-load me*, I think he means.

"You'll do it?" I can hardly believe he's suggesting it. I find myself walking around to the passenger side before he changes his mind.

"Except, from the sound of it, Evie, I think you need to be prepared—"

I'm back in the car with the door slammed before he can finish that sentence. I don't want him to voice the possibility that, when we arrive in Newcastle, I might not find what I'm looking for.

An hour later, we're crossing the Hawkesbury River bridge. That first glimpse of the sunlight dancing on water dotted with houseboats and fishing vessels and water-skiers was always a symbolic promise that I was heading home. All those years boarding in Sydney as a scholarship kid, I'd watch excitedly for this view, proof we were truly north of the city and heading for the Central Coast. I used to imagine that bridge was magical. A portal between school and home.

Today, there's no magic as we cross. Instead, I'm increasingly anxious about what I'll find when we get to Newcastle. Or what I won't find.

I envisage a car crash, and my body flinches.

Drew glances at me from the driver's seat. "You okay?"

I see my parents gone, instantly, like Oliver. Mathematicians would say the probability of that is low when I've just survived a fatal car crash myself, but right now life feels precarious and explosive. Stats don't mean a thing.

"If my parents aren't alive . . ." I can't continue the thought. If they're gone, I'll have already wrenched myself through the indescribable grief of losing them once, and now I'll have to repeat that agony, from scratch. Can a human body even put itself through something like that twice over?

Drew focuses on the freeway as he threads in and out of traffic and overtakes semitrailers. "Try not to second-guess it," he says, settling back into the left lane.

Second-guessing is all I've got, thanks to this horrible sinkhole in my memory. This not knowing has made me so hungry for answers that a spontaneous road trip with a strange man seems like the safest option, despite my intimate knowledge about serial backpacker murders along a stretch of road just like this. Each time we pass another turnoff down a dirt track into a national park, I breathe a sigh of relief that Drew isn't swinging into it.

His phone, cradled in a holder on the dash, lights up with a call. Someone called Chloe. Is this that "frequency illusion" phenomenon, where you've never heard of a certain word and suddenly you hear it three times in a week?

He slams the red button fast, sending poor Chloe straight to the purgatory of voicemail. Sudden death. Have I ever evoked that reaction from a man?, I wonder.

"What's your last name?" I ask him.

"Kennedy."

I resist the temptation to google him right here. As if he's a step ahead, he elaborates: "I'm at DK Imaging, if you want to verify me."

"Why is a serious photojournalist covering a funeral?" I take up his invitation and type his business name into the search bar.

"Did I tell you I was a serious journalist?"

"Come on, everything about you screams brooding, artsy content." Black car. Dark windows. Restless energy. "I bet you're big on monochrome imagery. Haunting shadows. Negative space . . ."

I seem to be spouting artistic terminology like I have some idea what I'm talking about. The psych team warned me that this could happen. Pockets of unexplained knowledge can burst through the fog. It's like those cases you hear about where people have a head injury and wake up fluent in Spanish or rattling off piano concertos, except nothing that impressive, in my case.

But as soon as Drew's landing page fills the screen, the images take my breath away. My instinct was right about the black and white. But there's also vibrant color. Clifftop sunbursts and crashing ocean waves. Wintry scenes of gnarled, high country snow gums. Deep, lush forests—mist curling through ferns and over waterfalls—and even photos of nebula and constellations and stunning aurora skies . . .

I drag my eyes away and look at him, still focused on the road, not giving the slightest hint of these depths. The artistry only makes me more confused about why he was mixed up with the media pack at Oliver's funeral. Because he's right. He's not *that* kind of journalist.

"Drew, these photos . . ."

He shakes off the compliment in my tone.

"If this is the kind of work you do, I don't understand why you were at the church. Do you moonlight for the tabloids?"

Silence.

"What were you doing there?"

He frowns. Am I skating too close to an off-limits topic? Next thing I know, he's pulling off the road again, into a deserted rest stop beside the freeway—one of those places visited only by overwrought travelers who can't stay awake until the next coffee opportunity, or have a sick kid, or need to discuss something that can't be said in a moving vehicle, in our case. There's a battered wooden picnic table and no other signs of civilization. I grab the dashboard to steady myself.

He shuts off the engine and opens the window. The buzz of

cicadas pulses as hot air rushes in and I put my window down too, trying to make the inside of the car feel more spacious. Between the exquisite photography and the erratic driving, I've never felt more alive with someone, or more on edge.

Meanwhile, he grips the steering wheel, even though we're stationary. It's like he's buying time, turning words over in his mind in a thoughtful, steady way that only makes me nervous.

"I wasn't at the funeral in an official capacity," he explains, eventually. He looks . . . is *tortured* too strong a word?

Unsettled?

*Unnerved.*

"I *am* a journalist," he reassures me. "But I wasn't there for the story."

Even the cicadas go silent as he twists his body to face me. It takes just one second of looking into his intense brown eyes for me to catch up with the fact that I am not the only one here who is suffering.

"Evie, I was there because of my history with Oliver."

# 7

***Drew***

She stares at me from the passenger seat, processing my words. We've sat in cars like this before, windows down, the hot breeze a distracting cocktail of her perfume and eucalyptus. We've had difficult conversations. I've waited while she's collected her thoughts and I've watched them play out across features so familiar to me, they're etched into my brain. Watching her now—scared stiff, messy bun windblown from having the sunroof up and the windows down, mascara smudged, accusatory expression forming as she realizes what I've just admitted—my head is scrambled again, like everything happened yesterday.

"You *knew* him?"

I can see the cogs whirring. I knew her husband: ergo, I can help her get her memory back.

When Evie and I fell out, she made me promise never to speak to her again. She's already forced me to break that promise once, and here we are again. She might have had a serious knock to the head, and I know she's lost her husband, but I'm not the savior she thinks I am. I need to quash the hope that's breaking across her face.

"I can't help you," I say quickly, and her expression falls. "It was all a long time ago."

To be fair, it wasn't *all* a long time ago, but it won't help her to know that. There's not much I could disclose to Evie about the two of us and her husband that she'd actually want to hear. Yet she's searching my face for details. Scrambling to read between lines that aren't there, because I've worked so fucking hard to erase them.

"What was he like when you knew him?" she asks.

"Evie—"

She wants confirmation of the fairy tale and my whole body aches from holding it back.

*One exposure, and he swept you into his orbit.*

*It was an inevitable collision course.*

*He reeled you in the way he reeled in everyone: with that deep, inherited cellular knowledge of how to disarm people.*

Seeing how hungry she is for him, even when she can't recall a scrap of an actual experience with the man, only goes to show how powerful he is.

*Was.*

"I'm sure your memory will return," I tell her. Memories of Oliver are too commanding to be thwarted by a little bump to the head, at least in my experience. They'll find a way around the bruises. They'll forge past damaged neurons, push through whatever carnage the accident caused, and slide sinuously into an area of the brain that will explode into recollection. I know her and I knew him. The amnesia doesn't stand a chance.

"Why didn't you go inside the church?" she asks. She's clutching the strap of the seat belt like we're still in motion.

"Well, I would have," I answer. "But some woman hijacked my car, so . . ."

She almost smiles. And slightly loosens her grip on the belt. "You were going to pay your respects?"

*I was going to get closure.*

"Sure," I tell her.

Something like regret creeps into her body, shifting muscles awkwardly, and I try to stifle it before it takes over.

"I can do that some other way," I reassure her. "Funerals aren't for everyone."

She doesn't seem convinced but nods.

I look over her shoulder and out through the open car window. Really, I chose the most inauspicious location for this conversation. It's nothing but a dusty road and a picnic table, but that's the thing with Evie. She blurs backgrounds. When we were younger, she'd let me practice street photography down dirty city alleyways, beside dumpsters and graffiti-covered walls. Even now, I want to take pictures of her, raw and messy and anxious. I'm shocked at how easily I could let her slip back into the role of muse in my world. For so long, she was the story I wanted to capture, until the images corrupted and all the editing in the world wouldn't rally the happy ending I'd hoped for.

"Thank you for . . . going along with the hijacking," she says. "If you hadn't—"

My journalistic colleagues are out for blood. Since the accident, Evie has had a target on her back. Add to that the uproar her exit would have caused in the family itself, and I can see why she took a chance on me. That, and the fact she has no idea who I really am.

Evie's childhood home is a turn-of-the-century terrace house in Cooks Hill, Newcastle, just a block from the bustling cafés and boutiques of Darby Street. The weatherboard cladding is sporting a fresh coat of duck-egg-blue paint, and the wrought-iron fence is rusty, its hinges squeaking as she pushes through the gate.

"Every crack in the concrete is familiar." She places a hand on the trunk of a fig tree beside the front steps, tracing the knot in the bark as if she's greeting an old friend.

I watch as she scans the items on the veranda. Terra-cotta pots filled with tired annuals. A white macramé hammock chair, swinging in the afternoon breeze. Her body stills at the sight of a blue-and-red plastic tricycle. Then she knocks on the door, hard and sharp. Ready to put an end to this agony.

Footsteps approach.

"It's not them," she whispers before the door opens. Footsteps are like fingerprints. Indelible proof of a person, locked in from years of tramping the earth.

A woman is standing there barefoot in a faded denim sundress. Late thirties. Fractious toddler on her hip. The little girl is wielding a yogurt-covered spoon, which she drags through her mother's blond hair, and along what looks like her last nerve.

Evie can't seem to speak.

"Hello," I say, stepping forward.

The child beams at me, and the mother shifts away from us, wary. "I'm not buying anything," she says, already reaching to close the door. "Sorry, it's not a good time."

It looks like it never would be.

"We're not selling anything," I offer quickly, worried she'll shut us out.

"I grew up here," Evie adds, her voice thin. "I'm looking for Christine and David Hudson?"

The woman visibly relaxes after hearing Evie's parents'

names, now that it's clear we're not hawking solar panels or eternal salvation. "Oh, yes," she says more openly, shifting the toddler to her other hip. "They were the previous owners."

Evie's body stills as mine moves unconsciously into the gap between us.

"Was this a deceased estate?" she asks, her hand shooting to my arm.

"Gosh, no! I couldn't buy a house from dead people!"

There's visceral relief. Evie lets go of me, then smooths the creases she made in my sleeve until I shrug her off and step back. She's always been touchy-feely to my keeping people at arm's length.

"No, the Hudsons were lovely." The woman pops the squirming toddler on the floor at her feet. When she stands again, her face is a picture of compassion. "Did you know them?"

Evie tries to answer, but chokes.

"It was a reluctant sale on their part," the woman continues. "They said there were too many memories here, in the house. And in the city. Moved north, I think. Or maybe west?"

"Too many memories?" Evie asks.

The mother glances at her child and puts her hand to her chest. "Yes, poor loves. Grief can destroy you, can't it?"

Evie takes a step back as my muscle memory kicks in and braces against her proximity. Her scent. Every tiny movement she makes, from the way she tucks her hair behind her ear to the curve of her back as it arches against the world when things are hard. I've seen it all before. I thought I'd successfully blocked it from my mind, but the familiarity of her is almost overpowering.

"I don't understand . . ." she says. And suddenly I don't want her to.

I silently implore the woman not to utter the next sentence, but of course she does, and everything happens very quickly. Evie's weight falls against my body as the truth tumbles out and catches alight.

"I'm sorry to break the news," the woman says, "but the Hudsons lost their daughter."

# 8

## *Evie*

I don't know how Drew gets me back down the steps and up the path. I'm losing feeling in my limbs as we walk to the Range Rover. He takes my elbow gently and prompts me to get in, passing me the seat belt, which I don't have the strength to pull across my body. Without a word, he reaches over me to latch it, his concerned face inches from mine. Then he gets in and drives to the Merewether Beach parking lot, where he pulls me out of the car again and makes me sit on the grass in the sun on the clifftop, overlooking the ocean.

*They lost their daughter.*

"What does that even mean? They lost me?" I'm right here. *Aching* for them from inside the shakiest situation I've ever faced, longing for their steady hands. Their wisdom. Their love, which let me mess things up without ever messing *us* up. What could possibly have brought us to this point?

Someone's selling coffee from a vintage caravan in the parking lot. Drew checks his jeans pocket for his wallet. "I'll get you some water," he says. "I'll be right back."

A flock of seagulls settles on the grass nearby, fluttering and squawking like preschoolers tumbling out of the bus on a school excursion. I watch the ocean as it drags in and out over the sand and salt spray whips across my face.

I used to come here, right to this spot, as a teenager and stare at that beach and this ocean, whenever things were worrying me—which they often were. I was always a little anxious, I think, despite the rock-solid foundations I had at home. Perhaps it was some kind of psychic premonition about this moment in my future, the cocoon of love that sheltered me for the first sixteen years of my life smashed open by some invisible force I can't fathom. Every atom in my body is dislodged. I'm disassembled into billions of microscopic pieces, none of which add up to a life I know, or even like. And I'm totally alone.

Well, except for Drew, who hands me a bottle of Evian water and sits on the grass beside me, taking "strong, silent type" to a whole new level. *His* atoms are entirely intact. His grip on the world is robust. Which it needs to be, because he brought me an hour or two up the freeway to Newcastle thinking he could leave me with my parents, and now the plan is in tatters. He's staring at the ocean too, dark brows knitted against the blazing sun. Or perhaps against the blazing problem.

"What will I do?" I ask him, after a long while. Maybe he's come across similar mysteries in his career as a photojournalist and will know exactly what process to adopt when your husband is dead, your family has ghosted you, someone has frozen your accounts, and you've lost your memory.

He checks his watch. The innocent action flares my growing anxiety. *Don't leave me.* You're meant to notice the small things to calm your heart rate. I fixate on the way the wind ruffles the sleeves of Drew's T-shirt. Zoom in on the dark hair on his forearms and clenched muscles that are the only indication that perhaps he is not as well assembled as I thought.

When I meet his eyes again, he's observing the audit I appear to be taking of his upper body, which now includes defensively crossed arms. "Are there people you could ask about where your parents might have moved to?"

He's right. Someone must know. They were entrenched in this place.

"We should find somewhere to stay, shop for a few basic supplies, and spend tomorrow on this," he suggests.

*Tomorrow.* He's buying me one more day before he flings me into this new reality, alone.

This man owes me nothing. Maybe it's Oliver he owes? Either way, I'm suddenly panicked about what will happen when he leaves.

"Don't you have photos to take or news to break or something?" I ask.

His focus is pulled to the spectacular view in front of us, from the sheer cliffs and rock pools out to the blue-on-blue horizon. How does a photographer sit here without his camera?

"That's the benefit of being freelance," he explains. "I'm actually taking some space at the moment while I weigh up a job offer from a New York magazine."

Wow. *What could there possibly be to toss up?*

"You're so grown-up," I observe. It sounds so silly. We must be about the same age, but he's talking about a midcareer move, while it feels like I'm effectively stuck at the preuniversity stage, wondering if I'll even get my first-preference course.

"So are you," he replies.

Yes. And no. Suddenly I'm wildly envious. Age-old ambition courses to the surface, white-hot. Hunger for the level of success Drew has, and that I always imagined and strived for whenever I saw myself scaling the path I was so set on. And here he is, with what might as well be overnight success from where I'm standing, while I'm stagnant, *years* behind where I want to be.

"A proper magazine job in New York sounds like something that happens after a full chapter of a career has passed," I clarify.

"It has," he admits quietly. "Anyway, Evie, the point is I can take a few days off and nobody's chasing me."

"I wish nobody was chasing *me*. Social media feels like death by a hundred thousand DMs." I'd throw my phone off this cliff right now if I wasn't clinging to the tiny hope that my parents might call me. If they even have this number.

A flash of memory jostles to the surface. Losing Breanna in a crowd at a party. I'd been far too introverted to be untethered from my best friend in a large group of our high school peers, and I remember the escalating panic as people who took up more space and sound than I did pushed past me, their laughter brash, their bodies confident. They seemed to own the air we shared in a way that sucked it from my lungs. The "big people," I used to call them, secretly.

Wait. *Was* I alone?

It's not a proper memory, just a mirage of one. More a feeling than anything specific. That sense of loneliness and abandonment when Breanna went off being swept away and replaced, in an instant, by something else. Light. Warmth. Enough to block out all the other people . . .

But now the light is so bright I can't see. Like a starburst on a lens. Brilliant. Overexposed. A boy's silhouette. And this all-consuming, extraordinary emotional *rush* . . .

"Evie?" Drew says.

His voice snaps me back to the clifftop.

"I asked you what you thought about staying in Newcastle tonight. We can start the search tomorrow? Seems pointless driving back to Sydney."

His words break the spell. I can't recapture that glimpse from the party, despite how intensely I want to. I'm not even sure it was real and not some subconscious longing for absent connection. In any case, Drew is right. We should make a plan.

"I've got a notebook and pen in the car," I offer. I've been using them to collect random assumptions about my life.

"Do you drink, Evie Roche?" he asks.

It's a simple enough question. I assume I do—I used to. Breanna and I once wrote ourselves off with Smirnoff Double Blacks at sixteen. It's a miracle the amnesia didn't set in then. My stomach churns. I'd be amazed if I ever drank again in the years following that mistake. Maybe I'm one of those wellness fanatics now who drinks only the green smoothies with ginger and turmeric that keep being pushed at me online . . .

I check my body. No, I do not look like a wellness *fanatic*, exactly, more someone who has a passing acquaintance with a gym. The type where I use the treadmill occasionally and the coffee shop more often. Mainly as a backdrop for Instagram.

"I probably do drink," I deduce, on balance. My jaw clenches and I try to ignore the dull pain in my chest, a deep ache from the exertion of trying to figure out my life.

Meanwhile, a man is asking me to a bar. I wouldn't even know what to order! I assume I graduated from vodka cruisers to something more sophisticated, like wine? But white or red?

And what about all the different varieties? What even is sauvignon blanc? How do you pronounce *sauvignon*? I don't even know my own palate . . .

"We'll have a beer," Drew says decisively. "There's a craft brewery on King Street."

Right.

"Come on, Versace."

And he stands up and pulls me to my feet.

# 9

***Drew***

Why am I offering her *days*?

I'm promising to help her unravel a mystery I already know the solution to. I could level with her right now. But I've dumped big news on someone once before. I can't go through fallout like that again. Surely it's safer to let the truth sneak up on her in gentle little episodes, however her mind wants to piece it together. Preferably in the company of her parents. Not me. I'm the last person she should lean on. The last one she'll *want* to lean on, once she remembers . . .

And now a jolt of guilt slices through me. What if I'm not protecting her at all, but selfishly carving out time with "the old her" while she stays ignorant? A precious limbo, before everything crashes in and we're back where it all exploded.

She used to be strong. The Evie I first met in boarding school, at sixteen, was the most focused person I knew. The kids around her didn't know their plans for the weekend; Evie had hers locked in years ahead. She had every course in her undergraduate degree selected before Sydney Uni even established a timetable. Ironclad rules that would lead her straight to the goals she'd tacked on her bedroom wall in Castle Hill.

Now she's staring at the schooner of beer on the trestle table, all wide-eyed and incredulous, like I've asked her to swallow poison. The whole vibe of the place—wooden floors, loud music, massive stainless-steel fermenter tanks—seems overwhelming to her and I'm gripped with guilt. Should we be somewhere this stimulating so soon after her hospital visit? A kid topples a massive wooden Jenga puzzle, pieces clattering onto the floorboards near us, and she jumps.

"We don't have to stay," I tell her, looking for the nearest exit.

She snaps her attention back to me. "I'm not sick. I wasn't badly injured." She tugs at her shirt sleeve to cover the purple bruises on her wrist, wincing. "The doctors said there wasn't a head injury. They did a whole lot of imaging to prove it."

Surely that's impossible. The woman has lost her adult life. She's adrift in a world that has stormed forward and left her without the experience she needs to wrestle reality. Even if she did have her full faculties, this situation would be a struggle—the sudden loss of the only partner you'd ever known.

"They think the amnesia is psychological. Apparently my conscious mind wants me to forget my life." She shivers at the admission.

I take a long sip of my beer, not prepared to admit I'm partly jealous. It's the whole fresh-start thing. The blank slate. You could create something completely new. Forget every mistake you ever made. A lowlight reel of my own mistakes blasts across my mind. Some of them make my heart plunge. One, in particular.

"They call it *dissociative amnesia*," she proceeds. "You're able to function pretty much normally in the present. You're still yourself and you know who you are. You can remember parts of your life, but there's a localized memory gap about a certain event, or series of events."

"Right."

"Thirteen years' worth of events, in my case."

Almost half her life. A lot to lose. "What triggered it? The accident?"

She shrugs. "I guess so. They said it can come on from extreme stress. Or trauma. I did plunge down a cliff in a car."

*And whatever came before that.*

"It will probably come back soon." She looks around the room as if she's expecting her memory to walk in the door, pull up a seat, and explain itself. If I could march outside, wrestle with it in the alley, and drag it in here for her, I would. But after that, I'd have to walk out of this brewery, break the lease on my Surry Hills apartment, and bolt straight to New York. If anything could boost the allure of the job offer I've been tossing up, it's this unwanted minibreak with the one who got away.

"Did the doctors say how long it might take?"

*How long am I going to be responsible for you?* That's what I'm really asking, isn't it? Because if we can't find answers tomorrow, what am I going to do? Abandon her?

"They couldn't be sure. It might be sudden and complete, or gradual, in pieces," she tells me. "It's not like the memories have been corrupted. They're all still there. I just can't access them right now."

Let me get this straight. At any moment, and in one crashing hit, she could retrieve every second we've ever spent together? Our lives flash before my eyes and I picture an unthinkable scenario in which they suddenly flash before hers. All of it. From our fraught first day through to that last heartbreaking email. I need some sort of emergency exit. An ejector seat, for the moment Evie Hudson looks into my eyes, sees the truth, and hits the roof that I didn't tell her.

"Is everything all right, Drew?" She must clock the fight-or-flight I'm battling. I used to be better at hiding how I felt.

Everything is not all right. A collision of memories can pound into you, sweeping away in an instant all the ground you gained in the time it took you to systematically forget.

"Is there any chance you won't remember at all?" I ask. *Please.*

I don't really want to rob her of a decade of her life just to make mine easier, but the older you get, the less space a batch of years takes up in your timeline. Plenty of people want to forget their twenties, don't they?

"Psychotherapy should help me join the dots."

All those dots will lead to Oliver. Once she met him, he filled almost every moment of her waking consciousness. The Evie I first knew, as determined as she was, still basked in the bright light of her boyfriend's existence. She was supporting actor to his leading role. It was a miscasting right from the start, in my opinion, not that my opinion on Evie's romantic choice was ever popular.

"So I'm meant to stick to routine," she explains.

I don't see how fleeing a funeral and gallivanting up the coast with me could be classified as routine, but I hold my tongue. She takes a sip of her beer. Struggles with the taste. Takes another sip. Sets it down on the sticky table.

"Looks like beer is not your thing," I say, although I've seen her drink it before. Maybe her taste buds have amnesia too. "I can get you something else."

"It's okay. I just don't know . . ."

*. . . who she is as an adult.*

She reaches into her luxury handbag and pulls out a note-book, scoots closer, and pushes a cloud of Chanel into my nostrils. I reach for her discarded drink and drain about a third of it. The woman has no idea what she's doing to me, every unintended touch like a spider's silk, dragging me back into the web we spun together—an invisible structure that held me safe, then entrapped me.

"I've started taking notes. Trying to piece it together," she explains.

It's like watching someone drown. I could piece a lot of it together for her in minutes, but who am I to ride roughshod into her brain and do the psych's job? I know from experience how much damage you can do when you raise the past. It's damage I refuse to inflict twice.

"I've scrolled back years," she explains. "Looks like I'm one of those people who routinely deletes everything and starts again, and apparently I have this whole curated color scheme going on." She holds out her phone and shows me the coastal neutrals of her Instagram feed.

"Artistic." I'm glancing at tiles I already scrolled through last week when news broke about the accident.

"I have two accounts," she explains. "The other one I can't even look at. It's all criminology, linking to my podcast. I watched one of the videos . . ." She shudders. "I can't bear seeing evidence of all the knowledge I had. Being an expert in forensic linguistics is everything I always wanted."

I know. And she'd been brilliant at it.

"You'll get your expertise back," I promise her, though it's unfair to be so confident when I have no idea which parts of her memory will return, or when.

"Anyway, there's no reliable record on my socials from early on, but from what I can tell from my in-laws, I met Oliver when I was seventeen," she says.

*Sixteen.*

I watch her pore over patchy notes in handwriting as familiar to me as the focus on her face while she scrambles for answers.

*But you met me first.*

## age SIXTEEN

# 10

***Evie***

The Photography Club meets on Wednesdays in the art studio at the boys' school. I've just signed up and Bree thinks it's only for the potential formal dates, but, honestly, it's because I want more extracurriculars on my CV and my dad gave me his old DSLR camera. I'm genuinely keen. On photography.

I mean, I'm keen on boys, *in theory*. Just not any boys I've actually met. Not a single candidate has measured up to the boys from the pages of the period dramas I wish I lived in, so until someone does, I am romanticizing straight A's.

Crossing the quad at the boys' school, I tighten my ponytail and pull at the hem of my skirt. The boys move in packs. Kicking balls and hacky sacks, shoving and headlocking each other, deep voices reverberating off the brick walls—their energy on high alert, tension ramped up at the sudden flash of a maroon uniform amid all the gray and navy.

"None of these boys could dredge themselves out of a pond looking hot in a white shirt if their lives depended on it," I tell Bree on the phone as I walk. "They're more likely to dredge themselves out of the gutter they've fallen into drunk at a house party."

It's all about subtlety for me. Slow-burn, will-they-or-won't-they tension. "You don't appreciate how incredibly sexy not having sex is," I tell her, keeping my voice low in case a teacher, or, worse, a boy, hears me. "I want romance that's *forbidden*. When it all seems *hopeless* . . ."

"IT ALL *IS* HOPELESS!" Bree shouts back. And maybe she's right. I should be more careful what I wish for. "We're so far behind, Eves! Neither of us has even had a first kiss!"

"That's not true! Lachlan Montgomery hoovered my face off at the interschools' disco, remember?"

"Yes, and you said that was like a cardiopulmonary resuscitation attempt!"

I end the call as I reach the art studio, attempt to muster confidence, and open the door. There's a seat near the front, which I slide into. I zip open my pencil case and extract my favorite pen, trying to ignore a trio of obnoxious Year Nine boys, who of course are the absolute *worst*, their cracking voices grating on my skin as the minutes pass. Anxiety swells as I realize I might be the only girl in this room.

Quietly, I'm beginning to regret being so obsessed with my marks and my portfolio. Maybe I should have pushed myself to go to more parties so I actually know people. And dropped my standards to the reality of twenty-first-century boys.

Any contenders? Breanna asks by text.

Unless a boy opens the studio door right now and presents himself in a white shirt, breeches, and boots, horse tethered to the bike rails behind the quadrangle, I'm not interested.

On cue the door bangs open.

I look up from my front-row desk as the newcomer ambles into the room without a shred of urgency. He is, of course, not in period costume. Truth be told, he's barely managing the school uniform—blue-and-gold striped tie hanging loose around his neck, slate-gray shirt tails flapping, camera bag swinging from his shoulder like he's rolling in from a tabloid shoot.

The only thing remotely eighteenth-century hero about this boy is his brooding expression. He has troubled brown eyes and a general air of having *a lot going on.* I expect him to slump in a chair in the back and withdraw from the whole thing, but he dumps his stuff on the table at the front, kicks the teacher's swivel chair out from the desk, and sits in it.

Right. So *he's* running this? Of all the qualities this boy is giving off, "leadership potential" isn't blaring.

"Hey, Kennedy," someone calls, waving a camera in the boy's face. "Smile!"

He doesn't bite, totally unfazed by his tormentor in a way that I want to emulate. "Mr. Dalgleish will be here in a minute," he announces, unzipping his camera bag. "He told me to get us started."

Suddenly I wish *I* was hiding in the back corner, not sitting right up front under the flickering fluorescent light, fresh notebook on the desk beside my camera, perfectly aligned with the angles of the tabletop. This Kennedy person with the scruffy, dark hair and sullen expression glances at me as he clicks a lens onto the frame of his camera, then leans back in the chair and puts his feet up on the teacher's desk. I notice his laces are untied. Typical.

My own feet are planted firmly underneath the desk in polished black school shoes. My pleated skirt hovers just below my knee as per school regulations and my crisp white shirt is ironed—and not just the scalloped collar poking out from the navy sweater. No shortcuts here. If someone from the uniform supply company knocked on the door right now, needing a model for an urgent photoshoot, they'd extract me in a heartbeat. Not because I look like a model, but because I carry off the whole studious schoolgirl thing to utter perfection.

The teacher bursts into the room, flustered, and snaps me from my insecurities. He's carrying a pile of essays and a pair of drumsticks and is wearing a bow tie with music notes. "Ah, good. Kennedy. You've got this under control!" he says, and shuffles to a spare desk in the back corner. "Forget I'm here."

I know from my brief foray into the combined schools' orchestra that Mr. Dalgleish is the music teacher, and not a good one. He spent most of the time tapping his plastic baton fruitlessly on the metal music stand, attempting to control the flirting epidemic that erupted in the coed band room. All I know is Shostakovich's "Festive Overture" was technically beyond us and the least of our priorities—I'll never hear a trumpet fanfare without my heart bolting at the memory of Isaac Rickman winking at me across the woodwind section, from behind his bassoon.

"Principal Walsh wants us to organize a photojournalism exhibition for first term next year," the boy up front announces flatly, as if the very idea is sucking the life force right out of his body. "That means planning it this term. So we have to agree on a theme by the end of this session. Go."

His brown eyes hold me firm. So firm that my own gaze takes flight to avoid his. I cannot seem to stay focused on him, no matter how hard I try, and now my heart is thudding erratically. I feel my face flame and the pressure descend, like this is a trick question. *Does he mean me?*

"Er, s-sure?" I stammer, on behalf of everyone.

"On what theme?"

I'm like Elle Woods in *Legally Blonde* when she goes to that first lecture and hasn't done the assigned reading. I don't know anything about photojournalism. I just want to take better pictures, not that mine are bad, exactly, but . . .

He's waiting.

"The patriarchy?" I panic-suggest. Bree and I have been obsessed with patriarchy-smashing since Year Eight. Why not attack it right at the source?

From behind me snorts an outburst of testosterone-laced laughter. My earlier nerves skitter aside, making way for a familiar sense of anger, because here we have to go. *Again.*

"Sorry—" I start, turning to glare at the perpetrators.

"Forgiven," one of them replies, winking.

"I forgot I was at an all-boys' school last seen on a prime-time current affairs show, scrambling to explain a scandal involving intrusive photos of female staff."

Someone whistles, ahead of a sudden hush in the room. I blink back angry tears because this is *not* just about the teachers. When I turn to face the front again, I notice a shift in Kennedy's eyes. He takes his clodhoppers off the desk and leans forward. "How about *Girls* as a theme?" I suggest.

This whips the fourteen-year-olds into a frenzy. "We already took photos of girls," a Year Nine boasts. He finds himself immediately hilarious, as does his audience.

"Yeah, we're famous for it," another chimes in, fist-bumping his neighbor. *Why did I think this was a good idea?*

"Not the kind that get sent around group chats until the school is forced to bring in a rep from the police station for a consent lecture," I say. "The antidote to that."

A memory blazes of that time last year when I discovered Bree, shaking and speechless in the corner of her bedroom after a boy from this school pressured her into sending photos of herself that he then uploaded to that horrible website She Loves It.

"I'll fix it," I'd promised her, when she looked at me desperately and cried so deeply no sound came out. But we couldn't go to the police. Bree and the other girls could have gotten in trouble for sending the photos too, so the website has stayed this massive, ugly, unfixable secret hiding in plain sight and, more than anything else in the world, I want to blow it to pieces.

"So, unfiltered portraits of our friends?" Kennedy suggests, trying to unpack my idea.

My imagination instantly conjures his female fan club, artsy girls with names like Sage and Mila and Blyth. I give them quirky plaits and *Amelie* fringe, dress them in black, with tartan skirts and ripped tights, while they listen to prog rock from the seventies and get high with him in an abandoned warehouse.

I've never been high. My toes squirm inside my school shoes, which now feel even more perfect and shiny beside the nonregulation Doc Martens Kennedy's harem would obviously wear, and I wish I'd broken the school's policy on makeup and put on some eyeliner or something. Not that I'm the policy-breaking type. Or any good with eyeliner.

"Friends, girlfriends, sisters," I clarify, "doing random things that they love, you know? No pressure. As if the camera isn't there."

Maybe we'd even reclaim She Loves It. Of course, in my head this is already bigger than a photography exhibition because I can never just do something *simple*. I want to dismantle what they've done and take the power back. "We could start a blog!

Shift the narrative? Go behind the scenes of private schoolboys looking at girls through a new lens?"

Kennedy stares at me. In fact, everyone stares, and not in a good way. I'm so used to the girls in our school talking fiercely about feminism and misogyny in classes and debates, but it's brutally obvious that the same conversations aren't going on here, where they're most needed.

"Wow," someone says from the back. "You're intense."

*That's it.* A volcano explodes inside me and I appeal to the only boy in the room who doesn't seem to be laughing at me.

"I'm not intense *enough*. You have no idea how much damage you do."

I don't mean him personally. Not unless he's like the rest of them, which, let's face it, is statistically likely in a culture like this.

"Isn't your school in economic jeopardy from all that bad publicity? I bet the board would throw money at a project like this." I seem to have shape-shifted into a forty-eight-year-old mother at a PTA meeting, but I'm not some weird economics genius. I know this stuff because it came up in a commerce class last week.

"I'm sorry, who *are* you?" Kennedy asks.

"Evie Hudson?" My response seems to come with a question mark, which is exactly the problem. I'm a person with top grades and an apparently "stellar future," according to my latest report card. The announcement of my name should come with an exclamation mark, but when you're the only girl in a room full of boys like this, it's shocking how quickly your confidence plummets.

Kennedy looks like he's seriously contemplating my idea. Of course, it's the only idea anyone has suggested, but still.

"We could do *Girls*," someone says from the back, "or we could do literally any other theme and it would be way more interesting."

"Yeah. *Girls* will get completely out of control," another says. "Like the time Kaelan O'Keefe snuck his girlfriend into the school chapel and took photos of her with the Virgin Mary."

More laughing and a couple of high fives. "Legend!"

Kennedy is even less impressed than he was when he walked in here ten minutes ago, and I watch as the spark I saw in his eyes dies out.

"Any other ideas for a theme?" he asks, with an apologetic glance in my direction.

# 11

***Drew***

It's no secret St. Dominic's has a reputation problem. Between a leaked video of a misogynistic war cry on the public bus to illicit photo sharing, the school has been in damage control.

The *Girls* exhibition idea is actually brilliant. The principal, Dr. Walsh, would probably go for it, and Evie is right—it could be the good-news story we need. The problem is, looking around the room, I have no faith that the members of St. Dom's Photography Club are capable of the emotional nuance needed to pull it off. What they *are* capable of is handing another school scandal to the media when the exhibition is unveiled, revealing another sacrilegious threesome in the school chapel—or worse.

She hasn't looked back at me once. She's slumped in her chair, frown on her face, texting someone furiously, and I feel like I've caused this.

I'm already dreading next week's session. I wouldn't be volunteering to run this club except that I need leadership experience to try to offset my sliding marks in visual art. Academically, I was tracking well all through Year Eleven until

Mum got sick again, but the art and photography school I'm striving for is mega-competitive, so this cocurricular club was meant to tick a box.

"I'm sticking this on the wall," I announce, pinning a blank page to a pinboard. "Everyone add one exhibition idea before next week's session."

Evie sighs and looks at the clock above the door. I should be able to lead this thing with my eyes shut, but I didn't expect to encounter Wonder Woman here, who's threatening to ratchet up the work involved and wreck what was going to be a cruisy semester.

I have to get this club back on track, and it's not like Mr. Dalgleish is helping. I need a minute or twenty or preferably the remainder of this meeting in solitude to get my head together.

"It rained this afternoon," I tell them. "Maybe go outside and take some shots in the reflections?"

They pick up their gear and tumble out, Evie included, and once the door slams shut, my forehead meets the desk. Three slow and deliberate times. I don't have the bandwidth for this girl.

I make sure the paper on the corkboard is secure and glance out the window. She's the only one who's really doing what I suggested, crouched on the asphalt, camera low to the ground, capturing red bricks and blue sky in a puddle of water. Ugh. I've got a weakness for earnestness.

"Evie, I'm sorry," I say, catching up with her in the quad on the way out to apologize. "I think your idea is great."

She frowns and keeps walking toward the bus stop.

Something about her makes me want to straighten my tie and pull up my socks. "So great you immediately dismissed it?"

That's not exactly true. I thought about it, listened to the boys' views, imagined trying to supervise the whole thing, and started steaming toward a panic attack. "It would go badly in their hands," I argue. "You heard them."

She stops walking and faces me. Up close, she's sort of terrifying. Bright. Intense. A "take no shit" attitude that's at odds with the fact that she couldn't even look at me straight in the classroom. And that had been fine by me. I don't want a girl looking at me. I haven't got time.

But that's when the truth hits me in the gut. That life deals you a certain hand and you find yourself, at seventeen years old, with no headspace for friends. Especially girls like this—the type that makes you feel like you're hovering at the starting line of a hundred-meter sprint, in those nerve-racking seconds before the gun goes off.

I don't need this level of nervous energy. The fear that I'm going to mess this up before it's even begun. I've known her only an hour and I'm already scared she'll scale the wall I've built that's kept all the others out.

"Walking past that behavior is as bad as doing it," she challenges me, fierce blue eyes pushing the controlled burn of my life beyond containment.

*Please make it stop.*

Evie doesn't understand. I've got nothing left in the tank. I just need everyone on board with some innocuous, paint-by-numbers exhibition—sunrises, trees, sports, I don't care. Anything easy.

I can't afford to unleash a wrecking ball in Photography Club. Or in my life.

• • •

I've seen the inside of the principal's office three times in my five years at this school. First, at the introductory meeting in Year Seven. Next, in Year Nine when Mum was first diagnosed and we were signing off on an Individual Learning Plan for modified assessment. And now today, the morning after encountering Evie Hudson.

I tried the spineless music teacher, Mr. Dalgleish. But he wouldn't commit to the exhibition theme.

"Nobody wanted it, Drew. You were there."

"The fact that they didn't want it made her point," I argued, and he said I should run it past Dr. Walsh. The only person with any guts appears to be Evie Hudson, whom, inconveniently, I haven't yet managed to evict from my head.

"Tell me, how is your mum?" Dr. Walsh asks. My heartbeat seems to lurch into my ears. It's taken two years of practice to be able to hold myself together at school, and now is not the time to test that.

"This is about something else."

It's not just Evie's frustration that motivated me. Doing something this worthwhile might pull me to the surface—even distract me for a minute from the quicksand at home.

"This isn't my idea," I make clear at the start. "There's this girl . . ."

Dr. Walsh braces in his seat. An automatic response, probably, to the last few girl-related crises he's had to defuse.

"The public photography exhibition you want us to do needs a theme. Evie suggested we all take pictures of girls."

Frowning, Dr. Walsh sets his pen down on the desk. "No, Drew."

I forge on. "Sisters, friends, mothers . . . lost in the moment, doing things they love."

His focus fixes on some point on his leather-topped desk.

"Pictures of girls . . . as people." My insides twist at the idea of having to drive home this obvious point. It's what I loathe about the culture here.

"It's a PR risk, Drew," Dr. Walsh says, after a very long pause, during which I assume he undertakes an imaginary visit with the school's legal team. "But this idea of yours may have merit."

"It's *Evie's* idea," I remind him.

"Who is this girl?"

I googled her last night. She only came up in videos of inter-school debates and mock trials and for some historical society she's in. She's one of those "world at her feet" people. Clever and articulate. Driven in a way that I used to be once, and want to be again if I can ever get Mum through this crisis.

"I've never seen her at cocurricular stuff before," I explain. But then I rarely go. And now half the school is asking who the girl is "who went off in photography."

"She wants to change the world," I tell him. *You have no idea how much damage you do.* "Starting with fifteen boys at a school that acutely needs an image overhaul."

*She's basically your hero.*

# 12

## *Evie*

LMFAO's "Party Rock Anthem" blares and my fingers clutch Bree's arm as she drags my introverted soul through the throbbing living room. Brilliant white strobe lights seem to pixilate the writhing bodies that lurch against me, beer splashing on bare skin as a glass bottle smashes on the timber floor, voices shrieking.

We burst onto the floodlit pool deck of the Pritchards' mansion. It's not an actual mansion, but it's the biggest house I've ever been in and is currently hosting the wildest party I've ever been forced to attend.

*"Relax!"* Bree screams above the music. She knows this is not my natural habitat. Put me in front of the class for an English oral and I'll smash it, but at a social event I suddenly can't seem to choreograph my limbs and lose command of the English language.

"Come on, Evie! It's fine! We can't hide in the library forever."

The library sounds good to me, but Tom Jenkins is at this party, and that's why we're here. Well, it's why *she's* here. My role is basically keeping her drinks safe and trying to find a normal way to stand while I count down the minutes until we can go.

"Back in a sec!" Bree buzzes off for drinks, leaving me

stranded. I pull out my phone and attempt to look casual by texting someone (Mum) about something fascinating (this house).

Check out the fairy lights! I type, sending a photo of delicate lights threaded through the branches of a fruit tree in a giant planter. Mum and I once spent a whole weekend overhauling a corner of the backyard with lights and potted plants and old wooden furniture we found at the dump and brought back to life with vibrant paint.

When she doesn't reply, I call her.

"Sorry, sweetie, your father and I are watching *Antiques Roadshow*."

"Mum, did you see the photo? This pot is *at someone's house.* You'd only ever see it in the foyer of the Hilton Hotel or somewhere."

"Are you at a party, darling?" she asks. "Try to focus on your friends."

I wish I was sitting beside her now, on the comfy sunken couch in our Newcastle terrace watching cozy British TV. Or back at Bree's. I endured the first four years of high school in the boardinghouse, until Mum and Dad came to an arrangement with Bree's parents and the school that I could board with them. It suits my social anxiety *way* better.

"I know you're not keen on big groups," she continues, "but I'm sure if you just try to strike up a conversation with someone nice, it will all be okay."

She's right. What am I doing, standing here talking to my mother about garden ornaments and feature lighting while everyone else gets happy on whatever Max Turner tipped into the punch?

"Stop gawping at that pot and try to look normal!" Bree instructs when she returns with a paper napkin full of cheese and crackers. She's caught me fidgeting with the black midi pencil skirt and cropped emerald cami she made me borrow, even though it's unexpectedly cold.

"Oh, God," I say under my breath when I notice that boy, Kennedy, from the Photography Club. "What's he doing here?"

Bree follows my line of sight across the pool to where Kennedy's standing, looking exactly as humorless as he did last week in the classroom. Definitely not in a party mood. I doubt he ever is.

He's talking to some girl. She's *well* into the party and clearly also into the whole moody Brat Pack thing he's got going on. She knows precisely how to wear a dress without fidgeting and where to put her legs and arms, which is basically all over him at every opportunity, while flicking impossibly shiny platinum hair over her shoulder at regular intervals. Exactly the hair I wish I had instead of this mass of wild curls that took Bree an hour to straighten.

"Is that *him*?" Bree is fascination personified. "The photographer?"

I hadn't realized my blow-by-blow account of the whole train wreck had painted him quite so clearly in her mind. "He's cute," she decides.

*Hardly.*

"He's just like all the others." I shrug and stuff a cube of cheddar into my mouth, washing it down with a swig of the beer she brought me in a red plastic cup, the sour taste biting my tongue.

"I don't know how else you expected your exhibition idea to go," she says.

But isn't that exactly the point? Bree knows why this matters, although now is not the time to remind her of the website half the boys at this party have probably seen her on or of how scared it made her feel.

That girl is *still* trying to get Kennedy's attention. He looks a hundred miles away as reflections from the pool dance across his stern face. I suppose if you dressed him up in trousers instead of jeans, ditched the leather jacket for a long, dark cloak and thigh-high boots . . . with those waves of dark hair, he might be at home traipsing across the moors, dark and tormented, in a Brontë novel.

When I look back at Bree, she is studying me from under her precision-straightened black fringe. Her on-point, cat-eye liner crinkles as she smiles knowingly.

*No!* "Bree! He put me on the spot in front of everyone. And then he let my suggestion get howled down." Wherever she's going with this, she's dead wrong.

Luckily, someone screams annoyingly over by the punch, which distracts her. She takes a sip of beer and plots to overthrow what she calls the "fangirls holding Tom Jenkins hostage near the drinks table." I had no idea she was so interested in Tom. It's not like her to let a group of girls stir her up this much.

"Don't look now, Evie," she says, softly. "But your nemesis is staring at you."

My heart thumps, and of course I *do* look.

"Hey! Evie!" he calls across the pool.

I watch as he removes the girl's hand from his person and points at me, as though I'm his long-lost best friend. Right when I'm galvanizing myself to reject his olive branch, a brawl breaks out behind us. Bree and I spring out of the way, only to be crashed into by the drunken boys, who push us to the edge of the water.

And then push me into it.

# 13

## *Evie*

Beneath the surface, it's shockingly cold and blissfully peaceful, dance music muted. Shadowy figures converge on the water's edge above me, distorted through ripples of water.

Underwater, there's a boy—perfect face and blond hair floodlit, blue eyes fixed on mine as we ricochet off each other and time stands still. Just for a second or two, but long enough for me to lose myself in his attention, before instinct hits and I try to kick my legs in this awkward skirt, wedge-heel shoes striking the pool floor, and start to panic.

The boy's expression shifts. His arms pierce the water as he powers toward me, a sense of relief washing over me. *I'll be okay.*

But just as he arrives heroically at my side, a pair of strong, leather-clad arms reach into the pool from above, scoop me under the shoulders, and wrench me to the surface.

I gasp as I'm dragged out of the water, dripping, and am swarmed upon by Bree and several others, who help me to my feet. My outfit clings to my body, hair bedraggled, as chlorinated water runs off my face.

I pull off wet shoes, the straps of which have been biting into my ankles anyway, and wring out my curls, laughing now.

The boy in the water swims to the edge and looks up at me,

eyes roving over the damage. "Thanks for taking this so well," he says, smiling.

Never mind my ruined outfit. I have moved swiftly onto the next crisis because *He. Is. Gorgeous.*

Those striking eyes—I'd thought blue, but maybe they're green?—fix on mine again. His face is entirely symmetrical, in that Hollywood way that is totally unfair to everyone else, and there's something kind of "retro boyband music video" about him, fully dressed and saturated in the pool. It reminds me of the time Mum showed me Backstreet Boys videos one Saturday morning, trying to explain her twenties. I half expect him to launch into the chorus of "Quit Playing Games (With My Heart)," as he plants his hands on the pool deck and starts to push himself up out of the water. Effortlessly. Because of course he has the sort of shoulders that can manage a task like that with ease.

Bree and I hold hands. For emotional support. And to communicate what we are both thinking.

*It's the wet-white-shirt phenomenon.*

Time seems to slow as he emerges from the water, shirt now totally transparent over the chiseled muscles of his chest . . . *oh my God.*

It's Colin Firth in *Pride and Prejudice.* Dan Stevens in *Sense and Sensibility.* Rupert Friend in *The Young Victoria.* And now this extraordinary boy emerging from McKenzie Pritchard's swimming pool, somehow rivaling all of them.

I'm vaguely aware of Kennedy, butting into my line of sight. "Evie, are you okay?"

It's static noise on my periphery as White Shirt hoists himself up from the edge of the pool. The Regency fantasy falters slightly at the sight of his *perfectly fitted* jeans, but I overlook that because the rest is just . . . it's honestly so glorious I'm speechless. In this moment, I want to take back all I'd ever said about twenty-first-century boys. Every time I'd rolled my eyes and judged girls for their laughable Insta Love obsessions. And I emergency-revoke my No Romance rule.

"Drew," the boy says to Kennedy. I'm still mesmerized as water drips off the tips of his dark blond hair, down his cheekbones, and runs off his jaw, onto his shirt and his jeans, pooling at his feet.

Bree clears her throat to break me out of my trance.

"Oliver," Kennedy says.

*Such* a heroic name. Reminiscent of Oliver Twist, except of course *he* was a penniless orphan and this Oliver goes to an expensive school and doesn't seem remotely upset about the fact that his leather boots are currently waterlogged.

It's clear there is no love lost between him and Kennedy—or Drew, apparently. It's like one of those moments in old movies where they "take it outside" with dueling pistols, and for a few amazing seconds I pretend their antagonism is for some reason inspired by me—even though one of them hasn't even met me yet and the other one probably doesn't like me after our altercation on Wednesday.

Now that my outfit is ruined, I feel way more confident than I did when it was spotless.

"I'm Evie," I interrupt. No question mark this time. No trouble focusing on Oliver's sparkling eyes.

"We met," Drew says. "In Photography Club?"

He thinks I've forgotten. And that I'm on speaking terms with him. Ironically, the way I look right now is exactly the type of photo opportunity I meant for the exhibition.

"I'm Oliver Roche," White Shirt says. He puts his hand

briefly *on my arm*. "And you need a towel." He glances hopefully toward the house, as if someone might appear with one, and then back at me, like he cannot bear for us to be parted while he goes and gets one himself.

I hold out my hand to shake because I am—what, exactly? A businesswoman about to conduct a meeting? This is why I can't do "sixteen" properly. Bree frowns at my hand, willing me to do something less professional with it, but that's when Oliver saves me.

His mouth draws into half a smile as he takes my fingers in his, brings my hand to his lips, and *kisses it* without ever breaking eye contact. So that's that then, isn't it? I'm clearly going to fall in love with him. What else am I meant to do in these circumstances?

Someone brings towels at last, and Oliver, who is *still* holding my hand, lets go, says, "Excuse me," and starts stripping his shirt off right in front of us. I imagine myself having an attack of the vapors and Bree having to fetch the smelling salts or raid McKenzie Pritchard's mother's medicine cabinet for a Valium or something to snap me out of it.

"You are *imprinting*," Bree whispers. "Like in *Twilight*. Rein yourself in."

But I'm already in trouble.

I *cannot* let myself fall in love at first sight. No, I *hate* that. I'm a romantic, but it's the slow burn all the way for me. Tortuous, intoxicatingly drawn-out courtships during which we *pine* for each other amid multiple misunderstandings. None of this unambiguous freaking out on the pool deck microseconds into one smile.

I'm pro-school. Pro–hard work. Pro–focusing on the big goals on the chart I've made for the wall in my room, none of which include going all goose-bumpy over a two-second glance from a spectacular potential boyfriend, if I may be so bold as to label him that.

I've never been psychic. I don't believe in that stuff, just like I don't believe in love at first sight. But in this exact moment, as crazy as it sounds, and while I can't explain how or why, I know this fact: Oliver Roche is my future.

# 14

***Drew***

When I open the latch on the sliding door out the back of our place, I try to be quiet. Mum is asleep on the couch. I pull the blanket over her and adjust the cushion under her head, and she barely moves—she's out of it, after back-to-back night shifts.

I scoop up the empty wineglass, which has fallen over on the threadbare forty-year-old carpet beside the lounge, switch off the late-night talk show on the TV, and flick the kitchen light as I head toward my bedroom.

Minutes later, I'm lying awake in bed, wondering if she took her medication. I just want to roll over and sleep. But she can't skip it. If she goes off her meds, the side effects are horrible and I can't miss any more school if she ends up in the hospital again.

I drag myself back up, stagger down the cramped hall to the kitchen, flick on the light, and check the plastic medicine pack on the chipped Lamin-x bench, near the swollen patch where I once left a hot saucepan. Mum loathes this kitchen. It's about three decades overdue for a renovation, but there's no way that fits into a budget swamped by medical bills.

"I can recommend our builder," Mum's work acquaintance

offered when she dropped her off the other night. "I have one that's probably more affordable than your private school fees."

Mum didn't tell her we don't pay the fees. My absent father does. And that's all he does too. I'd try to get him to pay her hospital bills instead, but legend has it he's an "Old Boy" at the school. That tells me everything I need to know.

The three evening tablets are snug in Saturday's capsule. I pour a tall glass of water, carry it and the tablets into the living room, and shake her gently by the shoulder. In my hand, her bones are too prominent. I wonder, briefly, how this woman was ever strong enough to bring me into the world. How she's strong enough to convey herself through it now. And whether she even wants to.

"Mum? Wake up."

Nothing.

"Come on. You need your meds."

Eventually she stirs and looks at me like she's lost track of what day it is. She's actually lost track of a lot more than that. Graying brown hair falls out of its ponytail and across her face, which, even this worn-out and unwell, lights up when she notices me. She's not one to worry about coloring her hair. Can't afford to, either. And she's exhausted from work, but she ran out of sick leave months ago, and there are only so many hours after school and on weekends that I can cram full of café shifts.

Mum smiles, but the glow doesn't quite reach her eyes, and my body's fear response kicks in as usual.

*How much longer will you hold on?*

"How was the party?" she asks, attempting to inject some brightness into her tone.

"It was fine," I lie. I'm as bad as her. We do this theater piece, each of us trying to fool the other that things are okay, both knowing it's an act. She's anxious for me to enjoy life, despite her illness, and so I pretend to, so she won't blame herself.

"Meet anyone nice?" she presses.

There's an unwanted flash of Evie Hudson and her friend across the pool before she and Oliver plunged into the water, destroying that skirt and top and her hair, and any hope I had of talking to her.

I needed to speak with her too, after the debacle with Alicia, who'd been haranguing me all night and invited me to the St. Ag's formal. Somehow, in turning her down, I think she got the impression I was already going—with Evie. I'd only meant to wave at her and warn her that the guys were throwing punches behind them. *What a mess.*

"Nobody special," I tell Mum.

I help her sit up and pass her the glass and tablets. She takes them in shaky hands and downs all three in one gulp.

"Thanks, darling," she says, and I pull her to her feet. She's stronger now than she was a year ago, though that's not saying much. We rarely stray onto the topic of her long-term prognosis, but you don't need a medical degree to know she's nowhere near out of the woods. She's got chemotherapy-induced peripheral neuropathy. Burning, shooting pain from damaged nerves in her hands and feet. It's why she's been relegated to admin duties at work instead of proper nursing. It's also why she takes so many painkillers. And the antidepressants.

I hate this for her. All of it. This fragment of the life she deserves. The hull of the person she's become, clothes drooping off her frame. Every day, she seems to disappear further, while my fear bolts and I try to imagine living in a world where our tight little unit of two is halved. It's unthinkable. I'm seventeen and everyone assumes I'm one of those mentally tough kids who could easily exist independently. The type to set off on a gap year and not come back until Christmas, when I'd lope in on the last flight and turn everyone's year around. I don't want to admit, even to myself, how far from the truth that is. How much I *need* her, even at this age.

"Are you sure you haven't met someone, Drew?" she asks. Her health might be the first thing on my mind, but it's the last thing on hers. "You seem different."

Mothers and their supernatural abilities!

I pause, for too long. She smiles—for real this time. "You *have*!"

I can't. Not the way things are here. Not with six work shifts each week outside school. And not now that Oliver Roche is on the scene.

"It's really nobody," I inform her.

"Uh-huh." And there's the real smile, after all.

# 15

## *Evie*

It's been three days since Oliver Roche exploded into my consciousness and this is my twenty-seven-thousandth confession: I can't stop thinking about him.

I topped Year Ten biology, so I know what's going on here. Adrenaline, causing the racing heart. Dopamine, flooding me with feel-good chemicals. Phenylethylamine, unleashing a million butterflies. It's like I've *inhaled* Oliver and he is now officially taking over my system, jangling my nerves, welding to my atoms.

I refresh my feeds again. But there's not a single trace of evidence that I got under his skin in the way that he got under mine in our fleeting interaction by the pool. This boy really knows how to play it cool.

I click on his profile photo. It's a particularly good one of him running across a rugby field, hugging the ball, his thick, muscular thighs plastered in mud. I zoom in on it an unhealthy number of times until my fingers slip and I accidentally tap the thumbs-up. Oh, *God*!

"Bree! I've liked his profile pic!" I barely recognize my high-pitched, frantic voice. "Help!"

*Do I undo it, or will that only draw further attention when he sees his notifications?* Elizabeth Bennet never had to worry about such romantic politics.

I hold up my phone to show Bree the evidence, hand shaking, stomach plunging with embarrassment. "What was I supposed to do?" I add, pointing at his thighs.

She frowns at the photo, and at me. "Scroll past?"

Ugh. This is why I've always had the rule. No boys. Because I am an all-or-nothing person. And that *all* has always been about being the first person in my family to go to university. A top one. To build a career in forensics that will take me somewhere I can make a real difference. Mum tells me to study less and spend more time in the world with other people. They enjoy their jobs—Mum's a medical secretary, Dad's a public servant—but they're counting down to the day they buy a retro 1960s caravan and travel from one beachside camping ground to the next.

I fling myself onto Bree's bed, head buried in the Justin Bieber comforter I'm sworn to secrecy about. If there's ever an emergency, like if she dies or falls in love and unexpectedly arranges to bring a date home, I've promised to race here and strip her bed.

"But he hasn't even contacted you," Bree says, pointing out exactly what's been keeping me awake at night. "We probably didn't even register on his radar the other night, Eves. Didn't you see him? Everyone is obsessed with him."

Not the way I am obsessed with him.

"He's old-fashioned," I explain to Bree. "It was the way he said that thing about the towel . . ."

She stares at me like I've lost it. Maybe I have.

"He kissed my hand. He's not the type to sext me," I add.

"He's also not going to saddle up a steed, gallop to your front door, sweep you up behind him, and ride off into the sunset," she says. "I know you and your weird horsey fantasies!"

I'm not a horsey person. I just like the idea of a hero riding into my life on horseback. He'd be instantly lovestruck by my intellectual banter and wild hair. He'd ask if I was lost, but I would simply be strikingly independent. It would be part of my *allure.*

"Drew seems nice," Bree says, interrupting my latest fantasy.

*Who?*

"Oh! Kennedy?"

"You know you totally brushed him off," she lectures me. "After he pulled you out of the pool."

*That was him?* "It was chaotic," I say, trying to defend myself.

"You were too goggle-eyed over Wet White Shirt to even notice."

Wednesday arrives and there's still no contact from Oliver. No friend request. No follows. No liking my profile pic in return, which I've changed three times. I'm beginning to think I imagined the chemistry and that Bree is right. He probably looks at everyone that way—as if you're the single most gorgeous person he's ever encountered.

I drag myself to Photography Club after school, dejected. After last week, I was going to quit, but I'm hopeful for the vague chance of running into Oliver on campus. I dawdle from the bus stop to the art studio, stealing glances and acting like I have all the time in the world. No luck.

My heart falls as I approach the classroom. I see Drew inside, still looking moody. I feel a pang of regret about being rude on Saturday night.

"Hi," I say as I walk in.

"Hey," he replies.

It's no wonder I'm so disappointed in modern banter.

"Evie, there's something I wanted to—"

"Drew, thank you for dredging me out of the—"

We both speak at the same time, but before we can draw breath to try again, I hear another voice. "Miss Hudson?"

Both Drew and I turn, and a wave of excitement spreads through my entire being. Can everyone see it? I feel like they must. How does Oliver even know my surname? Oh, that's right. From my public display of affection over his profile photo . . .

But he's standing there with an enormous black eye! And then he places a hand on his chest, and sort of . . . bows. Who in this century bows, other than people meeting royalty and karate participants signaling peaceful intentions? It's almost as if he's done his homework on me, found out my obsession with period drama, and is deliberately communicating in my mother tongue. It's *so* much better than "hey."

"What are you doing here?" I ask.

He produces a camera from his backpack, and I hear Drew sigh.

"I'm here to take pictures of you," he says. "For the *Girls* exhibition."

*What exhibition?* "Oh! That idea didn't get over the line," I tell him, trying not to glare at Drew.

"Nuh, it did," someone says beside us. "The sports theme would have been so much more interesting."

I'm confused. Drew is studiously polishing a lens. Did he make this happen? Is that what he was going to tell me just now?

"You know what would have made a great photo for the exhibition?" Oliver says. "You on Saturday night, drenched, with all the pristine girls blurred in the background."

*All the pristine girls blurred in the background.*

He *did* notice me. I hadn't imagined it. And now he's here, at Photography Club, greeting me with the politeness of a Jane Austen hero . . . bad-boy black eye, poetic compliments, and wanting to take my photo, acting like my dream boyfriend come to life.

"Oliver, what happened?" I reach out and almost touch his face, but he flinches before I make contact with his skin.

"There's a story there," he admits, with a half smile. "It sort of involves you."

# 16

***Drew***

Watching Evie pretty much fall in love with Oliver Roche in real time, right here in the art studio, just after he's stolen my thunder about the exhibition theme punctures any excitement I had for this club.

I'd wanted to tell her at the party, but that was thwarted by black-eyed Darcy here, who I'm certain has never taken a photo with a proper camera in his life. He'll have it set on automatic and the photo will be nothing like what I'd achieve if I spent time properly balancing the light, capturing just enough detail in her face, at just the right angle to tell a story.

"Who hit you?" she asks him, and even I am intrigued.

"Tell you later," he answers, master of the cliff-hanger, directing her toward two free seats.

"When did we decide we're doing my idea?" she asks me, after they get cozy in the second row.

"We didn't," one of the other boys answers, annoyed.

"Is anyone new to crafting artist statements?" I ask the group. It's met with a complete lack of enthusiasm. "Sometimes having a statement in mind can help in finding the subject. Like authors imagining a book cover before they write. It helps you work out what you want to say."

Oliver casts Evie a warm smile, as if he's composing his artist statement on the spot. Some brilliantly worded bit of poetry, no doubt; he's top in English. You can't fault the way he pursues a girl. It's like he conducts a forensic search of her history and morphs into exactly the person she wants. Theater-obsessed when he was seeing Bethany. Outdoorsy with Rowena. Now he's apparently taken with photography and eighteenth-century English literature.

"For today, let's practice portrait shots," I tell the group. "Try to experiment with aperture and how it changes the focus of the background. Sometimes you want the subject in focus and the background blurred. Other times the background is part of the story."

I can't bear the idea of talking anyone through the complexity of the exposure triangle when I just want to escape the real-life triangle of Oliver, Evie, and me. Not that it's actually that shape. It's more linear. Between just the two of them.

"Speaking of background stories," Will Marshall says, with a glint in his eyes, "what's this I hear about you going with Evie to her formal, Kennedy?"

The air is sucked out of the classroom. Everyone falls silent, and she looks at me, startled.

"Alicia Brown is telling everyone," Will continues. "She said you told her at the party."

*That's not what I said.*

My stomach churns as I look apologetically at Evie, who seems hit by a jolt of electricity as Oliver stretches his arm along the back of her chair.

"Alicia thinks you made it up," Will says. Everyone laughs, but the only one I care about is Evie, who is staring at me, trying to work out what's happening.

"I thought you only socialized with your mum!" Lachie Bowen jokes, and this one statement pushes every last button. Nobody knows about Mum's illness here except the teachers. The unexpected mention of her strikes me hard in the chest and the composure I've held so tightly cracks. I reach for the lens cap and my camera, but my hand is shaking and I can't quite get the two to align.

Eyes bore into me. Including Evie's. *Do not fall apart in front of her!*

There's a disconcerting moment where we lock gazes—worlds, really—and I feel completely, horrendously exposed. It's freefall. Something shifts between us as if she's caught a private glimpse into the life I've kept so meticulously hidden from everyone else's view.

"Alicia is wrong," she explains calmly, without breaking eye contact.

I should never have let Alicia get that idea. Where else did I think this would end up but here?

"He didn't make it up," she adds, while I look at her, confused. "Drew and I *are* going to the formal together."

*This* makes no sense. The girl couldn't be more obsessed with Oliver, whose mouth opens and shuts, before he looks back at me too, eyes narrowing.

Magically, all the sniggering stops. The pounding in my head eases. The noise and panic and some of the pain just evaporates. Even Oliver and his testosterone-fueled territory marking fades from view.

I don't know how this happened, or why, and if it will work out. All I know, right this minute, is that I'm aware of no one else in the room but me and my rescuer.

# 17

## *Evie*

All friends have an origin story. I suspect for Drew Kennedy and me, it will be rescuing him from the formal date fiasco.

I don't even really know what compelled me to do it. Every conscious thought was saying *Oliver*, and then I saw a flicker of dejection in Drew's eyes and instinct took over. He looked haunted. I had an overwhelming sense, right that second, that this couldn't go wrong for him. That it would be too many wrongs for him.

We're practicing manual focus and I'm working with the late-afternoon sunlight as it streams through an archway when Drew catches up to me. I might not know much about photography, but I do seem to have a natural eye for light. The softness here contrasts with the sharp lines and angles of the red-brick architecture.

"Let me explain." He still looks tormented, which adds to the whole Heathcliff vibe. Not the villainous, vengeful, revenge-fueled stuff—just the untamed moodiness and unpredictability.

"It's fine," I tell him. I'm not sure that it *is* actually fine, but I'm committed now.

"You don't have to do this," he says. "It was a conversation with Alicia that got out of control. I never actually *said* I was going with you. I just . . . looked in your direction."

He's so sincere. Giving me an out, despite the embarrassment it would cause him. Behind the weariness in his eyes, there's something intriguingly dark.

"We'll go as friends," I tell him, to make it clear. "Think of it as a thank-you for making the exhibition happen."

He shrugs, like that's nothing, but I suspect life was complex enough before my bright idea added to his load. "They need shaking up," he says, with a nod toward the bulk of the group, messing around across the quad.

I focus my camera on a nearby magnolia and launch into my disastrous formal backstory. "I went to the Year Ten formal with my friend's brother, who I'd never met, and it was so awkward we barely spoke all night. To be fair, this guy's mother forced him to go with me because he spent too much time playing *Call of Duty*. She was worried he'd become completely nocturnal and celibate—while living at home until he was forty."

When I look from my viewfinder back at Drew, he seems slightly stunned.

*Too much information?* I always talk a lot when I'm nervous. I don't know why I'm nervous with Drew when it's Oliver who actually freaks me out. I'm keenly aware of where he is, in the group across the quad.

"I missed our Year Ten formal altogether," Drew says, saving me from myself. I'm about to ask why, but he follows my line of sight and says, "You sure you wouldn't rather go with someone else?"

Is he already pulling out of the formal he invited himself to? Truth be told, the whole idea of going with Oliver absolutely thrills me. But it's also terrifying. Drew seems safe—around Oliver I feel like I'm likely to lose control and my *entire mind.*

"I'm thinking of doing some astrophotography on Saturday night," Drew says, and I realize I didn't answer his question. "Maybe you could come?"

Join a boy from the notorious St. Dom's in the dark, on my own, five seconds after we've met?

"Sorry," he says. "Of course it would be weird . . ."

It actually wouldn't be all that weird—I used to tag along when Dad would do astro in Newcastle. I'd talk his ear off, pointing out constellations, wishing on shooting stars. Sometimes he'd even let me press the shutter, but this was before I cared much about photography. I just wanted to spend time with him. I miss it.

"I was thinking of taking my mum," Drew says. "She loves stargazing." His face reddens, probably remembering that horrible comment in the classroom. "Evie, about her—"

"Sounds like fun," I cut in, wanting to save him from having to explain. "If your mum doesn't mind."

He smiles. A genuine smile that transforms his face instantly and prompts me to pick up my camera, drawn into the moment.

"You said to practice," I argue, when he puts his hand over the lens and pushes it out of his face. "Come on. Smile, or I'll uninvite you to my formal."

"I'll uninvite you to stargazing."

"What are you going to do? Ban me from the sky? Smile, Kennedy . . ."

The corners of his mouth curl and it's the first time I've caught light in his eyes.

"That wasn't so hard," I say. "Was it?"

# 18

***Drew***

I lift the camera out of Evie's hands and zoom in on the photo she took. The person staring out of the image, smiling, feels unrecognizable. It's a lightness I haven't seen or felt since . . . I can't remember when.

But instantly it's chased by a warning. *Don't get attached.*

I have a shaky relationship with permanence. My father has never been on the scene, except on the other end of the tuition invoice. I've lost count of the hours I've wasted poring over the school's old annual magazines, searching for someone who looks even a little bit like me. And I'm in constant fear of losing Mum, who was pretty much cut off by her parents after she got pregnant with me. My whole life I've felt this *longing* for a family. So starting a friendship with a girl who makes me smile like *that* is dangerous.

When Evie takes the camera back and asks for my phone number, blue eyes sparkling, curly hair backlit by the sunset through the archway, everything tells me not to let her take a single step closer.

"I'll text you the photo when I upload it later," she says. She then chases this with an easy smile—the first she's properly bestowed upon me—and the plan not to get attached to her is already imploding.

I pass her my phone to input her details, secretly glad there'll be an excuse to message her later, cursing myself for my total lack of willpower.

The whole time we're talking, Oliver is watching us across the quad—a juggernaut about to mess with her world. He's looking at her as if the deal is already done, like bright, shiny Evie Hudson is his latest prey.

"Can I help you with the exhibition?" she asks. "Maybe we could be codirectors?"

I'd planned to get through this Photography Club commitment with as little interaction with other people as possible. But now she's standing here looking at me expectantly, with five times as much enthusiasm as I'm likely to be able to muster, and she'll probably do a much better job.

"Sure," I say, shrugging in a way that I hope downplays the flash of exhilaration I feel at the idea of us working together.

Oliver starts prowling toward us, floppy blond hair catching the dying rays of the sun against the ivy-covered red bricks on the walls behind him. I can practically feel the sparks flaring off Evie's body at the sight.

"A few of us are heading to that new café on the corner after this," he announces when he reaches us. "You want to come?"

This is directed pointedly at Evie and delivered with certainty about her positive response. He adds belatedly, "You too, Kennedy." I can think of nothing I want to do less.

"I can't," I say, then look back at her. "See you Saturday night?"

I can't pretend there's not a part of me that sees it as a minor triumph over Oliver when she smiles and says she'd love to.

# 19

***Evie***

We sit in a corner booth at the café, and everyone else gives us space in a way that makes me feel like we're already a couple. Oliver orders a glass of iced water as well as a hot drink, so he can hold it against the bruises on his eye.

"Are you going to tell me about that?" I ask. I'm dying to know how the story involves me, and have spent the last hour carried away with the delicious notion that maybe he's been fighting off admirers I didn't know I had.

"Well, everyone was talking about you at school after photography last week."

*Not in a good way, I bet.*

"And you know your friend from the party?" he continued.

"Breanna?"

"Those two guys in the fight were talking about having seen her on a website." He looks at me cautiously, as if he's testing how much I know.

My heart thuds through the floor. How much I know should be obvious from the way the mention of the site makes my hands tremble in some mashup of panic, fear, and molten anger. They were talking about her? I feel sick, and scared, and helpless that I still haven't found a way around the problem that chipped away all the most confident parts of her.

"When I saw you at the party and realized you were friends," Oliver says, leaning closer, "the exhibition theme made sense. You want to avenge for the wrong done to your best friend." He's speaking like a knight of the Round Table, which is doing all kinds of things to my insides, but yes. YES. "This is what matters to you most?" he guesses.

"I just want to erase this whole chapter. But I don't know how to fix it without landing her in trouble too. She was fifteen. The photos were illegal, even on her own phone."

He listens calmly to every word. It's the first real conversation I've been able to have about it with anyone but Bree.

"Is this from that fight?" I ask, my fingers hovering carefully near his injured face. I lean closer this time, and get a better view of the shiny, bruised skin around his eye and cheekbone and at him. My crush is galloping out of control.

"Evie, this is because I found out who was responsible for the She Loves It site," he says quietly.

My insides heave, and I instantly imagine blue and red lights flashing at Bree's front door. "Are you going to report them?"

She can't be dragged through this. The whole thing is a giant, murky mess reliant on fear and silence to keep it hidden, and suddenly I'm terrified it's all going to blow up.

"It's gone," Oliver says simply.

*Gone? How?*

I grab my phone, type the address, and instead of recoiling at images that make me shake with rage, I get a business page saying the domain name is available. Then I look back at him, and at his black eye.

"You got the domain deregistered?" I say.

"It's just an email to the support team," he explains.

An email he made someone send under duress, by the look of it. And I realize what he's done, that he's done it for Breanna, *because she is my friend.*

Everything is blurry through tears of relief for her. And gratitude for him. The risk he's taken, not just physically, but in going against culture. "I don't know what to say," I whisper.

"Don't be too impressed," he says, hanging his head. "I should have done it months ago—I knew about the website." He looks back at me, guilty. "But it wasn't personal then, Evie."

His words are so loaded my mind can barely grasp hold of them. "I don't want to make a big thing about it, okay?" he follows up. "I wish I'd stepped in before."

So now he's heroic *and* humble and honest about his missteps and he's confiding in me about rushing in and saving my best friend from an impossible situation and being beaten up in the process . . . *And it's personal.*

"Can I just text Bree?" I ask him.

He nods, and I pick up my phone, ready to type two words that feel spun with gold: It's over. I attach a screenshot of the domain page, and, as the phone whooshes with the sent message, my eyes return to Oliver's. She doesn't know it, but she is eternally in this boy's debt. And by extension, given just how much I love her, so am I.

Thursday afternoon, Oliver meets me at the library because I have an English essay to write about Shakespeare and it's his best subject. It's my best subject too, and I don't actually need any help, but sitting across from him in the study area, coming up with points about Shakespeare's use of rhetoric in *King Henry IV*, is just about the most romantic thing that has ever happened in my time on this planet.

"Why has it taken me until Year Eleven to discover you?" he asks. Something about his use of the word *discover* instead of *meet* delights me. He's helped himself to one of the gel pens I use to take notes, and he's twirling it between his fingers. I know I'm going to isolate that pen later and keep it as a souvenir of this occasion.

"I've been here all along, flying under your radar, obviously," I reply, even though it's more that I've been totally out of the loop. "Where have *you* been?"

He puts the pen down and leans forward, looking at me through black-rimmed reading glasses as if I fascinate him. I've never fascinated anyone, except maybe my parents.

"I think I've been waiting for you," he admits.

It's a romantic idea. In reality, I very much doubt that it's true, what with the parade of girls featured in his Instagram feed, but I hang on to the notion anyway.

Friday night, he impulsively suggests we go to a movie. Our thighs touch the *entire time* and I can't focus on a single scene because I'm so busy trying to stop myself from trembling. It's electric. Then afterward, in the lobby, we run into a group of St. Dom's boys, and while he talks to them, his hand goes to the small of my back and stays there until they're gone. It *thrills me.*

By Saturday morning, the falling-in-love process is pretty much complete. I can't think or talk about anything else and Bree is bearing the brunt of it. And that's when her doorbell sounds. It's a courier with a box, addressed to me. I open it, and inside are several forensic linguistics textbooks from my online bookstore wish list. I'd shared my login details with Oliver at the library, because he thinks someone's purchase history is a window to their soul.

"Textbooks?" Bree asks. "How romantic, Evie."

"It *is* romantic. Textbooks are expensive," I argue. Getting ahead on this reading is all part of the plan to win a university scholarship. "I'd rather have these books than roses. He understands me."

"Also, you shared your login details—and my address—with a boy you barely know?" Bree asks, evidently less enamored by the delivery than I am. "Did we learn nothing from my website nightmare? This is . . . a lot."

"Your address was already in the bookstore account from last time," I explain. "And Oliver's the one who *saved* you from the website nightmare."

"If it's really gone," she says, under her breath. "How do I know my photos aren't saved on some hard drive somewhere?"

Why is Bree being so unsupportive? I've been there for every crush she's ever had for years, and this is the first time for me. She of all people should understand my current mindset.

I'm getting out my wide-angle camera lens for the astrophotography night with Drew and his mum—a social event that comes with Bree's wholehearted approval—when I get a message from Oliver. We were going to meet up for an afternoon walk.

"I can't come, Evie. I've got a migraine."

Immediately, I want to make him feel better. It's inevitable that I will go to his place even if I have to move mountains to get back in time to meet Drew.

"I'm on my way."

• • •

Oliver and I sit on a cane sofa on his giant Lane Cove terrace. I've got a huge thing for cane furniture and giant terraces. Something about the old-world charm of sprawling Southern mansions, which the Roche's twenty-first-century Sydney residence rivals.

"You didn't have to come," he says, in the muted tone of a person with a throbbing head who did, in fact, keenly want you to come. "This happens every so often," he tells me. "It's usually stress."

I can't think what he could be stressed about. He gets straight A's at school, and with all his bonus leadership stuff, an early-entry offer to university is practically guaranteed. He lives in a colossal house and his parents don't have to scrape money together for uniforms or field trips like mine do, even though I'm on scholarship. He's been voted incoming school captain in a massive landslide, because literally everyone *adores* him.

"Can I get you a sandwich or something?" he asks, even though he's the patient.

"Do you want one?"

He shakes his head, then grasps it, as if to settle the pain, and I make him lie down and rest his head in my lap, looking up at me. I don't want to have to work out how to eat in front of him, anyway. Things get stuck in your teeth. You can drop mustard on your top. You could choke! I don't think we're ready for that level of chaos.

"Is this okay?" he asks, gesturing at his head on my legs. I'm the one who directed his head into this position, so the unnecessary request for consent only skyrockets my crush. First he takes down my best friend's nightmare website. Now he's navigating physical touch as if my boundaries actually matter.

The fact is, I want to run my fingers through his blond hair, and then, well . . . *everywhere.* But I don't. We're not up to that yet. Are we? I've never done this before. I do risk a quick brush of his forehead with the back of my hand, under the guise of checking his temperature, like I'm a nurse from World War I and he's a hero dragged in on a stretcher, wounded on the Somme.

It seems normal. His temperature, that is, not my historical fantasies.

The French door onto the balcony opens, and an enormous man in a suit steps through it, frowning. I get the impression that his frown is not wholly about having found us here like this, but more habitual.

"Hello," he says, not really looking at me, his voice abrupt.

Despite his headache, Oliver bolts upright and shifts along the bench a little way. I feel exposed, suddenly. And very definitely not enough.

"This is Evie," Oliver explains, standing now, as if the man's presence is a cure for his migraine. "Evie, this is my father."

It's oddly formal. And as Oliver didn't tell me his dad's name, I don't know what to call him. I'm assuming Mr. Roche? Or was he "Doctor"? I think Oliver said he was some kind of specialist. I settle for saying nothing, which is also wrong, and now the silence is awkward. Oliver's whole demeanor has shifted, like he's waiting for the ramifications of being found here, idling with a girl.

His dad tosses a nod in my direction out of minimal courtesy, and I feel about as small as one of the ants marching around on his balcony. I check my watch. It's getting late in the afternoon, and I need to get back in time to meet Drew.

"N-Nice to meet you," I stammer. I turn to Oliver. "I can't stay much longer. I have to be somewhere by six."

I can tell he's deflated. The fact that he's going to miss me is both unbelievable, after such a short time, and enthralling. And flattering, given this is Oliver Roche we're talking about, king of everything. But there's something else too. A sense that he wishes I could stay for other reasons, maybe. Safety in numbers?

"Oliver, can I have a word?" his father asks. He closes the French door so forcefully after his son that I feel the vibrations on the deck. I can't hear what they're saying, but I can see their body language. Oliver is a solid six feet and a rugby player. Technically he's standing eye-to-eye with his dad, but somehow he still seems overpowered. His father is doing all the talking, and even from outside I can see Oliver's broad shoulders dip under the weight of whatever's being said.

As soon as the conversation is over, he comes back outside, smaller, somehow. "Do you really have to go?"

It's a strangely vulnerable moment, and I feel like I'm being given a glimpse behind that popular, confident facade that everyone adores. I think of Drew and his mum, and his grateful expression when I agreed to our formal date. I really should go tonight. Plus, it's obvious something major is going on with Drew. If I'm going to follow through on the offer to be friends, I need to find out what.

"Sorry, of course you should go," Oliver says when I don't answer. He starts looking for my bag. "I'll just miss you, Evie."

Emergency: he's moved up *so* close I'm almost certain he's going to kiss me!

This has never happened before, other than that one-sided shambles in Year Nine, and I have absolutely *no* idea how to do this. I can feel the warmth of his breath brush my skin as a heady cloud of pine-scented aftershave swirls into my nostrils. His eyes travel across my face, and he sweeps a strand of my hair behind my ear, where it refuses to stay because of my *exasperating curls*, but I don't even care about that.

"Can I ask you something?" he says, pulling back. The lack of the kiss shifts *kissing Oliver Roche* to the top of my bucket list, immediately knocking off *get a book published* and *be appointed to the UN*. This fact disgusts pre-Pritchards'-party me, but the girl I was last week is fighting a hopeless battle against the onslaught of first-love brain chemistry.

"Ask me anything."

"You and Drew Kennedy?"

Heat rises to my cheeks. "Oh, we're friends," I garble. *Barely.* "What's the story between you two?"

He glances back inside the house. "That's all my father. You know how they pick up that there's a kid at school who might be a threat academically?"

I don't, but I nod anyway.

"Drew got a higher mark than me on a science test in the first week of Year Seven and I made the mistake of reporting that at home."

"But that was years ago," I argue.

"He's never let it go. Drew is always the one to beat."

I feel a rush of love for my uncomplicated parents and almost feel guilty for the easy way I've been raised. They would never pit me against another student.

"Can I see you first thing tomorrow?" he asks, blue eyes eager behind the blond waves of his fringe.

I think of my several assignments and the in-class test I have on Monday that I haven't started studying for, and the promise I made to myself never to let a boy stand in the way of my grades.

Will I see him tomorrow? Or any time he wants? And every spare second?

"Yes," I whisper. *Yes.*

# 20

***Drew***

I'm not even sure why I invited her stargazing. Maybe it was because the way things have been with Mum, I wanted backup.

I've been struggling with this for so long on my own that I'm fraying at the edges. It would be so easy for someone to pull gently at the threads of my life and unravel everything. They'd see how bad things are, not sleeping, coming home from school with my heart in my mouth, holding my breath as I unlatch the flimsy back door with holes all through the fly screen—symbolic of our life, really—wondering what I'm going to find.

"It's nice that you've invited a friend," Mum says to me now. "Or girlfriend?" She looks at me carefully.

"Mum! I only just met her." I leave out the bit about the formal. She'll take that and run with it.

Evie is standing in front of her friend Breanna's place when I swing by to pick her up, camera bag slung over her shoulder, tripod in her hand. A late-spring cold snap means she's in jeans and a bulky blue sweater, knitted beanie rammed on her head like it's trying to contain the wildness of her curls. It's such a contrast to how she looked at the party around the pool. I wish I could take a photo of her right now in the car's headlights, for the exhibition.

She opens the back door and slides in, pushing her bag along the seat beside my gear.

"Hello, lovely!" Mum starts. She calls everyone "lovely." I found it annoying until she explained that it saves her from trying to remember names. Her medication gives her brain fog. She's going to gush over Evie, badly. "Call me Annie."

*Please don't say "Drew has told me so much about you."*

Predictably, she does exactly that, and I refuse to meet Evie's eye in the rearview mirror.

"Nice to meet you, Annie," Evie says brightly. She's in a great mood. "Thanks for letting me crash your family night out."

This girl seems as set on rescuing me from socially awkward situations as Mum is to dump me into them. Mum looks sideways at me now and winks without a shred of discretion.

I was fourteen when she first showed signs of something being wrong. She was always tired, but then she worked a lot of nights and was raising me as a single parent. That Christmas, she'd covered extra shifts—probably to have a bit more money to spend on me. The day after Christmas, things went downhill. When she collapsed, I called for an ambulance and she was admitted straightaway. That's when they found secondary tumors. We'd missed the primary altogether. Not that it's the cancer I'm most worried about now . . .

I turn up the music in the hope it will stop Mum from talking.

It doesn't. "Busy day?" she asks Evie.

Evie is looking out the window, a dreamy expression on her face. "Not too busy," she says. "Lazy afternoon with . . ."

I can guess.

". . . a friend," she concludes.

I snort. Can't help it. The chance of Oliver placing Evie in the friend zone at this stage is less than zero. I saw the way he looked at her before he even got out of the pool.

"Coffee?" I ask, pulling a thermos out of my bag, waving it at Evie. We've set up on the beach, down one end near a cove, sheltered from the breeze by rocks. The ocean roars as waves crash onto the sand and I inhale the salt spray close to the water's edge. She's standing near her tripod, arms crossed as if she's cold. "I came prepared," I add.

*Who am I? Lord Baden-Powell?*

"Thanks," she says, taking a mug from me, but then her phone pings with a message.

"Sorry," she says as she checks it. It might be dark, but even in the glow of her phone screen I can guess who the message is from. She's wearing the same expression she had in the art studio on Wednesday when Oliver turned up and while we were driving here tonight. She types something back, smiling, and puts her phone in her pocket.

I dig the thermos into the sand and pick up my camera, twisting the focus ring on my lens as stars blur before sharpening to pinpricks. With a twenty-second exposure I should capture a good amount of detail in the core of the Milky Way. "Everything okay?" I ask Evie once I've pressed the shutter.

She looks guilty. "Yep! What are we shooting?"

I let the camera capture and process the image, then show her the photo in playback mode. She looks up the beach a little way. "Do you think we could try to get that driftwood in the foreground?" she asks.

Mum is building a campfire on the sand a little way up the beach and playing ABBA on the portable speaker. "Dancing Queen" is just audible over the pounding of the waves as she sways in the firelight.

"Is this how you and your mum usually spend Saturday nights?" Evie asks.

It makes me cringe. "About Mum . . ." I begin, kicking the sand at my feet, unsure how to explain this without breaking Mum's confidence.

"I think it's nice, Drew." Evie looks like she means it.

This conversation seems refreshingly unrestricted by the gauntlet of teen rules I'm used to navigating.

"I'm just happy to get her off the lounge for a couple of hours," I explain. "She has a very small world at the moment."

We're setting up for the shot when Evie's phone starts ringing. She ignores the call at first, because she's attempting that long-exposure wave photo, but the ringtone bursts through a second time.

She moves a few steps away toward the shoreline to answer it and I watch her body language change. Every movement speaks volumes. The way she touches her hair and shifts her weight, accentuating her hips in those jeans. Pity he can't see it.

*What am I doing?* I'm here for the stars. And for Mum. And to get to know my platonic formal date so the night isn't an unprecedented disaster.

"Okay, tomorrow! All right? I have to go now, seriously," she says, then she laughs, her voice catching on the evening breeze before it's swallowed by the roar of the ocean. "Let me take photos, Olly!"

She ends the call and hasn't had time to clear the elated

expression from her face before her eyes find me and acclimatize. She adjusts her tripod to get the driftwood in the shot, tilts the camera, checks the focus, and turns to me. “Drew?”

“Yep?”

“Do you happen to know if Oliver Roche has a girlfriend?”

# 21

## *Evie*

"Pretty sure he's single," Drew says, as he looks back in his camera's viewfinder. "He had a thing with Bethany for a while."

*Is it completely over?* He didn't kiss me earlier, so it's hard to be entirely certain.

"He seems nice," I say, and watch Drew's shoulders slump a tiny bit before he straightens again. I wonder if the rivalry Oliver described runs both ways.

"He's a prefect."

That's not what I'm asking at all.

"He's on track to be Dux of Year Twelve. He's school captain. Captain of the first fifteen rugby team . . ."

"I don't want his CV," I explain, laughing—I've already committed that to memory. "I want information about his love life."

Drew stops looking into the camera and turns to face me, dark hair blowing across his forehead in the breeze. His face is open. Expression clear. I can see what Bree meant when she said he was good-looking, although it's in that interesting way that grows on you, unlike Oliver with his indisputable, movie-star attractiveness. "I don't think there's one particular girl," he confirms.

It's not exactly the answer I wanted. I imagine all the girls

Oliver might have kissed, or more, and when I see myself joining that club, I feel like I'm standing on the edge of one of those tiny paths on the side of a cliff face, scared to open my eyes.

"You auditioning for the role?" Drew asks.

"I don't know," I reply.

I do know, though. There's something about Oliver that feels inevitable, so much energy between us I literally have to catch my breath. Between how he looks and all the attention he's paying me, after I've been totally starved of romance my entire school career, he's irresistible.

"How about you?" I ask. I want to know why he's not spending late nights on the beach with Mila and Blyth and Sage from my imaginary warehouse. I watch as he sets up his camera to capture some star trails, swirling circles of light as the earth rotates.

"Nuh," he says, as he presses the remote trigger carefully and steps away from the tripod, focusing back on me. "Don't really have time."

I know that's not true. "You've just set up one photo that's going to take a full thirty minutes. Time is *not* the problem."

He glances back at his mum, who is very unsubtly giving us space by the fire. Tension creeps into his stance as he runs his fingers through his dark hair, like he's uncomfortable with the direction this conversation is taking.

"Alicia was clearly interested!" I tease him.

"Ha! Can you imagine Alicia out here, doing this?"

An awkwardness descends between us, before he adds, "Not that this is, like, a date or anything."

No, this is definitely not a date. I've learned from my very limited and recent experience that dates feel terrifying. Not relaxed.

"Seeing you and your mum together is making me homesick," I admit. "I've been at school in Sydney for five years now, but I'll never really get used to the distance. This is the kind of thing Dad and I would do at home in Newcastle."

It's also a stark contrast with the way Oliver was with his father earlier.

"People don't get how important parents are," Drew says, while he checks the viewfinder. "Until you've never known one, or you're at risk of losing one . . ."

My hand finds his arm, just briefly. We're cocooned in the ocean's noise, and in this private truth. Moonlight plays across his face and I think how attractive it is when someone shares their secrets.

"Toast some marshmallows?" he says, clearing his throat.

I carry my camera toward Annie and the campfire. He lays out blankets on the sand, where I sit across from the two of them and stick marshmallows into the fire on a long barbecue skewer. I can't help thinking how much more in my element I am here with Drew and his mum and the roar of the waves, the warmth of the fire, and a thermos of coffee than I was at that party with the loud music and flashing lights and alcohol.

My marshmallow catches alight, and I blow out the flame and slip it into my mouth, a sweet, gooey mess that makes me broadcast some primitive, guttural noise that I follow up with a snort of laughter. It's so different from the sandwich anxiety earlier.

Drew smiles and throws me the whole bag of marshmallows, goading me into a repeat performance.

I catch Annie smiling at him, and there's a whole history conveyed between them when their eyes meet.

"How often do you do this?" I ask.

"Not often enough. I haven't been well," Annie says, and I stop chewing and swallow. "It's taken so much time away from Drew's social life."

He groans.

"It's why he's never had a girlfriend."

"Mum!"

"What? It's true, Drew! I know you're not a saint . . ."

"MUM!"

"But as for long-term girlfriends . . ."

I watch him squirm. "I'm sorry you've been unwell," I tell her, saving him, desperate to decode his tormented expression.

"I've had a lot of treatment," Annie continues. "I just . . . It's hard, sometimes, to get motivated."

Firelight plays across Drew's face. He's reassumed that serious expression I noticed the second I met him. The heaviness. The depth. Even with this tiny glimpse into what might be going on in his family, I'm suddenly glad I acted on instinct and covered for him over the formal mix-up. It feels like it's one small thing I can lift from his plate.

He catches me looking at him, and there's a brief spark in his eyes, like the flicker of an engine about to roar to life. But I'm distracted by my phone buzzing again. He watches me resist it as I lie back on the blanket, staring at the stars.

# 22

## *Drew*

If I hadn't set my camera to capture that star trail, I'd take pictures of her. She's on the blanket, legs bent, her head resting on my jacket that she's folded as a makeshift pillow. She didn't ask. Just went ahead and helped herself to a piece of my clothing like we've been friends for years.

I *have* to stop. I can't be sitting here imagining this is more than it can be.

She's got a thing for Oliver. And if he has a thing for her, then that's the start of that. And the end of this.

Mum is staring at her too. I can read her thoughts. *Evie is lovely. How wonderful that Drew has met such an interesting girl, and she's into all the same things.* She tries to get up off the sand and struggles. I leap up and pull her to her feet, wrapping her jacket around her shoulders, remembering all the times a minor cold sent her to the hospital.

"I'm going for a little walk along the beach," she announces, obvious as hell.

As I sit down on the sand again opposite Evie, she rolls onto her side and cradles her head in her hand, watching the fire. She pulls the beanie off and shakes out her curls, casting spiral shadows on the sand behind her.

"Pass me your camera," I say. "And don't move."

It's hard to get the right exposure with the brightness of the flames; I have to try a couple of angles. But she's patient. She knows this is about the challenge of working out the shot. And she just lies there, watching me do it.

"Is your mum okay, Drew?" she asks, breaking my focus.

I take a shot, but it's blurry.

Mum is probably even less okay than she seems.

Evie is looking directly down the lens. I'm looking directly into the viewfinder. The camera should be a barrier between us, but instead it only draws her closer.

"I don't think she is," I reply at last, clicking the shutter just as my words land and her expression softens. "No, she definitely isn't."

I'm grateful she doesn't ask the obvious follow-up question: "Are *you* okay?" I haven't been okay for so long. I haven't told anyone how hard it's been, or how much of a mess I've become. There's always a risk it will get back to Mum, and it's meant to be the other way around with us. *I* worry about *her*. Care for her, apart from the couple of times we've been able to arrange respite or her nursing friends have dropped in when she's really bad. I'm not going to be the one to push her over the edge. This is why I keep to myself a lot.

I look at the photo. It would be perfect for the exhibition. I'd caption it *Compassion*.

But there are some moments that are too private for public consumption. And some unspoken conversations that need to stay that way.

When I put the camera down and look at her for real, I know that this one, small admission has chipped open a new friendship. She's not pushing. Not prying. Not telling me she knows exactly how I feel and sharing some vaguely relevant personal anecdote of her own as if this is a problem competition. She's just lying here on the beach with me, noticing my life.

News travels fast at school on Monday. And by "news," I mean some bizarre mash-up of the truth involving Oliver stealing Evie right out of my arms—as if she was ever in them. Apparently, I've come out fighting, still taking her to her formal, which surprises everyone. *Isn't Drew Kennedy that loner?*

And who is Evie Hudson anyway? Nobody heard of her until she stirred up the Photography Club and Oliver made her high school famous by asking her out. They can't even find her on Instagram. Probably because virtually no one knows she only has a photography account. Oliver's not even following it.

Saturday-night stargazing with her was beautiful. Sunday too.

Come over after lunch and we'll edit the photos in Lightroom? I'd texted. It had taken me a full ten minutes to construct that sentence and another twenty to get the guts to send it.

She did come.

I shut the blinds and darkened my room, the cramped space feeling even smaller with her in it, while I hoped she wouldn't notice the peeling cream wallpaper and creaky wooden floorboards. It's a space I've shared with girls a couple of times, but never like this. Working on our photos together felt a thousand times more intimate as we crouched beside the screen, not touching unless she reached for the mouse to adjust something or I leaned in closer and brushed her shoulder as I tried to see a tiny detail in the frame. I focused on pulling out the whites in the images and upping the texture and clarity, bringing the universe alive together—not on the scent of her perfume, or the sight of her legs in shorts, crossed under my secondhand wooden desk, or the way they brushed my thighs whenever she got excited about the images and forgot where she was and who she was with.

"I can't believe I took these," she gushed, leaning closer to the screen, touching my arm for emphasis, marveling at the resolution. It had felt so good to watch her confidence come together in real time, beside me.

Mum brought in drinks and snacks. I showed Evie my portfolio.

"Sounds pretentious to call it that," I said, "but I'm applying to the School of Contemporary Art next year." Provided everything is okay with Mum.

"You'll definitely get in with these," she'd replied, taking her time to flick through the pages and analyze each image in detail. She might not have had formal training, but she has a strong eye and spouted technical terms like a pro.

"Look at the harmony in this one . . ." She pointed to an image I took of some boulders in the snow on a school excursion to Thredbo last year. We were supposed to be skiing but I couldn't afford to rent the gear and had convinced the PE teacher that I should document the trip instead, for the school magazine.

"You know I have a darkroom set up in the garage," I explained.

She was beside herself. She'd never been in one. "I've never even taken film photos!" she admitted.

I reached high on the shelf in my room and brought down an old camera and a fresh roll of film. "You feed it in like this,"

I said, our heads close together over the open door of the camera while I showed her how to hook the roll onto the spool and move it along.

Next, we were rambling through the streets, taking photos of each other in the local park. Silly shots of her hanging upside down on the monkey bars and jumping off the swings. Semiserious artsy shots and gritty street scenes, while overnight freight trucks thundered underneath us on the overpass or streetlights flickered in alleyways.

Then we'd wandered home, where I set up the chemicals and we watched the images develop, playing music, talking, waiting for them to dry.

Standing in the red glow of the light with her, watching our faces materialize on the paper, seeing myself smiling, for real, after not smiling much for so many years . . . It's the first time in my whole high school experience that I felt vaguely "normal." In a way, it made me sadder about everything I've missed.

So now I'm stuck in math, trying to focus, looking forward to Wednesday's Photography Club. Worrying about the fact that I'm getting too entrenched in this friendship. Hoping Oliver will lose interest in photography, fast, and just leave this one thing for us.

I'm used to everything being transient. I can't get attached to ideas, or plans, or people. I'm used to the ever-present threat of things being swept away from me. It's just easier not to depend on anything.

Getting to know Evie breaks all my rules.

"Why don't we call the exhibition *Pictures of You*?" she suggests on Wednesday. "And each photographer can write a caption *to* their subject, instead of to the audience—you know, in the style of an old-fashioned letter. In their handwriting."

Predictably, the boys in the room groan at this idea, all except Oliver, of course, who is the Perfect Boyfriend and making a show of doing anything she asks. The dynamic has shifted in the group since his arrival—the boys in the younger years look up to him.

"I know we're doing this as a school photography exhibition," Evie adds, pulling herself up onto the desk to face the room, suddenly more confident in this setting than I've seen her before, "but we could turn this into a social media campaign. You know, people post their own photos and personal notes to the subject. Maybe a blog? Or a newspaper campaign. It could go viral."

It could be a total mess.

"What if people start trolling the concept? Sharing horrible photos, bullying messages?" I ask, and her face falls. I don't want to be the person responsible for her disappointment. "Just playing devil's advocate." Trying to protect her.

I wish I hadn't said it.

"It's genius," Oliver says. "*Pictures of You.* Poetic descriptions. A viral campaign." She smiles and he spins her into his arms, kissing her as if none of us is there. I can practically see her goose bumps across the classroom.

# 23

***Evie***

Being Oliver's girlfriend is dazzling. I feel like we're living in a rom-com. He's the king of grand gestures.

*You are gorgeous, Evie.*

*Let me drive you and Bree to the movie.*

Flowers.

Chocolates.

Books.

Tickets.

I've never felt so wanted and desired and needed.

He and I want to spend every moment together. School itself is *torture*, just an exercise in waiting to see him again. I am utterly and wholeheartedly, outrageously captivated by him.

"I thought your boyfriend's name was Drew," Mum says on the phone.

*What?* God, she can be hopeless. "Mum! Drew and I are *friends*."

"Photography Drew?"

"Yes!"

"I thought you were more than friends," she says. "The way you were talking."

Why would I be interested in *Drew* when I could be with *Oliver*? Wait till she meets him. That will be persuasive.

"How's your study going?" she asks.

It's something I usually wax lyrical about. The driving force of my life these last five years. I need to talk to Oliver about this. I don't know if he understands how much getting top marks means to me. I know he's committed to his own study and getting into Arts Law, but I need him to understand my commitment to mine too. Because right now, I cannot let landing the Boyfriend of the Century distract me from the future I've dreamt about forever . . .

"Oliver," I say, pushing him away from me on his bed one Thursday afternoon after school. We're not having sex. Not yet. I'm nowhere near ready. But we spend a lot of time in his room kissing, with me imagining it. "I'm worried I'm going to fail."

He sits bolt upright. Seriousness personified. "Fail at what? This?" He gestures at the bed. And at us.

I laugh. "What? No!" I mean, yes, secretly I am worried I'll fail at that too, but I'm talking about my schoolwork. "I'm trying to get a scholarship," I admit. "You're distracting me. I mean, *this* is distracting me. You and me."

Do I imagine the flicker of annoyance?

"Evie Hudson: I won't have this," he says, taking my hand and squeezing it. For a second I panic and think he's going to break up with me. "I'm going to make your scholarship my project."

I laugh with relief.

"Pass me your phone," he says.

I hand it over and watch as he does something with my calendar.

"All right, I've shared your calendar with mine. Now I'll know exactly when every assignment is due. I'll know when to leave you alone so you can study," he says. "I'll help you get the scholarship, Evie."

I need him to do exactly what he's saying, but I don't *want* him to leave me alone. I worry if I'm not directly in his line of sight, some other, more incredible girl will walk into his life and steal him away from me while I'm off cramming for a modern history exam or trying to balance chemistry equations. I see the way they all look at him, everywhere we go together.

I want to show my mum this boy. The way he supports me. The way he is as dedicated to the future I'm trying to create as I am.

He pulls me into yet another breathtaking kiss that sends me into some other world. This time it's deeper, and faster. He rolls me onto my back and pins my thigh to the mattress with his knee. I push my leg up underneath him, testing that I'm not trapped, and he immediately releases me.

His hand trails down my throat toward the button on my school shirt, playing with it. It's tantalizing, and terrifying, and I wonder if he's waiting for me to stop him.

"I'll always look after you," he whispers. I'm not sure if we're still talking about the scholarship, but my heart races either way as his fingers deftly flick the plastic button and the top of my shirt falls open, exposing the lace of my white bra underneath.

He's looking at me as if I'm the first girl he's ever seen. "Is this okay?" he asks.

I need more information. If he's talking about just that top button, then yes? I think so? It's just that I'm frozen right now and can't utter any response one way or the other.

"Do you know how gorgeous you are?" he says.

I do not know that.

His finger trails along my skin, teasing the lace. "I think I'm falling in love with you," he says, simply, while I stare at him. "Is *that* okay?"

He kisses my neck, and then my chest, and then I'm swooning like all those eighteenth-century girls, in the very best way. I know it's been only a few weeks, and they've been intense, but he *loves* me? Already?

"Maybe we're soulmates," he suggests. "There's never been anyone else who's made me feel like this, Evie. Never. Seriously."

I get it. I do. Soulmates. What else could something this powerful possibly be?

I want to tell him I love him too. I really want to. I should. It must be true—I'm entirely obsessed with him, after all.

His leg pins mine again, the weight of it heavier this time as he looks into my eyes with a silent intensity. I try to push back but can't, panic flooding my chest until I open my mouth and say the three little words he's expecting.

And the pressure from his leg instantly lifts.

# 24

***Evie***

The Book Cottage is a block up from Darby Street, in the shade of a large red maple. The tree drops so many leaves that they pile around the cart in front of the shop and its owner, Rose, has to brush them off the books. How can I remember the name of the bookshop keeper but nothing else from the past decade? It's maddening.

According to my high school plan, I was meant to be through my undergrad degree at Sydney Uni, and ultimately a PhD, which I would have completed in three years—the minimum time. I should have spent semesters overseas in postdoctoral fellowships at Yale or Brown or Oxford, and by now I would be working as a forensic linguist, solving crime by day, writing bestselling thrillers by night.

*That* was the plan. Not becoming a supporting character in my high school boyfriend's story with nothing discernible to show for my life except a giant diamond ring that I hate, a clinically decorated mansion, a viral podcast, and a gorgeous Instagram aesthetic.

I pull on the familiar brass handle and predict the exact moment the door will creak, and it does. The scent of old books and the whirring of the vintage fan above the counter send me straight to my childhood. It feels like home.

*Hold it together.*

Drew steps into the shop behind me, tall and broad. *His* scent is far less familiar. I turn and glance from the dark waves of his hair to the stubble on his jawline and picture him in *Wild* magazine—some glossy profile on the rugged photographer behind the beautiful landscape imagery—and instruct my imagination to stay on track. I'd had to do the same last night, standing beside him at the counter of a beachside hotel. The sixteen-year-old in me ran away with the whole notion of it—my being away in another city with a *man*—until he checked us into separate rooms and, admittedly, a sense of relief washed over me.

Walking tentatively toward the counter now, I see Rose serving a customer and my heart quickens. She hasn't changed. A bit rounder, maybe. Still wearing her light brown hair in that tight, messy bun, brown eyes still twinkling when she talks to people about books. Right now, the soft-spoken, middle-aged former librarian is the only connection I have with anyone from my past. I want to throw myself into her arms and stay there until everything rights itself and she hands me the scoop on my parents' whereabouts . . . but at the same time, I'm terrified. What if this is the moment that breaks me?

She looks up and her familiar features crumple into an unreadable mash-up of emotion. I want to step forward, but something stops me—as if sudden movement will scare her off.

Someone steps on a floorboard in a nearby aisle and it creaks, breaking the moment. Rose swallows and takes an audible breath. "Evie," she says at last. She comes around the counter, walks up to me, and touches me on the cheek, as if she can't believe I'm here.

Hot tears well, and I struggle to contain them. I want to keep my act together almost as much as I want to fall spectacularly apart. I need to know about Mum and Dad—now. But just as I'm about to ask that question, Rose turns, takes a step sideways, throws her arms out, and says, "Drew!"

Rose *knows* him?

And if he knows Rose, why didn't he say so?

But Drew looks just as taken aback as I feel. He moves a half step away from her, brows knitted as if he's trying to work out how he fits into this picture. "I'm sorry," he says. "Have we met?"

She'll have none of his reticence, drawing him into a deep hug, and he looks at me over her shoulder in wordless surprise. He's either a brilliant actor or he really doesn't know who she is. My heart is hoping like mad it's the latter, because Drew is the one person in the world I feel like I can rely on right now.

"Look at the pair of you!" she says. "All grown-up."

*The pair of us?* We are not a pair. We're not even friends. We're barely acquaintances. He's just an innocent victim, caught up in my unwitting chaos, trying to untangle the disaster that is my life, so he can get on with his. In New York.

*And why does the idea of him doing that suddenly make me so bereft and anxious?*

"Rose—"

"Come on!" She cuts me off and bustles us outside to the tiny courtyard garden, where I sink into a wrought-iron chair with a flat, faded yellow cushion and watch as Rose pulls up a chair from another table, sits down, and takes my hand.

"Now, Evie girl. How are you? I was sorry to read of your loss."

Does she mean my parents? My heart almost explodes in

fear before I ask, "You mean Oliver?" She nods. "Rose, I can't remember anything that's happened since I was sixteen!" The words gush from me. It's a massive relief to give the truth air. "We went back to the house but there was another woman living there with a baby. I don't have phone numbers for Mum and Dad or Breanna or *anyone* from here . . ."

Tears surface, hot and fast. Fear-laced tears. *This* is my loss. All of this. Not a husband I can't remember. A whole life that I've lost. A whole family.

Rose gets up and throws her arms around me while staccato sobs gush from my throat.

"Are Mum and Dad . . ." I can't even finish the question.

"They're well," she says. "They're okay."

Relief floods through my veins, bottled-up emotion erupting violently. They're okay. They're alive. *My life is salvageable.*

I'd been up early this morning, and had skipped across the road from the hotel, through the concrete tunnel toward the beach. It was all so wonderfully familiar. Finally, something I truly understood. Sand. Salt. The gentle spray of sea mist on my face, the pink of the sunrise kissing the navy-blue horizon, dotted with freight ships heading for Newcastle port.

I wandered down the Shortland Esplanade along the coast toward the Ocean Baths, where there's a pavilion with an art deco facade I've always loved. I learned to swim in that pool. I learned a lot of things. How it feels to dive under the surface and hide when the sun is too bright and your skin is too hot. What it's like to be out of your depth.

When I was seven, I'd been overconfident in the water. We were at the baths with a group of family friends, and I was the youngest. It was one of those situations where all the adults think someone else is looking out for the kids, and I guess nobody was. And when the older children I idolized went farther into the pool, I followed them. It was fine at first, then my toes couldn't reach the sandy floor. Pretty soon I was going under, panicking in the green water, kicking, gasping for air. It felt like years but was seconds, probably, before a stranger pulled me from the depths and I staggered out of the pool and ran for my parents. Bolted for them. Desperate for the safety of their arms.

This morning, I stood there on that same concrete, on the safety of dry land, and had been drowning anyway. Wanting their arms around me. I was home. And I'd never felt so far away.

So to hear now from Rose that they are *alive* . . . I can barely cope with the relief.

Drew reaches across the table and touches my hand. Just once. Silent communication that returns my attention to him, and the fact that Rose recognizes him, which makes no sense.

"How do you know Drew?" I ask, after Rose hands me a box of tissues and I blow my nose with gusto, face feeling all red and blotchy. *Now* I look like a proper widow.

"Yes, I'm sorry, Rose—I don't remember," he adds politely. I'm starting to worry that the amnesia is contagious. We cannot have two of us down with it.

She laughs. "Oh, we haven't met in person."

He's as baffled as me.

"But you showed me all those pictures of him, Evie. In high school."

# 25

## *Drew*

God, here we go. I'm nine parts intrigued about what sixteen-year-old Evie might have said about me to Rose, and one part gearing up for an explosion.

Evie stares at me, dumbfounded. "We *know* each other?"

I have to rapidly work this through. I can explain everything, obviously, but the story is so complex, and she's so emotionally compromised, I don't know how or where to begin. Or even if I should.

*Pretend we never met. Promise me, Drew. If we ever meet again, you will pretend you don't know me.*

Do promises pre-amnesia mean anything? What if they've been overtaken by more dramatic events? I can't just keep the whole story from her. Not now that Rose has given her such a compelling teaser.

"Well, it's complicated," I begin, ineffectually.

Color rushes to her face and I recognize a flash of the old Evie, ready to take incomplete information and run with it.

"We met at school," I say quickly. It's like throwing a snack to a wild animal to pacify it while you try to work out an escape plan. "At a school photography club."

"So were you and I . . . What were we?" She's gesturing wildly between us.

An old wound rises and lodges near my heart. It's like a long-lost battle scar that arcs up only in stormy weather. I did not want this. This reprise of Evie Hudson in my life.

But she needs it. Even this tiny preview into our past has her cheeks burning—maybe in anger, to be fair—but she's grasping onto our history, snatching at threads so thin, everything could fall apart.

"Wait, was I a photographer too?"

Photography changed her DNA. She barely saw the world except through a lens, and what she could do with that lens just on pure instinct used to floor me. I was always half amazed, half envious at how easy she seemed to find it.

"You loved photography," I confirm. "You were great at it. And you and I were friends."

Rose scoffs. "*Friends?* Come on, now! Drew was your best friend, Evie. Don't you remember?"

Evie looks from Rose to me, devastated. In trying to protect her from the truth, I've hurt her. Again. I can't seem to get this right.

"You acted like we didn't know each other!"

*Yes.* But I *don't* know her anymore. Not this version of her. When she jumped into my car at the funeral, she might as well have been a stranger—and, in my defense, I didn't ask for this rescue role. I was just trying to get some closure and move on.

"We fell out," I explain hastily. "We haven't spoken in a long time. It didn't end well. These days, we're barely in each other's lives."

I can see her freaking out. Asking herself if she can trust me.

Wondering if I'm going to hurt her. If only she knew our distance the last few years was at her command. Obeying that command is more about my own self-preservation. Can *I* trust *her*? Is she going to hurt *me* again?

"It was your choice," I add, my mind flashing back to the last message she sent me. The coldness of it. No fight left in either of us. Just a sad parting of ways that I regret but was powerless to prevent.

She's still confused, and I know we can't avoid this conversation—or him—any longer.

"Evie, you chose Oliver."

# 26

***Evie***

I'm grateful for the cool breeze flowing through the brick courtyard as I try to calm down. I can't even *look* at Drew right now.

Rose, having realized her blunder, shifts the topic. "Your parents have moved to Adelaide."

*Adelaide?*

"But we don't know anyone in South Australia," I argue.

She pats my arm. "I think that was the point."

A sense of dread creeps in, slowly at first, then rushes through my body. Why would my parents want to escape? What could they possibly be running from?

*They lost their daughter.*

I can't imagine what could have happened that was so bad that my parents and I have no contact, or that they had to leave the city they love and start a new life in another state. The only person who might have a clue is Drew, who has been keeping the truth of our own relationship secret too. Now I feel even more alone than I did yesterday.

I catch Rose and Drew exchanging worried looks. Are they protecting me because of my health, or is the truth really that bad? How far off track can a life possibly *get* in the decade or so since school?

Suddenly, I'm too scared to find out. Not here. I just need to get to Adelaide, see my parents, and ask them to set me straight.

Drew picks up his phone and starts tapping on the screen in a way that enrages me. Maybe he's texting that Chloe he was so keen to dismiss when she phoned on the way to Newcastle. Is my rapidly deepening crisis boring him?

I study him as he scrolls. He is annoyingly attractive, in that effortless, oblivious way, absorbed in the phone, sipping his coffee while dappled light filters through the canopy overhead and dances across his deceptively innocent face. I try to cast myself in his past, remembering the sort of girl I was—a person not in the slightest bit effortless about anything. Oblivious, no doubt in *many* ways. Anxious. Cautious. Studious. And I struggle to see us hitting it off.

"Rose, I don't understand *anything*."

She nods kindly. *She's* still talking to me, so surely whatever I did can't be that bad? Forgivable, at least?

"There's a four p.m. flight from Newcastle, via Melbourne," Drew says, looking up from his phone, which he was apparently using to help me. I can't read any situations right anymore. "Rose, would Evie's parents welcome a visit?"

Yes. I can totally cast myself as the prodigal daughter. "I could surprise them?" I say, hopeful of a happy ending. Maybe I could film their reaction and it would go viral on SnapTok, or whatever it was everyone was talking about at the hospital, showing me videos, trying to cheer me up.

"Hmm," Rose says, in obvious doubt.

"Yes?" Drew says, looking at me for the official go-ahead, finger poised over the booking button. How does he know my personal details? Does he need my birthdate? Oh. Of course. He knows more about me than I know about myself now, and that's terrifying. He could influence the whole narrative if he wanted to. How would I know the difference?

Seconds later, the phone beeps with a confirmation of the purchase. He looks at me and nods, and I don't know what he expects. *Thank you*, probably. *Thank you for keeping me totally in the dark and making me feel more insecure than ever?*

"We've got a few hours before we need to be at the airport," he says, his voice calm and even.

"We?"

He looks taken aback. Like he thought I'd know that he was coming too. Aren't we "barely in each other's lives"?

"Like it or not, we're in this together now," he says. "You claim you haven't had a knock to the head, but I'm not so sure."

*Flattering!*

"You've lost your memory. You're in no state to travel on your own—or at all, probably. And you don't know what's going to happen at the other end, in a city you're unfamiliar with. It's a recipe for disaster . . . as usual."

The "as usual" is muttered. And it stings.

I *will not* cry in front of this man again.

He's looking at me like I'm a liability. But when he sees me struggling to keep my emotions together, his expression softens. He looks like he wants to tell me it will be okay, but no words come out. Maybe because it won't be.

"I'll write down the address and phone number for you," Rose says, scurrying away to get the details.

I know I should thank Drew for the tickets. And for coming. But instead, I just accuse him. "What kind of best friend *are* you?"

"I used to be the best kind," he explains. There's something deeply resonant and believable in his tone, and I can almost see the younger, less confident version of him that I must have known. I'm cut up that he didn't tell me when I first got in his car, or when we pulled over and had that discussion about "where to next." Why not last night on the clifftop, or over dinner, or when we were in the store getting supplies? Why did he keep from me the one piece of information that would have made sense of every moment he's spent looking after me?

"And then what?" I ask. "What went wrong between us?"

*What did he do?*

I wish I could unsee the hurt in his eyes.

# 27

***Drew***

When Evie cut me loose, I had to let go. That meant almost no contact. Trying to resist social-media stalking. Finding a new "first person to call" when I had any kind of news. Being out of her life for good was hard, but if I'd stayed, it would have been worse. Besides, it's not like she gave me a choice.

"Here's your mum and dad's details." Rose passes Evie the information, written on the back of a bookmark from the shop. Evie holds the card like it's precious. "Don't phone ahead, okay?"

Great. Apparently, it's more strategic just to blindside them. Her advice hardly fills me with confidence. My mind skips forward to what I'll do if Adelaide is a bust and I'm stuck picking up more pieces.

As we exit the shop, Evie is shooting daggers at me. I want to explain why I kept it from her, but I don't know how to say it in any way she'll find palatable. *You ditched me. Pretending I didn't know you was the playbook you handed me . . .*

The real reason is scarier. *What if I tell you the truth and you completely unravel?*

I've done enough of that for both of us. You spend years getting over something—a betrayal—and rebuild your life, thinking it will never implode again, because you'll never allow it to. That's how I feel about this woman. She seems innocuous and fragile now, but history has shown she has the power to destroy me.

I need a plan to keep my head for the Adelaide trip. And to keep her at arm's length. Because this version of her . . . This is the person I first knew, and first liked. It would be so easy to be swayed.

We've got a few hours to kill before our flight, and what I'm craving is time with the camera. More specifically, time and space away from Evie. Photography is the only thing that keeps me grounded when everything else is out of control. Through the viewfinder, I forget who I am and can focus on whatever's in the frame. Tiny details, caught in shifting focus. Tricks of the light.

But right now she's standing in front of me, glaring up into my face in the street. A whole world of tiny details is being revealed across her features and blasted at me. All of them point to her being furious.

"Evie, I didn't know how to tell you without . . ."

*Confusing you? Destroying you?*

"How do you expect me to trust you now?" she challenges me, fairly.

"All I can say is I had your best interests at heart. Even if the execution was off."

*"Off?"* she splutters. "Drew! First, I thought you were an Uber driver. Then a paparazzo, then some sort of long-lost mourner at my husband's funeral. Now I find out you knew Oliver from school. Then that you knew *me* from school. Worse, that you were my *best friend*. And, apparently, I hate you?"

I recoil at that. "*Hate* is a strong word . . ."

"And what about Bree? Did you know her too? *Do* you know her? Is she in on this mystery?"

I wish I could fill this part in, but I haven't spoken to Bree in several years. We didn't fall out. It was probably just that staying in touch was too painful and we allowed ourselves to drift apart. "I'm sorry. I wish I'd kept in touch with her."

A light seems to go out in Evie's eyes. I can see how much she's been hoping her other best friend will ride in to salvage this situation, but unfortunately she's got only me.

"Whose judgment do I trust here?" she powers on. "Sixteen-year-old me who first made you her best friend? Or twenty-something me who shut you out of my life for some reason you refuse to divulge?"

I try to place my hand on her arm, but she shakes me off, and I get that familiar sense of dismay that I felt toward the end, when everything collapsed. My phone starts vibrating again with a call from Chloe. This time I can't ignore it.

"Maybe try twenty-nine-year-old you starting fresh with someone who is just trying to help you. I promise," I say, lifting my phone to my ear. "Sorry, I have to take this call."

# 28

## *Evie*

*This man!* I find it impossible to believe I would ever have seen something in him that suggested "best friend potential" when he is so cagey about our background. Yes, he's been doing a lot to take care of me, but he's been keeping *years* of history from me in the process.

Now he's wandered along the footpath, having a *very* earnest phone conversation under a tree outside the antiques store, presumably with the woman who called yesterday in the car. He doesn't realize the breeze is carrying his voice.

"I'll take Harriet to the zoo on the weekend," he promises. "How's Sunday?" He glances over, notices me staring, and angles his body away. It takes me back to primary school and the time I was inexplicably dropped by my two best friends, who'd whispered about me behind their hands and left me stranded awkwardly on the playground, trying to look busy.

"Sure, put her on!" I hear him say. There's a pause, and then a shift in everything as he turns around. Tone, volume, body language. He's like a whole different person. Guard down. Lit up. "How are you, sweetheart? How was kindy?"

There's a long pause while he listens and I catch the smile on his face, crinkling the skin at the corners of his eyes and washing away all the stress of our encounter to date. Eventually he gets a word in.

"I thought I could take you on an adventure," he suggests. And even I can hear the squealing, a few feet away. As he holds the phone out from his ear and laughs, his gaze falls on me, and I'm the recipient of a full-bodied smile so genuine and warm it floods me with refracted adoration. But the smile dissolves just as fast, and I find myself willing it back, wanting to bask in its warmth even a second longer. Wishing I wasn't its kryptonite.

I'm certain that child is Drew's flesh and blood. Which means Chloe is whom, exactly? His ex-girlfriend? Worse, his existing partner?

"I'm not running away to Adelaide with somebody's boyfriend!" I announce forthrightly, once he ends the call.

My statement catches him off guard and he stares blankly at me for a second. "Chloe and I aren't together," he replies. "It's—"

"Complicated?" I accuse him. Of course it is. She might be his ex-girlfriend, but Harriet is her daughter. *Their* daughter. Why else would he be taking her to the zoo? "She's not your sister?" I confirm.

"No."

"So, just a friend?"

"Evie!" He's exasperated now.

Is he daring me to ignore every red flag he's waved at me since yesterday and just trust him? I don't know much about my almost thirty-year-old self, but I hope I haven't become this gullible. I was always attracted to men of honor, with manners and standards. Yes, they were mostly fictional, but isn't art supposed to imitate life?

*Friends? Come on, now! Drew was your best friend, Evie. Don't you remember?*

Rose's words echo in my ears. Rose, whom I *do* trust.

I survey Drew again, sunlight beaming through the giant Moreton Bay Fig tree behind him. His earnest brown eyes bore into mine, trying to convince me to believe in him. A big part of me wants to, the one who has nobody else. The part who doesn't want to get on a plane on my own and face the music in South Australia. The part buried deep beneath this unrelenting amnesia, violently trying to push its way out of it.

# 29

***Drew***

We decide to call a truce and take a head-clearing walk on the beach before our flight. As I sling the camera bag over my shoulder, slam the trunk, and walk down the path toward the sand dunes, images of our old photography rambles flood back.

She's taking photos with her iPhone, using the wooden fence to create strong leading lines, unaware how good she is at this. Photography is an art she intimately understands. Surely that will come back. You might lose your memory, but it doesn't change how artistic you are. I think back to our first time at the ocean together, when she captured the driftwood under the stars.

As we make our way toward the bottom of the cliffs, water washing over the rocks and pooling in valleys, I pass her my camera to hold while I put the bag up the beach a little way, paranoid a rogue wave will destroy my expensive lenses. When I turn around, she's kneeling on the sand, focused on the shells of some tiny periwinkle snails barnacled to a rock, but I can tell that's not what she's really trying to capture. It's the miniature starbursts of sunlight that hit the still water in the rock-pool. In the soft focus of the background, she's creating sparkles of bokeh as light hits the ocean, a spray of white foam rising into the sky.

She admires the shot, and smiles in surprise. "Look at this!" she says, eyes wide and sparkling in her unexpected achievement, and holds out the camera to show me, strap still around her neck. I have to lean in close to see the image, the wind flicking her hair into my face, a cocktail of strawberry shampoo and salt.

"I expect nothing less," I say, stepping back.

Now she's flicking back through the last few stored images from a shoot in Sydney last weekend. Raw, unprocessed photos of an intergenerational initiative between an aged-care facility and a local preschool—bright-eyed four-year-olds bounding exuberantly through the wheelchairs and walkers, among wrinkled smiles and wistful glances.

Since she's confirmed her parents are actually alive, she's relaxed. I think in her mind it's a simple matter of knocking on their door and all will be well. I don't know what exactly led to their estrangement, just that estrangement was a common theme. First Breanna, then me. And later, presumably, her mum and dad. I don't think she realizes this isn't over just because they still exist.

"You're very good," Evie says, handing me my camera.

I flash to our long afternoons lazing by the pool in Year Twelve, dreaming up futures that didn't pan out as planned—for either of us. She walks into the water a little, while I hang back and fire off a few shots of the cliffs, then pan around until I find her in the frame.

It's like she's never left the ocean. She's in a world of her own, making patterns in the wet sand with her toes as the waves rush in and carve ditches in the sand around the hollows of her ankles. I imagine my own memories carving a similar path in my heart, pumping through my veins until they've flooded every cell. Again. And I find myself capturing her, until she turns and sees me and smiles. One perfect moment in the middle of our extraordinary mess.

# 30

***Evie***

As I turn around and he takes the photo, I'm thrown back in time. Another beach. Another photo. Him behind the camera. Me . . .

This time, the memory isn't a blur. Not like it was last night, while I was grappling to hold fragments of memories about Oliver. This one is sharp. And it's not about being awed and overwhelmed by light. It's a sense of peace. Safety. A feeling of being more *myself* than I've felt with any other person, even Breanna.

Maybe he *was* my best friend.

"We've done this before," I say.

He looks out from behind the viewfinder.

"You and me," I say. "At the beach, with a camera."

He drops the lens away from his face and wades into the water where I am, denim cuffs of his jeans getting wet. "You remember?"

The way he's looking at me, you'd think he'd struck gold. Not me in a rare lucid moment. The closer he stands, looking into my eyes like he's searching for the real me past the glaze of amnesia, the surer I become: I know this man.

"I saw you. Younger you."

Same height. Smaller breadth. Lanky. Smooth-skinned . . .

I reach out, involuntarily, and graze my fingers across the stubble on his chin, amazed that he needs to shave at all. Forgetting he's not a boy anymore. The hair prickles the skin on my fingers, and I retract my hand quickly. "Sorry!" I say, embarrassed. *What am I doing?*

"We were on Bronte Beach," he informs me. "A Sunday afternoon in the Easter holidays. It was still hot. We'd been for a swim."

I can imagine it all. I read once about a condition called *aphantasia*, where people can't create mental imagery. It's not a challenge I ever faced. My mind is bursting with images and sounds and tastes—the imaginary world as intense as the real one.

"You'd just finished an English essay," Drew says. "I proofread it. It was annoyingly perfect."

More than a decade later, this thrills me. Academic praise has always been my love language.

"Then you bolted onto the sand. I took a photo when you turned around, splashing through the waves. I entered it in an exhibition we put on together."

"We put on an exhibition?"

It sounds exactly like me. The spirit of me.

Suddenly, if this is the caliber of my teenage past, I'm thirsty for more. More information. Details. I want to hear everything about every moment Drew and I have ever shared, in the hope that it will dislodge this mental block and open a torrent of remembering.

"Do you still have the photo?" I ask.

His face clouds, jaw clenching. He seems to realize the cuffs of his jeans are getting saturated and steps back out of the waves, annoyed. "Oliver bought it," he says. And, just like that, the magic is broken.

# 31

***Drew***

Oliver's buying my photo was a power move I never forgave him for. He couldn't stand to see me with something he wanted, even if it was my own intellectual property. I guess it was a mutual sentiment. It wasn't just me who looked at Oliver Roche and saw a whole world to envy. Splashy house in Lane Cove. Luxury car at seventeen. Two parents invested in his life. And yet he managed to stay down-to-earth enough to be universally likeable. Or loveable, in Evie's case.

I don't know what he did with the portrait. It was never on display. The reason it won didn't have anything to do with my photography skills; it was all her and the joie de vivre she had back then. She'd lit up the moment I pressed the shutter, but she would have done that with or without a camera stuck in her face.

"Maybe the portrait is at the house I shared with Oliver," she suggests, walking backward away from me, as if she's pulling me into a stroll.

I amble toward her, sand clinging to my feet, wet denim rubbing my ankles, every shred of common sense telling me to stop following this woman up the beach, into our past. I think she'll be disappointed if she goes looking for that portrait, but it's not my place to accuse Oliver now. Never speak ill of the dead, they say.

Dead. It's weird to think Oliver is gone. Even weirder that I'm the one here with Evie. Life twists and turns and things you never imagined possible strike in an instant. Suddenly you're on a totally different path. Not that this is still our path. It's a diversion. Get her memory sorted, and that's it. I can't let her get any closer than she already has. No more brushing my face with her fingers.

She's down the beach a little way now, inspecting rock pools. I resist the temptation to take more photos. She's similar to the teenage girl I remember—always in a world of her own—but now with the body of a woman. Every move she makes puts thoughts in my head that don't belong there, not in these twisted circumstances. She looks up just as I'm banishing yet another idea. My body has always been under her spell, but it's my mind I worry about more.

I have to snap out of this. I pull out my phone and search for *dissociative amnesia*. The more I know about what she's grappling with, the better, although what I find only plunges me into a world of concern.

*Severe memory loss that can't be explained by a medical condition.*

*The patient can't recall events or people from their lives, especially from a time of distress or pain.*

*Can't recall upsetting events or traumatic experiences.*

*Increased risk of self-harm . . .*

"Did you keep anything from when we were at school?" she asks. "Concert tickets, programs from school plays, photos?"

Armed with new details of her condition, I'm wary about how to answer. "Why?"

"It's just, I don't have anything. I think it's all been thrown out. Apparently I'm a minimalist now? Can you imagine?!"

"I remember your car. Books, journals, school assignment instructions . . . I can confirm that you loved stuff."

"Maybe you really did know me," she says, wonder lighting up her face. It's better than fury. But now she's looking at me expectantly, perhaps hoping she meant enough to me that I've stashed away evidence of our friendship for safekeeping.

"I kept a few things," I assure her, though I'm not ready to tell her what. Not even sure I should, if this glitch in her mind is preventing her from accessing a whole period of her life for her own emotional safety. *Why?*

I wonder if she has any idea of all the ways she could break me. *Has* broken me. The fracture of our friendship was the catalyst for a decade of chasing the wrong relationships, gravitating toward situations I knew would fail before they even began. Always holding out some crazed hope that something massive would shift and a miracle would happen and we'd get our plan B start. An idea so far-fetched, given her marital status, that it always seemed impossible . . . and because it was impossible, *safe*.

# 32

***Evie***

The flights to Melbourne and Adelaide pass in a blur. Drew tries his best to make conversation, but all I can focus on is landing and going straight to my parents' place. I need this agony to be over. Surely my memory will return once I'm back in my comfort zone with them?

It's after 9 p.m. when we hit the tarmac, and a wall of unexpected heat slams into me outside the terminal. Fading orange and pink clouds merge into deeper purple and blue, punctuated with the first of the evening's twinkling stars.

"The 'blue hour,'" Drew says, while we're waiting in the queue for transport. It's not clear if he's talking to himself or to me, until he adds, "This perfect, tranquil soft light . . ."

Is he serious?

"Do you *remember*?" he asks, dragging his eyes from the sky and settling them on my face.

"Remember what?"

"About the blue hour?"

"Are you trying to give me a photography lesson in the midst of my crisis?"

Or is he just lost in it? I think of his photography website and how *in the world* he is. And I have a pang of regret about my own approach, so "head down" to his "looking up." I'm always focused on the next thing, endlessly worried about where I might be tripping up or falling short. I've never made time for finding the poetry in the world, the way Drew does.

"You seemed to recall some things about photography," he says. "Negative space and all that. I thought you might remember this. Maybe photography could be the way back for you. A positive trigger."

"A glimmer?" I tell him. The psychiatrist mentioned those. The opposite of triggers. Moments of joy or calm that ground you. I'm hungry to feel some. I wish the blue hour meant something to me, but it only hands me another piece of information I should know and don't.

According to the address Rose gave us, my parents live thirty minutes from the airport in a suburb called Mawson Lakes. I try to distract myself during the drive there. The psychiatrist at the hospital told me to stay "in the moment" by noticing details about my surroundings and telling myself what I'm seeing. The sandstone architecture. The churches. Quirky shop fronts. Street art. The pale green sundress I'm wearing, purchased in a dash to Kmart with Drew. My own nerves. Drew's hand resting between us on the back seat. The bones in his knuckles. The way he clenches and stretches his fingers every so often. Maybe he gets repetitive strain injury from holding the camera so much? My gaze travels up his forearm, over the definition of his muscles. The sleeves of his T-shirt. Up his neck and the square of his jaw, the dark hairs on his chin, Adam's apple bobbing in his throat as he swallows when my exploration of him reaches his brown eyes, which are observing me closely.

"It's anxiety," I explain, quickly. "Sorry. I'm meant to pay attention to things. Little details, you know? You're just . . . an available stimulus."

He doesn't seem convinced.

"You never could keep your eyes off me, Hudson," he jokes. At least I assume it's a joke. Either way, I'm mortified.

The closer we get to my parents, though, the fewer of the city's charms I take in, and the more nervous I become. Drew remains a solid presence beside me in the back seat, but even he wipes his hands on his jeans and takes a breath when we pull up outside the house.

It's so different from our home in Newcastle, but I can see Mum and Dad's influence all over it, even from the street. Mum's favorite Pierre de Ronsard roses climbing along the side fence in the garden. Dad's old armchair on the veranda—even though Mum thinks it's an eyesore. Such normal, middle-aged "parent" things that a vastly less grateful version of me used to find cringey.

Drew opens the door and gets out of the car like a man on a mission. He is a "rip off the Band-Aid" type of person, leaving me to clamber across the seat after him as he grabs our things. As the car drives away, he gestures for me to go first up the garden path, but my feet seem planted to the driveway, so he takes my hand and pulls me these last few steps to the front door. I have déjà vu from doing the same thing together in Newcastle. How could it be only yesterday?

I knock tentatively. Then stronger.

I should just walk in. I should have a key.

There's scrabbling on the other side, and Dad's voice saying he'll get it, then Mum saying not to get up, him telling her he's already up. They always do this performance. Forever trying to make each other's lives easier. Finally, the door swings open and Mum is standing there, tea towel in hand, staring at me, speechless.

"Who is it?" Dad calls. "Christine?" He rounds a corner, carrying two cups of tea, and stops dead in the hallway. He looks almost comical with his beard, in an apron and shorts and a gray polo, and I'm hit by the scent of something delicious from the slow cooker—all wrong for this time of year, but all right for my parents.

There's a protracted silence before I drop my bag, fall across the threshold, and throw my arms around Mum, her shape exactly as I remember, and sob. Just her fragrance is enough to fling me back to every age I've ever been. Four, and twelve, and fifteen, and . . . no, that's where the memories start fading. It's so *frustrating*.

She takes moments to catch on, then holds me by the shoulders and pushes me back so she can look at me. "You're here?" she says. Her voice is strained.

Mum looks *years* older than I remember. Middle-aged, when she was always so youthful. She's in white capri pants and a vibrant top scattered with sequins. Of course she is. What would have once had me rolling my eyes now looks utterly perfect to me, in the wake of Gwendolyn's classy polish. I can handle the lines across Mum's face, and the graying hair. What I can't handle is the arm's distance.

She isn't hugging me back. Dad isn't rushing to my side, either. There's a scary silence that should be exploding with the reunion of our dreams.

They look at Drew, and back at me.

"Why?" Mum says.

*Why?*

It's the last question I expected. Far from being delighted, she looks hurt.

Dad puts the tea cups down, walks over, and stands behind her, placing his hand on her shoulder. It's a gesture I've never noticed him do before. Protective. Calming. But protecting against what? *Me?* His lip is trembling and the tears in his eyes are contagious as my heart plunges.

"I'm sorry, Evie," he says after an unbearable few seconds of silence. His voice is cracking. "Your mother just can't do this anymore."

# 33

***Drew***

Evie stumbles out of her parents' front hallway and over the threshold as her dad and I step toward it. I don't know what has gone on here, but I can guess. As horrible as it was being on the receiving end of her hot-and-cold behavior, I still want to save her from the consequences of it.

I put my hand on the wood paneling of the door to ensure that it stays open. "Mr. Hudson, please give us a minute to explain," I say, surprised at the firmness in my tone. I spent a long time swallowing abject envy about the love-filled family Evie grew up in and the relationship she had with her dad—such a stark comparison to my complete lack of a father figure. Is it because of that that I can't contend with the idea of them rejecting her? Or can I not contend with the idea that I'll be stuck with her?

He pushes from the other side. "I've said no, Drew. I'm sorry."

My heart bolts at the notion that he recognizes me. We've never met, but she's clearly painted enough of a picture of me over the years that he knows me on sight. The emotion in his voice is unmistakable: this is killing him.

Evie sinks onto the concrete beside me, back up against the metal fence, defeated.

"I need to prioritize my wife's mental health," her father says. "The last few messages Evie sent . . ." He can't continue. I can hear Christine crying now, in the hall.

"What messages?" Evie asks from the ground. "Dad, I don't remember anything!"

"Look, we're only just back from Sydney," he says, his voice low. "We got in the car as soon as we heard you were in the hospital, Evie. Aimed to get to the service, of course. But when the media started harassing us . . . There's only so much more your mother can take."

"You *came*?" She looks from her dad to me and appeals to me silently, willing me to grab hold of this morsel of hope.

"We also have to prioritize Evie's health," I find myself arguing, and I feel her father's hard pressure on the door give a couple of centimeters. It's like a standoff. I didn't mean to swoop in like this and I appreciate that this is a strain on them, but I'm genuinely worried about the impact of this stress on Evie's already fragile mental condition now that we're away from her medical team. "It's post-traumatic amnesia," I continue. "She can't remember anything about Oliver. I've spent the last twenty-four hours with her and can promise you, this is the daughter you used to know."

Evie is looking at me as if I'm dishing out even more scary news. I offer her an empathetic smile that goes nowhere. Her whole body is shaking. "What have I done?" she asks. Her innocence skewers my heart—a reminder of why it's dangerous to get too close.

David lets go of the door.

"It's okay," I assure her, taking her hand and pulling her to her feet again. "It's going to be okay."

The problem is it might not be. I can't get my head around

how she can come back from the last thirteen years with any of her core relationships intact. I feel like we're at risk of her memory snapping into focus at any moment, and then we'll lose this version of Evie all over again. The first time nearly destroyed me, so I completely empathize with her father's standpoint.

"Dad?" she begs. "Please help me. I've got nowhere else to turn."

That admission punches me in the gut.

He lets the door fall wide open. "I need you to know if this gets out of hand, or if Mum can't cope, I'm going to have to ask you both to leave."

I get it.

"It's not just my wife's mental health I'm worried about." He directs this to me. "She's got a blood pressure thing. Stress can make it worse. I can't risk her health for—"

*Evie.*

"She's your daughter," I point out. "She needs you too."

He looks me up and down. "She's got you, by the look of it."

*No.*

*No!*

"She's in crisis," I point out. "I promise if it gets too much, we'll leave, but please try."

He dips his head. Defeat. Then he nods reluctantly, pats me on the shoulder as if to communicate the elaborate mess we're in collectively, and invites us across the threshold. "Probably should have been you all along," he says.

# age SEVENTEEN

# 34

## *Evie*

I'm such a mess seeing Oliver and his parents off at Sydney Airport that I land on Drew's doorstep at nine o'clock on a Saturday morning in a flood of tears. It's been a whirlwind two months, and somehow I scrambled through both my driving test and the end-of-year exams with my mind partially in gear and mainly in a love-induced freefall. I've emerged with my license, thanks to Bree's parents and mine helping me get my hours up in Sydney and with long drives back and forth to Newcastle. And miraculously I haven't totally wrecked my grades this semester.

But Year Twelve will have to be different. I'm barely holding on to my rational mind! I might be in love, but I'm also determined to get into Sydney University and study forensic linguistics. I *have* to get my head together, or the intensity of the relationship will do the one thing I always predicted. It will tear my life down.

For now, though, summer holidays stretch before us. Starting with me being totally bereft about Oliver's family trip. It's not just that he's going away. It's the way his parents acted with him in the departure lounge. Criticizing everything from the way he packed his bag to what he was wearing, the music on his iPod, and how he slumped in the chair.

"We're giving you a first-class trip to Europe," his mother said. "Why don't you ever appreciate what we do for you?" She was as put together as always. Brunette bob. Pearl earrings. Judgmental expression etched on her face. I've tried to get along with her, but my breezy Newcastle vibe just doesn't seem to cut it in Lane Cove. "Do you see other families giving their teenagers this experience?" She glared at me then, as if I were Exhibit A of the less fortunate.

"Sit up straight and look like you actually want to go," his father demanded.

"He's gone for six whole weeks," I explain to Drew without preamble, crying, when he opens his front door. "How am I supposed to survive?"

He stares at me like I've lost it. He's in flannel pajama pants and a white tank. Bed hair. Dark, school-holiday stubble on his chin, like he's an actual man. There's a huge bowl of cornflakes in his hand, as if he'd starve in the time it took to answer the front door. Entirely unbothered by my predicament, he shovels an obscenely large spoonful into his gob and mumbles through it, "Do you need a GoFundMe?"

I want to tip the cereal over his head. Someone as unromantic as Drew could never appreciate that Oliver is the first thought I have waking up or that I drift off to sleep inventing romantic scenarios starring us both. In the mini-screenplay in my head, I take some classes at the boys' school, so it's all secret longing looks over the flame of a Bunsen burner, or heads bowed, wrangling quadratic equations in the library's study nook at recess . . .

We've spent so much time together since the pool party, Oliver's existence on this earth seems to have woven itself inextricably through my own. First love will do that. Particularly for someone who spent years with her nose stuck in literary romance novels, thinking this happened only in books.

"It's six weeks, Eves," Drew says, crunching cereal in a way that makes me want to murder him. "Pull yourself together."

I stop crying simply because I'm now outraged at his lack of empathy. He and I might have become close friends, but he was my second choice of comforter. Bree has a work shift at the markets this morning, so I'm desperate—and the way he's receiving me here, I'd have to be.

"Come on," he says. "It's fine. I'll distract you." We walk inside to the kitchen, which looks like it always does—a little worse for wear.

"Can you *stop chewing* like that," I beg him.

He smiles.

He *knows* I get enraged by the sound of unnecessarily loud chewing. It's made worse by the way he's tapping the metal spoon on the ceramic bowl between mouthfuls. And the fact that he's leaning back against the kitchen bench instead of *leaning into the problem.*

"I don't know why I expected you to get it," I say. "It's not like you've ever had a girlfriend."

He feigns offense. "How dare you! I've had girlfriends!"

He has mercifully finished the cornflakes but positions the bowl as if to slurp the remainder of the milk and looks at me like this is a challenge.

It's a step too feral for me. I leap up and snatch it out of his hands.

He towers over me and smiles.

"Being with a string of different girls isn't the same as having one special person, Drew."

"God, you make it sound like I'm a player."

Yes. Well. Given I've technically been with precisely no one so far, sexually speaking—not even my own boyfriend—anyone with any experience is a lothario from where I stand.

He shifts me out of his way, then feeds four slices of bread into the toaster.

"I can't possibly eat," I tell him.

He frowns. "It's not for you."

He's eating four slices of bread *and* the cereal? Where does he put it? My eyes flit over his taut physique. Seeing him practically undressed only calls to mind my other problem. Sex. And the fact that Oliver is expecting us to have it for the first time when he gets back from Europe. First time for me, that is.

We would have done it ages ago if he'd had his way, but whenever I imagine stripping off my clothes, I get worried I won't know what to do and where to put things, and when, and in what order, while he compares the shambles of being in bed with me to all the other girls he knows.

"Bloody hell, Hudson, your boyfriend has been out of the country five seconds. You look like you want to devour me," Drew teases, breaking me from my ponderings.

I am *mortified*. "Sorry!" I blurt. "I was thinking about sex."

The toast pops up as if it can't miss a second of this exchange.

"Not with you, obviously," I clarify.

He picks up the toast and burns his fingers. "Shit!"

"Oliver wants us to . . . when he gets back . . ."

He busies himself attacking the toast with butter. Meticulously slicing tomatoes and cheese. Cutting the bread into precise rectangles. Then he carries the plate to the kitchen table, drags a chair along the tiles (cue more internal rage from me), sits down, and says, "Are you sure you don't want some?"

"Er . . ." Now I'm truly flustered. "I mean, part of me does, obviously . . ." *For the love of God, do not elaborate, Evie.*

He pushes the plate across the table toward me. Oh! He was talking about toast. He covers a smile by biting into a piece. I can tell he's trying to eat less annoyingly this time, and I feel myself soften toward him, despite his teasing.

"What do *you* want?" he says, after a while. We're off toast and back on sex, I think.

I want to tell him I'm terrified. That I'm scared of showing someone my body. Scared I won't know what to do with it, and that my lack of experience will ruin everything. But while Drew and I have become mates, that's a conversation for me and Bree. He continues anyway, before I can think, and says, "Because if you're not ready, he needs to respect that."

*I'm definitely not ready.* The thought rushes at me, loudly.

"But I told him I loved him," I explain.

Drew puts down the toast and pushes away the plate, defeated. He looks squarely at me. "You did?"

It's like I'm under a spotlight in a police interview and he's asking me if I meant it. Do I love Oliver? I must. Everything about him and me is like all my fictional dreams come true. He has everything in the world going for him and he's literally *obsessed* with me. Whenever I'm with him, I feel like I've lost my grip on this earth. It's this exciting, scary sense that I can't predict our next steps.

"Whether or not you do is irrelevant," Drew says, barging on. "You can still say no if you're not ready. End of story."

"I think I'm just scared," I admit. I'm such an overthinker

when it comes to this stuff, and I hate this about myself. I wish I had the confidence of other girls. "I'm sure it will be fine."

Now he's standing up and dumping leftover toast in the bin. "It needs to be more than fine," he says, clattering the dish into the sink as he shoves the tap on too fast. "Fuck!" he says, accidentally spraying water all over himself. "Sorry."

Drew always apologizes for swearing. It's cute and unnecessary, because I also swear—with him, at least. Not with Oliver. It's like I try to portray a version of myself with my boyfriend that is his ideal girl. I look back at Drew and his messy hair, wiping his torso with a tea towel as the hot morning sun beams through the kitchen window. And I can't help feeling slightly envious of the girls he's no doubt very patient with during "more than fine" sex.

# 35

***Drew***

I wish she would shut up about having sex with Oliver.

Everything about how she's talking bothers me. The lack of enthusiasm. The sense of obligation. The expectation he obviously has and the deadline he's forcing on her.

I look at her. She's puffy-faced from all the crying at the airport. She's confused and intense and vulnerable and worried and *not remotely ready*, and I am fucking furious.

And jealous as all hell.

We need to get out of this enclosed space before she reads my mind. She has no idea the thoughts I've started having about her, nor will she ever find out, because I'm scared she'll push me away. Being around her as a friend is better than not being around her at all, so I'm resigned to it.

"Will we take the cameras out?" I ask. It's become our go-to whenever one of us is stressed about school (in her case) or her boyfriend (in mine). It's not just that I'm jealous—even though that's absolutely true. It's that I'm worried. Everything about the way she reacts to Oliver seems extreme. This response to his departure is just the latest example. Second-guessing herself all the time. Overthinking. The story she tells herself about him being out of her league, when clearly it's the opposite.

"Do you know what I want to find?" she asks. "Ghost fungus!"

*Ghost fungus?* She is alight.

"Glowing mushrooms . . . in the dark!" she adds, assuming my silence means I don't know what she's talking about.

"I know what they are. I think you can find them in the Blue Mountains." I am so up for a photographic adventure, crawling around in the dark together.

"And also bioluminescence in the ocean . . . I've seen photos from Jervis Bay." She picks up her phone to show me images and shoves it in my face, along with the intoxicating scent of coconut body lotion. Long brown hair falls over her shoulder and wild curls brush the skin on my arm as I stand beside her, invested in her bioluminescence quest, knowing my own quest is futile.

"Look at this!" she says, eyes shining, playing a video of someone walking through the waves in the shallows, stirring up the neon-blue phosphorescence at their feet. "I want that, Drew!"

*And I want you.* It's crazy how much.

It's way more than physical attraction. Evie and I are completely on the same page. We don't just want to hang out, watching movies and eating snacks. There's a purpose to our friendship—we have goals and a creative understanding, which adds up to a depth I haven't felt before, with anyone.

"I'm in," I tell her. I'm all in for anything she wants. "As long as you shut up about Oliver and quit being pathetic about the next six weeks."

She laughs. "What kind of friendship is this?"

I want to tell her it's an Oliver-free zone. That the next six weeks are ours, around work and the Sydney-Newy commute.

This might be the first and last summer holiday we ever have, depending on the choices we make at the end of next year. But saying any of that would be pathetic.

"God, fine," I say. "I'll *be there as a friend* and all that sop. Whatever you need. Ride or die. *When Harry Met Sally* blah blah."

"You can't just quote random eighties rom-coms."

"Rom-coms? It's the one where they're platonic friends, right? Mum loves that movie."

She looks at me weirdly. At least she's stopped crying. "You're completely unqualified for this conversation."

She gives me the once-over, and I indulge in a fantasy that her gaze snags for a moment on the muscles across my chest.

"Get your camera ready," she demands. "And put some clothes on. Geez."

Maybe she's not a hundred percent immune, after all.

# 36

### *Evie*

A few weeks later, we've borrowed Drew's mum's car and driven three hours to Jervis Bay, during which time I performed a one-woman show for him featuring a lot of One Direction. But now, standing on the white sands of a secluded stretch of beach in the dark, there's no need for music. I'm so overwhelmed by what I'm seeing, I forget to take photos. Glowing bioluminescence. Sea sparkles. Every wave that breaks in the dark lit up in magical neon-blue light that swirls around our ankles on the shoreline.

"Should we be standing in this?" Drew asks.

I shrug. "I probably wouldn't drink it."

He's so careful about health stuff. He once told me when someone you love has ended up at the wrong end of a statistic, you're more focused on what could go wrong. But there are more dangerous things we could be doing on a Friday night. We could be taking drugs at a party. Not that I would know. In any case, I'm fully distracted by the way my calves are glittering in the moonlight.

"There are worse ways to die than being killed by luminescence," I announce without thinking it through. I immediately kick myself for blundering into the sad stuff. "Sorry! I shouldn't have said that."

"No, you're right. I should lighten up."

That's not what I was saying.

"Let's focus on how lucky we are to be here." I grab his arm beside me in the shallows. "This is notoriously so hard to find!"

"Not when you're following the live blogs as obsessively as we are. You've just got to be ready to jump in the car when there's a chance."

He walks a little way up the beach and strips off his shirt. Without worrying anymore about whether we should or shouldn't wade in here, I pull my dress over my head, throwing it on top of the camera bags on the sand. I am literally the last person to have planned how best to Instagram this turn of events, but even I have to admit my choice of white bikini top and boy shorts against the fluorescent blue in the water tonight was inspired.

Drew runs into the ocean, flicking up the brightly colored water, sparkling with chemical reactions, and I splash after him through mystical waves. It occurs to me, briefly, that while I'm anxious about undressing in front of Oliver, I have no such problem around Drew—probably because this whole thing couldn't be more platonic. I completely trust him.

All around us, the water lights up in eddies and swirls, as if we're in an otherworldly animated movie or living on some distant, undiscovered planet. I spin, trailing my fingers through the water, light swirling all around me.

Drew is standing nearby, looking more relaxed than I've ever seen him. It's as if the phenomenon is distracting him from everything that makes his life so hard. "We need to see fireflies next," he says.

"Yes! And the aurora, of course. Let's start a list."

As a wave breaks behind him, his body is silhouetted against the bright light. It's all just so incredible and beautiful and so *once-in-a-lifetime* I start to lose the battle against composure, my eyes filling up.

"Missing your boyfriend?" he teases, and I slam some neon water at him.

For a few moments, I'd almost forgotten Oliver existed. Now I struggle to imagine him here in this scene. Drew will stay here in the water all night if I want to. He's big on wondrous things—it's the photographer in him. We're kindred spirits on this stuff, and I can't help wondering whether Oliver would rush me through it.

"Can I take your photo?" Drew asks. "Not for the exhibition. Just for you?"

He wades onto the sand, dries his hands off, and grabs my camera. Not his. I know he'd never share these photos, but this ensures it.

As he lines up the shot, I realize it's the little things like this that I like about him, not that I'd voice that aloud—he'd think I was weird. I want to take back my initial accusation in the art studio at his school, when I lumped him in with the other boys. They would never ask for consent to take these photos. They'd take them and share them and do God knows what with them.

Knowing it's only Drew, I come to life, scooping the shining water, spinning and dancing in it as if nobody is watching me. Not even him. Then I traipse back through the water to see what he took, laughing at the couple of failed shots where I've got a weird look on my face or my eyes are shut, but I'm so genuinely happy and confident in the others, I barely recognize myself.

"You are really good," I say. "*Really* good." I've told him this before, but I never think he quite believes it. He basks in the praise, reflections from the water flickering across his face in the moonlight.

"Spin around," he says, never one to dwell on a compliment. On our mission to create the perfect shot, I twirl so many times I lose my balance and fall over, into him, pulling both of us down onto the sand, laughing, while he holds the camera aloft.

We end up sitting at the shoreline while the luminous water washes in and out on the beach. By a million miles, it's the most precious experience of my life.

"The day I die, when my life flashes before my eyes," I tell him, "this scene will be the finale."

# 37

***Drew***

This is the standout night of my life. The water is luminous. But so is she. All in. Confident. She doesn't care how she looks. Just throws herself into everything without giving a second thought to what I'm going to think. It's this gusto for life and this freedom that I covet because my own life feels so constrained.

"Promise me, no matter how old and boring you get, or where you go, or who you're with, you'll never stop looking for this," she says.

She means bioluminescence and its ilk, not the way it feels to share it with her. I try to imagine myself with someone else in the future and already know it will never measure up. A pretty tragic thought, at seventeen.

I shove a wave of water at her. "Thanks for the vote of confidence in my future personality."

She smiles. "It's not you personally. Won't we all get old and boring one day? You know, when we have to worry about mortgages and bills and why our kid is being excluded from the friend group at lunchtime?"

"You speak from experience?"

She looks at me tentatively. "I was completely on the outside when I moved to Saint Ag's," she admits. "I really didn't have any friends until one of the teachers forced Bree to work on an assignment with me. Even now she's my only close friend."

"Well, thanks," I say. "What am I then?"

As she looks at me, I realize I don't want to know her answer. Whatever it is will never be enough, and while she doesn't confirm it, I can always hold out hope.

"Anyway, why are you thinking about mortgages and kids?" I ask, hoping to divert her attention.

"Don't you? I mean, not all the time, obviously, but don't you sometimes fast-forward into your future and imagine a partner and babies and—"

"I'm not going to have kids," I confess quietly. It's something I've never told anyone else.

She pulls her knees up and hugs them, leaning toward me. "Why not?"

I think of everything I have to do for Mum, and the way illnesses run in families. And then I'm imagining some poor future kid lying awake at night scared of finding me, the way I'm scared of finding her . . .

"I don't want to end up a burden," I say. Inside that admission is a confession I've never voiced before. Guilt punctures my chest just saying it, and I wish I could take the words back. "Mum is not a burden," I say hurriedly. "But she's . . . hard work. Her *illness* is hard work."

"But she's sick," Evie replies. "None of this is her fault. And you're amazing with her."

Who else has she got to take care of her? Certainly not my dad.

"It's okay to admit you find things hard," Evie says, her serious eyes on mine. I want to tell her exactly how hard I find it and outline all the ways Mum's illness frightens me. But I'm scared of what might come out of my mouth if I start. Worried I'll say things that even my conscious mind hasn't been brave enough to voice.

We sit there in silence for a long time, in the gentle shallows, light all around, until the waves move farther out and the breeze stills and I become aware of my phone ringing just up the beach.

"Sorry," I say, getting up. "Someone's calling me."

I stagger to our stuff on the sand, relieved that someone else on this earth knows even a tiny part about how I feel at long last. And I find my phone.

Four missed calls. One from Mum and three from a number I don't recognize. They've also left a voicemail, which I listen to while watching Evie play with the fluorescent blue on the water's edge, knowing the spell is about to be broken.

My heart falls.

"It's Mum," I call to Evie. "We have to go back."

# 38

## *Evie*

Bree and I didn't plan on spending our summer holidays hanging around in a hospital cafeteria, but a week after Drew and I had that almost religious experience together in Jervis Bay, she and I fall into a routine where we visit him in the café most lunchtimes.

"Are your parents okay with you staying here a bit longer?" she asks me as we're walking from the bus stop. She knows they're not. My mum has been on the phone to hers, and we listened down the hallway while her mum made the argument for me staying just a few more days in Sydney while we support our friend.

"Drew is on his own with his mum. How would it look if they told me to ditch him?" I ask.

She pulls my elbow and stops me on the path. "You and Drew are getting pretty close?"

I don't understand the question. "I thought you approved of him." Why is she always acting like my gatekeeper with boys?

"I really do," Bree says. "And he really likes you. Be careful, Evie."

"I'm with Oliver," I remind her.

She looks at me like she's unable to think of a response to a statement this obvious. It's the look of a person with tons on her mind, but nothing will make its way through her vocal cords and come out of her mouth. "Yes, on that," Bree starts. "With the formal . . ."

"Oh, there he is!" I wave at Drew near the hospital entrance, quickening my step. "We can talk about the formal later."

"It's a forensics necklace," Oliver explains weeks later, as I unwrap the silver chain he's brought me back from a police museum in Amsterdam. There's a tiny silver fingerprint pendant hanging beside a microscope and a strand of DNA. This is a million times better than some sort of gemstone. It represents the future I want to create. And the fact that he *knows* this about me—and how much it matters to me.

I throw my arms around his neck, my fingers threading through his still-wet hair. He's freshly showered after the long flight and smells of shampoo and some expensive cologne that's so different from the Lynx Africa other boys reek of.

He pulls me even closer and kisses me like a person who's been forced to go on a six-week European trip with his parents when he wanted to be in Sydney with his girlfriend. It's a six-weeks-in-one kiss, and when we emerge from it, we're both hot and flustered and I barely know which way is up.

"We need to talk about our gap year," he says breathlessly, between kisses, pushing me across the luxurious room, past the doorway to his own en suite and walk-in wardrobe and toward his bed, the back of my calves hitting the mattress as I tumble and land on his pillow. It's like a scene from a movie where they're *hungry* for each other—and I am definitely as hungry as he is, just also anxious, which is making me feel sort of nauseated, but I don't let on because right now I'm the main character in this big love scene that's playing out in Oliver Roche's lavish Lane Cove bedroom. *Just grow up, Evie. It's fine.*

I've already planned my gap year with Bree. We've been working on the itinerary since Year Eight. Fly to London, do a Jane Austen tour of Bath, attend a live screening of *Pride and Prejudice* on picnic blankets at Chatsworth House, where the Pemberley scenes were filmed, then Paris and Prague and Venice and tossing coins into the Trevi Fountain in Rome, wishing for everything we've always wanted . . .

"Travel with me," Oliver says. He's been staring into my face while I was running through the trip in my head, and his statement takes me by surprise. I mean, of course he'd imagine we'd travel together. That's what gap-year couples do. But in every version of the itinerary Bree and I invented, neither of us accounted for a future romantic lead.

"Oliver, can we talk about . . ."

He kisses me on my neck, and I lose track of the sentence.

"I just, I'd already sort of planned . . ."

His lips close over my mouth and I can't say the rest of the words as his hand travels down my neck and across my shoulder, sweeping aside the shoestring strap of my top in a way that thrills me and scares me and makes me forget about Pemberley and picnic screenings and my best friend.

"We don't have to think about it now," Oliver whispers. I'm relieved, because I don't want to argue about anything. That said, given the dangerous route his hand is now traveling, I'm tempted to reraise the topic. Or any topic. And slow this down.

"Oliver, wait . . ." I try to sit up, but he shifts his weight, and I can't. So I place my hands on his chest and push him back. "Oliver, stop. Please."

He does stop. He moves back. I feel really bad, because I know this was the plan. He'd get back from Europe and we'd do this. *Look at him!* As far as your first time goes, he's a knock-it-out-of-the-park partner.

"I'm sorry," I whisper. I'm close to tears now.

"It's okay," he says, flopping back on the bed beside me.

But it's not okay. "I don't know what's wrong with me."

He takes my hand, and I try to stem the tears and prevent myself from becoming even more pathetic in this already mortifying situation.

"Evie, it's fine. I'll wait."

And we lie there in silence, while I play with the forensics pendant around my neck, imagining Oliver is reliving all the times he's had sex with less-awkward girls, probably wishing he wasn't stuck with me now, while this gap-year clash looms impossibly in my head. I resolve to be a more courageous and less uptight girlfriend in the future.

Starting tomorrow.

# 39

***Drew***

"It doesn't have to be a whole suit," Evie says. "Just get pants and a nice shirt." We must be the only two students at Dom's and Ag's worried about our formal budget.

"What's your dress like?" I ask. I don't know why—I don't know anything about dresses or what I'll do with this information when she gives it to me. The formal committee has gone for a "great couples from literature" theme and fancy dress is optional. Or compulsory in Evie's case.

"I can't decide. There's one that's pinks and oranges, kind of floaty, but sexy, with tiers, sort of a floaty go-go girl situation, you know? Could be a sixties vibe, if we could think of a flower power couple . . ."

I am none the wiser.

Formals—fancy dress or otherwise—aren't my thing. I'm more comfortable in a darkroom or under a dark sky. Definitely behind the camera and not in front of it. And not dressed up. With small talk. I've been this close to telling Evie just to go to the formal with Oliver so many times, but something always stops me. I think it's stubbornness. Right or wrong, there's something about being invited by Oliver Roche's girlfriend to her own formal that gives me some kind of kick. So that's how I find myself in a suit store with Evie on a Friday after school in February, determined to put myself into a social situation I'm going to loathe.

She pushes me into a changing room with a handful of shirts and snaps the curtain closed. "The other dress is this whole *Pride and Prejudice* vibe—Empire waist, soft blue, super-feminine."

I can see her as Lizzy Bennet, with her hair up, curls framing her face.

"I haven't worn it since . . ."

"Since what?"

"Never mind."

She's gone uncharacteristically quiet, and I open the curtain, even though the white shirt she handed me is still flapping loose. "Okay, go-go girl. What are you hiding?"

It's so not like her to be coy about something.

"You have to promise not to tease me about this," she begins.

I try to resist smiling. She has me captive now.

"How bad could it be?"

She steps forward, her fingers brushing my skin while she threads buttons through the holes on my shirt, and she looks up into my face, as if she's about to share a state secret. "All right, Drew. Here it is. Ready?" She takes a deep breath. "I'm a card-carrying member of the Regency Literature Reenactment Society," she whispers. "We get dressed up and hold balls and dance La Boulangere."

I stare at her. This was not the confession I anticipated. It's also not a surprise, since I discovered this when I googled her the first day we met. "Fascinating . . ."

She twists my wrists so she can fix my cuffs. "Yes, it is." She glances at me, as if to check how I'm taking the news that she's even more of a nerd than I'd allowed for.

"Are you searching for a suitable husband?" I ask.

She thumps me. "If I was, you'd be struck off the list!"

"I wasn't aware I was in the running. Also, I'm seventeen?"

"Anyway, I haven't been lately. I've just been . . . busy."

Ah, yes. Busy with the future husband material that is Oliver. Can't see him showing up at a Regency ball. Not even for Evie. I guess we have that in common.

"What other weird hobbies don't I know about?" I ask.

She rolls her eyes. "All right, then, if we're putting it all on the table," she says. "I propagate plants."

"Huh?"

"Plants. I take cuttings and grow them in water until they strike roots, and then I plant the seedlings. I've got two lots on the go—one at Bree's place and another set in Newcastle that Dad looks after while I'm here!"

"You are positively middle-aged."

"You are positively irritating. I should just go to the formal with my boyfriend!"

*Here we go.* "Do you want to?"

*Please say no.*

She looks straight at me, like she's considering it. I silently will her to choose me.

"If you wear your costume," I say, before I can stop myself, "I'll dress up too."

What. The. Fuck. I don't even want to go in the optional modern dress. Now I'm offering to fulfill all her Mr. Darcy fantasies?

Her eyes brighten. "You would do that? Dress in period costume?"

I guess I'll have to now.

She is *delighted*, and throws herself at me in a vigorous hug, before grabbing me by the wrist and dragging me through the store. "We need to get you a poet shirt."

I regret this already.

"And a waistcoat. And a neck cravat. You can just wear normal straight-leg pants."

"Thank God for that. I thought you'd put me in breeches . . ."

She looks at me thoughtfully. "Would you *wear* breeches?"

"Evie!" I grab her arms and spin her to face me. "I really like you, but there's a limit."

She laughs. "Yes, okay. Normal pants. But the poet shirt is a must."

"For when I emerge from a pond?"

"Are you a closet Regency romance fan, Drew?"

Hardly! "*Pride and Prejudice* is Mum's comfort watch," I explain.

Her smile widens. And suddenly I don't care what I wear to this formal. Or who's there. Or what they think. I just want to make her this happy, all the time.

# 40

***Evie***

After Drew's revelation at the suit store, it was inevitable that I would invite myself over to his house to rewatch *Pride and Prejudice* with his mum. So now Annie and I are binge-watching the BBC version on a Sunday under blankets on the couch and having homemade pumpkin soup and crusty sourdough. My social life has left the building, entered a time machine, and emerged somewhere in my fifties.

Every so often Drew saunters through the room on his way to the kitchen or down the hall, until eventually we tell him to either stop it or join us. He flops down between us on the couch, acting like it's a total burden.

"Did Drew tell you this was my go-to distraction during chemo?" Annie asks. It's the first time she's acknowledged her specific illness in so many words.

"He did say it's your comfort watch," I answer. "It's mine too."

"She gets dressed up in period costume and goes to balls, Mum. She's fanatical."

"It's not just me dressing up," I explain to Annie. "Drew has agreed to wear period costume for the formal!"

I wish we could take a photo of her face. She is elated. And so pretty; I can see where Drew gets his looks from. I love the idea of doing something small to brighten her life.

My phone pings on the coffee table and Drew passes it to me. It's Oliver. Don't forget your modern history exam tomorrow, it reads. See, this is why I like him so much. He *listens.* I sigh, and Drew's body stiffens beside me.

"Are you reading my messages?" I whisper.

"Stop waving them in my face," he says. "Has he committed your exam schedule to memory, then?" He isn't hiding the snark in his tone.

"He wants to support me," I explain. "He knows how much my results mean to me. He synced our calendars so he can help me stay on track."

"Shush," Annie says, just as Elizabeth starts bickering with Darcy at the Netherfield ball.

Drew frowns. "Evie, you're a straight-A student. You don't need help. You need space. He just wants to know where you are."

That is such an outlandish accusation. Drew is ruining what was a beautiful afternoon. I get up and collect the empty soup bowls so Annie can watch in peace.

He follows me into the kitchen, trying to take the bowls from my hands, but I won't let him.

"I'm sorry," he says. "Maybe you're right and he's just being supportive."

The idea of Drew criticizing Oliver just makes me *furious.* Olly has been nothing but amazing to me since the moment we got together. And extraordinarily patient.

"You don't hear conversations in the common room from other girls about boys they date," I tell him. "The only ones who ever seem happy are dating girls! Oliver could run master classes on how to be a boyfriend."

"I'm sure he could," Drew says, but I can tell he's just trying to stop me from arguing.

"They complain that boys won't listen and forget important things and are generally awful."

He nods.

"But Oliver is constantly aware of every aspect of my life."

He folds his arms.

"He's attentive and generous . . ."

"Evie . . ."

"He's forever checking in."

No response.

"Nobody else would love me the way he does." I puff up defensively. "He said so!"

"Try not to read too much into it," Oliver says, two hours later, after I've given him the executive summary of my first real argument with Drew. "If he's getting a bit intense, maybe give him some space?"

*This* is why I'm into Oliver. Drew has openly criticized him, yet he's being so reasonable.

"He's always been emotional," he adds. "Misses classes. Goes away for days. Flakes out on group assignments. Maybe he thinks you're the only thing he can control in his life . . ."

*Control?* I hadn't thought of Drew's behavior that way. But maybe Oliver is right; he seems to be about most things.

"I can't give him too much space," I explain. "We've got the exhibition opening in ten days. And the formal next month."

"You've got the exhibition under control, haven't you? And I'll be at your formal." He pulls me into a hug, but I push him back, surprised.

"You'll be there?"

"Bree and I were going to surprise you," he admits.

*Bree and Oliver?*

"Since friendship dates seem to be a thing . . ."

I don't know how I feel about this.

"She was so cut up about Tom Jenkins asking Madeleine Dupont, I thought I'd offer to go with her. Obviously just as mates. And you and Drew will be there. Bree seems to like him."

*In what way?*

This whole development is head-spinning.

"Evie, any other boyfriend would be insanely jealous about his girlfriend going to the formal with someone else, but I reckon we could just make a party out of it. Makes sense, doesn't it?"

I think it does, even though it's doing multiple weird things to my insides trying to put it all together.

# 41

***Drew***

"The media has asked for two students to be spokespeople for the exhibition," Dr. Walsh says, at the students-and-parents-only preview of *Pictures of You*. "Evie, obviously, as this was your idea . . ."

She looks sick at the thought. I can practically see the color drain from her cheeks in real time. "Oh, I don't know?" she says.

"You'll be fine! Take the credit," Oliver says.

He has no real understanding of how much she hates being in the spotlight.

She glances at me, panic in her eyes. I send her a brief, encouraging smile, and a nod. It will be okay. I don't like the idea of media attention any more than she does, but we've worked so hard over several months, curating this. She deserves to be the one to show it off.

"Oliver, as school captain, you should join her," the principal adds.

Now it's Evie who's sending me a silent sign of her disappointment. We've been in each other's pockets the last couple of weeks, putting this all together, making sure the photos are displayed in the most creatively logical order, the lighting is right, and the narrative story behind the exhibit makes sense. The argument we had in the kitchen seems to have been forgotten, but I'm aware for the future that Oliver is a hot-button topic.

"Should it not be Drew who's interviewed?" she says emphatically. "He's done all the work!"

Oliver pulls at his collar, as if it's suddenly tightened around his neck, just as a team from Channel 9 starts pushing through the door of the atrium, with their cameras and tripods and big black bags bursting with lenses and reflector panels. There's no time for anyone to argue.

"We're on a tight schedule to get this to air at the end of the six-o'clock news," a young reporter explains, while the camera operator fiddles with the lights. "We just need a quick interview and some B-roll footage of parents perusing the art. Who's up?"

Oliver and Evie are pushed forward.

"Straighten your tie," Dr. Marsh says. "Where's your blazer?"

Evie fiddles with her ponytail, tightens the maroon ribbon in her hair, and smooths her dress down. She looks like she's being swept out in a rip.

It all feels like complete chaos until the spotlight flicks on, the camera rolls, and the reporter says, "Tell me about the genesis of this exhibition."

Evie rises to the occasion in a way that makes me want to punch the air for her.

"This is a joint exhibition from students from Saint Dominic's and Saint Agatha's. Drew Kennedy and I wanted to rewrite the script on the way girls and women are often seen through the male gaze," she explains, looking in my direction. "It's an opportunity to showcase images of the women in our lives without a filter and capture the stories behind ordinary moments."

"The images are for sale," Oliver adds. "All proceeds from this weekend's exhibition will go to our local women's shelter to help women and children escaping domestic violence."

He looks good on camera, spotlights shining off his blond hair. The poster boy for women's issues, apparently. And for the school. And for boyfriends everywhere.

"Boys from Saint Dominic's have been volunteering at the shelter, packing emergency supplies for families, and offering manual labor in the gardens," Oliver says. "Violence against women affects more than one-third of women globally, and this exhibition and the activities around it will raise awareness of these issues in our school community and more widely."

It couldn't be going better. Dr. Marsh is positively beaming as he watches the interview unfold. The reporter leads them to the wall of images and pauses at mine. A photo I took of Evie on the beach one weekend.

"This is you?" the reporter asks.

Evie squirms at the attention. She can't bring herself to even look at the image, even though privately I think it's my best work. "You should talk to the photographer, Drew," she begins, pointing in my direction. But Oliver takes her elbow and sweeps her farther along the row of photos, drawing attention to any portraits other than mine, while she looks over her shoulder at me and has to give up on trying to get me involved in this.

Walking along the wall in their wake, I pause in front of my print. Below it, a red circle is stuck on the wall, meaning it's sold. And I look up just in time to see Oliver's satisfied, off-camera smirk. Simmering annoyance flashes into silent rage. I was intending to buy this portrait and give it to Evie for her eighteenth. He'll probably stuff it in a drawer. To him, it's probably not about her. It just represents everything he hates about our friendship.

Three weeks later, I'm in the garage sifting through a metal trunk of Mum's old stuff, searching for my great-grandfather's old army belt for the formal. I can't stop thinking about Evie. The white poet shirt is on a hanger over my bedroom door, advertising how ludicrously far I'll go to impress her, as lines from our argument persist in my head. *Constantly aware. Forever checking in. Nobody else would love me the way he does.*

Worrying about her distracts me from worrying about Mum. Her latest test results came back stable, so she should be in a good mood, but I feel like she's slipping. I know the drugs she's on to balance her hormones make her feel sick and sore, but a light has gone out. It's like she's letting them defeat her, while together we're sliding down a cliff face and I'm furiously pulling on tree roots and grasping unstable rocks to break our fall.

She's crammed so much stuff into this old trunk, it's like a time capsule. Old receipts. Notebooks. Photos. A nice change from prescriptions, pills, and oncology appointment reminder slips. My memories of Mum revolve around her forever trying to make ends meet when I was little, and then always being sick. Her life since she left home at eighteen is still a mystery to me in many ways. I know she went interstate from Queensland to go to uni, but it was also to get away from her parents' shouting. By twenty-two she was pregnant with me. Alone, and trying to work as a first-year nurse, she had virtually no support.

All I know about my dad was that he was a specialist doctor at the hospital. Older. Married not long after they broke up, to someone else. He's bankrolled my school fees, presumably out of guilt, but appears to have been unable—or unwilling—to be present in my actual life.

I find one of Mum's nursing textbooks in the box. She's stashed various things between the pages: old movie tickets, a couple of photos of her with friends. I turn the book upside down and fan it out, shaking the pages until everything tumbles into my lap—including a photo I've never seen before.

It's of Mum with a man. She's smiling and confident, and he has his arm around her while she stares up at him, enamored. I wish this was digital so I could zoom in. The sun is on their faces and they're squinting, so it's hard to make out his features clearly.

I go back to my room, get my camera, and take a photo of the image. Still, when I zoom in, the original is of too low a resolution to see details, so I take it over to my desk, wake up the computer, and feed the memory card into the slot.

In Photoshop, I tweak the image, crop it, and zoom in.

And I feel sick.

The way my mother feels about this man is unarguable—she's practically fangirling over him. I check the date on the back of the photo. It's about eight months before I was born.

But it's the man himself, now that he's more clearly in focus, that causes the bottom to drop out of my world. The blond hair. The penetrating blue-green eyes. The perfect bone structure. The expression of sheer confidence and domination. Even the way he's standing is wildly familiar.

By the look on Mum's face, and the date on the photo, I'm certain I'm looking at my father. But I'm equally certain I could be looking straight at Oliver.

# 42

### *Evie*

It's formal night. Drew is picking me up from Bree's in an hour and I'm still curling my hair. It's naturally curly, but in that way that looks like you have no control over your life, and I want it sleeked up with perfect Elizabeth Bennet curls and a ribbon.

Even with the fancy dress theme, Bree thinks I'm brave wearing the Regency dress, but this feels like my one chance to pretend I'm living in the fairy tale of a different age.

Ripples of our parents' laughter float down the hallway while they sip champagne. Dad has gone overboard and brought the camera and a tripod, which is majorly embarrassing, but Mum said this is a key moment in parenting they didn't want to miss and we're going to be glad we have the photos later, as if every kid at this formal won't take a hundred photos of their own.

All good for 7pm pickup? I text Drew. I'm still feeling bad about the way he was sidelined at the exhibition.

I'll bring the carriage around then, he replies. It makes me smile, and I send back an emoji, which isn't very Regency of me, but I'm sure Jane Austen would have embraced social media, given the opportunity. She'd have *owned* social media, actually.

My phone rings. It's Oliver.

"Just checking all's okay," he says when I click the speaker button and get back to my hair.

"My hair is not okay," I reply. It really isn't. I am not a hair person, and whatever I'm trying to do here is actually making it worse.

"I'm sure it's gorgeous."

Bree is the one who is stunning. She is in an amazing slinky black dress, absolutely rocking it. I'm a bit nervous about how it's going to go with Oliver and Drew, but Oliver promised it would be fine from his end.

Forty-five minutes later, my nerves have skyrocketed. This whole formal scene is just like the parties that make me so uncomfortable, but on a much grander scale. I'm so anxious I'm inhaling the scent of the jasmine plant in front of Bree's house. I read that it's as powerful as Valium for calming anxiety. In fact, I grab the secateurs that I use for my plant propagation, chop some off, and stick it in my hair.

Oliver arrives first. Looking like his usual self, except even more incredible, if that's possible. As he gets out of the car, grabs his jacket from the back seat, and walks toward me, I honestly want to chop every single branch of jasmine from the plant and smother myself in it to calm down. He and Bree are going as some sort of glamorous James Bond and Bond girl pairing. It's off script for Bree to choose a theme in which she is not the main character, but there's enough weirdness around this formal already without me questioning that.

"Look at you," Oliver says, standing back and taking my outfit in. "Wow."

I'm hoping it's a good "wow" and not "wow, I can't believe my girlfriend is going out in public looking like a Mr. Collins magnet." It's hard to tell what he's thinking, until Bree emerges and I notice a bit more "wow" in his tone when he sees her dress.

I smooth down the silky blue fabric of mine, over the high Empire waist that suddenly feels frumpy beside Bree's Bond girl sleekness. There's no way around it, the black dress with its plunging neckline, and low-scooped back are showstopping. And she is his date, technically, but wait till he sees the whole picture with Drew in his outfit. *Where is Drew? He should be here by now.*

Seven o'clock passes.

Seven-fifteen.

Seven-twenty.

I've messaged him twice, with no reply. "You two should go. I'm sure he must be on the way," I tell Oliver and Bree.

"We'll wait," Bree protests.

But we're meant to be at preformal drinks already. "It's fine!" I say. "I'll see you there soon."

They get in the car and I hover near the jasmine, obsessively checking my phone every five seconds. Still *nothing* from Drew. I try to call but it goes straight to voicemail.

Oliver messages me a few minutes later. Any sign of him?

Not yet. And he's not picking up.

I'm a ball of nerves as Oliver types and deletes and retypes his message.

I thought this might happen. He's just unreliable, Evie. He misses class a LOT. Want me to turn back?

I can't do that to Bree, who has been longing for this night for months. I'll give him ten more minutes and then I'll . . . what? Go by myself? Do I dare walk into a formal in period costume *alone*?

Maybe I should change into the other dress. It's still "me," but not quite this unconventional. Or I could just not go. It doesn't take much for me to pull out of a social event.

The phone bursts into life and I'm so nervy I drop it. It's him. Drew.

"Where *are* you?" I burst out.

"Evie, I am sorry to do this," he says, his voice strained. "I can't come."

*Can't come? At ten to eight he tells me this?*

"Why can't you?" I say, trying not to sound as angry as I'm starting to feel.

"I really can't explain it," he says. It's totally insufficient. He owes me a proper explanation. Is he on drugs? What could possibly have come up in the hour since he put a smile on my face telling me he'd bring the carriage around?

"Is it your mum?"

"Sorry, I can't tell you."

I don't have time for this. I hang up on him. Furious.

He's not coming, I text Oliver.

I'm on my way, he types back.

I have a flash of the expression on his face when he first saw me in this dress. And I walk upstairs and change.

# 43

***Drew***

Evie ends the call abruptly and I turn back to the paramedic. He's got Mum sitting up on the sunken couch now, her hand gripping the worn wooden armrest, and he's given her something to calm her down. I wish he'd give *me* something. I've never been so scared in my life. And I should never have been so reckless as to ask her about that photo when I was meant to be heading out to the formal.

All I wanted to know was who it was. It has to be Oliver's dad; they're practically identical. Though I need to stop jumping to conclusions. Just because it's a photo of Mum with Oliver's father doesn't mean . . . God, I can't even say what it doesn't mean.

But I didn't expect her to react quite as badly as she did.

"Where did you get this?" she said, collapsing into one of the kitchen chairs as she held the photo in her hand.

"It was inside a book in a box in the garage," I explained. "I was looking for that old army belt to wear tonight. Mum, who is this?"

The color drained from her face and her breathing seemed to constrict. Within seconds, she was physically shaking. "I . . . can't," she said.

*Can't what?* "Mum, is this my father?"

The woman staring at me wasn't my mum. She was the ghost of a person. Was she having a heart attack? She just froze. I couldn't shake her out of it, and in the end I called the paramedics—I didn't know what else to do. By the time they arrived, she was a mess.

"Your mum's heart rate is starting to slow down now," the paramedic explains kindly. "That's good."

I'm used to seeing her in medical settings, just not inside our own little house. Having paramedics walk through your own kitchen, past unwashed dishes still stacked in the sink, recycling piling up next to the bin, while they set their equipment down on top of your history essay is a whole other thing. Home is meant to be where we're safe. An escape from all of this. They're like intruders here. This feels all wrong.

"Given your mum's medical history, we're going to take her to the hospital," the paramedic explains after they've made their initial assessment. "They're well equipped to handle a mental health crisis."

*Mental health?* I thought it was her heart.

"Did something trigger this panic attack?" he asks, as I follow him back down the hall to get the paperwork he needs. "It's pretty severe."

*I* triggered this by showing her that photo. She's still agitated, though not as much with the Valium they've given her, and I'm racked with guilt.

We get to the hospital, Mum in the ambulance, me racing behind in her car. Everyone stares when I walk through the ER waiting room. Maybe I should have changed after all.

I tell the nurse behind the registration desk that I'm Annie Kennedy's son, and she presses a button for the automatic door and directs me to the critical care ward. *Aren't we just here for a panic attack? Why critical?*

Mum is parked on the bed in the corridor. She's even more washed-out and fragile than normal, hair stuck to her forehead from where she's sweated through the anxiety, brown eyes dulled from the sedation.

"I'm sorry," I say. I mean that I'm sorry for showing her the photo and upsetting her. But even mentioning it stresses her out again and I decide just to shut up about it altogether. I hold her hand and tell her it will be all right. I have no idea if it will be or not—probably not, the way things have been going. But I say it anyway.

As the sedatives really sink in, she starts to doze. I try to compose a message to Evie. It's not as simple as telling her Mum isn't well, because I know she'll ask for details and I can't share the trigger for tonight's collapse. And if I tell Evie where we are, she'll appear here in an instant. It's not fair to ruin her night. But that leaves me with no valid excuse for ditching the formal at the last second, when I'm the one Evie rescued after Alicia Brown first spread those rumors.

In the end, all I can do is type It's Mum. I'm really sorry x.

But the message won't send.

A couple of hours later, they've done a blood test and they're a bit concerned about Mum's white blood cell count.

"It could indicate an infection," the doctor explains. "Your mum is immunocompromised from the chemo, as you know. Emotional stress weakens her system further and makes her more susceptible to whatever's going around."

My own blood pressure rises. *Is this all my fault?* I'm *never* going to tamper with someone's past again. The speed with which she collapsed after I showed her the photo leaves me with zero doubt that it was the trigger for the panic attack that led us here, though she must have already been struggling with the infection.

My skin is clammy. I'm hot and cold and shivery and finding it very hard to breathe. I've felt alone with Mum during various emergencies in the past, but never more than now, when I can't even voice my guilt. It's tearing me up.

"Listen, we might keep her in overnight and get some IV antibiotics into her, just to be on the safe side. She's sedated and peaceful now. And you look like you have somewhere to be . . ."

I really don't want to go to the formal *now*. But if my message isn't going through, turning up in person and apologizing may be my only option. I can't afford to blow up this friendship.

There are plenty of odd looks once I arrive at the venue. The staff in the hotel foyer direct me to the function room. It takes a minute for my eyes to acclimate to the dark, and, as I scan the room, the room scans me. I feel like I'm never going to forget the blue-green patterned carpet in this room. The chandeliers. The round tables adorned with candles and flowers. The dance floor and lights. Muffled laughter. People staring and pointing at the billowing sleeves of my shirt—so out of place beside every other boy here, most of whom have ditched the theme and taken the less attention-seeking route, not that I care.

Finally, I see her. She's in the center of the dance floor, under the twinkling lights of the disco ball, lit up.

In the sixties-inspired go-go dancer dress.

Wrapped around Oliver.

# 44

*Evie*

Whenever I imagined Rome, it wasn't like this.

I saw myself and Bree tearing around the city on mopeds, in vintage dresses à la Audrey Hepburn in *Roman Holiday*. We'd attract the attention of two sophisticated Italian boys who'd order us pizza and wine and entice us into hot holiday flings that we'd brag about to our grandchildren in seven decades' time when we'd totally lost our filters in the nursing home.

Instead, I'm crying in front of the Trevi Fountain in the heat of the Italian sun, under perfect blue skies, with the perfect boyfriend. Miserable. I sold out on our gap-year dream.

"If he really loved you, he'd wait," Bree had argued when I first broke the news. "That's proper romance! Putting you first . . ." It had sent me into a defensive spin that ended with us both in tears.

"I guess Italy will always be there," she'd added more softly, trying to fix it a while later. "We can still meet up and do Pemberley, Evie. He wouldn't want to go to that bit, anyway."

"The Trevi Fountain was *our* dream, though," I'd conceded. We'd infused some sort of incantation into it, as if tossing in those coins together would cement our friendship for the rest of our adult lives. I just feel so guilty about ditching her. And age so torn, because Oliver has otherwise been handing me the trip of my dreams. The entire itinerary has been thoughtfully planned to maximize all the things I want to do, with hardly any of the stuff he's into.

"I've been before," he'd argued. "I want your first time to be special. This is all about you, this trip. I want you to be happy."

Water splashes from the fountain into the pond, hundreds of coins glinting in the sunlight. All those wishes. That *hope*! A busker plays an Italian folk song on the accordion nearby, as tourists make wishes and cram in for photos. Eventually it's our turn. I sit on the stone wall of the fountain and pose for a photo for Oliver—an experience that should be so iconic—but instead I burst into tears.

"Sorry!" I gasp, crying. "I love you."

He pulls me up and into a hug. "It's okay, I get it."

But does he? I feel like if he really understood, he wouldn't have insisted we travel to Italy, knowing how much it meant to me to do this with Bree.

All I can think about is my galloping fear of what I'm missing out on right now in London. Bree is there with Isabelle, Ella, and Olivia—friends whom we weren't deeply entrenched with at school but would sit with in classes if one or the other of us wasn't there. Seeing the photos she posted earlier of the four of them at a pub in Soho—beers full, smiles wide, arms draped around various hot strangers—made my heart hurt. She looked genuinely happy beside some new girl she'd gravitated toward, like she wasn't even missing me.

My photos probably look like that too. Shiny, sparkly photos of Oliver and me soaking up summer in Rome, devouring chocolate gelatos outside the Colosseum. Images of us in a gondola in Venice, my head nestled on his shoulder. Standing beneath the Juliet balcony in Verona. A seemingly blissful week in a tiny B&B in a Tuscan village near Florence, crumbling stone walls, vineyards, glasses of crisp white wine on white tablecloths—glamorous trappings disguising the true difficulty of that whole experience.

*Candles.*

*Rose petals.*

*A four-poster bed.*

*Me scrunching sheets in my fists.*

"Oliver, stop!"

Technically, he applied the brakes when he realized. I'm sure he did. Not long after, anyway. Maybe he didn't hear me the first time . . .

"You should see a doctor about this pain," he suggested when my unreliable body thwarted a second attempt. *Maybe I should?* "Or just try to get out of your own head, Evie."

Of course, the more out of my head he instructs me to get, the more inside it I seem to go, worrying he'll soon be sick of me if I can't fix this. I twist the sapphire and diamond ring that he splashed out on the next morning in a tiny jewelry shop on the Ponte Vecchio in Florence. It's on my right hand. I mean, obviously it is! I had a moment of panic when we started looking at rings, and a whoosh of relief when it became clear that this was just a gift and not something more.

"Just enjoy it!" he'd said, hugging me when I complained that it cost too much. "You overthink everything!"

He wipes the tears from my face now at the fountain. He hates to see me sad.

"Aren't you meant to make a wish?" he asks, fishing around in his jeans pocket for a coin. What more could I theoretically want? He's everything I always imagined. Or he should be. I mean, it's normal to have *some* doubts, isn't it? Traveling together in close quarters is hard work. Even for people who've been together for years. I read that in an online quiz I did the other day after I made too much of a fuss about his absence for a few hours and ruined the dinner he'd planned at a secluded little bistro near the Spanish Steps.

His mention of the wish sets me off again. Because this is Bree's moment. We were meant to stand in this exact spot, hold hands, and make this wish together.

"Close your eyes," Oliver says softly. The Italian sun is punishing. He's staring intently at me, wanting me to believe in the magic of this experience, and I just feel hot and tired and sad and—"Trust me, Evie."

I close my eyes as he presses the coin into my palm. He maneuvers my body so I'm standing with my back to the fountain. And he takes my hand.

"Okay, make a wish," he instructs, and even though I know I'm totally wasting this opportunity, I wish Bree were here. And that I were more assertive, and that everything would be okay. Is that greedy? It's three wishes for one coin, and I'm starting to feel like there isn't enough magic in the world to whisk away my anxiety. I know I had it before, in Australia, but over here, away from my moorings, it's taken on a life of its own. It's not so much about unfamiliar places, or the understandable challenge of being in a foreign country where I don't speak the language. I'm anxious about making mistakes. Taking wrong turns, figuratively and metaphorically. I'm beginning to feel as though everyone around me—all these locals and tourists, Bree and the others, the entire cohort of gap-year travelers in Europe—has their act together. Except for me.

When I open my eyes and wipe them, Oliver is standing in front of me. Not beside me. And he's got a silly grin on his face. I'm dazed by the harsh sunlight and wondering whose hand I'm holding if it's not his.

"Surprise!" Bree says, throwing herself at me so hard she threatens to tip us both into the water. I can hardly speak, as Oliver captures it all on video and all my fear just evaporates in this one incredible moment. *She is here.* The *relief.* She tries to break away from our hug and I won't let her. I pull her closer and hold her harder.

"How did you . . . What is happening?"

She laughs. "It was all Oliver's idea!"

I stare at her, and then at him.

"Isn't this exactly what you wished for?" he asks.

All my doubts seem to rush away in this instant. "You did this?" I ask him, still in shock that she's really here.

He smiles and pulls me into his arms. "I love you, Evie. I'd do anything to make you happy. You should know that by now."

# 45

***Drew***

Why I torture myself with Bree's Instagram post about her Trevi Fountain bestie reunion is beyond me. I don't follow Evie anymore. Not since I bungled that high school apology, she doubled down on her attachment to Oliver, and we fell out. And now I've scrolled through Bree's carousel of images of the two of them reuniting in Italy more times than is remotely healthy.

A memory returns of Evie on that dance floor in Year Twelve. She'd eventually looked up and seen me in the doorway to the ballroom. She'd tried to break away from Oliver to talk to me, but he'd grabbed her arm and pulled her back. I saw him shake his head and watched her listen intently to his pointed advice, and then the music changed and he pulled her into a slow dance from which her attention never reemerged, and I couldn't watch. So I left.

Evie had come over to my house the next day, but I was at the hospital with Mum. She called me, but I let it go through to voicemail. I couldn't have Mum overhearing my explanation and feeling even worse than she already did. I wanted to explain later. Wanted to tell Evie everything and lean on her through it, but how could I do that without sharing Mum's secret? My loyalty had to be to Mum. Every time I tried to set things right, the excuses in my head sounded either too flimsy or too outrageous. *Sorry, something came up at home. Sorry, your boyfriend's father got my mum pregnant, and when I found out, she lost her mind and wound up in the psych ward.*

In the end, by the time I worked out exactly what to say, it was too awkward to say anything. I backed away and hurt her until she stopped chasing me for answers. I'd already let her down once. She was better off without this complication in her life.

Even seeing Evie in a photo now triggers memories of that first night in the hospital. They'd shifted Mum from acute care to a ward upstairs. I'd thought, *Fine, we can cope with this—a few days and she'll be out.* But no. Once the psych team got involved and questions were asked about her panic attack, a litany of issues spilled from her secret.

"It was the whirlwind romance of my life," she admitted to me, sitting in the garden at the hospital one afternoon. "He adored me. He was obsessed with me, really. Fancy private dinners at his house. Weekends in secluded hotels. Gifts."

Part of me was glad to hear it wasn't just a one-night thing. He did actually have feelings for her. "But what went wrong, Mum?"

"I started making mistakes. I'd get held up at work and be late meeting him. He wouldn't believe my excuses . . . He was the specialist, so I had to fit around his schedule, but my job as a trainee nurse was demanding and I didn't have the flexibility I needed to adjust to his timing. And then he started to suspect things about other doctors I worked with. He didn't trust me. He'd have my schedule changed to avoid shifts with certain people . . ."

"And you didn't think it was time to get out of that relationship?" I asked her.

"I tried to leave," she said, pain seared across her face. "And that led to an awful argument, and then . . . well, in the end I was pregnant."

The way that hit me in the heart.

"You were never not wanted, my darling. But it was terrifying to think of telling him. When I did, the fallout was bad. He demanded a DNA test. And even when he had proof you were his, he said he couldn't be with me anymore. By that stage he'd met Oliver's mum. She was everything he expected. Good family. Established. Someone he didn't have to hide away on secret weekend breaks—because I was never good enough for him, Drew. My background didn't fit his future."

The heartbreak in her voice was raw. It might as well have happened a week ago, not twenty years in the past.

"He drew up a contract saying he would pay for your education if I walked away. I took what I could. I knew I'd never be able to provide much for you myself. I was young and stranded. I had no one advising me, and I signed something saying I would never disclose his identity. Because, of course, by then, Oliver's mum was pregnant too . . ."

I was furious.

She could see it. "Drew! You can't tell anyone about this. Especially Evie."

The terror in her eyes broke me.

It was all too messy. Besides, I had more pride than to try to convince Evie to cram me into her increasingly happy existence. Our feelings were never going to align, in a way that was always going to be worse for me, so I pulled the pin on the whole friendship. A sudden explosion seemed easier than her gradually peeling off the Band-Aid.

Bree and I stayed friends, though. And following her gap

year online hasn't been an issue until now, because they ended up having separate trips. But opening the app while I couldn't sleep tonight and being hit in the face with their reunion in Rome slammed me backward. So much happiness on Evie's face. And the caption: Surprise of the year with @Evie_Clicks #Trevifountain #boyfriendgoals #tears #bffsforever.

And now the light of my phone has disturbed Esther, who rolls over beside me in her bed that we're sharing in the shoebox of a flat she rents, her long leg draped across mine while I try to stay still and not wake her.

Esther and I met at work about a month ago in the café beside the photography studio in Manly, where I'm hoping to hold my first solo exhibition. She's an artist too. A couple of years older than me, at twenty-one, and ridiculously cool in that "couldn't care less what people think" way that oozes confidence. Tall and fit, with dyed black hair to match her black tank tops and black jeans and boots. In fact, she is the embodiment of the girlfriends Evie admitted dreaming up for me, except probably even better, and I can't believe she's concocted a "colleagues with benefits" arrangement: *Nothing serious, Drew, don't get attached.*

Given the way my heart is pounding, not by the sight of Esther's bare leg stretched across me but by the unexpected appearance of Evie's face on my phone screen, there's very little chance of that. And then my gut churns remembering Esther and me in this bed last night, and where my mind wandered when it shouldn't have.

My deciding to stay in Australia during my gap year to work and create and exhibit my photos was less about my career, I regret to admit, and more about putting a whole hemisphere between me and the girl who broke my heart. And got away.

Plus every other lovestruck cliché that could possibly be applied here.

"You mean you weren't even together?" Esther quizzed me, not long after we first started working the same shifts and I mentioned Evie one too many times. "And you're still hung up on her a year later?"

I'd opened my mouth to argue, but she said, "It's a high school thing, Drew. Move on." Then she backed me up against boxes of coffee filters and bags of beans in the storeroom and kissed me in a way that convinced me we weren't in high school any longer.

When she'd finished with me and we were adjusting our clothes and righting the collateral damage on the shelves, she kissed me once more and whispered, "Evie who?" in my ear, before swanning out of the storeroom like she owned it, the entire world, and me. But her methodology was flawed. Being with her only made me crave Evie more, because it turns out there's more to a friendship than mind-blowing trysts among the café inventory.

*What if I never get past this?*

# 46

***Evie***

"You're not a little bit worried?" Bree asks, while we sip strong black coffees and share a slice of amaretti and sultana cheesecake at an outdoor café hidden down a little cobblestone alley not far from the Colosseum.

My hackles rise immediately, the cake losing a touch of its sweetness on my tongue. Chewing and swallowing buys me some time. "Worried about what?" I ask lightly.

I know what she's talking about. She's been in Rome half a day and already the cracks have started to show.

"It was all amazing when we were pulling off the surprise. The photos for socials are all smiles. But you're not even slightly concerned about the way he's been since?"

"He literally flew you over here from London!" I say defensively. "He planned everything. It's the most romantic gift imaginable, to fly my best friend to the Trevi Fountain instead of just keeping the experience to ourselves. He knew how much this meant to us!"

She sits back. Am I protesting too much?

"Evie, he's known all along this was our thing—ever since you started talking about the gap year with him."

"And maybe he shouldn't have insisted I go with him

instead, but he obviously realized in time to invite you and make it happen," I argue.

She puts her coffee down and focuses on passers-by, gathering herself. "Sorry, Evie. I don't mean to be critical," she says gently. "And I appreciate this trip. Of course I do. It's just . . . now that I'm here, he seems irritated."

I've noticed that too but can't bring myself to admit it. If I raise it with him, I'll just look ungrateful.

"It's like he flew me in for the photo shoot and the accolades," Bree continues.

*Wow.* "He's just got a lot on his mind right now," I explain.

Bree shoots me a look as if to say she's heard this excuse before. Ad nauseam. I don't know whether Oliver has a lot on his mind or not—just that it seems that way, and it's an excuse I dredge up every time a social event goes wrong. Which is quite often, lately.

"You would tell me if things weren't okay," she says soberly, leaning across the table. "I could help you get out of this."

*Get out of what? The trip? Or this relationship?* My stomach churns at the thought of a breakup. I don't have a valid excuse for one. Suddenly, I'm claustrophobic just sitting here in this conversation. "If he's been irritable lately, it's because I've been quiet. Missing home. And missing *you*!"

Visions of my latest fight with Oliver assault me. Although *fight* is the wrong word. He just goes silent. That's how I know I've done something wrong, and then I'm floundering, trying to work out what it was and how to fix it, flinging haphazard solutions at him until I crack the ever-shifting secret code.

"He's invested so much thought and money into this holiday," I add.

"Yes? That's been his choice," she says. "You don't owe him anything."

Maybe I just need to be a bit more animated. I think I take him for granted. He said he doesn't know what more I expect from him, when he already gives me so much, and sometimes I feel like some kind of entitled brat.

"It's not Oliver who's the problem, Bree. It's me. I've been moody. He's just bouncing off me."

She frowns. "You lit up when I arrived. Now he's jealous. He's always jealous, Evie. Remember what he was like about Drew?"

I don't want to be reminded about him. Not now, when I'm barely holding myself together through this conversation. The way he ditched me and never explained himself still stings.

"Oliver was just trying to protect me. He knew Drew would disappoint me—and he did. He wanted to save me from the inevitable fallout from the loss of a friend, so I stepped away before I could get hurt. It's called having boundaries." If I think about it too much, I will cry.

"Boundaries are something you put around yourself," Bree says quietly. "When someone else puts them around you, it's called a prison."

The analogy makes me gasp. I pull at my sky-blue T-shirt, trying to get breathing space. It's the top Oliver made me change into this morning because he thought I'd be more comfortable in something less tight. Isn't that what he said? It feels tight regardless.

Then she goes in for the kill. "Your parents are worried. We all are."

*My parents?*

This is not how Rome was meant to be! Instantly, at even the mention of them, emotions I've repressed erupt. An explosion of heat cracks through the surface at this fresh criticism of Oliver. I feel entirely ganged up on. As if Bree's coming to the Trevi Fountain was just a Trojan horse for a parentally sanctioned psychological intervention.

*I'll just try harder. They'll see.*

Suddenly it's obvious to me that he's been right all along. It's everyone's constant picking at our relationship that's the problem. Backed against the wall in what feels like a deliberate campaign to make me doubt him, I vow to prove everyone wrong! About Oliver. About us as a couple. About everything.

"I know what I'm doing!" I declare, so confidently the people at the next table turn around to look at me. "And I can do without all this judgment!"

As the words stampede ferociously out of my mouth, I feel myself slipping further from my best friend and my parents. And ever closer to Oliver.

# 47

## *Evie*

"Let's go to bed tonight and tackle this fresh in the morning," Dad says firmly, once we've brought in our bags and he's made us each a cup of tea. This is a level of leadership he usually reserves for Mum, and their change of guard unnerves me. "We've got the couch, and the spare room . . ."

"Thanks, Dad."

I feel like one of those people who returns home after a fire engulfed it to sift through the remains, hoping to find something salvageable. I don't find what I'm looking for in Mum's expression, her eyes downcast as she fidgets nervously with her sapphire engagement ring and the understated eternity band Dad presented at their tenth anniversary. She looks a lot more than thirteen years older—worry lines carved on her forehead, hair gray, light gone from eyes that were always sparkling. *Is this my fault?*

"Thank you for letting us in," I add softly. There's a politeness in my tone that belongs to acquaintances. Not family. I hadn't thought it would be this hard. I lean across the kitchen table and grasp Mum's hand, hoping to breathe life back into our relationship somehow, desperate to revive it.

She gives me a tight smile, but it's as if the unconditional love she's always shown is trapped behind a wall of self-preservation. She curls her fingers around mine, then slowly lets my hand fall—our bond now weak—and heads off to bed with Dad.

An hour later, Drew is exhausted beside me on my parents' couch. We've been drinking some herbal concoction designed to help anxious people sleep, even though I didn't know either of my parents ever had a problem in that department.

His eyes shut and he dozes. Sleep hasn't wiped the frown, and I take the opportunity to really look at him, hoping to provoke my memory. I've still had only that one glimmer from our past on the beach. Maybe if I study him up close, something will trip in my brain and the rest of our friendship will come rushing back.

His long legs stretch out in front of him, ankles crossed. Even weary and stressed, his face is kind. Like me, he's showing the earliest signs of creasing at the corners of his eyes, fine lines etching across his forehead, like he's spent time looking into glaring views. All that landscape photography, probably. Or worrying. I examine the dark hair along his jawline and imagine him clean-shaven. Then shaving. After a shower . . .

"Are you staring at me?" he mumbles without even opening his eyes.

I sit back. "I was just trying to remember you," I admit. I leave out the imagining him in nothing but a towel bit. I am a *widow.* Surely I should have eyes only for my husband, even if he is dead and completely absent in my memory. *I wonder when the world will let me notice someone else.*

I move to get off the couch, but Drew grabs my wrist and

pulls me back down beside him. He pivots us so we're square on. Then he looks straight into my eyes, takes my face in his hands, and says, "Remember me now?"

I think he wants me to remember him as much as I want it myself. The clock in the corner ticks as the breeze brushes the sheer curtains against the frame from the open window. The faint soundtrack from the TV is an undercurrent, and, for a few moments, it doesn't feel like it's only the past that I'm reaching for. It's whatever comes next.

"You made me feel safe," I tell him. The words fall out of my mouth as if disconnected from my conscious mind, and I wonder what deeply held truth they're reflecting.

He drops his hands from my face and edges back. "So ironic," he murmurs. "You made me feel wildly unsafe."

I don't want to touch the delicate ecosystem from which he has finally shared something real. I can't speak or move in case I disrupt the environment that has caused him to open up.

"We met in Photography Club after school, as I said."

I nod.

"I needed to flesh out my CV. My marks had dropped. My mum had been sick . . ." He falters, just briefly, and I notice the slightest catch in his voice. "You were in the classroom. Front row. Notebook on your desk. Making up all sorts of weird fantasies about me . . ."

"What?"

He laughs. "You told me later; you'd imagine all these girls I'd been friends with, and you'd been jealous."

I scoff. "*Jealous?* Of imaginary girls?"

He smiles like he's pretending to be God's gift and shrugs. "I'm just reporting it like you told it, Eves."

*Eves.* His use of the nickname seems to shift us closer.

"Anyway, I had to lead this club for the semester. I was just going to phone it in, and then you showed up and complicated everything. The exhibition we planned. You were always reaching for the stars, and you dragged me with you at a time when . . ." There's that pained look on his face again. "I didn't think I could be dragged."

I've been so preoccupied with my own situation these last couple of days, I didn't stop to wonder about his.

"You pulled me back into life. Maybe that's why I'm here. Because it's you who needs to be pulled back into *your* life now, and I owe you."

I don't want him thinking that. I want him here because he wants to be. Not in this mess, exactly, but in my life . . .

"What was unsafe about me?" I ask.

"That's easy. Once you'd dragged me out of the shadows, I worked out what I'd been missing. I worried you'd leave me stranded there."

I did leave, though. He said we went years without seeing each other. And I need to know why, but he moves the conversation to my parents instead.

"It might take a while before you gain their trust. I know you want more information, but I've been looking this up. I think we need to remember the good stuff first. Go gently into this memory-retrieval exercise." Unexpectedly, he places a hand on my arm.

Something flutters in my chest, and I feel sixteen and completely inexperienced again. A gesture like this could have had me replaying it for weeks—analyzing what it means. I don't have weeks now. I need my memories back. "Drew, were you and I ever . . ." I want this information so badly.

He looks surprised. "No. It wasn't like that."

He says the words, but why can't I shake the feeling that there's something else between us here on my parents' couch—and in this cavernous white space in my mind?

"Never?" I whisper.

# 48

***Drew***

*Almost never.*

I don't know what she's picking up, but I'm not going to let her run with it. I do want her to remember—but *not this part.* I'm here to help her through this crisis and then we'll be going our separate ways. I've wasted too many years on this woman already, and now I'm thirty and drawing a line—she's got to stop looking at me like this, innocent eyes full of possibility.

"Evie, I'm moving overseas in six weeks," I announce. Nothing like putting a firm date on it. "I'm going to accept the magazine contract."

These words are news even to me. But the way she's editorializing us . . . *I can't go there.* I have to commit to the path I know I deserve. Not this half-life, endlessly looking over my shoulder, hoping the future I imagined will catch up with the present and bowl everything over.

"I'm happy for you," she says, but her tone conveys the exact dose of genuine disappointment that younger me would have clung to for months.

Visions of New York fill my head. Working in the magazine's Fifth Avenue office. Lunchtime jogs in Central Park. Brunch at the Met. Maybe I'd rent a condo in New Jersey and travel on assignment, chasing stories and images and a whole new idea of what life could be . . .

"It's time for bed," I suggest, realizing my hand has now traveled to hers, clutching it, almost as if I'm preparing to pull her into this shiny new vision alongside me.

I let go, but she's looking at me like she's still snooping around in our past, trying to dredge up a bit of romance. She's going to be disappointed. Besides, her husband just died. He was always the leading man, not me.

I pick up the mugs and carry them into the kitchen, rinse them at the sink, and exhale a long, deep breath. It's not something I'd say aloud, but I used to imagine what it would be like if Oliver were dead. I thought I'd feel all kinds of things—triumph, relief. But it's not like that. If anything, I'm sad about what could have been—that the brotherly bond I'd craved as an only child became a twisted, one-sided rivalry right from our first scholastic joust. "Complicated grief," they call it. Someone you're problematically tangled up with dies, and it's all about guilt, regret, and resentment. Everything you're meant to feel, you don't.

And here's Evie, who should have complicated grief and instead has nothing. No grief at all, except for the life she's lost. A life I can't say for sure she *would* grieve if her memory does come back. Not that it's my place to judge how happy or how miserable she might have been. Maybe the misery is a touch of wishful thinking . . .

She sets the crockery on the bench, and I help her carry in a pile of sheets and blankets her parents left on the kitchen table to make up a bed on the sofa. Her face is pale, like she's wrung out. She starts pulling scatter cushions off the couch, dumping them in a pile in the corner of the room.

"I'll do it," I say. "You go to bed. You must be exhausted."

But she's already unbundling a white sheet and fluffs it out, so I pick up the other end and we tuck it into the couch cushions. She shakes the light blanket and tucks that in, then throws me a pillow and stands in front of me, beside the makeshift bed, admiring our work.

There's a moment of awkward silence, while she looks at me, presumably assembling a good-night speech in her mind. My own mind is attempting to banish the thoughts I'm having about pulling her onto the bed we just made—still trying to line up the woman she is now against the girl I knew. A catalog of reasons why that cannot happen presents itself, starting with the fact that obviously she's not in her right mind, and, once she remembers everything she'll be a grieving widow to my half brother. Now I'm flashing back to that summer she told me Oliver was pressuring her about sex—an episode in her life that she's forgotten. I mean, there's simply no way I'm charging headlong into this much confusion and inexperience.

"Thank you, Drew. For coming here with me." She takes a step toward me and looks like she's contemplating a hug, but she rethinks it at the last moment.

My arms reach around her anyway and draw her close, just for a few seconds, her body melting into mine while I inhale her scent and remember us. But then I pull back too. And there's nothing but the static electricity where the hug should still be. The longer I linger on the memory of the last time we did this, the more my common sense evaporates.

# 49

## *Evie*

I'm seated in the auditorium beside my peers, nervously adjusting the mortarboard on my head and hoping I don't trip when it's my turn to cross the stage. I've felt so clumsy lately. Even this morning, Oliver and I visited his grandfather on the way to him dropping me off at my graduation, and I flopped enthusiastically onto a small couch, sending it skating into the buffet table behind it, triggering a bunch of ornaments and photo frames to topple loudly onto a crystal tray.

"Never mind—it's just stuff," his grandfather had said. He's the kindest person in the extended family. But in the car afterward, I received a lecture.

"Be more thoughtful, Evie. You're always charging through places."

That comment makes me even more nervous about all eyes being on me in this packed hall. I'd rather be the woman down in the front row with the clipboard, ticking off names as we parade past. Or, if I'm honest, I'd rather be recording a podcast in my room. I'd have never predicted a group assignment about gender-based violence would lead me down the podcasting path, but I love it—it gives me something to focus on and people to connect with. I guess I became so absorbed in my research I hadn't noticed I was lonely.

The ring on my left hand flashes under the stage lights, and I want to cover it up. I'm anxious not to advertise the choice it represents as I look along the row. Of course I'm the only person wearing one. I haven't even said yes yet.

"Marry me, Evie," he'd said, at an expensive oyster bar in The Rocks. I don't like oysters, but they're his favorite, and he'd ordered a dozen and expected me to try one.

As I placed the globule in my mouth and it slid down my throat, practically making me gag, my first response to his proposal was no.

"What do you mean, no?" he'd said.

"Well, I mean no. Not yet. We're twenty-three, Oliver!"

"And we've been together seven years. It's time. At least try it on. It was expensive."

He wouldn't let go of my hand until he'd forced the diamond onto my finger, which sparkled obnoxiously under the restaurant's fancy overhead table lamp.

"Wear it for a while. See if the idea grows on you," he said, before calling the waiter over. "We'll have a bottle of your best champagne."

I tried to pull the ring off and give it back. I wanted to ask him for time to think. But he covered my hand and stopped me. "Give it a go," he whispered. "And don't make a scene."

I smiled at the waiter and thanked him when he congratulated me, every little step in the charade entrenching us further along a path I wasn't ready for. Wearing the ring today is absorbing mental energy I should be throwing at graduating.

My phone beeps with a message from Bree. You did it! it

reads. Next grad with the floppy hat I want to be there! Love you! Revel in all your success!

The floppy hat reference is about the PhD I'm about to begin. The idea of starting a doctorate at twenty-three feels much more like me than getting engaged. This was the plan all along, and academia is the one place in my life where I don't feel totally out of my depth.

Bree, I have other news, I type. I take a quick photo of my left hand and send it to her.

There's silence at her end for a full minute. Eventually, three dots start blinking. The longer she takes, the stronger my anxiety becomes.

*What am I doing with my life?*

As I look up, I'm startled by a massive camera flash a couple of rows in front of me. I can't see anything at first except stars, but, as my eyes adjust, a blurry vision of *Drew Kennedy* materializes.

I haven't seen him in years!

He wasn't taking the picture of me. It's of a girl two rows away, whom he's smiling at. More widely than I ever saw him smile at school. A broad, open smile that lights up everything, brown eyes dancing as he flirts with her, and I stifle feelings I have no right to experience. Particularly not while I'm wearing this ring.

Drew is here, I update Bree by text. Now I need help with that too!

She and I had workshopped my falling out with Drew, over and over. She didn't like agreeing with Oliver, but if Drew had had a legitimate excuse for ditching me when I was just trying to help save him from social embarrassment—something to do with his mum, perhaps—why wouldn't he have told me?

How does he look? Bree types.

My heart hurts and the ring feels heavy on my finger. I think of that night with the bioluminescence and wonder how we drifted this far.

He's taking pictures of a girl, I write. I crane my neck to get a glimpse of her. Blond hair, super glossy, and falling over her shoulders in perfect waves, the way I always wished mine would.

Pictures of her, and not you? ;-)

Bree's joke falls flat, and I can't explain my sense of loss—I *won't* explain it. I am snared on the path I've chosen with Oliver and can't seem to pull myself free. And it's unreasonable, anyway. Drew and I were only ever friends, and for a few months, really. He left me at the high school formal equivalent of the altar and never explained why. That should have been the end of it.

I hope he didn't inadvertently get me in the photos, staring at my trial engagement ring, having an existential crisis about what I am doing with my life. It's not the look I imagined for this defining experience on my timeline.

And it's definitely not how I wanted to feel.

# 50

***Drew***

I sit back in my seat in the supporters section and flick through the photos on my camera while we wait for the official ceremony to start. Meg is radiant. Beaming smiles. Confidence. I've been tempted to make some kind of move but haven't yet and won't today. It's all about her and her graduation. She's got enough going on without a romantic overture from me detracting from her success.

The lighting is all wrong in here to get good photos, but I can fix the red eyes later, and I'll get some good images of her outside in the garden party reception after the ceremony.

I'm about to switch the camera off when something catches my eye in the corner of the shot and makes me look over to that section of the auditorium. Is that . . . *Evie Hudson*?

The sight of her twists my gut. I haven't seen her in almost five years. I knew she went to Sydney University but hadn't expected her to be at Meg's ceremony—I thought Evie was studying criminology. This is the day she used to dream about. She should look luminous, like Meg, but instead she's fidgeting and anxious, and so am I, now. It's all intertwined. Evie. Mum.

The night of the formal. The aftermath with Mum's health. And then my mind flashes to seeing Evie having the time of her life with Oliver on that dance floor, and to the decision I made in that moment not to let my unpredictable trajectory mess with hers, and I'm seventeen again.

I hope she's happy.

I look at Meg, who smiles back. It's such an uncomplicated, safe friendship. No arguments. No drama. No possessive boyfriend monitoring our every move.

I let my eyes travel two rows back to where Evie is sitting. She's nervous. Probably hates the idea of being in the spotlight She's straightened her curls and perfected her makeup. I check the photos again. Zoom in on one where she's brushing the hair out of her eyes.

*Is that . . .*

I zoom in further. A ring? A giant one. On her left hand. *What the fuck?*

The lights in the auditorium dim and everyone stands as the official party parades in. Academics in bulky robes. The vice chancellor with the guest speaker. But my heart and brain have bolted, even though they have no right to, from any angle. I'm meant to be cheering on my friend's graduation, and instead all I can obsess about is this one thing: Evie Hudson is getting *married*?

The ceremony seems to take years. All the while, she's just over there. Meters from me. On the precipice of what I can only presume is an enormous mistake, depending on who gave her that ring.

I'm having alarming visions of clambering across all these rows of people and extracting her from this auditorium and demanding to know what she is *thinking*. I hope we get out of this without bumping into each other, particularly if it's Oliver who bought that piece of jewelry. Is he here? Even thinking about him raises my blood pressure.

We sit through an original composition from a student in the music school, which I'd be impressed by any other day. Instead, I'm just getting more and more agitated. I've imagined this moment—seeing her again. But I thought I'd be more composed. What does it say that she still sets me off like this?

I whistle as Meg crosses the stage. We met last year at a community festival gig; I was the official photographer for the event. She was working behind a pop-up bar and slipped me a free beer when her boss wasn't looking. It was friendship at first sight, not just because of the free beer. She brings out a lighter side in me and never takes anything too seriously. It's all just *easy*.

"Evelyn Hudson," the MC announces a few minutes later, and a few people burst into applause farther back in the auditorium. "Evelyn graduates with a Bachelor of Arts, with First Class Honors in Linguistics and the University Medal for Linguistics. She has received the Lilian Barnes scholarship for postgraduate research in the school of Linguistics, specializing in forensic linguistics."

In other words, she is completely on track.

It's the exact academic career she always imagined. Prizes. Scholarships. And her personal life also tied up in a bow. No scrambling for competitive arts grants. No doomed relationships. No clawing for glimmers of success in photographic journalism that still seems wildly out of reach, even if I've been shortlisted for a major award . . .

So why, when her eyes meet mine walking down the steps after she's crossed the stage, does she look so comprehensively despondent?

# 51

***Evie***

*Shit, shit, shit.*

I didn't mean to look in his direction on my way down the stairs. Drew Kennedy and I have never had secrets. Well, we have, but most of them were glaringly obvious to each other. I know, without exchanging a single word, that he's just seen right through my blazing academic achievement and plowed straight into my heart. Where things are *not* right.

I don't know when the anxiety escalated so much. I had it as a kid, I guess, and it got worse on our gap year, but this full-blown worry about everything has crept up on me. And I didn't realize how bad it was until now—trapped in Drew's scrutiny. Seeing him again feels like a natural measure of how far I've fallen.

He, meanwhile, looks annoyingly good. Or did, when he was admiring his girlfriend. Glancing at me, he's tense and grumpy. I try to smooth it away with a half smile, but he doesn't smile back and that only heightens the strain between us.

I thread my way back to my seat, sit down, heart thumping, and contemplate the fact that I have everything I've ever wanted. The metal cylinder in my lap containing my degree, the scholarship, the place in the research program. I'm studying forensic linguistics—a fascination that has gripped me since I first started watching crime shows as a teenager. I'm researching how a criminal's speech patterns can expose them. It's enthralling. And even though I've only just started my PhD, I've been nominated to speak at my first national conference later in the year, because, apparently, I'm the linguistics department's "rising star."

And I have Oliver. Still.

He couldn't come to the ceremony because they gave us only two tickets each and my parents took those. We had a fight about that—"I'm your *fiancé*, Evie, or will be once you see sense"—but we're meeting outside for drinks in the garden afterward.

The law faculty held their graduation last week. His mum was sick, so I went to his ceremony with his dad and his mixed signals. Utterly proud in one way but also totally distracted—he kept looking at his watch and typing emails on his phone. It hit me again that Oliver has never really been loved. Not like I am. There's a part of me that's been increasingly worried this lack of example in his life is going to creep up on us—or that it already has. But that's probably just my being paranoid again, as he loves to suggest.

I push through the crowds on the way out, looking for Oliver. Knowing I need to find him first, in case we run into Drew.

Carried by the wave of people down the stairs, I'm thrust out into the sunshine, where everyone's milling about having photos taken, throwing mortarboards into the air, clinking glasses. All these years of hard work, and it's over. Well, not in my case, as I've gone straight on, but this feels like a major milestone.

"Still a nerd, Hudson." Drew's voice is clear, behind me.

I turn around and he's the only person standing still in the bustling crowd, sunlight refracted onto his face from the shiny terra-cotta tiles at our feet. He's taller than I remember, and he looks into my face with a mix of teasing and pride and silent apology. He knows exactly how much these academic results mean to me. And for a moment we're frozen in time.

*I miss him.*

He steps forward and draws me into a hug. "Congratulations," he whispers. "You did it."

I don't want to let go. I clutch my degree, my arms tightening around his neck. In the privacy of this embrace, everything else seems to fall away—the crowds, the noise, the anxiety, the decision I have yet to make about Oliver's proposal. Well, his statement, really. I get this crazy vision of Drew picking me up in my graduation gown and carrying me out of here, taking me away from everything. Escaping.

But that doesn't happen, of course. The moment is broken when his girlfriend approaches with two glasses of prosecco and a sunny expression.

"Congratulations!" I say to her, pulling out of the hug and brushing my gown down.

She beams back. "And to you! Wow! Impressive results. I'm Meg."

At face value, she's everything I would want for Drew. There's an open warmth to her. Of everyone I know, Drew deserves warmth.

"Meg, this is Evie," he says.

"Wait!" she says. "High school Evie?"

He looks uncomfortable. I scan the crowd for Oliver, who is nowhere to be seen. I hate to imagine the story Drew has given Meg. *This is my former best friend who never really spoke to me after I was two hours late to her formal for secret reasons I've never divulged.*

I wonder if he's divulged them to her. No, why would they even have talked about me? I belong firmly in Drew's past.

"Evie the photographer?" Meg asks. "The *Pictures of You* exhibition?"

Maybe the story he gave her wasn't all bad.

"Oh my God, we *idolized* you at my school!" she gushes. "Smashing the patriarchy, one boys' school at a time!"

I laugh. That's exaggerating it slightly. "It really wasn't all me. And I'm not sure how much we really smashed."

I think of being interviewed on the news with Oliver. I feel awkward even remembering the way that happened, and how Drew was sidelined after he'd done the lion's share.

"Drew did all the work," I explain hastily. "He made it happen." I'd said so on camera, but they'd cut that bit from the interview.

"Your idea," he reminds me.

"Good team?" Meg suggests.

Neither of us confirms or denies it before Oliver shows up, clearly irritated at encountering his nemesis. "Hello," he says tersely. They shake hands, Oliver deliberately twisting his hand on top of Drew's, asserting dominance, which for some reason makes me unspeakably angry. And embarrassed. "What brings you here?" he asks.

Drew throws his arm around Meg, drawing her to his side, triggering a massive smile. "This is Meg," he says.

Oliver smiles at her. "Hello." His tone is warm now—he can be so charming. "I'm Evie's fiancé."

*Fiancé?* I mean, yes, I'm wearing the ring, but only on trial, as we agreed.

Drew's eyes drop to the diamond sparkling on my hand and I feel myself covering it with the certificate. He gulps his drink.

Meg's eyes widen. "Ooh! When's the big day?"

"We're not rushing anything," I explain, perhaps more quickly than I intended to. "In fact, technically—"

Oliver cuts me off. "She wants to establish her research first."

Am I making things more difficult than they need to be? He makes it sound like I've taken up a PhD just to annoy him.

"Still mucking around with that camera?" he asks Drew. The condescension makes me cringe.

Meg snuggles in and places her hand on Drew's chest proudly. My heart thumps. "Drew is an award-winning photographer!"

I'm instantly thrilled for him.

"Emerging photographer," he corrects her, humble as ever.

"Shortlisted in the Australian Photography Awards," she brags. "You should own it!"

I reach out to grip his arm. I remember his telling me about this award years ago, and how competitive it was.

His eyes fall to my left hand and its adornment on his forearm, and the muscles stiffen through the sleeve of his shirt. "Anyway, it was good to see you," he says. "Congratulations, Evie. Meg—should we find your mum?"

She nods and slips her hand around his back. He does steal one final glance over his shoulder that doesn't quite reach me as they walk away, and pieces of my heart break off as I lose sight of him in the crowd.

Lose sight of myself, really.

# 52

***Evie***

Oliver has booked a table for two in the window of a prizewinning restaurant overlooking the Opera House. After the stress of today's graduation, I'd rather stay in and order pizza, but instead I change into the sleek black dress and heels that he placed on our bed for me to wear. My feet hurt before we've even made it across the pavement from the cab.

It's really a gorgeous setting. Enormous picture windows offer an unobstructed view across the harbor, and I watch as the Manly ferry pushes out, imagining the lives of the people onboard, wishing I was any one of them.

"Champagne?" Oliver asks. It's not really a question. Of course we're celebrating. Not just my graduation but his, and our big plans for the next chapter: the position he's nabbed in a commercial law firm, my PhD. And I suppose our personal plans.

As a waiter pops the cork on a bottle of Veuve Clicquot, piano tinkling in the background, I try to peruse the menu, distracted by the sparkling diamond on my finger. Who knew something so beautiful could weigh so heavily?

"What are you thinking?" Oliver asks. Does he mean about the menu choices, or my life?

"I'm really not sure . . ." I begin. Not sure about any of it.

"We'll have the seared foie gras to begin," he tells the waiter, before I have the chance to contemplate it any further, "followed by the wagyū beef for my fiancée, rare. I'll have the lobster, and bring us sides of truffle mash and greens."

"I'm not sure!" I exclaim quickly, every bit of his sentence unappealing. I'm *really* not.

The waiter, who had been rearranging the cutlery on the table, pauses.

Oliver's back arches across from me, brows furrowed over his steel-blue eyes. "Is there something else you'd prefer?" He looks apologetically at the waiter and adds, "I'm sorry. She's incredibly indecisive."

I shake my head. "The beef is perfect, thank you. But I'd like it medium, please."

And that's it. That one correction is enough to tip him over.

"How do you think it looks that I don't know how my wife-to-be likes her steak cooked?" he hisses after the waiter has gone.

"But you do know."

"It's better rare, Evie. It's meat in its purest form."

Do *any* of my preferences matter? For steak, or for movies, or for holidays? Even this engagement ring is nothing like what I'd select myself, but of course I wasn't consulted on that, either.

He catches me twisting the ring. "Oh, poor you, having to wear a two-carat diamond. God! I give you *everything*!"

"And I'm grateful, Oliver, but this isn't what matters to me!"

He's raging now. "What does, though? You're impossible to please!"

Phosphorescence springs to mind. Beaches. Sunrises. Conversations. Photography.

"Do you expect me to believe you only ran into Drew today?"

Here it comes: the accusation that has been brewing for hours.

"I haven't seen him since Year Twelve," I say as calmly as I can.

The practiced, steady gaze can't hide the way his hands are shaking, heat traveling up his neck, barely containing the boiling rage. "He was never good for you, Evie. Don't let him back in now."

Drew *was* good for me, though. And apart from the formal, which, yes, was hugely disappointing, he didn't let me down once.

I pick up the champagne flute and take three large mouthfuls in quick succession, the bubbly warmth sliding down my throat.

"Go steady," Oliver chastises me, glancing at the diners at neighboring tables. I take another sip. Oliver's bad mood has ruined the night I've been working toward for years. Nothing about this celebration is about me. Instead, I'm being led into a conversation we don't need to have, about another nonexistent situation with a man.

"Oliver, if it's not Drew, it's my peers at uni. Or my tutor."

"What?" He frowns at me, as if I'm talking nonsense.

"There hasn't been a single platonic, casual, or professional acquaintance I've had in the last three years that hasn't gotten your hackles up."

Whether it's having seen Drew so suddenly, after all this time, or whether I'm just tired, I know for certain now that I can't keep this up. This being on edge all the time. All this *explaining.*

"I need a break," I tell him, twisting the ring off my finger as

I say the words. So much freedom and lightness and hope from that one tiny action.

He stares at me, shock crashing across his features. "A break?"

I know it's not just a break I'm asking for, it's a breakup. And it's years overdue.

I place the ring on the white tablecloth between us and push it toward him. An action so calm. So precise. So unambiguously final, my heart lightens and bolts with relief.

"What are you doing, Evie? You don't mean this."

I do mean it, though. I can't be with someone who won't trust me. I reach for my bag, and he grabs my wrist under the table.

"Don't go!" he says, his voice low, but laced with urgency. "We can work this out. I'm sorry. It's just . . . Drew triggers me. Always has."

"Because of a Year Seven science test?"

His nostrils flare. "You know it's not just that."

I sigh. He's not getting it. "Let. Me. Go."

His eyes are urgent now, the same eyes that were so cutting just moments ago. He searches my face, looking for hope. Or perhaps looking for a weak spot, through which he can stampede, as usual, and bring me back into line. "Tell me how to fix this," he begs.

A memory pops up of one of our earliest kisses in his bedroom in Lane Cove. The way he trapped me with his leg until I told him I loved him. I knew then that the words were premature, but he forced me. The way he pressured me, saying he could wait, but was unrelenting until I finally slept with him. The way he's tried to control every decision I make since my friendship with Drew ended, and the way I've lost track of which thoughts are mine and which are his, while he orchestrates *everything*, drowning the melody of my own life with the searing crescendo of his . . .

I've let this relationship drag itself incrementally toward this crisis, where the damage is so deep it's ingrained in our everyday existence. More evidence flashes before my eyes. The elation of Oliver's surprise at the Trevi Fountain, followed by his unexpected coolness the next day, when he thought I seemed happier with Bree than I had been the whole trip with him.

"You'd always arrive early to pick me up from lectures," I remind him.

"You hate it when people are late!" he counters.

"You'd sneak in through the back door of the lecture theatre, to check where I was sitting. Or who I was sitting with." My skin crawls at the recollection. The way everyone's face would turn to check out the overprotective boyfriend. "You were antisocial with the few friends I managed to make at uni, all of whom ended up being transient because you'd *always* find ways to push me away from them, or create events to clash with our plans." It was rarely anything obnoxious. Just being overly quiet, to the point where I was forever making excuses about his "headaches" or all the "stress" he's under. It was easier for us just to drop out of the social scene altogether, which perked him up to no end, because he had me all to himself. Subtle bad behavior that I *always* excused.

As I shake his hand off my wrist and watch his frenzied attempt to cling to the dregs of this fairy tale, I realize it snowballed so fast in the beginning, it completely absorbed me. By the time the cracks started to appear, I was stuck. Imprisoned in the kind of airbrushed relationship everyone else thought they wanted, every wrinkle ironed out, every blemish smoothed until no part of this glossy picture resembled real life anymore. I was always scrambling to rebalance it. Forever adjusting the light. And when I inevitably failed, it felt like me who was wrong, or confused or crazy—while all along it was him. He was the artist. And now I've caught him here, with the camera in his hand, blaming his tools.

"I'm done," I say, resolution rising through the exhaustion in my voice as I pick up my bag, sweep my coat off the back of my seat, and leave the diamond on the table. "Truly, Oliver. We are through."

# 53

***Evie***

I wake before dawn in a house my parents have made their own, without me. I feel like a visitor rather than a daughter. Dad is snoring down the hall, a familiar drone that I could have sworn I heard only last week. The spare room looks like it's been entirely furnished by Kmart's home décor section—dusty pink glass vases and pointless little ornaments, and a muted pastel print of a flower on the wall. Staring at it from bed, all I can think is how much more striking one of Drew's photographs would be hanging here.

Beside me on the dressing table are framed family photos. Once again, I have this sense that my lost memories are just beyond a veil. So close. They'll push through soon, rushing in and swamping me. The anticipation is torture.

I get out of bed in the dark, creep down the hall, and open the sliding door onto the back veranda. It's been one of those long summer nights that never really cools off. There's a big swing seat out here with overstuffed yellow cushions, and I ease into it, one foot still on the deck, rocking gently.

A soft light flicks on in the kitchen and I look up to see Drew through the window as he tries to figure out the coffee machine. He doesn't know I'm out here, and I watch as he potters around, looking for the ground coffee, opening and closing doors quietly, searching for a mug.

Even first thing in the morning, with bed hair and several days' dark stubble, he looks good. I'm suddenly aware of having crawled out of bed after a bad night's sleep, my own hair a total mess, skin drawn, bags under my eyes . . . just the total opposite of how put together he looks even in gray pajama pants and a T-shirt. I don't believe him when he said there was never a spark between us. That might be true for him, but teenage me *must* have had a crush, surely?

As he waits for the coffee to percolate, he peers out the window and notices me. His face shifts in an instant, softening, before he can catch himself. Looking at him, I'm suddenly overcome by an unspecific sense of sadness from our past. No, it's even worse than that. I feel bereft. Not about him. *For* him. *What am I remembering?*

The first fuzzy images sift to the surface. A younger Drew, standing at a kitchen bench like this, looking at me. Torn right open. Completely vulnerable. Right now, I feel the same emotions as I must have back then—heart-wrenching pain for him, coupled with a terrifying sense of not knowing what to do.

*What has he been through?* What happened to make my heart remember hurting this much for him? I want to console him right now, except obviously he's not distraught right this second. But, oh, he *was*.

It's grief. It has to be. This futile desperation. I ache for him. And I hope with everything I've got that a younger version of me stepped up to the plate and didn't run away from this anguish. Because that would have been my instinct, I'm sure.

Suddenly, his focus is drawn. Inside the house, another light flicks on, and his face breaks into a *dazzling* smile. He's talking to someone I can't see in the front doorway. It can't be one of my parents—this is not the smile you bestow on someone you just met. It's got years of backstory behind it.

And then she comes into view. All I can make out from here is her short-cropped platinum-blond hair and the build of someone who has just stepped off a catwalk in Milan. That, and the fact that she is throwing herself into Drew's arms.

Is this Chloe? The woman he insists isn't his girlfriend, but whom he's spoken to or messaged several times in the last two days? It has to be. They're obviously together—look at the body language! They're *still* hugging. And now the brokenhearted compassion I felt for him seconds ago has been replaced by something entirely unfamiliar, unwanted, and unwarranted: outright jealousy.

*What the hell is wrong with me?!*

He puts this woman down and stands back at arm's length, admiring her hair, more smiling, then they hug *again*. Ugh!

But as they drag themselves apart at last, he pulls her over to the window and nods in my direction, as if to say, *Sorry, I've got a green-eyed monster outside, excuse the hair and pajamas, she's not in her right mind . . .*

He slides the door open and I run my hand through my curls in a flustered and ultimately hopeless attempt to smooth the frizz. As he walks out onto the deck, he pulls her by the hand through the doorway, face triumphant, eyes alight like they're a royal couple emerging onto the balcony of Buckingham Palace.

It's only in the soft light of sunrise, outside, that I can make out her features. The unusual, feline shape of her eyes. The jet-black roots under the platinum blond. The sophistication crumbling on sight, falling away to reveal the twelve-year-old I first knew. The one who rescued me for that group assignment and helped me through every assignment since, and who is here, at last, to help me through the biggest assignment I've ever faced.

She falls into the swing seat with me, hugging me so hard and so long, not saying a word, that I know instantly, just from this one, desperate embrace, just how much trouble I must really be in.

# 54

***Drew***

The relief I felt when Breanna walked through that door!

They're still hugging, Bree looking like she's stepped out of a *Vogue* shoot, and Evie reminding me of all the times she'd turn up on the doorstep for a sunrise photo trip as a teenager, half dressed, half asleep, wholly unaware that this disassembled, not-ready-for-the-day vibe just made me want to take her back to bed.

"Macchiato, Bree?" I ask. I've already made one for myself, and I've seen enough of Bree's gap year foodie posts to know what she drinks.

Evie opens her eyes and locks gazes with me. Probably wondering how I know Bree's adult coffee preferences but didn't know hers. And why Bree drinks the strong stuff now and she doesn't. I can read this woman like a book, even after all this time, and I give her an encouraging little smile. *It's just coffee, Evie.*

"How did you know I was here?" she asks Bree, finding her voice at last. "Where have you *been*?"

Now it's Bree who looks unsure. I can see she's trying to stamp down the anger. Where has *she* been? Where has *Evie* been? I hope she can hold on through this turbulent reunion.

"Your parents called me last night," she explains. "Pretty much went straight to the airport. The only flight was a red-eye from Perth via Melbourne."

"Perth?"

"I play there now."

"Don't be modest, Breanna," I cut in. "She's first violinist with the West Australian Symphony Orchestra."

Evie's eyes widen and her hand shoots to her heart. "This was your *dream*!"

"It was a nightmare to get there. A lot of hard work. A lot of rejection," Bree starts explaining. She's always been transparent about her success.

"Please tell me I helped you through that . . ." Evie says, leaning toward Bree. She's going to be disappointed.

"Make it a double shot, Drew?" Bree asks, letting go of Evie's hand to readjust the cushions.

Evie, once again, looks worried. And Bree is wary, the way I am. It's like Evie's wearing a bomb and the two of us are SWAT operatives attempting to dismantle it. We know where the wires go, but we don't want to trip something and have the whole thing explode.

"I'm sorry about Oliver," Bree says.

"I don't know Oliver," Evie replies bluntly. "I don't miss him. I don't know anything about us. I sat there and watched the slideshow at the funeral and didn't recognize any of it. I didn't like it, Bree. How in hell did I end up here?"

"I'm not on social media much anymore," Bree explains. "We've been deep in rehearsals. We're doing one of those *Star Wars* movie screenings, playing the soundtrack live, you know?"

Evie doesn't know. She looks confused.

"So I didn't hear about the accident."

"Would you have come to the funeral?" Evie asks. She looks at me, knowing that I almost made it up those steps but didn't quite, and that her parents were similarly defeated.

To her credit, Bree holds it together, while years of hurt flash through her eyes and diplomacy floats to the surface.

"I'm here now."

# age TWENTY-THREE

# 55

***Drew***

After Evie's graduation, I spend the next two days writing and deleting a text message to her. The basic gist is, "Why are you so unhappy?"

It's not my role to intercept her mistake. But I keep flicking through those photos on my camera and all I see is my former best friend, trapped.

*Walking past that behavior is as bad as doing it.*

It's her annoying line, but it's apt in this instance. I can't walk past her making a mistake of this magnitude without trying to sow even a small seed of doubt in her mind. What if she's just waiting for one person to question everything? This whole thing reminds me far too much of the way Mum described her relationship with Anderson. Suddenly, it's Mum who I really want to ask for advice.

Her blue Mazda is parked in its usual spot under the carport. The bins are empty and still on the road—the last ones left in the street. I drag them in, before clearing the mailbox and tossing the catalogs in the recycling. She never reads them, and the no junk mail sign doesn't seem to deter the ten-year-old pamphlet deliverers.

I knock on the door to warn her I'm here, then let myself in.

"Mum?" There's no immediate response as I walk across creaking floorboards through the hall into the laundry, where a load of washing is waiting to be taken out of the machine and hung on the clothesline. On autopilot, I pull out the clothes, dumping them into a basket. She has a caretaker in twice a week to do this stuff for her, and I check in several times a week myself. It's still not enough, but she's too proud to consider full-time care.

"Mum?"

She's not in the kitchen, either, but I finally see her in the garden, lazing in the bright blue easy chair I gave her last Mother's Day. There's a book on the wrought-iron coffee table beside her, the pages flapping in the breeze, along with a half-empty glass of water.

The clouds have come over and she's in short sleeves. I head out the back door and down the steps past her prize roses and fragrant jasmine, onto the lawn.

"Mum!" I say again, before I realize she's asleep.

I touch her arm, gently, so as not to startle her. She's freezing. And I look toward the blanket box she keeps under the wrought-iron pergola.

I feel like I've been looking for blankets to cover Mum for most of my life. Nothing is ever warm enough. Everything I do to try to help her falls short. But even as I'm searching for something to wrap her in, part of me knows the deep truth that my subconscious mind is scrambling to protect me from.

Something wasn't right, just then, when I touched her.

My fingertips are like ice, responding to how cold she felt, my mind taking a few seconds to catch up with the monstrous knowing that's erupting in my body.

How still she was.

How silent.

I walk slowly back to her side, scared to approach her. "Mum?" My voice breaks, her name fragile in the crisp garden air.

No response.

I put two fingers on the paper-thin skin of her neck and wait for it to pulse.

I lean forward, near her slightly open mouth, hoping for a brush of air on my cheek that never comes.

Then I shake her, gently, expecting her arm to flop off the armrest, limp.

It doesn't. It's stuck.

When I rock her a little harder, in a last-ditch attempt to wake her from this nightmare, her entire body rocks with the stiffness of a store mannequin, and I reel in abject horror. Stagger to the rosebushes. Throw up.

Seconds later, I grab my phone. Dial the number.

"Ambulance!" I say, my breath coming fast as my heart pounds. "But I think it's too late."

*I know it is.*

"Is the patient breathing?"

"No, she's not."

"I want you to move her onto the ground and lie her on her back," the person instructs. They don't understand.

"It's too late," I explain again. "She's gone."

"I want you to give CPR until the paramedics arrive. You'll want to know you've done all you could."

Mum looks completely at peace, in a way I don't recall ever having seen her—not in all the years she struggled with her broken body and fractured mind.

"Place the patient on the ground, flat on her back," the operator instructs me again.

"It's too late," I reiterate helplessly. I don't know why I can't just say the words: *rigor mortis*. Maybe if I speak them, the truth will cement itself into this place and time.

The place and time of Mum's death.

Her *death*.

"Put the patient on the ground," the person insists relentlessly, and I find myself silently apologizing to Mum as I do as I'm told, dragging her body from the chair, stumbling with it as we fall onto the grass. I brush the hair out of her eyes. I know how much it always annoyed her.

"Now put the heel of your hand in the middle of her chest and do compressions in time with my count, okay? One, two, three, four. One, two, three, four . . ."

I become unhinged from time. Past. Present. Future. All time is now, swollen seconds in this unspeakable, desperate agony. I will pump her lifeless chest for eleven whole minutes, which is what the police officer will note on the death report as the period that elapsed between this call and the arrival of paramedics.

*One, two, three, four.*

One of them will tramp over her azaleas in the backyard and set down his gear as he reaches us and asks me to move over.

*One, two, three, four.*

I won't move. And he'll touch her just once as he tries to coax me aside.

*One, two.*

He'll feel what I felt. The stiffness.

He'll shake his head at the other and turn to me and tell me he's sorry, while I make one final attempt to rally her broken heart, frantically trying to undo this and bring her back to me.

*One.*

That's when I'll hear the crack of her rib and feel it break into pieces underneath my hand. A sound and a touch that I know will haunt me for the rest of my days.

I'll fall onto her frail body, sobbing. *I'm sorry, Mum. I'm so sorry.*

Then I'll notice the silver bracelet, shining on her wrist under the ambulance officer's headlamp, three words engraved on it that will hit my heart with a regret that seems to spread cancerously through my entire body, poisoning my spirit, cell by cell.

do not resuscitate.

# 56

## *Evie*

"I came as soon as I could," I tell Drew, fighting back tears as I dump my handbag onto the kitchen table. I probably haven't been in this room since I last studied for an English exam there, when there would have been textbooks and junk food spread all over. Drew is standing here, in adult form, exactly where he used to annoy me as a teenager, eating cereal and teasing me about Oliver.

There is no teasing now. And, despite the lapse in our friendship and the awkwardness of our quick reunion just days ago at my graduation, I throw myself into his arms. "I'm so desperately sorry, Drew."

I'm not just sorry about his mum. I'm sorry about my silence. Sorry I didn't try harder to clear up what happened that night he abandoned me. Sorry I listened to Oliver. And I'm sorry we let our lives decouple from each other's so convincingly it's taken a tragedy to bring us back.

When I go to pull out of the hug, he grabs me harder, holding me to his chest. I wrap my arms tighter around a body that feels unfamiliarly tall and broad, despite how close we used to be. His heart is racing. And breaking. I could tell the latter just by the torment on his face when he opened the door. The haunting shock in his eyes as he looked straight through the gap in our fractured friendship and met me here in this moment.

"Evie, it's me," he'd said on the phone. "Can you come to Mum's? I need you."

I hadn't asked why. Hadn't needed to. I knew from the tone in his voice what had happened. That almost telepathic connection, intact after everything else had been shredded between us, brought me up sharp on the way over in the car as I turned onto his street and arrived to the glow of lights from the paramedics. The knowledge that, even after we fell out, I'm still the first person he calls suddenly means everything.

They have Annie on a gurney. My heart aches at the sight of her. She's smaller than I remember, her skin drawn, lips a bluish gray. I've never been exposed to death up close like this. When my grandpa died when I was little, I went to the funeral, but Mum and Dad shielded me from the burial.

I don't want to be this close to it now, and I feel myself shaking. But this is not about me, even though Drew shields my face, aware of my response to her.

"Cup of tea?" I manage to ask, turning the other way.

Drew doesn't look like he wants tea, or that he'd say no to a cup. He is completely and utterly lost, as if deciding one way or the other on tea would be beyond him.

I fill up the kettle and sit beside him while a police officer asks questions.

"Do you know what she last ate?"

Drew shakes his head.

There's half a sandwich on a plate on the bench beside the kettle. The bread is dry, the cheese curled up at the edges. "Perhaps that?" I offer.

The idea of the half-eaten sandwich almost undoes me. That we could just step out of life one day, unfinished. Books half read. Wet washing still in the machine. Places unseen. Ambitions unmet. Grudges held, long after they should have been . . .

The sandwich seems to undo Drew too. It's the simplicity. She deserved something scrumptious for her last meal. As he stares at the stale bread, I grieve for the years of support he's needed in my absence. I have every intention of making up every moment we missed.

"We need to check the air vents in the ceiling," the officer says. "Standard procedure. Can we see what medication she was on?"

I glance at all the packets and bottles on the bench. Pain relief that never quite worked. And I don't have a clue what to say. I want to make it better. Lighten it. Soften it? Obliterate it altogether. But somehow I hold back that impulse and manage just to sit with it at the kitchen table, while the kettle sings.

The officer excuses herself and says she's going to check the garden before it gets dark. Why can't people just slip off at home in peace? All this suspicion, when it's abundantly clear from her frail appearance, the wad of medical records Drew fetched from the study, and the fact that she's frequently visited by in-home caretakers that Annie had been sick for years. I'm stung by even more guilt that I stepped so far away and left him struggling with this.

"I'm so sorry," I tell him again, slipping my hand into his. "About your mum, but about so much more."

He leads me through the cluttered house and out into the front garden, where we sit on a bench seat under Annie's favorite silver birch trees. Turning to face me, he says, "Evie, the night of the formal . . ."

I can't believe he's raising that now. "It doesn't matter, Drew, honestly!"

"No, you don't understand. Mum sort of . . . collapsed that night. She ended up in an ambulance. They admitted her."

The horror of this news descends over me. The idea of Drew at seventeen rushing his mum to the hospital while I became more and more incensed that he wasn't collecting me for a trivial dance . . . My thinking at the time that *he* was the bad friend.

"I felt so bad that I let you down, but I knew if I told you, this would happen."

"What?"

"You'd end up here with me."

He's right. Of course I would have. I'd have bowled up to the ER in my Jane Austen dress before even conceiving of getting changed and going to meet Oliver. I'd have pushed my way to Drew's side.

"The thing is, it was my fault," Drew admits. "That night, and the way her health plummeted afterward. I triggered it."

That can't be right.

He takes out his phone and scrolls through the photos.

"You don't have to go through this now," I tell him, gently. But he ignores me, and when he finds what he's looking for, his expression contorts again.

"This is a photo of Mum with my father." He passes the phone over.

I look at her first. So young and pretty and light and *alive.* So like Drew. Sunlight bouncing off her face, upturned and looking at . . .

I zoom in. Then look back at Drew.

This can't be.

I know that stance. That set of the jaw. The steely glare at the camera, annoyed at having to pose for a photo. I know it, because I saw precisely the same body language play out last week when he was asked to pose for a photo at Oliver's graduation.

# 57

***Drew***

Evie's obvious shock at the photo of my parents is overtaken by Mum's doctor turning up to perform the formalities. *Pronounce her dead.* I have to say it to myself to believe it, and even then it doesn't seem real.

"I'm sorry, Drew," she says, after she hands the form to the police. "This was not unexpected."

*But it was.*

I shake her hand. "Thank you for coming out tonight."

*Even though we knew it was coming. Even though we'd talked about it. I don't understand why I feel like I'm in some sort of shock, despite neon billboards blaring this exact outcome at us for years.*

"Are there some clothes you'd like your mum to wear?" the funeral director says when we're back inside. In this cast of thousands, I hadn't even noticed his arrival.

I stare helplessly at Mum's current attire—the old trousers with faded knees she used to wear while gardening, a tear where a rose thorn shredded the material at her thigh. An old button-down check shirt, the fabric thin from years of wear.

When I don't answer, Evie places my phone down on the kitchen bench and comes to my side. "May I help?"

I'm barely processing the clothing task, when it occurs to me that Mum's hands are dirty from pottering in the garden. I touch her fingers again and try to rub soil off her skin with my thumb, but it won't budge.

Evie disappears into the hallway for a minute, and I hear the door of the linen press dragging along the carpet as she opens it. She reemerges seconds later with a washcloth, and runs the kitchen tap, waiting patiently for the water to warm up.

Mum doesn't need the water warm. But Evie is making sure it's at the perfect temperature anyway. She wrings out the excess liquid and holds the cloth out for me. I just stare at it, as if it's somehow beyond me to know how to do this.

"Annie, I'm just going to pick up your hand," Evie says softly, stepping close to Mum beside me. She cradles it gently, respectfully, in her palm. I assume she's going to do the job herself, but then she reaches out and takes my hand too. Places the warm cloth in it. And helps me begin. It's as if she instinctively knows I'll want to remember I did this myself.

While I'm wiping the dirt off Mum's skin, Evie fetches a nail brush and squirts some liquid soap onto it, running it under more warm water. This part she does do, and we follow that with some lavender hand cream that Mum had in the bathroom—each taking one hand and smoothing the lotion into her skin.

All of it is unnecessary. The people at the funeral home will take care of her. But it's somehow the most intimate, bonding performance among the three of us, and seems to go some way toward making up for the violence I inflicted on this same body, only hours earlier, trying to save her life.

Evie leads me into Mum's bedroom and flicks the light switch. I can barely enter the room, with its unmade bed, clothes draped across the chair in the corner, books stacked on the floor. She pulls open the wardrobe and beckons me to stand beside her as Mum's floral scent spills into the room.

"She always looked lovely in this," Evie says, reaching for a long, colorful dress in swirling blues and greens, with delicate, floaty sleeves. "What do you think?"

I feel the pressure of someone's hand, placed gently on my shoulder.

"Yep?" I say, turning around and expecting to see the funeral director with another question about Mum's wishes. But there's nobody there.

"What was that?" Evie asks.

"Someone touched me on the shoulder," I explain quietly. It was both impossible and unambiguous.

"It wasn't me," she says. Both of her hands are on the coat hanger holding up Mum's dress, so I know that.

I face her, confused. But also hopeful that the hand belonged somehow to Mum, with a sign of approval, perhaps? A silent thank-you for all that I did to look after her? A final goodbye, sending me forward into the rest of my life just as she leaves hers? *You'll be okay, Drew.*

Evie's eyes fill with tears. For a fleeting moment, in this sacred space, while she holds Mum's dress with the gentleness of an archivist handling a priceless garment in a museum, it's just the three of us. Me, and the only two women I've ever loved.

*That* realization hits me hard in the chest and my heart bolts wildly. Maybe that's what Mum was acknowledging here. What she was endorsing. Evie is now carefully selecting a pair of silver earrings from a glass plate on the dresser and looking to me for permission to open Mum's underwear drawer. Nobody tells you how pragmatic death can be. I'm at a loss to know how I would ever have made it through this process without her.

I'm plunged into fresh turmoil at the sight of Mum lying on the gurney in a body bag minutes later, while the director carries a plastic bag full of the clothes Evie has helped me choose. As I help him push her through the house, careful not to bang her against walls and doorways, I realize this body we're maneuvering *gave me life*. It carried me and pushed me into the world, and now it's left me here—on my own. There's something about seeing Mum pulled over the threshold of the home she loved, despite its faults, one last time, that just about breaks me.

Evie walks beside us out to the funeral director's van. We each place a hand on Mum, on top of the thick fabric of the bag she is in now.

All the words I want to say escape me, and I simply pat the bag and lift my hand off her again. The very last touch. The bond severed.

The director nods and bows at Mum, then shuts the van door.

That's it. The end.

And it's just Evie and me now, standing in the driveway, with the feeling you get when you wave off loved visitors after a beautiful stay. Except it's forever this time. And I'm devastated.

Without words, we turn and walk back inside. Evie slides down to the floor in the living room, her back against the couch, signaling that she's not going anywhere.

I check the time. "Do you need to get back?" I ask. The last thing I want to do is set off Oliver.

She shakes her head. "I have nowhere to be. Oliver and I broke up."

The admission hangs in the air. It's only now that I notice how pale and fractured she looks, at such odds with the strength she's displayed all night.

*They broke up?* My heart leaps at this news, only to be chased by a massive dose of guilt. Mum just *died*. How can I dredge myself so quickly out of grief and into any form of optimism, however fleeting?

"Sorry," she says. "It's not the time to talk about this. But he left. I threw him out. I can stay as long as you need."

My eyes flick to her left hand. It's bare. I have the preposterous thought that this miracle is Mum's parting gift to me, that she arranged it, somehow, like some ethereal matchmaker from the afterlife. There's something so poetic about the notion that I came into the world out of a relationship gone wrong with Oliver's father, only to be handed a glimmer of hope with Oliver's former fiancée, right when I'm at my lowest ebb. Hope, rising out of the ashes of loss.

"How are you feeling, Drew?" Evie asks, swiveling to face me.

I can't admit the thoughts running through my mind. But I'm getting ahead of myself. Evie isn't leaping into my arms. She looks as messed-up as me. "Overwhelmed," I answer truthfully.

"We don't have to think about anything tonight. I'm going to help you through this," she tells me. "I have a lot of ground to make up as your best friend."

Her friend. *Yes.*

"Although, what about Meg? Shouldn't she be here instead?"

I should call her, I know. It's just that she'll try to fix this somehow. She's one of those intensely optimistic people. Exhaustingly so, at times.

"Meg and I are just friends," I assure her, even though she didn't ask. *Not friends like this.*

I go through the open doorway into the kitchen and get two wineglasses and one of the bottles of cabernet sauvignon Mum had been saving for a "special occasion." The irony of this being that event . . .

I wave it in Evie's direction, and she nods.

"Yes, I think we need alcohol to discuss how you're *Oliver's brother*."

"Half brother, technically. Born ten months apart."

"Drew . . . Oliver has absolutely no idea about this, or he'd have said. He'll hit the roof."

Of course he doesn't, and yes, he will. Why would our father destroy the perfection of Oliver's world just to include me in it?

"Can you imagine? Oliver has always had it in for me," I say.

"Because of me," she explains, cautiously.

I look at her, wondering what she means. It's not like there was ever anything for him to be jealous about here; it was very much the other way around.

"Will you confront him about it? Anderson, I mean." She shivers, and I wonder what she's witnessed in the Roche household over the years. "Presumably he has no idea you found out?"

There's no way I'm going to confront him. I don't need someone in my life who values me so little. I pass her the wine and sit on the floor beside her, then reach for Mum's laptop on the coffee table in front of us. I need to start thinking about how to tell people.

"He controlled Mum the entire way through that relationship. He's a narcissist. He always knew exactly where she was—he tracked her."

"Tracked her? With what technology?"

"Private investigator. I think he was terrified she'd undo him."

Evie's mouth falls open. She lifts the glass to her lips and takes a large sip.

I open Mum's email account. It's full of spam and unread newsletters. "He had access to her bank accounts, long after he abandoned us. He wouldn't go near me as a father, but he sent her rules for raising his son."

Goose bumps rise on her arms.

"She met someone when I was about six. He was this wonderful man who made her happy. The only man I've ever looked at as anything resembling a father figure. Anderson destroyed that too." I pick up my phone and look at the photo again. "The woman my mum became was nothing like that vibrant young nurse. She was anxious. Depressed. Paranoid."

Evie has all but drained her glass during my monologue and holds it out to me. I splash in a large serving of wine and top mine off too.

She picks up her phone and fumbles through the settings, getting frustrated.

"What's wrong?"

She shakes her head. "Nothing. Don't worry."

I do worry. A lot. I've tried not to go there—thinking the apple doesn't fall far from the tree, but there have been signs all along. "Are your calendars still synced?" I ask.

She looks at me like she's stunned I remember that. Or that I'd raise the trigger for our first fight, all those years ago. "I don't want to un-sync them," she admits, and my heart plunges. "I don't want to provoke him."

*Provoke him to do what?*

Anger stampedes up and surpasses my state of shock,

blistering through the denial. The idea that Evie is willing to stay tethered to Oliver after a breakup to avoid antagonizing him makes me furious.

"I can create a second calendar and use that," she suggests, stifling tears. Trying to put on a brave face. "Sorry, tonight is meant to be about you."

That's just it, though. So much of who I am is about her. I've grieved in the silence between us. Craved her company. As ludicrous as it sounds, I feel like we're a team. A partnership. Not a couple, exactly . . .

I stretch my arm across her shoulders and pull her against me, stroking her mess of curls, and she lets out a strangled sob that is probably about Mum and Oliver and her and me and just how *complicated* life can be, and it breaks me all over again.

# 58

***Evie***

"I'm sorry," I say, over and over, anxious to pull myself together. Until tonight, I hadn't known how severely I missed Drew, and how quickly he steadies me. It's like coming home and meeting an earlier version of myself. One I liked more.

From some deep, sensible, grown-up part of myself, I dredge the self-control I need to reverse out of this meltdown and morph into his support person. The wrong shoulder is being cried on. "What can I do?" I ask.

"Take it one step at a time . . ." he suggests.

"No. What can I do to help *you*?"

He shrugs, defeated. Stares ahead. Sips his wine. In my imagination, he's that sixteen-year-old boy again who ambled into the art studio and put his feet up on the desk, not wanting to be there, difficult home life looming larger than everything else, while I pushed him to do even more.

"Come with me to Mum's funeral?" he asks.

"Of course I'll be there," I assure him.

"I mean come *with* me," he clarifies. "Sit with me. Stand beside me while I shake hands and make small talk with people I've never met."

Like his *date*? No, that's not what this is. Funeral dates aren't a thing.

I take his hand. "Ride or die, remember?"

I'm so glad he bamboozled me with that camera flash at my graduation. It seemed to startle me out of my reality. That we saw each other, just days before he needed me for this crisis, feels somehow fated. Of course, meeting up with Drew is exactly what tipped Oliver into a silent rage before he ruined the celebration dinner.

"You need to eat," I announce, aware that the bottle of wine is disappearing fast, along with my inhibitions. "What do you feel like?"

"I feel like not making a decision," Drew says, rubbing his forehead. His hand is shaking; he's probably in shock. I rack my brain for first-aid information. What am I meant to do? Watching someone drown in freshly inflicted grief is the hardest thing I've ever done.

I google the Thai takeaway we used to love, while Drew occupies himself reading emails on his mum's laptop. I haven't had Thai in years. Oliver hates it.

As I scan the menu, I realize it's the first time in months I've been free to decide. How has it taken me so long to see all the ways Oliver chipped away at my preferences? And my friendships. *Did you see how quickly Drew ran away at your grad? It's the formal all over again. He's hiding something. You can't trust him, Evie.* It's only now that I'm realizing the extent to which he's been planting doubt in my mind, convincing me to let everything go, piece by piece, while he replaces the discarded parts of my life with larger and larger pieces of himself.

I place the food order, put my phone down, and twist my body to face Drew's on the floor next to me. He's staring at the screen of his mum's laptop, expression falling, eyes welling.

Without even speaking, he passes the computer to me. His head drops to my shoulder, hot tears seeping through onto the fabric of my shirt as I read the opening words of the message on the screen from his mum, written this morning.

"Darling Drew . . ."

# 59

***Evie***

We contemplate the letter, and what it means, in silence. Maybe if we don't speak, we won't weld into reality the truth about how Annie really died. Maybe the timing of the letter was a coincidence and it was just a love note to her son? Perhaps she sensed she was dying and rallied for one last beautiful communication . . .

Eventually, the window lights up with the headlights of the delivery driver's car. I clamber unsteadily to my feet and answer the door. Except when I fling it open, a chill blasts over me. It's not the delivery driver standing there. It's Anderson Roche. And I am clearly the last person he expects to see.

His face clouds in confusion, until he straightens, clears his throat, and says, "What are you doing here, Evelyn?" He's such an imposing man. It's the habit of leaning his torso slightly forward whenever he talks to you, so you feel talked down at.

I hear Drew set down his wineglass on the coffee table in the living room. His footsteps approach, and I feel his hands on my waist, moving me aside so he can face his father square on.

"Andrew, isn't it?" Anderson says. The faux innocence enrages me. I'd never noticed the similarities in their names. Never heard Drew's full name, actually. Not in all the years I've known him. "I've seen you at school with Oliver . . ." He extends his hand.

Drew crosses his arms, edging closer to me. He must sense that I am about to volcanically erupt on his behalf, fueled by his mum's cab sav and the sheer audacity of this interaction.

"Is your mother home?" Anderson blusters on.

*Bloody hell.* I suck in a sharp breath and it catches awkwardly in my throat, causing me to cough. Anderson frowns at me. He's always frowning. He's never liked me, not from that first day we met at their house when Oliver and I were teenagers. Nobody was ever good enough for his son, especially not an anxious, introverted girl from a family of nobodies in Newcastle.

"Why are you here? What do you want with my mother?" Drew asks. There's no trace of intimidation. Or of the grief Drew has just shown me, so acutely, in the other room. The measured way he's rising to this confrontation astonishes me. It impresses me, given the crash course I've just received about their background. If I were him, this would be a shouting match by now—accusations of paternity flying.

"What's going on with the two of you?" Anderson fires off, as if that is the worst problem we have as a trio. "Is Oliver here?"

"When did you last see my mother?" Drew steps toward him, into a moment of ice-cold silence charged by twenty-three years of rejection—much of it in plain sight. Sports sidelines. Prize-giving assemblies. Parent-teacher interviews, where they all must have brushed past each other like strangers. And I watch the dawning realization in Anderson's increasingly panicked eyes the longer his son stares him down with the knowledge of all they have missed: *Drew knows.*

"Where is she, Andrew?" he says at last, a slight crack in his voice the only sign that he is rattled. "I haven't got time for this."

There is *no* love here. None. Not in either direction. It's all so dry and callous and fraught. Anderson glances back at me, as if he's trying to piece me somewhere into this puzzle. Has Oliver not told him we've broken up? That would be entirely typical. He probably thinks it's a temporary glitch. *No need to inform the family.*

"Mum is in the morgue," Drew announces in a way that shocks even me, and I already knew the information. It's not a word you throw into normal conversation. *Morgue.* It's ugly. Cold. *Is that even where they took her?*

I shiver, and Drew's arm comes around me. I'm instantly scared of Anderson's reaction to the gesture, and Oliver's response if he somehow finds out. Drew doesn't take his eyes off Anderson and we watch all color drain from the man's face, so much so that I'm worried he himself will drop dead on this doorstep.

"What do you mean?" His voice is different now. All the power bled out of it.

"I don't know how many interpretations you need," Drew replies. "She's dead. I found her here, dead, this afternoon."

Anderson reels back. Stumbles. He reaches for the doorframe to steady himself as decades of history play across his face. He is horrified. Devastated? I can't quite pick the exact emotion.

"What happened?" he asks, at last. "Was it the cancer?"

Drew's body stiffens again and he pulls me closer to his side, preparing to voice aloud for the first time the awful truth, in light of his mum's note.

"No," he answers simply. "It wasn't."

# 60

***Drew***

This note from Mum has me gutted. It's flung me into a reality I can't yet face or talk about.

I've seen her close to giving up on life too many times over the years to count. Part of me is racked with guilt that I didn't see the email this morning and get here in time to intervene. Part of me is relieved that she's succeeded, and her torture is over.

All of me puts the blame firmly at my father's feet. I didn't know he was back in her life, but showing up here tonight proves it. It explains the way she's been acting.

Anderson trips backward down the garden path and into his BMW. He slams the door. Runs over the curb, flattening one of Mum's flowerbeds as he screeches off. As he turns the corner at the end of the street and the roar of the engine fades, we gulp the silence, then retreat inside the house.

Evie and I stare at each other in the hallway.

"She had shriveled recently," I tell her. "Not from the cancer or the treatment. Shriveled in her soul. It was as if she'd lost the strength to will herself through life."

"Given up the battle with her past," Evie says, as if she's been inside Mum's head.

I don't want her empathizing this strongly with the idea.

"Mum's life was so messed up, over so many years—largely because of that man—she couldn't find a way to make it bearable."

*Thank God Evie has split up with Oliver.* The pattern needs to break.

And I need to go through Mum's emails and work out how my *horrible* father pushed her this far. He might not have driven the final nail, but I'll bet he handed it to her. Why would he have turned up here on the day of her death, after avoiding her for years, if he wasn't tormenting her in some new way?

Evie steps toward me wordlessly. She places her hands on either side of my head as if trying to calm my thoughts. Then on my chest, over my beating heart, like she's trying to heal it as we stand here, in the wake of Mum's life, grief swirling between us and around us like a spell, binding us together. "Drew, I'm *so* sorry this is how it happened," she whispers.

Death is complicated enough, even when it's straightforward.

She leans in to me, head pressed against my chest as my arms come around her. Two human beings, holding each other through one of the most vulnerable passages a person can face: these first fragile hours after a loss, when the world has shifted on its axis and nothing will ever be the same again.

I kiss the top of her head and she lifts her face to mine. I lose myself in the sweet scent of wine on her breath, and her perfume, and the compassion in her eyes that I'd first noticed all those years ago on the beach, that night with Mum. I take in her features up close for the first time. We're both emotionally shaky and tipsy and wired, inhabiting this strange, afterdeath quiet together. I brush the dark curls away from her face, my thumb tracing her cheekbones, *all sense* leaving my brain.

She's startled when I move closer, and pulls back slightly, eyes flicking upward, surveying me. Questioning my intent?

I would think it was clear. My fingers slip through her hair. I draw her closer to me again, my lips finding hers as I push her back against the wall in the hallway, one hand traveling to her waist, squeezing it. Pulling her against me as I kiss her. Not nearly close enough.

A guttural sound emerges from me, part desire, part loss, part bargaining with the universe not to shatter this moment because, even now, the way she's responding to my touch, this feels transient.

"Drew," she whispers. "What are we doing?"

She has no idea about all the things I've wanted to do with her since I walked into that art studio and saw her perched at her desk in her immaculate school uniform with her meticulous life plan, challenging the status quo of the school. And my *life*.

The shadow of death blurs the rules, doesn't it? Her breakup. My loss. This ephemeral glimpse of a parallel universe in which it was always her and me.

"Evie . . ."

She places her hands on my chest and pushes me back. Gently. But decisively.

I know she can't. And I know why she can't. And it kills me.

I feel like I've lost the two women in my life within hours.

# 61

***Evie***

I'm almost ready for Drew's mum's funeral when there's a knock at the door of the terrace apartment in north Sydney, where I've been staying alone since Oliver rented a studio in Coogee "to give you space." Space is not what I've asked for. I want a complete severing of the relationship—a message that seems to be bouncing back, undeliverable, no matter how many different ways I say it.

Finding my own place is my top priority—it will send him the message that we are irrevocably done. How I'll do that in Sydney on a meager PhD scholarship and the part-time tutoring work I've been doing is not yet clear. Thank God I kept that café job he said I didn't need. But I can't stay here. Can't afford the rent, but can't bear to, either. Too many memories that left me ducking from words that stung and bruised as I swept away shattered promises. Papered over cracks. Apologized, excused. *Hoped.*

I open the door.

It's him, bearing an oversize bunch of flowers and an apologetic expression. "Let me in, Evie," he begs. "I've been so wrong. I'm sorry."

His eyes roam over the muted floral dress I've selected for

the funeral and I wonder how much his father has told him, if anything. I bet he still has no idea he even has a brother, let alone who it is and how hard this day is for him. I shudder at the idea of him finding out. The mere mention of Drew's name has always been a hair trigger for Oliver, a sudden disruption to his fragile stability.

"I'm just heading out," I tell him as he thrusts the flowers at me and pushes into the wallpapered hall, even though I don't want them—or him. I set them on the antique hall table I'd picked up on a weekend away in Moss Vale once, even though there was no room for it in the car and Oliver complained the whole way back to Sydney that I never thought things through. I have absolutely no intention of plunging the flowers into water. They can die there, with this relationship.

"This is important," he argues, pushing past me into our sitting room. "We can't just ignore each other."

"Why not?" I fling back. "Oliver, this hasn't been working. I'm sick of having to check myself constantly."

"Check yourself?"

"It's *everything*. Always questioning whether I've done something wrong. You sending copious messages every time I go out." *Where are you? Who are you with? When are you coming home?*

"Because I worry about you," he argues.

"You criticize me for not being lively enough at your work dinners. Or for being too animated. No matter what I do, I can't ever seem to hit the right note."

His hand on my shoulder feels like dead weight, pushing me down with his ever-changing expectations.

"It's not just me who you criticize. It's my parents. Friends.

Bree. The few friends you allowed me to make at university. You pick at people until there's nothing left!"

If he'd heard the chorus of advice my friends have given me over the years, he'd do more than verbally assault them. *Why do you stay, Evie? You're so smart! Just leave!*

"I'm sorry, Evie. It's not you. It's me. I've been seeing a counselor." The blue-green eyes I'd fallen into that first night at the pool stare at me now, just as intensely.

"Since when?"

"I don't think I had a good role model for relationships . . ."

*You don't say!* The anguish in his expression is almost convincing.

"The psych is talking me through everything. The way I was raised. I've never been shown how to love someone properly. I've spent my whole life trying to get my father's attention. I've never been enough."

This part is true. Anderson's behavior at Oliver's graduation was just the latest example of how hot and cold the love runs. He's either bragging obsessively about Oliver or ignoring him altogether. As long as I've known him, Oliver has scrambled to impress his dad, and has always fallen short.

"Evie, I'm doing the work, I promise. I'm begging you for a second chance. You're everything to me."

I've been Oliver's everything ever since we fell into the swimming pool. But I think I've been drowning every moment since. Every time I try to clamber to the surface, he finds a way to pull me back under.

"You don't have to marry me," he promises. "I can see that's too much pressure. But I want to support you through your PhD. You can give up your tutoring. I'll throw everything at getting you through this. You can have the career you've always wanted."

It's all too late. A hopeless afterthought without enough power to win me over. I zip up my purse and grab my keys.

"I don't think you understand," he pleads, stepping up to block my path. "I need you."

I glance at the time on my phone. And then at him. He looks like he hasn't slept in days. Such a disheveled version of that perfect, confident boy I knew.

"This last week," he says, more quietly now that he has my attention, "I've wanted to end everything."

*Don't take me down this path.*

"I can't face a life without you, Evie. And I've realized my father has set the very worst example of what it means to be a man. It's *him* I need to cut ties with."

He's right about his dad, at least. He takes both my wrists in his hands and clutches them, staring into my eyes with a genuine misery and need. "Please, just one more chance. We can take it slowly. Just let me prove to you that I'm learning. I'll do anything for you."

"Olly . . ."

He falls to his knees now, arms reaching for my waist. Our bodies know this choreography, intimately. This is the part where I always yield.

"If you push me away now, I'm not going to survive." There's a finality to his tone. A believability that forces me to fast-forward in my imagination to a time when there might have to be another phone call to the paramedics. More flashing lights. More questions. Another gurney with a white sheet on it . . .

And then forward again, to all the years after, where I'd always wonder if I could have stopped him.

*This is impossible.*

Oxygen fights to make it into my lungs as my chest seems to freeze, limbs tingling, brain aching from the desperation of this relationship. The car keys drop from my hand and clatter onto the floorboards beside Oliver, a hopeful spark reentering his eyes as he stares up into my face.

But this time, from somewhere deep in my subconscious, another vision pushes up and forces itself through all the sinews of this diabolical mess, until it takes a stranglehold and causes me to break eye contact, remove his arms from my waist, and pick up my keys again.

It's that same gurney. Those flashing lights. A body under a sheet.

And a soul-deep knowing that, if nothing changes, the body will be mine.

# 62

***Drew***

Mum's service was the hardest thing I've ever had to push myself through. Made worse because I pushed myself through it alone.

Evie didn't show.

I've never felt more crushed by something in my life. More let down. Or more surprised.

I know I shouldn't have kissed her, but when she left the other night, we were on good terms. Friends. She promised she'd come.

To have spent the service glancing toward the church door, hoping to see her walk through it—finding it empty, and knowing I'd just spent my mother's funeral thinking about somebody else—makes me inconsolably mad. At Evie. At myself. At the world.

And being mad at your mother's wake is a bad look. Everyone is throwing platitudes at me: *At least she's not suffering now, Drew. You're lucky you had her into adulthood, given how sick she was.* All I can think of is getting the hell out of here—preferably out of Sydney, or out of the country altogether—and starting fresh somewhere else.

I'm about through the refreshments after the service when the heavy wooden door at the back of the church hall swings open. When I turn around, Anderson is standing in it, framed by the archway, almost comically. Menacing by his pure presence.

I can't believe his nerve.

I cross the room and move him outside into the portico. "You're not welcome here," I say sharply.

I think of the email Mum composed the day she died. After scanning through some of her other messages, I'm more convinced than ever that Anderson is the reason we're all here. A cut-and-dried case of narcissistic personality disorder. Wanting to know she needed him. Offering to send her money to cover her treatment, late in the piece. Love-bombing, two decades after the first round. Going off on her when she refused his help. Retreating. Reappearing. She couldn't take it after twenty-three-plus years of control. And I don't care how we're related, I'm throwing him out.

Anger storms across his face, the way I imagine it does when he's about to discipline my brother.

"I'm not here about your mother," he says. Somehow this makes it much worse. This is her *wake*. "I'm here about you."

He's lying. He's here about himself. It's always about him.

"I know who you are," I tell him. "I've known for years."

He stares at me, thrown off.

"Drew . . ."

"I don't need you in my life," I say firmly. "Or want you."

He bristles. He's on the back foot now. "Oliver doesn't know about your mother and me."

Of course it's about Oliver.

"He doesn't know about you, Drew."

My muscles tingle, years of pent-up injustice coursing to the surface.

"Oliver might not know," I explain. "But surely he's felt it all these years? The rivalry you created between us, first in science class, and then fanning into every corner of our school lives." He opens his mouth to argue, hands balling into fists. "You primed him to compete with me over everything, Anderson. Relentless jealousy, fueled by genetics and guilt."

"You're wrong," he says, fuming.

But it makes total sense. "Oliver had to have it all. He had to win. Because you needed evidence you'd backed the right son."

This man, who looks ready to explode, does not deserve another moment of my time. He did enough damage while Mum was alive. I shake my head at him, and at this—all of it—and turn to go back inside.

He grabs me by the arm. I almost pity Oliver, having to put up with this. We stare each other down, and I have so little regard for him I realize there's nothing he could say to me now that could possibly hold any kind of power.

"I came here to ask you to stay away from Evelyn," he mutters.

*Except that.*

"She and my son are working things out."

*What?*

If there were ever a few words that could inflict more hurt, on multiple levels, I can't imagine what they would be.

"Oliver's in a tough space at the moment, Drew."

*Oliver is in a tough space? Has this man lost track of the fact that we are literally at my mother's funeral?*

"And he's in love with that girl."

When people say their whole world crumbles, they mean this. This devastating sense of everything sliding away. Mum. Evie. The bearings in my life. The light from it.

"Is there something you need, Drew?"

I assume he's not offering emotional support or twenty-three years' worth of parenting. But he can be assured I don't need to be *paid* to stay away from the woman who has just let me down in such a friendship-shattering, irreversible way.

"I won't ask you again to leave," I say.

He might be many things, but he's not the type to make a scene. Not in public. My attention is snagged on Evie. Working things out goes against everything she said the other night—and everything she seemed to feel. I won't take Anderson's word for it.

But just as I resolve to have one final shot at talking sense into her, I receive what is potentially the most bizarre and over-the-top text message she, or anyone else, has ever sent me. Reading the words, I realize I can't do this anymore. Can't let this woman or that family derail another second of my life.

Pretend we never met. Promise me, Drew. If we ever meet again, you will pretend you don't know me.

# 63

## *Evie*

"When did we last speak?" I ask Bree, still trying to come to terms with her short hair. She's stunning, but everything about her is different. Edgier. Older, obviously. She's one of those cool, accomplished classical musicians—I can picture her on an album cover in some pop-classical ensemble—flowy black pants and a sequined handkerchief top, violin propped on her knee . . .

She's pulling up our messages on her phone, and so do I.

"Let's see . . . Well, we messaged at your graduation . . . You'd just gotten engaged. Then Drew turned up and you were telling me he was 'taking pictures of a girl' . . ." She winks. What is the wink about? What girl?

"That would have been Meg," Drew says, matter-of-factly.

How many girlfriends has he *had*?

I scroll to the same messages, hoping she doesn't read them aloud.

"Then there's the one just after you had the fight with Oliver. You'd stormed out of the restaurant?"

"Which one is that?" I'm not seeing it in my phone.

She leans over and shows me on her phone: Bree, it's over. I've broken up with him. Where are you?

That message is not in my phone. "It's not in my history. Why did I delete it?"

She and Drew both look at my screen. Then at Bree's, and then back at mine. They put their heads together and scroll down, on both phones, comparing. Then Drew gets his phone out and looks through his own messages. There are none to compare them to on mine, as he's not in my inbox at all, but the two of them are wearing equally concerned expressions.

"Wow," Bree says softly to Drew. "Missing messages might explain a few things?"

She sighs and looks at me in a way she never has before. With pity and years of regret, almost as if she's on the verge of an apology herself. "Then you sent me a message from Drew's house," she adds. "The night his mum died."

*His mum died?* Looking at him now, I see it. That same feeling I remembered, looking through the kitchen window before Bree arrived. That sinking grief I couldn't place. "What did I say?"

She glances at Drew, and then passes the phone to me rather than reading aloud another message that's missing from my own record. It says, Bree, I'm with Drew. I think I've made a terrible mistake . . .

I stare at Drew on my parents' deck. What terrible mistake did I make?

And all this time I've been harping on about fictionally losing my parents and he hasn't told me to shut up, like I would have done if it was the other way around. Instead, he did everything he could to reunite me with my mum and dad. He saw my relief when we got here. He convinced my dad to let us stay.

"Is your dad still alive?" I ask him suddenly. I'm grasping at straws. It's not like the presence of one parent makes up for the loss of the other.

He looks out over the garden. Body tense. "It's messy," he tells me. Is there a single aspect of Drew Kennedy's life that *isn't* messy?

"You can trust me," I say.

He looks at me as if that isn't true. Again, I wonder where it went wrong between us and what I did to him. What was this mistake I made?

I watch as his body seems to harden in defense, and I can't tell if he's subconsciously bracing himself against his dad—or me. "He's not worth our oxygen."

I can sense the schoolboy I must have known. And the adolescent. Tangible memories try to push forward, for a friendship I remember only in glimpses. But even without distinct evidence, I increasingly trust this connection.

"I'm going for a quick shower before your parents wake up," Bree says. "We'll talk later, Evie." She moves off the seat and hugs Drew again on the way past, but my envy has evaporated. This is the best friend I remember and the one I forgot, and there's something beautiful about that.

"Do you want to talk about your mum?" I ask Drew, once Bree has closed the sliding door behind her.

"No."

I suppose I can't be allowed to walk back into our relationship just because I've finally been convinced it existed. "What's our happiest memory?" I ask, changing tack. The sight of Bree hugging him like she'd trust him with her life has helped me jettison my remaining doubt.

He rakes his hand through his hair. Trying to dredge up some happiness to share?

"Come on, Drew. We were best friends. We must have happy memories. I know you're scared to break me . . ."

"Because I've got form."

I wonder what he means. Did he break me once before? Or someone else? "Tell me something gentle, then."

He clasps his hands behind his head and looks at the sky as if I'm asking him for the moon. His T-shirt rides up and my eyes drop to the strong line of muscles making a V shape above his waistband.

"You all right?" he says, catching me staring.

Not as such. No, I haven't seen abs like that on a man outside a Calvin Klein billboard.

"All right. Bioluminescence," he says, tugging his T-shirt down. "We spent a night in Jervis Bay, splashing around in the water under the stars. It was . . ."

"Magical," I whisper. "It's on my bucket list."

"Technically you've already ticked it off," he explains. But he must notice how crushed I look. "You can always do it again. I just don't know if we can top that night. They say you should never go back . . ."

"But I have to go back! I have to redo the good stuff, or I'll lose it all."

"It wasn't all good. That night ended badly. Bad news about Mum."

"Tell me I went with you," I whisper.

He sits beside me again and puts his hand briefly over mine. "Of course you did."

The idea of anything going wrong between us at a critical

point like that makes my heart hurt. What we used to have was clearly *something*. Before I wrecked it.

He says we weren't together. That I was crazy about Oliver. So why do I feel so heartbroken over him? And what's this electric energy I can't ignore whenever I'm near him?

"Do you think we can start our friendship over?" I ask.

He looks guarded. And torn. And ten types of exhausted. He takes a moment, then looks at me with an intensity that stirs something inside me. It brings a bunch of feelings flooding back. A memory blunders forward that absolutely conflicts with the "we were just friends" narrative he's been spinning.

"We *were* more than friends," I tell him suddenly, breathless excitement shooting through my body. "Drew, you kissed me!"

# 64

## *Drew*

*Shit.*

It's like she's cherry-picking every aspect of my past that I wanted to bury. Including that fucking kiss.

And now I'm sitting here, trying to come up with a story that paints Past Me as someone other than a grief-stricken, uncharacteristically drunk twenty-three-year-old who kissed his best friend when we were both at our lowest.

"It wasn't like that," I say, even though it was exactly like that. And, after all this time, I can't go there again. Oliver hasn't been gone two weeks. What kind of person am I, even fantasizing about it?

She looks like she's mentally rehashing something she's not equipped to handle, which means she's shoveling in imagined details and coming up with some story that's probably even worse than the truth.

"It was one kiss," I explain. "It didn't mean anything."

*Not to her.*

Now she looks offended. And hurt. Instead of shocked, like she did when it happened.

Next thing, Evie loses the rest of her mind. Without any

warning, she leans toward me, takes my face in her hands, and drops her eyes to my lips.

*No.*

*No!*

*What is she doing?*

She threads her fingers through my hair, one hand dropping to my neck. Closes in, and draws me slowly into what can only be described as the kiss of my *life*. Even the initial tentative brush of my lips with hers sparks fireworks of memories.

"Evie . . ."

But she doesn't let me speak. And the taste of her lips assembles every thought I've ever had about her this way. *Every one.*

She pulls back. "This is . . ."

It's me who won't let her speak now. The gentleness gives way to something far more urgent that we fall into, our bodies angling to get closer as my hand slips under the hem of her pajama top, grasping her hip, pulling her toward me.

This is a New Year's Eve kiss with a stranger and it's a kiss with someone you've known several lifetimes. A thermal spring of brand-new passion colliding with recognition as it explodes to the surface.

Her fingers thread harder through my hair and her leg finds its way across my lap as she pushes me back against the end of the swing seat. She's kissing me like it's the key to getting her memory back. Like she'll plug herself into me and I'll transfer the missing knowledge. Like she's hungry and I'm her life source.

And I kiss her like . . . I can't think about how I'm kissing her, and what's running through my mind, because with every passing second, it's as though I'm losing more of myself to this woman who has already taken too much. I can't get close enough.

It's everything that first kiss could never have been.

This time she's not tipsy. Not straight out of a breakup. Not torn. I'm not newly grief-stricken. She's all in, without Oliver's shadow over her life, pulling me over the edge of a cliff I've been dragging myself back from for *years*.

"Evie," I say, pulling us apart, both of us breathless.

She's looking at me the way I've imagined and hoped she would since we were teenagers, breathless and flushed, skin prickling with goose bumps as she props herself up against my chest and stares at me, bed hair tumbling across her face, dazed by what we've just done. I've lost all direction from here, completely disoriented in my own life.

"You said this was nothing," she says quietly.

Silence hangs between us and I know my expression betrays me. If I could rearrange it into something resembling apathy, I would. But she's drained all sense out of me and I can barely breathe. Years of longing for exactly this moment can't match how it feels. And the dangerous realization crashes in that there's so much she still can't remember, and I am falling harder than I did the first time.

# 65

***Evie***

I know it can't have been my first kiss. I must have had a thousand kisses by now. But was it like that to kiss Oliver? Did I lose myself like that? Aching to be nearer to him and *part of him*?

Drew seems shattered.

"I've never done that before," I confess. It sounds like a line. Like I'm trying to say I don't usually throw myself at old friends on my parents' back deck before breakfast. "I've never kissed someone—"

He seems momentarily confused.

"Only you, Drew. Twice now."

"Evie—"

"That's the only kiss I properly remember." I'm not counting that horrendous experience from Year Nine.

What makes things true? I can imagine a whole world of experience missing from my memory, but if I don't remember it, did it ever happen? Aren't we meant to be the sum of our experiences? Surely that works only if our memories are intact. Piled up over years, shaping us into the people we become.

He's looking at me like he doesn't know what to do with me. Or with us. Up until now, he seemed in control of this situation, but I've blown that up.

"We can't do this," he says, shifting me from his lap, standing up and walking to the edge of the deck. "For . . . so many reasons."

"Because Oliver is dead?"

"Yes."

"Because of the amnesia?"

"God, yes." He's leaning back now, against the railing, trying to push more space between us, perhaps.

"Drew, that kiss was *not* nothing. Not even close."

He fails to argue back this time. Just looks at me, with some sort of hopeless acceptance.

Whatever the two of us had back then, it was special. This is years of chemistry, safely contained. Explosive agents sitting beside each other on a shelf, not allowed to mix until now. And this no longer feels like it's just about our past. It's about our future.

It's as if the loss of the last thirteen years doesn't matter at all, and we could just start right here, on this deck at sunrise.

# 66

***Drew***

Evie's not remembering *entirely* wrong. She's just not remembering her half of it. She never looked at me that way. The first time we did this, it barely got off the ground, because she realized it was a mistake and put a stop to it almost immediately.

The sliding door opens and Bree emerges with a second macchiato, caffeinating for a difficult conversation after a long night. She's a mere two steps onto the deck when she clocks Evie looking even more disheveled than before—cheeks flushed, pulling at her pajama top—and she stops still. Evie faces up to her best friend's experienced scrutiny and doesn't have to say a word. Bree's lips curl into a smile, which she hides behind her coffee mug, clearing her throat.

"And how are things going with you, Drew?" she asks, a glint in her eye.

*How does it look, Breanna?*

"Exploding head emoji, I think he said . . ." Evie responds.

"Having the time of my life," I assure Bree sarcastically. "And you?"

She smiles. "Actually I *am* having the time of my life." She puts her coffee mug down and gets a photo up on her phone to show us both.

"Who's this?" Evie asks, admiring the professional headshot of a woman with a flawless bronze complexion and a thick mane of dark ringlets, brown eyes sparkling despite the serious smile.

"This is Ivy. She's a cellist with the Chamber Orchestra."

"*The* Chamber Orchestra?" Evie asks. "The Australian one?"

Bree laughs. "Yes, but you're missing the central point!"

"Is she your new best friend?" Evie is trying to get on board.

"EVIE. This is Ivy, my partner!"

As the realization dawns, Bree doesn't get the reaction she was hoping for, because Evie just starts crying. Sobbing, actually. In fact, she absolutely *loses* it. "I'm sorry!" she cries, jumping up and throwing her arms around Bree. "I'm so sorry, Bree. I didn't know. I am the *worst* friend!"

"You've got amnesia," I remind her. "How could you know?"

"But how didn't I know back then? In high school?"

"Because I didn't tell you," Bree explains.

This sets off a fresh wave of tears. "Why not? Did you not trust me?"

"Evie, it's fine. I hadn't figured everything out back then."

This placates her slightly. "But what about the white-shirt thing? You know, Mr. Darcy. Were you just pretending?"

Bree and I explode into laughter at this point.

"I'm queer, Evie, but I can still appreciate a man in a white shirt."

"What was all that fuss about Tom Jenkins at school?"

"It wasn't Tom I was interested in. It was Madeleine!"

"That French girl?"

*"Mmm."* This time it's both Bree *and* Drew reminiscing dreamily about her.

"So now I'm in love with a woman named Ivy. Madly. She's

currently on tour in New York, or you could have met her. She's from Adelaide!"

"Drew is moving to New York," Evie says, between sobs. I don't pretend the tears are about me. She's still mourning not being beside her best friend when she first came out.

"It's a magazine job," I explain to Bree, and Evie dissolves into silent tears this time. Maybe these are a little about me? She can't possibly want me to reevaluate New York in the wake of one kiss, though. *Can she? Would I?*

"You should visit him, when you're well," Bree says in no-nonsense fashion. "You love New York."

The tears stop. "I made it there?"

"Shit, sorry, Eves," Bree says, backtracking. "I'm sure you'll remember. Though you'll probably have more fun next trip if you go with Drew instead of his brother. I know it's bad to speak ill of the dead, but . . ."

*Oh, no. Stop.*

"His brother?" Evie's voice is a whisper.

Bree's hand shoots to her mouth. She's appalled by her gaff.

"What do you mean?" Evie backs away from us both. She's dumbfounded. "Drew. What does she mean?" The slow and deliberate way she's speaking is more terrifying than the sobbing.

"Oh, God," Bree whispers, screwing up her face in remorse. "I'm so sorry."

Evie has barely come to terms with the fact that she and I were friends. We *just kissed*. And now this bombshell, which I was planning on breaking to her gently.

"Evie, listen . . ."

Her eyes are like saucers. *Filled* with hurt.

"When you and I were going to the formal together," I begin.

"You said we were never together!"

"We never really were . . ."

*"Drew!"*

"Just let me tell you this one thing, please."

She sighs, pacing the deck like we're caged here. I feel like we are.

"I was searching for a belt to wear to the dance and I found a photo with some old things of Mum's. It was from when she was young, with a boyfriend."

Trauma jolts to the surface like it happened yesterday. I can trace everything that happened to Mum back to that one moment when I forced her to face this truth. It's why I've been so studiously avoiding lobbing any triggers at Evie all this time. I can't hurt someone else I love like that.

All sensation leaves my limbs.

Someone I love. *Still?*

What else would keep me hooked for more than a decade, regardless of every relationship that has come and gone since. Why else am I even here, in Adelaide, pretending it's about "off-loading" her, but soaking up every possible second? I swallow down the revelation and force the next words out.

"The man in the photo with Mum was my father. And he was the image of Oliver."

Her mouth falls open. At least the shock has absorbed all the tears.

"I didn't want it to be true. There had been no relationship at all. No birthday cards. No expressed desire to meet. I was an inconvenience—the evidence of a relationship that should never have happened."

"You're Oliver's *brother*?" Evie says, finding her voice again.

She can't know how much I wish I wasn't. And that I hadn't kept this from her.

"This is why you were at the church? You said you shared history . . ."

"It's . . . a complex situation."

"You *think*? My God, the things I've been thinking . . ."

*What things?*

We're in the eye of a storm, everything whirling around us uncontrollably. Dangerously. "I need you to understand I couldn't just launch every chapter of your past at you. We needed time . . . If I kept things back, it was always to protect you."

"Every chapter? What else haven't you told me, Drew? Bree?"

She is wild now. Furious. Crushed at how I've betrayed her, even if it was all for her own good.

"Seriously, what other family secrets are you hiding? Are you going to tell me I've got some kid stashed away somewhere, because I swear if I am a mother and you haven't told me, and I've abandoned some child the way I've felt abandoned by all of you since I woke up in that hospital . . ."

Bree tries to rescue us. "Evie, stay calm. Take a breath, okay? You've never given birth."

Evie falls back into the chair again, white as a sheet and shaking. "And Oliver and I never adopted, either?"

Bree shakes her head. "You didn't adopt."

"Bree, stop," I say under my breath. Hiding the truth from Evie so far hasn't worked. It's only traumatized her even more to find out later that I lied. I've got nothing left to lose now—she needs to know everything. We have to tell her about Harriet.

# 67

## *Evie*

It's Saturday morning at home and I'm up early, as usual. Also as per usual, Oliver was out late working on some corporate merger in the city, so he slept in the other room when he eventually got in after 2 a.m., which is when I finally fell asleep.

*I'm worried about you, Evie—you're burning the candle . . .* Mum's words echo in my head as I try not to make noise while I set up the coffee machine and then watch as the liquid drips into the glass jug. It's her job to worry. And surely this insomnia is just a temporary patch.

But as I fill my favorite mug, it triggers what has become a daily morning observation: *Another twenty-four hours has passed and he hasn't left me.*

I seem to spend every day worrying about when the divorce asteroid will hurtle into our marriage's atmosphere and explode on impact. Surely he's as unhappy as I am? We come to life only at social events where other people are present, and that's only because it's easier to pretend things are okay than to explain ourselves.

My phone pops up with a reminder: Drew's mum's anniversary.

I set the annual alert the day after she died, so I'd remember to message Drew each year, tell him I'm thinking of him and apologize, again, for missing the funeral. He's ignored me every single time. Obviously, he took my instruction never to contact me again and ran with it. Probably blocked me or hid my messages, so it's futile reaching out.

A memory of that train wreck of an afternoon barges in. Me standing firm on not taking Oliver back, trying to get to the church to support Drew. Oliver utterly losing it, falling at my feet, and practically begging me to take him back. The classic playbook of short-lived promises: *I've changed, Evie, I'm working on myself, doing everything I can to deserve you.*

I'd stood firm. I left the house and got in my car and started heading for the church, determined to stand beside my friend the way I'd promised. But before I could get there, my phone rang with an unknown number. I shiver even now.

"Are you Evie?" It was some guy—a random jogger. "I've got Oliver here."

"Where?"

"The cliffs at The Gap . . ."

I made it there in record time and found Oliver prowling the clifftop, eyes wild, searching for me in the gathering crowd. He lurched at me when I got to him, gripped me by the shoulders, forehead pressed against mine, fusing us together in his desperation.

"Give me one last chance, Evie. Promise you will."

"Let me go, Oliver." I was terrified he would take me with him, over the edge.

"One chance. Just one." His voice was strangled as he shook me. And I knew there was no way out. The answer he forced out of me became the promise that locked me to this future.

But even that was not enough.

"Give me your phone," he said. That's when he typed that message to Drew about pretending we'd never met. He handed it back. "Send it."

"It's his mother's funeral . . ."

He held my hand and stepped back, closer to the edge, not even looking behind him. His foot shifted some rocks that tumbled over the edge and smashed at the ground. He was going to kill us both at this rate. "Send it, Evie."

"I'm begging you, let me send it later?" I felt sick about the timing, after I'd promised to be there for Drew. But I was caught in a hopeless, life-and-death situation with a man I felt responsible for. Wasn't it me, and my rejection of him, that had caused this? How could I walk away and have his inevitable choice on my conscience?

So I chose Oliver. Again.

And again, and again, and again. At every instance surrendering another piece of myself I could never get back.

The doorbell rings now, and I'm relieved to be dragged out of the memory. I set the coffee mug down. I don't know what kind of person visits a household unannounced before eight in the morning on a Saturday, and I'm surprised to open the door and find a woman about my age standing there, with a little girl asleep in a stroller.

"Evie?" she begins tentatively. How odd that she knows my name. She looks haggard—way worse than I feel, in jeans and a white T-shirt, gray cardigan and sneakers, simple ponytail sweeping mousy blond hair out of worried brown eyes.

"Yes?"

"I'm so sorry to barge in." She seems genuinely apologetic and genuinely distressed. "I'm Chloe? An old friend of Oliver's." She looks like she's hoping I'll know exactly who she is, but I don't. "I found you through a mutual friend of his on Facebook and they let me know your address."

I've never heard him mention her before, and we've been together since we were sixteen, so you'd think I'd be aware of all the old friends. I shepherd her across the doorstep and into the kitchen, where I can offer her some of the coffee.

"He had a late night," I explain. "He's still in bed."

She nods and checks on the sleeping child in the stroller, whose blond ringlets fall across her face as she sucks her thumb. When Chloe looks back at me, there's anguish in her eyes. My heart sinks, the way a heart can before a brain catches on. I don't know what's going on here, but it involves this little girl, and it's bad.

"I need to talk to Oliver," she says, blinking back tears. "I'm so sorry."

*Sorry for what?* All this apologizing.

I look back at the little girl, and several things strike me all at once. How pale she is. How blond. How she has dimples in both cheeks—like Oliver—and the same perfectly symmetrical features. All of that, and the fact that there seems to be some sort of catheter sticking out of her chest, covered in surgical tape.

*No. No, no.* Pieces of a puzzle I wasn't aware of until this moment seem to descend at once and my mind attempts to assemble it. I think I'm meant to feel enraged. Shouldn't I be *wild* with fury?

The little girl stirs and opens big blue eyes. Waking in an unfamiliar place, she looks for her mum. When she sees me, she stares for a moment, curious, before deciding she can trust me and breaking into an enormous smile. I am acutely aware that there are defining circumstances in your life that require you to rise above something very, very bad, for a higher good—and that this might be one of them.

"I'll wake Oliver," I say, unable to pull together my emotions, or even properly identify them at this point, let alone articulate them.

This is his child, I can guess that much. And while part of me wants to storm into the spare room and throttle the man, I suspect he's about to be faced with bigger problems than that.

"Chloe?" he says, startled, as he staggers into the kitchen looking annoyingly good for someone who just rolled out of bed. The sight of her wakes him up fast. His eyes dart straight to me, and he looks ready to gallop into a frantic explanation, but then he rounds the bench, notices the stroller, and his explanation morphs into questions.

There have been very few occasions when I've seen my husband at almost a complete loss for words, but here we are.

"This is Harriet," Chloe says. "I'm sorry I didn't tell you about her before."

Now she really is crying. I should be too, but there's just . . . nothing.

"How old is she?" Oliver asks.

"Three years and three months," Chloe explains pointedly, before looking at me. "He said you'd broken up . . ."

I'm glad I've had that coffee, because my brain needs the caffeine to do the math. Three years and three months, plus the pregnancy. It does put this back around the time I graduated. Around the time Drew's mum died. A flash of that kiss with Drew hits me and softens my burgeoning anger. I might have cut off the kiss at the time, but I've thought about it countless times in the years since. Clearly, Oliver did more than kiss this woman.

He remains speechless, which annoys me, but then he steps across the kitchen and stands in front of the stroller, examining Harriet. I watch as he crouches down, looking at her with wonder, no doubt seeing what I saw—a mini-replica of himself. I can't help feeling sorry for him that he's missed the crucial start of her life.

*Was* it while we were broken up? I'm recalculating, just to be sure, but coming up with the same timeframe. We'd definitely split; Oliver gets off on a technicality. But shouldn't my heart be shattering over this? It's definitely breaking, but not in the right way.

The dull ache in my lower abdomen heralds another month in which Oliver and I have failed to achieve what he clearly had no difficulty accomplishing with Chloe. Our marriage might not be conducive to raising a family, but secretly, selfishly, perhaps, I long for the companionship and distraction of a child in my lonely world.

What also strikes me, though, is the telling fact that I was hoping the dates were wrong. Wishing Harriet was somehow my "out." Wanting an excuse—something to nail him on. Blame to cast. A reason to leave . . .

Then Oliver looks up at Chloe, concern spreading across his face as he meets her devastated expression. "What's wrong with her?"

# 68

***Drew***

I must be a masochist, accepting their invitation to meet for lunch. I haven't seen Evie since the day Mum died, and haven't seen Oliver since that terse interaction at her graduation a few days earlier.

She sends me a text message every year on the anniversary of Mum's death, and I ignore it, just as she asked. I wouldn't be here today, wishing I were anywhere else, except that her text message this year was four days late: I thought of you on the anniversary. I'm sorry this is late. Things have been bad. Oliver and I are handling a life-and-death family emergency. And, actually, we need your help.

When I didn't reply, she sent another: Please, just give us an hour to explain. This is bigger than the three of us. I wouldn't ask if we weren't desperate. I'm sorry, Drew. For everything.

When they arrive in the doorway, I watch as he helps her shake off her coat and hangs it on the coatrack near the door. She's in white trousers and a cream turtleneck. Absolutely polished, down to the painstakingly straightened hair. She looks good. I wish she didn't. I hate myself for the way I react to her, every single time.

Oliver is moody and agitated, making sharp, nervous

movements as he waits for her to walk ahead of him. A stranger would see a man possessed with worry. But I know him. I don't have a shred of trust.

They weave through the restaurant tables and over to where I'm sitting. I stand up and confront Evie, not knowing how to handle this reunion, given it was never supposed to happen, at her request. Handshake?

She tosses her handbag onto the seat and throws her arms around my neck in a hug—clinging on for longer than she should in front of her husband, in that way that seems to communicate volumes without words. It's the same thing she did at her graduation, and I meet Oliver's unimpressed glare over her shoulder as I slip my hands around her waist in response. What am I going to do? Totally reject the woman the way she specifically instructed me to?

She lets go and the three of us sit down. I just want to get this whole uncomfortable catch-up over with. "What's this about?" I ask, before we can even look at the menus.

She glances at Oliver, as if they're about to launch into a prepared speech. "Drew, something serious has happened and we need to ask you for help," she begins. "I know this is awkward, but we all need to rise above that."

I'm not going to rise above anything. These two have caused nothing but problems in my life for *years*. I don't need a moral lecture now.

"I have a daughter," Oliver announces suddenly, staring not at me but at the salt and pepper shakers.

I look at Evie, confused. *Oliver* has a daughter? My heart skips a beat in anger. For fuck's sake.

"Congratulations?" I say, sarcastically. *Congratulations on being the arse I always thought you were.*

He shifts in his seat, trying to dampen his own anger.

"Drew, Harriet is sick," Evie interrupts, placing her hand over mine as if to will me to calm down. It has completely the opposite effect. "She'll be four in three months' time. Hopefully."

*Hopefully?*

I slip my hand out from under hers and sit back in my chair, arms crossed, the conversation having taken a complete turn. Oliver looks emotionally wrecked. He hasn't shaved, and he's wearing a crushed shirt, not in a trendy way but because he simply doesn't seem to care. He looks tormented. My compassion for him attempts to turn over, like an engine without oil trying to start.

"We're all having human leukocyte antigen typing," he says, his voice flat. "For bone marrow. They're looking for familial compatibility . . ." He chokes up.

"Oliver isn't a match," Evie fills in. "Drew, it's a long shot, but they're widening the search to other family members."

I look at her, and then at him. When his eyes meet mine, I know it's with the knowledge that we are brothers.

"How long have you known?" I expected it to feel different—having a brother. Instead, as I glance from him to Evie, I remember he has the relationship I've always wanted. And he's ruined that too. I loathe the man.

"My father only told me this week when none of us matched. She's his only grandchild. He's desperate."

Desperate. *His* father? Ready to acknowledge my existence, but only because he needs something?

"I know it's upsetting," Evie begins. The way she's trying to smooth this over infuriates me.

"Don't lecture me about what's upsetting," I tell her, folding the napkin, putting it on the table, pushing my chair back, and standing up. "*Our* father deserted me, Oliver. I suspect he gaslit my mother into her grave. He showed up at her wake and warned me off speaking to you, Evie. Forgive me if I'm not playing happy families here."

"Please, Drew," Oliver says, standing up and trying to block my exit. "*Please.* She's a three-year-old child."

I glare at him. I'm angry and hurt and more sidelined than ever. "Of course I'll bloody get tested, Oliver, I'm not a fucking monster. Send me the details."

And as I walk out into the harsh sunlight in the street, which is bustling with businesspeople power walking between meetings and mothers pushing strollers and cabdrivers honking horns, my breath rushes as I contemplate the fact that I had nobody left. No family. Not a single person since Mum died. I've been totally alone against everything, anchorless.

And now I have a niece.

# 69

***Evie***

My dad keeps *everything*, and it strikes me that he probably has a copy of my wedding video stashed somewhere in the house. I leave Drew, my *brother-in-law*, who I just *kissed*, on the deck and drag Bree inside by the hand.

"I can't believe he kept another secret from me," I whisper once we're in the living room. "And let me kiss him." And kissed me back. *Like that.*

"*You* kissed *him*?"

It was incredible. For a few delirious seconds, I slipped into a world of hope. Life wasn't just a confusing jumble of memory fragments and odd behavior. It was *connected*. I felt like, even if I couldn't remember my past, I'd caught a glimpse into some kind of delicious future.

But then that was confiscated too.

"Obviously, I shouldn't have."

"If you had your memory back, you'd know I was always Team Drew."

She looks alight with something, but I don't have time for this. I kneel on the floor in front of the TV cabinet, swing the doors open, and search through the mess. Honestly, it's like sorting through the National Film and Sound Archive. Old recordings of *Yes Minister* on VHS from the eighties. *Columbo. Fawlty Towers.* I have amnesia and even I know about streaming services! What's Dad's excuse?

Right near the back, I find a stash of family videos and DVDs. All the footage he took of me when I was little. Dance performances. Soccer matches. Band concerts. It brings tears to my eyes, thinking about just how loved I am. Or was.

My fingers find a DVD case with a photo of Oliver and me on the cover. The wedding dress is no surprise—I saw it in the slideshow at the funeral. I can see how I arrived at the choice. It looks vintage in style, but it's not authentic. It's a modern take on the drop-waist 1920s gowns I always thought were so elegant. Dripping with lace and pearls. *And hope . . .*

I slip the disc into the DVD player, grab the remote, and sit back on the couch beside Bree, my thumb trembling as I press play. It's a typically mushy production. Baby photos of us both as an introduction. Pictures from school. Photos of Oliver that I recognize from his funeral slideshow too—muddy on a sports field, wielding a shiny gold trophy. On stage in his fancy school blazer with blue-and-gold piping at a debate. In a cap and gown at a university graduation. Me in the backyard in Newcastle, sunlight streaming through the trees, chasing butterflies . . . That was always my mum's favorite photo of me as a kid, and I long to be that carefree girl again.

I fast-forward through this walk down memory lane, and through some footage of everyone arriving at the church. It's glaringly obvious at this speed that one side of the congregation is full and the other very sparse. I know I was never the type to have a huge bunch of friends, but surely I had *some*? My parents are there, obviously—well, I can see Mum. Maybe Dad walked me down the aisle—such archaic patriarchal symbolism. Teenage me was never going to allow that kind of thing in my future.

I slow the footage down when it gets to the procession into the church. Some strange woman walks in before me, in a bridesmaid dress. "Who's that?" I ask Bree.

"Oliver's sister."

"But where are you?"

She takes my hand. Was she not invited?

I was already staggering from the idea of her not being the bridesmaid, but she wasn't even there? It's starting to dawn on me that maybe I haven't been abandoned after all. Perhaps I was the one doing the abandoning. And if so, doesn't it speak volumes for them that they're here with me now?

The videographer has captured that classic moment when the groom first turns to see his partner at the foot of the aisle. Oliver was an incredibly good-looking man. Wildly good-looking. Surely he could have had any girl he wanted. An awful, anxious feeling begins to well in the pit of my stomach. Inferiority. Undeservedness.

*I'm your best bet, Evie. Nobody else will ever love you like me.*

Where did those words spring from? My stomach drops.

I focus on the screen. I can read my own face, even behind a veil. That smile is fake. That's fear in my eyes. I must have known even then that this marriage wasn't right for me, so why did I go through with it?

I feel sick as I watch myself promise to love him. Can't anyone see the cry for help in my eyes?

"Until death do us part . . ." I promise. Well, it's done that, now, hasn't it? And, like clockwork, I seem to have stopped loving him. This soon after the funeral, I think a widow is meant to be screaming into the void, aching for her love to be returned.

It's irrelevant, anyway. I suspect I stopped loving Oliver long before our car crash. Perhaps even before the wedding, the way I look in this footage. What I'm watching on the screen is not the fairy tale it's striving to be, and no amount of cleverly put together pew decorations or Instagram-worthy color-coding could salvage that. I'm gobsmacked nobody picked it up at the time. How much of my life was a lie?

I can't watch any more of this. My stomach is churning. I fast-forward through to the reception instead, hoping to catch a glimpse of *anyone* important to me.

But that's when I land on the speeches.

# 70

***Drew***

When I summon the courage to enter the house, Evie and Bree are trawling through her god-awful wedding reception. Obviously, I wasn't invited. Just seeing footage of my father and the way he idolized my brother sends blood pumping erratically through my veins. Oliver was always glued to that pedestal.

Strangely enough, this video is the first time I've watched Evie with Oliver without that familiar, gut-punching envy that's haunted me since we were at school. She does not look at him the way a bride should look at a groom. I'm fascinated. Behind the poise and the immaculate hair and makeup and that perfect dress, she's clearly as empty and miserable as I was that day. Just for a different reason.

"On behalf of my wife and I . . ." Oliver begins, and everyone groans at the well-worn speech opener.

"Not like you to allow a man to speak for you," Bree observes.

Evie squirms. "None of this is anything like me, obviously. What was I *thinking*?"

The sensible perspective she seems to have now is so at odds with the way she was then. Everything I knew leading up to this, from the moment she first met him, never made any sense to me. Her prickliness whenever I floated the idea that perhaps the relationship wasn't brilliant for her. The jumpiness whenever we were hanging out and her phone would ring. It was clear from the start how wrong the dynamic was, but the more any of us criticized it, the harder she defended it.

Now it's my father's turn to bore everyone senseless with his gushing, Oliver-centric monologue. "There are few things in life that have brought me more pride over the years than my blond-haired, young, clever boy."

"As distinct from his dark-haired son?" I say under my breath, unable to disguise the bitterness.

Evie pauses the video. Rewinds. And repeats that section. "'My blond-haired, young, clever boy.' That's very odd," she says.

"Not really. He's always simpered over the Golden Child."

"No, that speech pattern," she says, hitting the mute button. "The adjectives are out of whack."

"Is this one of your weird forensic linguistics things?" Bree ribs her. She's not actually mocking Evie's degree. We both always found her thoughts on this stuff fascinating.

"There's a natural pattern to adjectives in the English language," she tells us. "We don't learn it at school, we just know it instinctively. It's 'big red ball,' not 'red big ball.'"

She doesn't seem to have noticed that this knowledge is spurting effortlessly out of her mouth as if she's recalling it from university. Perhaps it's her memory starting to surface.

"Anderson is saying, 'blond-haired, young, clever boy.' That's wrong."

"You were always such a geek for this stuff," Bree says. "Do you think your memory is coming back?"

"Nobody speaks like this," she repeats. She doesn't seem to care about her amnesia right now.

"Yeah, but it's not a federal offense," I argue. "Are you going to turn that up?"

She just lets it run, muted while she paces the room, whispering the phrase under her breath, over and over. It's an extreme reaction to incorrect sentence structure and I'm starting to worry she's snapped.

"'Blond-haired, young, clever boy. Blond-haired, young, clever boy.' Where have I heard this before?" she asks herself.

"At the wedding," I remind her. "You were there."

That said, at the wedding she looked like she was a million miles away. I doubt she took in a single word. She looked like she'd disassociated from her own fairy tale.

"'Blond-haired, young, clever boy . . .'"

She stops pacing. Bree and I are both staring at her, probably both wondering the same thing. *Should we call the psych team?*

"'I love you, my brown-eyed, creative, tall boy.'" She says the line and stares at me. Suddenly, this is far more than a memory fragment. Her fascination and all the pacing and racking of her brain makes sense as everything inside me drops through the floor in realization. I feel like all the water from the ocean has suddenly been drawn away, revealing the entire seabed, just as we're about to be hit by an incoming tsunami.

She may not remember yet, but I know exactly where she read that line.

# 71

## *Evie*

Drew looks like he's going to throw up. All the color has drained from his face, and he seems at once younger and more vulnerable, but also like he's aged a decade in seconds.

"What is it?" I cross the room and sit beside him on the couch.

"That speech pattern," he says quietly, his voice strangely gruff and laden with concern. "How likely is it that two well-educated English speakers would use it?"

I shake my head. "They almost certainly wouldn't. Most people might not be able to tell you *why* it's wrong, but they'd know it was. It's a universal rule. Virtually inviolable."

Suddenly, I remember that notebook in my podcast studio. The words I'd written down and then crossed out hard. *Adjective order.* Who was I hiding that from? Was I already onto this before the accident?

"That can't be right," he mutters.

I take my phone and google *order of adjectives*. "See, it says it here. You don't say someone is wearing a green striking coat. It's a striking green coat. It's a specific order—the more abstract property first. We don't say a hot nice cup of tea. It's a nice hot cup. It's a quick brown fox, not a brown quick fox . . ."

I'm getting mildly excited that maybe I *am* recalling information from my linguistics degree. And excited just by linguistics itself. The enchantment of words and how cultures build languages. That someone's way with words can be so particular and unique that it's like a verbal fingerprint. *This* is what I loved. The mysteries of language. The secrets of communication, unlocked in little phrases and accents, in how we play with words and shuffle them to make meaning. Maybe my memory will start to domino back as I connect with things that mean this much to me.

Drew is not so excited. It looks like he's shattering into some kind of private hell. "Evie, we once had a conversation about the Unabomber."

I don't remember.

"You told me they cracked that case because he used a specific phrase?"

That sounds right. I think that's a lot of what forensic linguists do—look for patterns and quirky language uses to tie to crimes.

"He said 'You can't eat your cake and have it too,'" Drew says.

"Isn't it 'You can't have your cake and eat it too'?" Bree interrupts.

"No, that's what we all think, but, Evie, you told me he'd used the original version of the phrase, the way it used to be said in Middle English, which almost nobody ever uses now. That's what tipped off the FBI, because he'd used it somewhere else too . . ."

I don't understand what the Unabomber has to do with anything. Particularly with Drew. Or my father-in-law's wedding speech. But I'm fairly certain I did know, before the accident.

Drew looks at me. "That phrase, 'my brown-eyed, creative, tall boy.' Do you remember where you read that?"

I wish I did. All I know is it's oddly familiar to me, probably because it sounds so wrong and would have stuck in my mind.

Now he takes his phone and starts searching for something, scrolling a long way back. As I watch, it's as if his entire physique folds in on itself the further back in time he goes. He's rewinding years, becoming increasingly fragile as he reenters a time when grief was clearly all-encompassing.

"You don't have to do this," I say. I just want to make it better. Need to. I can't stand seeing this man suffer—it makes my chest ache.

He finds what he's looking for at last, reads the screen first to himself, and sighs heavily. Then he passes the phone to me with a shaking hand.

It's a screenshot of an email. And when I realize what I'm reading, I gasp.

# 72

## *Evie*

Drew is pacing the room, which is more than I can manage. I can't actually stand right now.

"Is this . . . your mum's . . ." I can't say it. Can't even think it.

"Yes," he confirms.

Neither of us seems able to say the words *suicide note* aloud. But there's that sentence, with the butchered order of adjectives. The inviolable rule, violated not once but twice, by not one but two intelligent, articulate adults . . .

"I found it in her Sent folder the night she died," he says, rereading the note on his screen. I suspect he's read it a million times since. "I hadn't read my emails in time." Refreshed pain sears across his features. He looks back at me, broken. "Evie, I know you can't remember your time at uni, but you were close to getting a PhD. If you had to dig deep and just take a wild guess?"

I know what he's asking. I just don't want to give him my answer. Perhaps he held on to these words from his mum for years. And without me raising this, he wouldn't be questioning their authorship now. Here he is, trying to get me through my crisis, and I'm creating one in return.

"Please, Evie—what do you think?"

I can't avoid it. "I'd guess the same person made the wedding speech and wrote the suicide note," I confirm without fanfare. "I'd guess, at the very least, your mum had help writing that note . . ."

"Help, or . . ."

Neither of us can say the word *murder*. Murder is for Agatha Christie. It's for *CSI Miami*. It's for How to Host a Murder parties. It's a group of crows. Murder is not something that happens *in our own family*.

And isn't that what Drew and I have become? Family? Sort of . . . even if he's estranged and we're not related, and he shares only half his blood with my dead husband.

I'm beginning to wonder if I even *want* my memory back. The trailer I'm being drip-fed about the life I've forgotten isn't inspiring me with much confidence or desire to return to it. Maybe I'll be one of the lucky ones whose memories never return at all. I could just draw a line in the sand and start from here. I could see out the rest of life as an incomplete jigsaw puzzle with the scary pieces lost. Like one of those cracked Japanese vases with the broken bits filled with gold.

"I found a note in my podcast studio at the house with *adjective order* written on it," I confess. The idea that I was already onto this before the accident suddenly seems even worse than the unexplained abandonment of my friends and family.

This news hits Drew hard. "Evie, you *knew*?"

"I don't know. I can't remember!"

He shakes his head.

"Maybe I was doing the same thing for you as you've been doing for me. Protecting you from the truth."

I'm worried that the dissociative amnesia will get him too. That everything I've remembered and that he's confronting will stretch him too far, like my life stretched me. Until his mind just ruptures.

We can't have that—one of us needs to stay together here. And that person needs to be him. No matter how much he'd like to share my luxury of an obliterated past.

# 73

***Drew***

I expected this trip would end with Evie's life in uproar. Not my own. I don't even know what to do. Who to talk to. The police?

No. I can hardly walk up and offer the vague expertise of an amnesiac after she's had a three-minute google and flicked through a linguistics article on Medium. She'd start raving about green coats and brown foxes and they'd have her admitted for psychiatric evaluation.

This is all just so incredibly, unimaginably hideous.

*Why* would my father kill my mother? What's the motive? She and I were never any threat to him, or to Oliver. We never demanded anything. We weren't going to make any trouble. Mum was the least likely person to make a fuss of any description.

"I can't believe I'm even thinking about words like *kill* and *motive* in relation to my own parents. It's absurd," I say aloud.

Evie is sitting awkwardly on the couch, looking guilty. "I'm so sorry," she says. "If I hadn't got out the wedding DVD . . ."

"We wouldn't know my father was a murderer?" I said it.

She flinches at my words. And looks lost. "I don't know how much I knew about this, Drew. All I have are two words, crossed out on a page."

"Should I make a cup of tea?" Bree asks.

"Yes, because tea is clearly the go-to beverage for the moment you discover you're descended from a criminal," I say.

Now they're both floundering.

"Sorry," I apologize. "It's just . . . imagine the field day the press would have if this got out. 'Prominent Sydney anesthesiologist charged with the murder of former lover, exposed by amnesiac daughter-in-law two weeks after she was widowed in a mysterious car crash . . .'"

Every aspect of this has tabloid fodder written all over it.

"Wait, is he an anesthesiologist?" Evie asks.

I nod to confirm it.

"How did your mum die?"

"According to her death certificate? Cancer. But she was on a concoction of pain relief toward the end, so . . ."

"Someone could tamper with that concoction pretty easily," she suggests. "Especially if they were a specialist in drugs that put the body to sleep. And perhaps he'd know how to do it in such a way that the toxicology report wouldn't raise any suspicion."

"There was no report. They never looked into it any further," I explain. "The doctor just took it as an open-and-shut case of natural death, with no suspicious circumstances."

She looks at me. "But the note?"

"We found it after they left. Everything had been signed off. The note didn't *say* she was going to do it. Just happened to have been sent that morning and was clearly a goodbye."

She doesn't seem convinced. Probably imagines herself as some sort of accessory after the fact. Something we all could be now—me, Evie, and Bree—if I don't take this information about Anderson to the police.

"I'd already put her through a round of CPR that haunts me to this day. She was closing in on the end of her life. I imagined, if anything, she just helped herself over the line. So we did her one last favor and kept her secret. I recall thinking, *What would it change?*

I'm cycling through almost a decade of grief, remembering the way I processed it all. The anger I felt at one point that she had left me, knowing I'd already been rejected by my father. And the guilt of wishing she'd held on even longer.

"But, Drew, everything could have changed," Evie says, quietly. "If this had been investigated at the time . . . if linguists were involved, and they'd found the note, they might have compared it with your mum's other correspondence. They would have known she didn't write it. And if there were other messages from Anderson, and he wrote this way in other places, he'd have been the suspect."

*All those messages I poured over in Mum's inbox.*

"If he'd been arrested . . ." she continues. "I mean, it's the butterfly effect, isn't it? Whatever else happened that week would have unfolded differently."

I think of Anderson turning up at Mum's funeral, warning me off Evie. And the text message she sent, ordering me to forget we'd ever met. If our father was in trouble, Oliver would have been reeling from the scandal and been preoccupied—rallying his legal mates.

Maybe she wouldn't have gone back. *Maybe she never would have married him.*

I look up and meet that same solid compassion Evie had shown me stargazing. Even after everything we've been through and all the ways she let me down, and with the fragility of her own mental state, I know she is here for me now.

"I'll need to report this," I tell her.

"I'll come with you."

I get a flash of the empty seat beside me at Mum's funeral.

"Okay, but this time, you need to see it through."

I can tell by the way the words seem to smart her skin that it hurts. Amnesia or not, she needs to take some responsibility for what she did, because the abandonment theme has loomed large in my life, and I can't take any more of it. And now here's Evie, historically one of the worst offenders, and I'm just handing her everything.

Experience tells me this can only end badly.

It also tells me I will be reckless enough to take the risk.

# 74

## *Evie*

Bree unmutes the TV and is about to eject the DVD, which has been playing a blank screen for the last fifteen minutes, but then it bursts into more footage. The first shot is of people's feet. The camera operator is walking through the crowd and getting the viewfinder lined up to focus on the church, and then it cuts out. What is this, the blooper reel? There's another shot where the sound isn't right and then one that's out of focus, taken before the service started, of people arriving for the ceremony. They must have included this raw footage by mistake.

"I wonder if anyone's ever watched this?" Bree asks.

We're about to turn it off. I've had enough. But then some audio begins of the sound guy looping up a lapel microphone before we went into the church.

"We picked these up in Japan," the tech is saying. "Neat, aren't they? Perfect for weddings. You don't notice them, and the sound quality of the vows will be top-notch. Testing, testing. Yeah? Right. Good to go!"

"Okay. I'm really doing this!" we hear me say nervously. My voice sounds young and unsure and shaky.

"You look beautiful," Bree is saying. But I'd assumed she wasn't there! "Are you sure about this?"

There's a pause, and I can imagine myself trying to assemble conscious thought. *No, I'm not sure, but it's too late to back out now. Everyone's waiting . . .*

Bree slams her finger on the stop button. "Oh my God. I didn't know they were recording that."

Drew and I snap around to look at her.

"Keep playing it," I say calmly.

"I don't want to." She's tearing up already.

"Press play, Bree."

"Please don't make me listen to it," she says. "If I could go back, Evie . . ."

I take the remote control out of her hand and aim it at the TV.

"Just say the word, Evie." Now it's Dad's voice. "We can call the whole thing off."

"You wouldn't have to lift a finger," Bree insists.

Now it's the muffled sound of me crying. "Aren't you meant to support me, no matter what?" I say. My voice is frail, laced with fear. Even without the full details, I want to tell myself to run. *Say yes, Evie. Let them stop this for you.*

Bree sits quietly on the couch, head in her hands, while I listen to her say, "Evie, I'm sorry. I just can't stand beside you and watch you make the biggest mistake of your life."

Then there's the sound of footsteps retreating and a door banging. Did she just *leave*?

It's only 10 a.m. and I'm mentally drained. The more answers that fall into place, the more confused I become, and my head hurts from trying to reassemble the picture.

"Drew and Bree have gone to the bakery for breakfast things," I tell my parents, after knocking tentatively on their bedroom door. Mum and Dad have slept in. Or maybe they've given us space. Either way, being alone with my thoughts is too much to bear, and I need them. "Can I come in?"

Years ago, I would have flopped onto their bed. But now I stand at the foot of it, contemplating the miles between us, even from a few feet away.

"He's always been a nice boy," Mum says.

"You never even met him, so how do you know?"

Her smile is the first I've seen since we arrived, and it's an extraordinary flicker of hope for me. "You talked about him all the time in high school. We were convinced you were in love with him."

She pats the bed, so I sit on the edge of it, contemplating her words. *Was I ever in love with him?* I fall back on the mattress, face to the ceiling. It's a good impression of a lovestruck sixteen-year-old, probably, but I'm also just emotionally exhausted from the constant confusion. And revelations! Do I dare drop the suspected crime into the conversation? There's only so much drama my parents can stand, and they barely accepted me into their house last night. The idea that their daughter's father-in-law is a murderer would exceed that capacity.

"But then you got together with Oliver, so that was the end of that," Dad tells me, straight.

I think of the way he offered to help me call off the wedding. "It feels like getting together with Oliver was the end of a lot more than that," I admit.

None of it feels right. The wedding video explained some of it. I can see the attraction between us. I saw how he looked at me—like it was *just* me, and nobody else was in the room. I remember craving an eighteenth-century love story complete with grand gestures, and I can imagine the impact of this superstar boy crashing into my life. It must have felt like he was sweeping me off my feet.

"He dazzled you," Mum says.

I roll onto my side to face them and start playing with the tassels on a throw cushion. Dad hates the cushions but patiently removes them from the bed each evening and places them back the next morning when he pulls up the bedspread. That's love, really. Putting up with someone's annoying little quirks. Simple acts of kindness that show you really understand a person. Surely that's the type of love I wanted all along?

"Why did I stay with him?" I ask. "I can't see it . . ."

Mum shrugs. "I never understood it, either."

This is no help—I need a reason. I'm a smart woman, or thought I was. It makes no sense that I'd marry someone when I was as unhappy as I looked in that video. Particularly after my father and my best friend tried to talk me out of it.

"I suspect you were trying to keep him alive," Dad says quietly. His words are infused with heartbreak. Even Mum looks surprised, as if they've never discussed this idea.

*Keep him alive?*

"He was very persuasive," Dad adds. "More persuasive than we could be."

I know how strong-willed I was at sixteen, and having just heard even a snippet of that determination on the recording, I can imagine exactly how that conversation went down. And I would have been too proud to admit I'd been wrong about him.

I don't want to get upset. I don't want to dislodge this conversation in any way. This is the first spark of my real family that I've felt, but there's someone ringing the front doorbell incessantly, so I roll off the bed, redo my ponytail while walking down the hall, and answer the door.

• • •

Standing on my parents' doorstep is a woman around my age in jeans and an oversize blue shirt who greets me with a warm smile. More than anything, I'm interested in the fact that she's holding hands with the little girl from my camera roll.

"Evie!" the child says, extricating herself and rushing toward me, throwing her little arms around my waist. She stares up into my face, blue eyes alight with the kind of recognition I wish I felt too, blond curls swept into Cindy Brady pigtails. I can't describe the relief that she seems to belong to this woman instead of me. Perhaps we're friends?

"Well, hello there," I say. I don't want to let on that I don't know who the little girl is—she's clearly obsessed with me and I don't want to confuse her.

"Harriet, let her breathe," the mother says, and the girl lets go and takes my hand instead, as if we're besties, staring at me that same, adoring way that she did in the photos. Then, just when the silence is getting awkward, she lets go and dashes inside my parents' house!

"Harri!" the woman calls after her, but she's disappeared from sight.

"I'm so sorry," I explain. "I'm having trouble with my memory. I can't place you."

The car pulls in with Drew and Bree at this point, and they climb out, white cardboard boxes brimming with pastries. At the sight of the two of us standing on the veranda, they stop dead.

Harriet's mum lights up seeing Drew, but her elation quickly dissolves, and she steps toward him, throwing her arms around his neck.

He passes the pastries he's holding to Bree and brings his arms around this woman, his hand cradling her head against his chest, comforting her, looking over her shoulder directly at me.

I try not to look how I feel. Wildly envious and incredibly confused.

Eventually he brings her back up the path, his arm still around her, and presents her to me. "Evie, this is Chloe," he explains. *This* is Chloe, with whom the situation is "complicated." Is it *Drew's* child who's currently scampering around my parents' house?

"Evie, I'm just so sorry," Chloe says. Is she apologizing for stealing the romance out from under my nose before it even begins? "I didn't know if I should come."

She definitely shouldn't have come! Because now I've kissed her boyfriend and raised my hopes, and the way he's holding her is making my insides buckle. I am furious at him! How could he let this happen, with me so vulnerable and confused and Chloe so ordinary and nice and with a *child* in the picture? And why is she so upset? Is she here to confront me?

"Look, Chloe," I say quickly and apologetically. "I didn't know about you two."

"No, I know you didn't."

So it's true, then? Is Chloe his *partner*? The man had not given off "in a relationship" vibes—particularly when he was kissing me.

All the air has rushed out of my lungs, and I can't seem to inhale enough to replace it. I need to sit down. If I had any doubt about my feelings toward Drew, it has evaporated right this second, imagining him—no, *looking* at him—with the mother of his child. My heart is torn to pieces.

Bree suggests that Drew and Chloe go inside and find Harriet, and she sits beside me on the chair on the veranda. "Come on, Evie. It's okay."

*Okay?* How can *any* of this be okay? And why am I taking advice from the best friend who walked out on me in the precise moment I needed her most?

"She had a baby with him," I say, gasping for oxygen, trying to regulate my breathing and heartbeat. "And I *kissed* him!"

Bree takes my hand. "You were married to him, Evie, obviously . . ."

"Married?"

Bree looks confused. "To Oliver? We just watched the wedding DVD this morning, remember?"

I stare at her. "Chloe had a baby with *Oliver*?"

Bree nods, and I cry again. Oliver is the dad? I suppose I'm meant to feel outraged, but these are great, heaving sobs of relief. "Thank God," I whisper, between breaths. *"Thank God!"*

Bree pushes me back to see my face. "Evie, who did you think she had a baby with?" And, as understanding dawns, she draws me into a tight hug while enormous waves of emotion seem to well up and spill out about someone I've known less than three days, plus half a lifetime.

# 75

## *Evie*

There's some sort of surreal family reunion going on in my parents' kitchen. Harriet is holding court, sitting on Drew's knee, with Chloe beside them. "Grandpa" has produced a box of crayons and some stickers. "Nanna" is "just whipping up a batch of mini-pancakes." It becomes painfully obvious to me, the second I see my parents cosseting Harriet, that this is not their first rodeo. And when I walk in with Bree, Chloe gets out of her chair for me. Chloe, who somehow had a baby with my husband, and yet we're all smiles?

"Look, Evie!" Harriet says, passing me the drawing she's done of stick-figure people. "That's me, Mummy, Daddy, you, and Uncle Drew."

The stick figure of "Daddy" is crossed out, with angel wings on his back, a sad face and the word *dead* written beside his name. *Dead.* Harriet is holding my hand in the drawing, and trying to hold his, but their arms won't reach.

*My God.*

Here is Oliver's grieving little girl, proudly showing me her work, appealing to the love she's so deeply portrayed between us on this page, and I have no recollection of a single second of our time together. Nothing that I've seen nor heard since the day I found out I was a widow has hit me this hard. I've been so obsessed trying to work out who I am and what carnage I seem to have caused that I've completely underestimated the way my husband's death has ricocheted through other people's lives.

Suddenly, I *have* to remember. Looking into her big, innocent, heartbroken eyes, I know I have to step up. The dormant adult within me needs to phoenix herself out of the ashes of amnesia and stepparent the hell out of this encounter.

"This is beautiful," I tell her, crouching to her level and then sitting on the kitchen floor beside her, cross-legged. She instantly scrambles into my lap, the way I suspect she has done a hundred times before, and pulls my arms around her waist. When I say her drawing is beautiful, I really mean everything in this room. The warmth I'm feeling in a tableau that should surely be filled with angst. Wouldn't I have been furious that my husband had this baby? Yet nothing about the celebratory reunion here feels forced or tense or wrong.

"Harriet, you are magical," I whisper. "Do you know that?"

She reaches back and touches my face with sticky mandarin-scented hands as I kiss the crown of her head, inhaling the scent of blueberry shampoo and sunscreen while love rushes into my drought-ridden psyche, flooding the parched spaces of my heart and pumping life back into my world.

*You are the linchpin,* I think.

"Daddy died," she says, completely matter-of-factly. "I typed him a message on my iPad saying, *Sorry you died, Dad.*"

My heart!

"But he didn't answer. It means we will never see him again. Evie, are you sad?"

As she asks the question, she jumps up out of my lap again and stands in front of me, taking my face in both her hands and looking directly into my eyes. Silence descends in the room during this inquisition, and I can almost read their minds. *Handle this like a seasoned stepmum, Evie. Don't botch this child's grief.*

"It's very sad that Daddy died," I begin. "It feels scary."

She nods. "I'm scared too."

I pull her into my arms. "Close your eyes," I say. "Can you smell those pancakes on the stove?"

"Yes?"

"Can you hear Grandpa's noisy breathing?"

She giggles, then nods.

"What about Mummy?" I ask. "Did you just hear her footsteps across the kitchen?"

"Yes," she whispers.

"And I know you can feel my arms around you, can't you?"

She hugs me hard. "And Uncle Drew saved my life," she adds. "But I don't know the other lady."

She means Bree, but I've lost track of this exercise now, my eyes open again, staring at Drew from the kitchen floor. *He saved her life?* He's sitting quietly at the table with tears in his eyes, looking at Harriet. He will not look at me.

Goose bumps spread along my arms. The bondedness in this group that I found so hard to understand just moments ago begins to make sense. I'd assumed we'd been through a lot, but this is more than I ever imagined.

"Uncle Drew saved your life," I repeat, even though I am a completely unreliable narrator. "You've got so much love around you, Harriet, even in this little kitchen, haven't you?"

*"Mmm."* She nods again, playing with my hair.

"And do you know what else?" I tell her. She looks up. "We can't bring Daddy back to you. I wish we could. But these are the very same people who help me when I'm sad and scared and don't know what to do."

"But you're a grown-up!" She is amazed.

"Sometimes I feel like I'm still a teenager," I confess. And now it's me with tears in my eyes, and Harriet's hug is giving comfort this time, not seeking it.

"That's okay, Evie," she says. "I'll look after you."

"Have we had more than our share of life drama?" I ask Drew, when we steal some time away for an evening walk.

"Everyone has drama. But hearing your story played back in fast-forward isn't helping."

He's right. All the big events that punctuate our lives are usually spread out. Not delivered over forty-eight hours, one huge twist after the other.

"Were you going to tell me I was a stepmother?" I ask. *Stepmother.* I can't even contemplate what that means, or how strange it is to know I've had a child in my life. The same child who I heard squealing down the phone when Drew promised to take her to the zoo. The one in the situation he described as "complicated" when I hounded him about it. His niece. My stepdaughter. Someone who very clearly loves us both.

"I thought you had enough on your plate. I didn't think Chloe was going to turn up here, but Harriet was already bereft without her dad and she thought you'd died too. I think Chloe was only going to let her glimpse you. Nobody expected that performance in the kitchen."

"Performance?"

"You were pretty impressive back there."

I smile. Actually, it felt fairly instinctive, which is weird because I've never even babysat a child that I remember.

We find a bench seat in a park not far from my parents' house and sit down.

"When Chloe kept calling you, I thought . . ."

He raises an eyebrow.

"You were being so mysterious and secretive. I thought she was your girlfriend, or that Harriet was yours. You were so gorgeous on the phone with her . . ." *Gorgeous in general.* "I thought there was a relationship situation you were keeping from me."

"There's no situation," Drew explains. "Not with me."

"But there clearly was with my husband?"

Drew shakes his head. "From what I know, it was a one-night thing the night you and Oliver had a massive argument after your graduation. You'd broken up. He was irate. She was there. It was never meant to be anything more than that."

"So we were together seven years, had one fight, and he accidentally conceived a child?"

Drew frowns and shifts awkwardly on the seat. "It wasn't your first fight, Evie."

"Yeah, but I wouldn't have run straight into the arms of another man, would I?!"

He seems unwilling to answer the question. "Anyway, several years later Chloe turned up begging for Oliver's help with Harriet."

"He bloody well should have helped her! Raising a child on her own, and he had all that money."

He rubs his forehead. "Harriet was sick. Chloe was searching for a familial donor. That's the only reason she showed up on your doorstep."

*My doorstep.* "Was I there?"

"Apparently it was your shining moment. You were very compassionate and forgiving." He looks at me kindly as he says this. An implied *Well done, Evie. That must have been hard.*

No wonder she's so normal around me, and lovely.

"Much like I hope you're about to be with me for keeping all of this from you," Drew adds.

I can't help it. I sort of swell with pride at the idea that I would have set aside what must have felt like a betrayal and handled a situation like this with maturity.

"Oliver wasn't a match. So that's when my father broke the news that there was another son."

*Oh!*

"Things only deteriorated after that. The chances of an uncle, particularly one who's a half sibling of the father, being a genetic match were incredibly low."

I let out a long sigh. I know Harriet is still alive, of course, so there must have been a happy ending to this story. I glance at him nervously. "She's okay now?"

"She's wonderful," Drew says proudly.

"And how did Oliver take it all—you being the donor?"

He winces. "Badly."

I'm not sure how many more ways my husband can disappoint me but jealousy, when the brother who had nothing gave you everything you needed, tells me all I need to know.

"Evie, the thing is, you let your parents fall madly in love with that little girl. Harriet used to rave about your mum and dad. You saw it today, the way they are with her."

It was everything I had as a little girl myself. Knowing I'd been able to take the higher ground over how she came into the world, and then seeing my family embrace her—it's everything that makes me proud of us. It's all so beautiful.

Drew's still talking, though. "But then you snatched her away from us all."

# 76

***Drew***

It's all going to come out now. The way Oliver pulled Evie and Harriet, inch by inch, from the family until he ripped that last shred of connection they'd all been clinging to. It was never just one thing. It was microwounds, inflicted over several years, always on top of scars that hadn't yet healed. Withdrawing Harriet from their world, like they did from mine until I reached out to Chloe, wasn't the only reason that, when we landed on their doorstep, they said they couldn't do this anymore. It was a big one, but after years and years of Oliver chipping away, digging at them, planting suspicion in Evie's mind, and manipulating emotions in both directions, it had been the last straw. They just had nothing left. Winning Evie back—only to risk losing her, and potentially Harriet, all over again—would take more emotional energy than they had.

"Once Harriet was well, Chloe and Oliver came to an arrangement," I explain. "You two had Harriet every other weekend."

Evie's eyes widen at the idea of having been a part-time parent. The reality is that she'd reveled in it. Even in high school, though she had no experience with babies, they'd featured in her long-term life plan.

"When Harriet got a little older, she stayed with you for half the school holidays. You'd take her to Newcastle. She had the whole 'Grandparent Experience,' as your dad used to call it. It was far more love than she ever saw from the other side."

Evie nods. "That makes a lot of sense. But I don't understand how this went wrong."

I sigh. She has to hear it. "Oliver became progressively jealous. He didn't want to share Harriet with other people. He never got over the fact that I'd been able to help his daughter in a way that he couldn't. He was already jealous enough before that, of you and me."

"You and me?"

*Always.*

"We were never together, you and I. We had that one kiss after you'd broken up . . ." *One kiss, before that kiss for the ages on the deck.* "But he was jealous of everything. And everyone. Even Harriet, in the end, and the love everyone lavished on her, particularly when she was having treatment."

And that was exactly the problem. The further Harriet wormed her way into all our lives, the more envious Oliver became. With a much older sister who was living overseas, he'd effectively grown up as an only child. And then along came someone who absorbed all the attention. It didn't matter that she was his own child, and deathly ill. He was that narcissistic.

"The focus on Harriet ate him up," I say.

"But she was his daughter! What kind of a person was I *married* to?" Evie asks. It's such an innocent question, and I'm stuck for a response.

"It reached a point where he closed you both off from everyone. By that stage, I think you'd lost the will to fight for us. You all but said so in the last email you sent to your parents."

# 77

***Evie***

Hours later, I'm still pondering Drew's words. He can't be right. I would never have stopped fighting for them. How could I let my parents fall in love with a surrogate granddaughter and then steal her away? No wonder they didn't want to see me. I must have completely worn them out—worn Drew out too. And driven Bree away after our argument at the wedding.

"Dad, I would never have done this," I tell him, after Chloe and Harriet and Bree have left, Mum has gone to bed, and it's just him, Drew, and I having a nightcap on the deck.

But I did. I did do it. The fact that I can't remember doing it isn't an excuse.

I pick up Dad's iPad again and reread the email I'd asked to see, clearly sent from my account.

> Mum and Dad,
>
> Things can't go on like this. We are constantly under attack. You've never tried to love Oliver. He's on edge when we're with you. He never felt good enough. And now Harriet asked why you don't like Daddy. I have to choose my family.
>
> Evie.

"The important thing is you're here now," Dad says softly.

"I didn't write this," I argue.

"It doesn't matter now."

"No, Dad. These are not my words. I don't write like this. It's the clipped tone, can't you hear it? And the sentences are all the same length. I don't speak that way or write that way—without any poetry to it . . ."

*Who wrote this?*

"Sweetheart, I hardly think you were considering the poetry of the message. You were furious with us!"

"I also never put a full stop after my name," I tell them. "In forensic linguistics, that kind of thing is relevant. You can hang a criminal case on punctuation! I'm telling you, I didn't write this."

Did *Oliver*?

Dad doesn't seem to believe me. I try to imagine my parents receiving the message, heartbroken, and me completely unaware it had been sent.

"But this is no different from the way you'd been messaging us for years, Evie. Every time you canceled a visit or didn't like the way we'd said something. Or when you'd write to tell us we were wrong about Oliver and laboriously explain his perspective on things. You blew hot and cold with us the entire marriage. And when it wore your mother down, yes, she'd step back. Just to catch her breath before you'd criticize her again, but you know, Evie, your mother is a person too. It was destroying her life."

"And were there full stops after my name in all those emails too?"

Both of them stare at me, then look at each other.

"Why didn't I just *leave*?" I ask, blowing my nose.

"Leaving an abusive relationship is not that easy," Drew says, and I stare at him. It's the first time anyone has used that word.

It looks like it's breaking his heart having to spell this out. "He always knew where you were. He tracked you. If any of us ever expressed a hint of a concern about him, he pulled you further away. You were scared of him, but you'd make every excuse for him. He had that hold over you. You broke up once, but then you went straight back—he was all promises, no delivery. Constantly apologizing, begging your forgiveness, 'working on himself.' Never with any discernible change."

I take this in. "So I was scared of being with him, but more scared of leaving?"

They both nod and I'm newly sorry for having placed them in such a horrible bind, regret and guilt rising up and breaking through the surface in the form of tears.

"And I lost all of you in the process?"

It's unthinkable.

They look silenced. Like they're ashamed they gave up on me.

"We tried," Dad says, choking up.

"The number of times I had to restrain myself from rushing in there and just *rescuing you*," Drew says quietly. "From high school onwards. The rage I felt at the hold he had over you . . ."

This new information piles in on top of the shame and guilt and hopelessness. The idea of Drew, enraged. The vision of him wanting to fix it. The way he looks now, brows knitted, jaw set, leaning intently toward me in one of the chairs on the deck, elbows on his thighs, hands cradling a glass of whisky as he talks about riding in and rescuing me, and by extension my parents, after he'd already done that in a different way, saving

Harriet . . . It's giving serious Darcy-saving-the-Bennets-from-ruin energy.

I want to tell them I'm sorry, but it seems so inadequate. I would never have isolated myself from them if I'd had any real say in it. But the idea that I could have reached a point with someone where I was so small that I'd lost my own voice is truly terrifying.

"I thought I was strong," I admit. I guess I was wrong about that too.

"No," Drew says. "Don't you dare take this on as if it was your fault. You're the victim here."

It sounds like we were all victims.

"I just want my memory back," I say, crying now. "I'm ready now. I've heard the worst. I just want it all back, so I can move forward."

Neither of them speak. Do they not want me to remember?

Or have I not yet heard the worst?

# TEN DAYS AGO

# 78

***Evie***

I gently push the covers off and swivel my legs over the side of our bed. Oliver's still asleep beside me, facing the other way. We've slept like this for years—if we're actually in the same room—each on the far side of the king-size mattress, clutching the edge of the sheet. I've perfected the knack of wrapping it around my leg, almost like a little hammock over the side, keeping me as far from him as possible, while preventing me from falling out.

That's if Oliver is at home at all. He spends a lot of nights somewhere else. "Work," apparently. I don't ask. It's reached a point where I don't care. Honestly, if he came home and told me he'd fallen madly in love with a partner at the firm and she was pregnant with triplets, I'd be relieved. This marriage is dead.

*I'm* dead, with it.

The death knell was when I read that the bioluminescence was back at Jervis Bay.

"Come with me?" I'd begged him. I remembered that enchanted night with Drew and believed that glittery water capable of anything—as if it held some supernatural power to draw people close. Perhaps it could save even us.

He did agree to go, reluctantly, and, as we pulled up the car, I turned to him. "Coming?"

"I can see it from here," he said. And technically we could see it shimmering and glowing in the distance. He doesn't like sand. Doesn't look at the stars. Doesn't *live*. "I'll make a few work calls from the car. Don't be long, Evie."

I walked to the water's edge and dipped my toes in. Thought how different this was. How wrong everything felt. How trapped I'd become. There was so little of me left by that night, I was barely able to mourn for myself. Couldn't rouse the pity I deeply deserved. Couldn't even cry.

I grab my silk dressing gown now, then tread down the hall and downstairs into the kitchen. Sunlight is streaming through the bay window I dreamed up with an architect when we built this place years ago. The house is perfect. A dream house. It's hard to believe something so beautiful can contain an existence this dismal.

Every morning, I psych myself up to ask for a divorce. Every night, as I close my eyes, I kick myself for chickening out. Fictional triplet babies or not, Oliver still seems fixated on me. Or maybe it's that a divorce would reflect badly on him. My own life has evaporated. I'm a plus-one in his. Constantly charming his clients, smoothing his path, calming his nerves, boosting his spirits, while my own direction is lost—the path so overgrown underfoot I can't find it.

I flick on the kettle, and it starts rumbling to life while I check my phone. As I scroll through the same mind-numbing wasteland as always, something catches my eye.

It's a post from the official school account from St. Ag's. Notification of the death of an ex-student, after a short illness. I remember her. She was in our year.

She was *thirty*. A vet. Always clever. She volunteered at the animal shelter, as I recall. I can picture her so clearly.

"Too young," I whisper. "So much life ahead. Several decades."

*So much life ahead. DECADES.*

My own future crowds in, swamping me with its awfulness until I gulp for breath and feel like I might die too.

I can't do this anymore. Not for one single day.

I have a sudden, unbelievable need to talk to Bree. Piece by piece of our friendship broke off every time Oliver couldn't cope with me going out, or thought I was on the phone too long or was sending too many messages. She got sick of me hanging up and canceling plans and not responding to texts. Even then she agreed to be my bridesmaid, but we fought at the wedding when I wouldn't let her help me call it off. The obvious choice, in retrospect. But Oliver convinced me afterward that she was the bad, unsupportive friend, and I was better off without her.

I open a message to her. Pippa Marsh died, I type. No "Hello." No "Long time no hear." No "Sorry I let my husband ruin everything we ever were to each other."

As I wait for her to respond, I scroll up and read our last few messages. Before the post-wedding silence, it's nothing but a string of broken promises and apologies from me. I keep scrolling. The further back I go, the longer my messages get. The less apologetic. Warmer. I'm more focused on *life*. Talking rubbish about inconsequential but, in retrospect, beautiful things. And I'm grief-stricken for having lost that. Lost Bree.

Not just her. My parents too.

And Drew.

I flick to my messages with him. I have to go a lot further back, but it's the same pattern. The air that was sucked out of our friendship in the later messages gradually coming to life the further back in time I travel.

Not just the friendship coming to life. Me.

And when the kettle clicks off, steam rising out of the spout, I decide I cannot spend another morning standing here at this bench, watching this kettle boil. Watching my precious life slip through my fingers.

I can't give another single day to this man.

# 79

***Drew***

It's eight at night and I'm stacking the dishwasher in my apartment in Surry Hills when my phone pings with the email from Sony. I can hardly bring myself to open it. I'd submitted an entry into the World Photography Awards—the most prestigious photo competition—and hadn't heard anything back, so I assumed it was another rejection.

I collect rejections. It's part of my strategy for success. Every time I enter something, or bid for an assignment, or take a risk, I write it down. I'm aiming for one hundred rejections in a year, which would theoretically mean a higher rate of success too. If you've got a modicum of talent, surely it's a numbers game? I open the email.

> Dear Mr. Kennedy,
> We are pleased to let you know . . .

I have to reread the start of the opening sentence because I'm sure I imagined it.

> We are pleased to let you know your photo series, Pictures of You, has been shortlisted from more than 170,000 entries

from 171 countries and is a finalist in the documentary project category in this year's award.

I sit back on the couch in silence.

This is it. The news I've imagined receiving ever since I started taking photography seriously in high school. So many photos. So much time spent learning how to improve. So many rejections and failures and setbacks. *So* many dreams and so much future career potential, even being placed as a finalist in this very competition.

Without thinking, I reach for my phone. *I'll call Mum . . .*

And then it descends, again. That sinking realization that I can't do that. That every good thing that happens to me now has this horrible flipside of loss. And she would be so proud of this.

"I always think it's about the climb for you, Drew," she used to say. "It's the striving for something. You're inspired by the gap between where you are and what you want. Getting there is almost an anticlimax, and then you want the next thing."

She was right, in a way. It is the climb that I love. But this summit is one I never really imagined reaching. It feels pretty bloody good.

*Although . . .*

The other sinking flipside is that I never actually believed I would get this far in the award, so I skipped the bit where you're meant to have permission from the subject of the images. I thought chances were slim. It wasn't worth the angst of rekindling any kind of association with Evie. Every time we're together it ends disastrously. I haven't seen her since Harriet's fifth birthday party, and what a mess that was. Harri clinging to me, “Watch me, Uncle Drew! Uncle! Look! *LOOK!!*” Oliver fuming in the corner. Evie trying to be diplomatic. Him silencing her efforts with one glare. I gave her the gift—a toy camera—and left early in the end. Promised I'd see her another time. Hoped I wouldn't see her dad and stepmum again for another year.

My photos are going to be printed and hung in the competition's public exhibition at Somerset House in London. And I implied that I had Evie's permission. I can't imagine the photos are good enough to win, but I also can't imagine the professional embarrassment of winning, only for it to come out that she hadn't agreed to being featured. Such an inexcusable error.

Contacting her makes me feel sick, though.

“Pretend you don't know me” had been the pre-Harriet instruction. Not “Blow up photos of me and broadcast them on the international stage.”

I'm going to have to withdraw—and implode the best career break I've ever had.

Or send her an email.

# 80

***Evie***

After my coffee, I go to the gym. I'm not going to let a little problem like ending my marriage disrupt my normal routine. Teenage me would be astonished about the exercise. I was hopeless at phys ed—devoid of any kind of prowess at ball sports, or patience, particularly for anything with a high chance of failure. I consider the irony of ending up in a marriage that has so spectacularly crashed.

The routine is all I really have these days. I hardly even do anything here, just walk absentmindedly on the treadmill and then adjourn to the coffee shop, usually, to read or to people-watch. Wishing things were different. Filling in another pointless day that's dragging me further from my dreams.

My anxiety got so bad after I pulled out of the PhD, Oliver convinced me to give up my job. "It only has to be temporary," he'd explained. "Just while you pull yourself together."

"I don't want to stop working," I told him. "It's the one place where my anxiety isn't bad."

"Find a hobby or something, Evie. You need a break."

Pulling myself together turned out to be a bigger task than either of us envisaged. I was far more broken than I'd thought. At least, that's how it had felt. I was bedridden for months. Too scared to face the real world. I think I feared that if a single person I knew saw me—really saw my face—they'd *know*. About the failed relationship. Failed PhD. Friendships. Family. Everything.

And if they found out, then I'd have no choice but to do something about it, which is where I am now. A deer in the headlights of an untenable situation that can't be tolerated a second longer but seems equally impossible to face.

I sit down in the café and get my phone out. It's always on silent and I hardly ever check it lately. Too scared of missed calls and messages. Too overwhelmed by notifications. Too sad, to be honest, about the messages that *aren't* there. The calls I don't get. The way everything went so wrong with my parents and Bree. And Drew.

I always separate him, I realize. It's always "My parents and Bree. And Drew." He deserves a category of his own, I guess. I remember when my parents thought it was Drew that I liked. Not Oliver. They probably heard something in my voice that spoke more truth than the bright lights and fanfare of the iridescent romance I was swept away by.

My mind flashes to the day Drew's mother died. That fraction of a kiss. Of all the thousands of kisses I've had with Oliver, not one has occupied as much space in my mind as that one with Drew that barely began. Even now, reminiscing about it, everything plunges inside me in delicious anticipation. And then loss.

I flick open my email app. It's full of marketing promotions and bill reminders and job-search notifications I never look at because it's too depressing wondering how to explain the growing gap in my résumé. It's not like I've had kids. We've tried. Oliver thinks our failure to conceive is all in my mind, that I'm too high-strung and emotional and that's what's stopping my body from just relaxing into motherhood. Perhaps it's more that I've been privately hoping things will change and the relationship will strengthen enough to give me the confidence to bring other humans into it. Every other weekend with Harriet is nowhere near enough parenting for me—she's the only sunlight in my life.

I'm about to close the app when I scroll back up. I'd skipped over the messages so fast, I hadn't noticed one buried between a spam message about a bogus phone bill and something from a meditation app I signed up for, thinking I'd start a daily habit about six years ago.

**FROM:** Drew Kennedy
**SUBJECT:** Pictures of you.

My heart leaps at our exhibition name.

I open the message.

Evie,
I know we haven't spoken in a while. I hope you're well, and Harriet.

This is a short message. And a confession. With a question.

My breaths come erratically. The idea of a confession and a question injects a level of hope into my soul that I haven't felt in a very long time. Hope that has no business being in my soul at all. Not delivered by Drew Kennedy. But I read on.

Remember I always wanted to enter the World Photography Awards? I told you my photos weren't good enough and you insisted they were? Well, on a whim a couple of months ago, I threw together a submission in the portrait category. I'd been cleaning up my storage on the computer and found a bunch of photos I'd taken of you over the years. Nearly deleted them, to be honest. But then . . .

Anyway, I've been shortlisted.

Now for the confession part. Before I submitted the images, I was supposed to get your permission. I never really thought I'd get this far, and the idea of reaching out to you felt overwhelming, so I didn't. I just submitted the entry. Evie, I'm sorry. I shouldn't have done that.

I've attached the images here. You probably should have them, anyway. I understand if you'd rather I didn't go ahead with the competition. Just say the word and I'll withdraw from it.

Let me know, either way?
Thanks,

Drew.

P.S. I had to write an artist's statement to go with them. For what it's worth, I meant every word.

I flick through some of the photos—from the first ones he took of me in Year Eleven, galivanting through the city with him that night we used the film camera, wild and exhilarated, to one of me at Harriet's birthday party, staring out the window, dead inside. I look like a princess trapped in a tower. He may not have meant this, but in chronological order the images strike me as a timeline of how much my life has shrunk. And just how far I've fallen.

I put my phone down on the table and stare at it. Suddenly I don't want to be at the gym while I look through the rest. I don't want to be listening to the grinding of coffee beans and the clanking of barbells. I need to be outside. And alone.

So I gather together my things—the gym bag at my feet, my towel, keys, phone. My heart is beating just as fast as it had on the treadmill half an hour ago as I rush outside, head across the road, and find a place in the park under some trees, where I will click on the file titled *Pictures of You—by Drew Kennedy.*

# 81

***Drew***

It's the artist's statement that worries me most. It's one thing capturing someone on camera and another doing it in words. *If I could reverse time, I'd fight for you . . .*

I like to think I see something in Evie that other people don't. Something Oliver definitely doesn't see. And as besotted as she used to be with him at school, I know she's never looked at him the way she's looking into the lens in every one of these shots.

*It was that time on the beach when you looked straight through the disaster of my life and stayed. When you understood me as I was and didn't want to fix me, or change anything, even though there was so much that needed shifting.*

*It was the night Mum died, when you stood at the kitchen sink waiting patiently for the tap to run hot to wash her hands. Mum, who didn't need warmth by then, but you provided it anyway. It was the way you said, "Annie, I'm just going to pick up your hand," as if Mum was still alive. And how you knew I would want to be the person to do that, before I knew how important that act was myself.*

*It was your utter delight in Jervis Bay, untethered from time or expectation, plunged into life so wholeheartedly, alight with the joy of phosphorescence, dreaming up our futures.*

*It was a million tiny things that add up to the resounding loss of the deepest relationship I've had in my life. It's the loss not only of what we had, and what we could have had—but of the person I saw in you, and the one you imagined becoming.*

*These are pictures of you, Evie, before your large life closed in. Before it folded in on itself, and then folded in again, over and over, until your dreams ran out of oxygen.*

*Pictures of the woman you could be again.*

I wrote those words down, until the document became less of an artist's statement and more of an artist's intervention. Likely the last straw in our relationship, but it had to be done.

I sent the email two hours ago and haven't heard from her. I guess she does have a life. She isn't just sitting there thinking how nice it would be if I dropped into her inbox for the first time in years and told her I was thinking of her. *Still.*

It wasn't a declaration of love. It was a declaration of radical friendship. A last-ditch desire to get through to her. And save her.

And, yes, the exhibition itself is also a career move. There's a quality in these photos that I've never captured in portraits of anyone else my whole professional life. Light seemed to radiate from her.

Whatever it was, I'm freaking out about having sent it now. Is it too late to recall the email? I should just ditch the competition, take the professional hit, and get the fuck over this entire situation once and for all.

People say you never forget your first love. At thirty, after never being quite able to commit to anyone else, and with a string of failed relationships and false starts with the wrong people in my wake, it's time I admit that's what's going on here. Maybe it would have been easier to let her go if I hadn't spent the last thirteen years worried sick.

I pull my sneakers on. I can't sit here refreshing my email all day. Besides, I have a corporate shoot at a bank at midday and need to organize my gear. I'll go for a run, clear my head, and move on with my life.

But just as I'm locking the door, my phone pings with an incoming email.

It's from Evie.

Drew.

You do not have permission. Do not use these photos for this award. Withdraw from the competition. And never contact me again.

Evie.

# 82

***Evie***

I get settled on the grass overlooking the lake, turn my face to the sun, and take a deep breath in a fruitless attempt to ground myself. Then I open my messages. More spam has entered my inbox in the five minutes since I left the gym, and I scroll through, looking for Drew's email.

I think of him often.

Even when things were amazing with Oliver in the early days, I never really felt like myself with him. I was always trying to be the person he wanted. Scared to eat in front of him. Worried about my body. Questioning every step, wishing I was different, or more, or better.

With Drew, I cared only about being alive in the world. I was present in the simplicity of our existence. Of course, at the time my immature teenage perspective interpreted this as comfortable. It couldn't be romantic because it was so stress-free and simple.

Oliver scared me, in a way I thought was all part of falling in love. The intensity of it was so exhilarating I convinced myself it was real because it felt dangerous. But Oliver's increasing vigilance over my life only pinched me further. He constantly chiseled pieces off me. Sculpted me into the woman he wanted.

But he carved out everything inside me at the same time, and now there's nothing left but the brittle shell I've become.

Where is Drew's message? I'm sure I've seen these emails from Amazon already, reminding me of books left in my cart. Yes, I'm now back at messages that came in overnight.

I type his name into the search bar and it filters the inbox. No results. That can't be right. The message from earlier should be there, along with others he's sent me over the years. One telling me he'd had the tests done after we told him about Harriet. Further back, something about the arrangements for his mum's funeral. They're not there, though. None of them are. Including today's with my photos.

I panic. I can't even remember his address. He's not coming up in contacts at all in my email app, so I switch to my texts.

There he is. I'm ridiculously relieved to see his name. Sad that the last messages we exchanged were four years ago, and only terse little snippets—me thanking him for doing the testing for Oliver. Him telling me he wasn't doing it for him, he was doing it for his niece.

"He's not seeing her," Oliver had said, once she was home again. "Family only."

"Drew *is* family," I'd argued.

"Immediate family, I mean." Oliver has always been intent on reducing everything to the smallest common denominator. Him and me. He'd been gruff and annoyed and all kinds of impatient. My pressing the issue about Drew had cost me days of silent treatment.

Drew hung around anyway. He never gave up on his niece. Then there were all the gifts he sent her, which she was never given. *We don't want to spoil her, Evie, just because Drew wants to buy her affections.*

It makes me shudder.

Could you resend your email? I've lost it, I type to Drew now.

Message failed. Tap to retry.

I tap.

Message failed.

How could it have failed? I open the internet browser and type: What does it mean when a message won't go through?

Result: You may have the wrong number. You may not have sufficient cellular service. The person you are messaging may have blocked you.

Blocked me? And recalled the email, perhaps? You can do that these days, can't you? I wish I'd replied at the gym the second I received it. I'm not prepared for how lost I feel without access to him, even though it's been years of struggling through on my own. Big tears well in my eyes and I choke down a rising sob. I just can't understand how my life went so far off the rails. I should have left Oliver *years* ago—when he first started closing in my life, needing to know where I was, shutting out all the people who matter most.

I shouldn't be almost thirty and crying in a park, wishing I was sixteen again and could go back and do everything differently.

I'm still having the existential crisis over my life choices when Oliver finds me. The car screeches into the lot, he slams the door, pulls Harriet out of the back seat, and tosses her onto his shoulders. I'd recognize his determined strides from a mile away. Determined, angry strides, in this case, even with his daughter in tow—though he has a knack for making everything feel fun with her, so she mistakes his mood for horseplay.

Harriet squeals at his blistering approach. I wish he'd put her down, and I wonder what I've done now.

The fear dries my tears. I sense my body tensing. Preparing. Gathering what little strength I have left in my muscles and mind and soul. The adrenaline starts its well-worn course through tired veins, sick of the fight or flight. Craving peace, I put on my "everything is okay" Harriet face.

"Thought I'd find you here," Oliver says when he reaches me, pulling Harriet down off his shoulders and scooping her through the air like she's coming in to land. He did not. I've never been in this park in my life. He tracked me here.

"Evie!" she calls, giggling. Falling into my arms, a welcome beam of sunlight. "Daddy took me to the *beach*! We had ice creams and went swimming and built sandcastles and he buried me up to my *neck*!"

I feel like he's buried me up to my neck, too, and that I'm forever trying to extract my arms and dig myself free.

"We forgot sunscreen," she confesses, holding out her little arms, investigating the redness.

"I put it on you," he says, irritated.

"Daddy, you said not to tell."

"Stop lying, Harri."

She looks crushed and confused, and I ask her what flavor ice cream she chose—practiced sorcery designed to distract and diffuse.

"Come on," he says, extending his hand and pulling me roughly to my feet by my wrist. He scoops up my gym bag and starts walking in the direction he came from, while Harriet grasps my hand and swings happily between us as we go.

"Let's get *milkshakes*!" she suggests, hopefully. I'm about to say yes, when Oliver turns around and drops her hand.

"You had ice cream. We need to take you back to Mummy."

It's not drop-off time until five. I hope we don't ruin Chloe's plans for a relaxing afternoon. It's a tough gig raising a child mostly alone, and I love having Harriet. I shiver at the idea of divorcing him and rupturing this second family of hers, even if we see her only every other weekend and during the holidays. Harriet is the only part of this relationship that is real.

As we follow Oliver across the park, I watch him unzip my bag, pull out a chocolate bar, and toss it into a bin as he passes. "You don't need that crap, Evie."

There are moments in life when everything comes into sharp focus. I've felt stuck in this nightmare for so many years that I blocked out much of it. You'd think it would be something big and obvious that would cause me to snap. His screaming at me for inadvertently leaving my phone on silent after going to the movies. Throwing a glass at the kitchen wall when I was home late. But in the end, it's the simple act of flinging a Mars bar into a rubbish bin in front of his impressionable daughter, whom he's just gaslit over sunscreen, that pushes me to a place where I've not only had enough but have dredged some lost pocket of courage I need to fight back.

We buckle Harriet back into the car and drive to Chloe's. She lives in the kind of ramshackle rental I'd adore right now. A little two-bedroom terrace with vines running riot up the bricks, potted plants crowding the front steps, and nowhere near enough room for all their stuff. It feels like a home should.

She flings open the door in shorts, a T-shirt, and headphones, like she's about to go for a run. "Oh, hi! I didn't expect you this early!"

Harriet disentangles herself from Oliver's arms and runs in to play with their new puppy. It's all okay. Chloe will just have to reschedule her exercise. Everyone has to reschedule and rearrange and fit in.

"I thought you said you'd taken off the tracking app?" I say, as we walk back to the car after saying goodbye. It's a bold statement, given the bad mood he'd been covering until we'd off-loaded Harriet. We'd argued over the app again recently, when I told him I was sick of him knowing my every move.

"It's to keep you safe, Evie," he says now. "That's all I ever want."

I'm not particularly unsafe. Not physically. At least not when I'm out in the world without him. Psychologically, I'm in real danger, but that's his doing.

"You're always underestimating risks," he continues. "People get obsessed with things—and with people that they can't have."

He is out of his mind. I'd suggest a psych evaluation for delusions and paranoia, but of course he'd never go for that.

"I love you," he tells me, for the millionth time. "I love you more than anyone else ever could." He means Drew, of course. It's *always* about Drew. In fact . . . right now, as I look at the jealousy contorting across Oliver's face, the penny finally drops. The explanation for why I've never felt good enough. Why I've endlessly wondered what he saw in me and why he held on so vehemently to our floundering relationship when he could have released me and had his pick of anyone else that he wanted. It was never about loving me. It was about hating Drew. From the moment Drew reached in and pulled me out of that swimming pool away from him.

"I just don't want anything to happen to you, Evie. I'm protecting you," he says now.

We've been around this buoy a thousand times. We never get

anywhere, other than into an angry mess, devolving into him going silent, eventually, and that is always the worst part. There's power in silence. More power, sometimes, than when things are explosive.

We reach his car and he opens the passenger door for me. Always the gentleman in public. An elderly woman nearby nudges her companion, hand on her heart, and smiles in our direction. I can almost hear her thoughts: *Look at that, Shirley! Chivalry isn't dead . . .*

Oliver's brand of chivalry is going to kill me.

I get in and pull my seat belt on, feeling even further restricted.

He swings into the driver's side, pushing angry energy into the car, his demeanor shifting again, plunging me into a familiar mental tussle as I attempt to work out what he wants from me and how I'm going to navigate my way out of this. Whatever I deduce is on his mind, it never seems to be that. Whatever steps I take to try to shift his mood, they're always wrong.

So this time I do nothing. I say nothing to try to change him. I disengage.

Of course, that's wrong too.

"What's up with you?" he says as he drives out of the parking lot, too fast, and into the slip lane.

I stare out the window. Where would I even start in answering a question like that?

"I asked you what's wrong," he repeats, his voice firmer this time.

He misses the turnoff to our suburb.

I look at him now. "Where are we going?"

"For a drive. We need to talk."

*We need to talk.* Such frightening words, usually. But so true in this case. And here is the opportunity I'm looking for to raise the topic I've avoided for far too many years.

He drives toward the freeway. It's not in the direction of home. I piece together the route we're taking and it looks like we're heading out of the city. We can't go away. I don't even have a bag packed. I glance into the back seat to see if he's thrown some clothes together for me, but it's pristine and empty.

"I agree we need to talk," I say, "but can't we go home?"

"I feel like driving."

It's always whatever he feels like doing. I'm never included in decisions like this. It's all so different from when we first got together and he put me center stage and did anything I wanted.

"Are you happy, Oliver?" I venture. I know it's dangerous, and that's confirmed when his fingers tighten around the steering wheel.

"What an odd question."

"I mean are *we* happy?"

His foot pushes the accelerator and I grip the sides of my seat. "Are *you* happy, Evie?"

How do you tell your husband you are miserable and it's his fault and you want out? Any time in the past when we've skated close to the topic of how we're doing, I've backed away. I've never been able to say these words, because I've always been so scared of the ramifications if I did. But suddenly, today, maybe because of the reminder of Drew, I'm more scared of *not* saying this. More scared of the status quo than of worsening consequences. My life, if I stay with him, is over anyway.

A long silence later, and he's heading for the Illawarra escarpment. Are we driving to Wollongong? Maybe he's taking me to Kiama or something. I'm increasingly nervous and certainly not going to continue this conversation while we're on this particular road. Macquarie Pass has always made me uneasy. Just a feeling I've always had on that mountain, ever since I was a kid. We'd go on coach trips for school excursions and I'd be terrified as the bus clung to the crumbling pavement, the ravine falling away to the side, fear stopping me from taking in the spectacular view of lush forest, sweeping into the valley, toward the ocean.

"You haven't answered my question," he says at last. He's gripping the steering wheel so hard now the whites of his knuckles are gleaming.

"Can we talk about this when we get there?" I beg him.

He looks at me, and I wish he'd look back at the road. It's treacherous.

"It should be a simple yes or no, Evie. You're either happy or you're not. I've given you everything you ever wanted."

*Does he know me at all?*

"All I wanted was to prove myself academically and get a job and make a difference. And I've lost that."

"Because you're mentally unwell."

He thinks he's been loving and generous to let me step back while he took care of things. I thought he was, too, at the time. But wasn't it just another way to keep me needing him? The more anxious I became, the more he seemed to enjoy taking care of me. My anxiety fed his need to be the one I depended on.

"Remember when we met?" he says. "You adored me."

"You flooded me with attention. You helped Bree."

"How?"

"Don't you remember? You got that horrible website taken down."

He laughs. "God, Evie, you've always been so gullible."

*What?*

"Oliver, tell me you had someone else take that site down." I can't let myself imagine what he means right now. His decision to step in and do this for Bree was a major factor in the infancy of my crush. It was the gallant act that I clung to, once the gloss of physical attraction wasn't enough.

He looks at me, veering off the road and back onto it, his driving getting worse by the second. "It took me five minutes to unpublish and cancel the domain name."

This can't be true.

"But the black eye? You said you got into a fight with the boy responsible?"

He laughs. "The black eye was from the brawl at the pool."

I stare at him, while a kind of rage I've never experienced erupts. *Oliver* was behind that site? *My husband.* Responsible for all that carnage in teenage girls' lives. And then he passed himself off as the hero and lured me into his web?

"Pull over, Oliver? I feel sick."

But he speeds up, taking the corners even faster. And I realize the sick feeling in my stomach isn't from motion. It's from some uncanny, almost psychic premonition that this is about to end in disaster. Because I know I shouldn't say this next thing. Not right here. I desperately want to stop the words even before they start pouring out of my mouth, but my brain has snapped and it's as if I can't undo the inevitable and, on some level, don't even care.

"Oliver, I want a divorce."

# 83

***Drew***

I don't usually watch the six-o'clock news. I reached a point around the time Mum died when I realized my quota of "darkness" was full.

Tonight, I have the television on in the background—probably for company—while I'm processing photos in Lightroom. This is the part of photography that I love most. Taking the raw files and creating art with them. Subtly enhancing the colors. Adjusting the balance. Wherever the mood takes me, creatively.

Monochrome tonight. Unsurprising, in the circumstances.

I'm trying to ignore the way Evie ended our friendship, for good this time. Her email had a level of formality bordering on callousness that I know I don't deserve. But rather than get angry, I just feel defeated. Defeated by an entire friendship that began with all the promise in the world and ended in inexplicable silence.

"A thirty-year-old man was killed this afternoon on Macquarie Pass when he lost control of the BMW he was driving on the notoriously dangerous stretch of road. A woman, twenty-nine, was injured in the crash and airlifted to Saint Vincent's Private Hospital, where it's understood she remains in serious but stable condition. No further details have been released about the accident, but police have urged any witnesses to come forward, appealing for dash cam footage of the crash."

My heart stills. Somehow, I know. Time shudders and lurches over some fault line in the universe.

Even before looking at the screen, I know I'll see images of Oliver's crumpled white BMW sedan. I'm already imagining her lying in a hospital bed. No, I'm already reaching for my keys and jacket. My body leaves my apartment and gets in the car before my brain can catch up with the plan. They hadn't even named the couple. I just *know*. And, as pictures of our friendship flit across my mind, I'm compelled to go to her. I don't even care if she pushes me away again. I just have to see her.

The drive to the hospital is clogged with traffic, and, when I eventually arrive, the garage is full. My blood pressure hits the roof. I don't even know why I'm rushing. She might not even agree to see me. I just want to see with my own eyes that she is alive.

Finally, I pull into half a car space at the end of a row and risk a fine. I slam the door and lock it, the sound reverberating off the concrete walls. I stride in through a maze of corridors and approach the reception desk.

"Evie Hudson," I say, then correct myself. "Sorry, Roche."

The receptionist types thc name into the computer and tells me Evie's in the acute-care ward. She points me through and I find my way to a nurses' station. It's all too reminiscent of being here with Mum.

"I'm afraid we can only let family in," she tells me.

"I'm her brother-in-law." I hate the words. I'm so much more than that.

She looks at me and shapes her expression into pity. "Oh, I'm terribly sorry for your loss."

The words punch me, before I realize she means Oliver. I stare at her and say thank you, even though Oliver's loss feels like nothing to me. Absolutely nothing. Just a static buzz where grief would be, if this had been a normal brotherly relationship.

I'm shown to a cubicle where Evie is unconscious, monitors beeping around her.

"You're the first family member to have been in."

"Has anyone called her parents?"

She shakes her head. "The only next-of-kin information we had was for Oliver Roche. I'm sorry, we didn't know there was a brother."

*Brother* still feels like an empty word. I shake it off and put my jacket over the back of a chair, moving closer to her bed.

She looks peaceful. A little battered, but not as bad as I'd envisaged. Her wrists, lying still at her sides, are bruised, and there's a red mark across her neck where the seat belt must have tightened against her. I brush the dark hair, straightened to glossiness from its natural curl, across her face, and her eyelids flutter as if they're going to open, but they don't. All I can think about is how much she's already been through, the traumatic way it ended, and what's ahead of her. My heart races the way it always does around her, but with an extra impetus this time, because I came so dangerously close to giving up on her.

I gently take her hand. "Evie? It's me."

The heart rate monitor beside her has a sudden uptick in resting pulse. The nurse walks in, checks it, and looks from her to me. "Her brain needs to rest," she says. "It might be too early for the excitement of visitors."

*Excitement.* I'm not sure that's the right word in this case, but the nurse reads my wretched expression.

"We'll tell her you stopped by," she says softly, then checks the equipment and pats me on the arm. "Judging by that monitor, though, I think she already knows."

# 84

***Evie***

It's four o'clock in the morning when Drew wakes me in my parents' spare room. I've had the most unsettling, horrible nightmare, but I can't hold on to it in my mind.

"Evie," he's saying, shaking my shoulder. "Wake up."

I open my eyes, and he's perched beside me on the bed, fully dressed, in jeans and a T-shirt.

"Get up, Hudson. Get dressed. Meet me in the car."

"Are we running away? What is it?"

"Just trust me."

He leaves the room and, a minute later, I hear him leave the house and close the door quietly, while I dash to the bathroom and pull on a dress I grabbed from Mum's wardrobe yesterday. Some white, shapeless thing that she's probably never worn, and no wonder. Not exactly the Bonnie and Clyde outfit Drew might be going for if we are, in fact, running away, but it's all I've got.

I slip outside and into the passenger seat and he wastes no time starting up the engine.

"So we're stealing my parents' car now?"

He smiles. "I promise we'll have it back by breakfast."

It's about forty-five minutes to Brighton Beach—less at this time of morning, particularly at the speed Drew is driving. We arrive and park, and if we're here for a beach sunrise, I wonder why he didn't pick a closer one.

He takes my hand once I'm out of the car and drags me down the sandy path toward the ocean. I'm not even remotely near the shoreline when I see why he's brought me here. With every crashing wave, the ocean is lit up in blue, sparkling phosphorescence. I stop on the sand and just watch.

"Every time I see it it's like the first time all over again," he says. I know this is for my benefit, because I was so brokenhearted to know I'd forgotten.

"How did you know?"

"Location-centric alert on a photography app on my phone."

I pull the slides off my feet and tear toward the water, running straight into the waves, stepping over them, falling into them full-tilt, splashing everywhere.

He's on the shore, watching, kicking his shoes off and carefully rolling up the cuffs of his jeans like he might step tentatively into the shallows. I'll have none of that. I wade out of the water and pull him out into the depths with me, waves crashing over our calves, and then our thighs, the hem of my white dress floating up in the water around me.

"Don't get it in your mouth," he warns, and I ensure that won't happen by dragging him close, throwing my arms around his neck, wrapping my legs around his hips, and planting my lips on his.

I feel like I'm floating as the ocean builds around us, waves rising as Drew stands firm on the sandy floor, hands at my waist. I shut my eyes, the shock of cold water swirling at my hips as white-hot flames catch alight between us.

"Did we do this the first time around?" I ask, between breaths.

He pulls me closer, one hand trailing up my back and through my hair. "No," he replies.

His mouth meets mine again. Not even the phosphorescence is enough to distract me from a kiss that seems to encompass every second of remembered and forgotten time. My hands cradle his face as he carries me deeper into the water, my mouth trailing along his cheekbones—strong contours, familiar even to the part of me that can't remember him. His lips explore my neck and my back arches, my legs falling from his hips and my feet finding the sand beneath the water. I burrow my face into his chest, holding him in a hug so all-encompassing it transcends the need I've had, all this time, to "know."

And then . . . from another place and time, stark, bright flashes of light and knowledge.

*Not now.*

My lips find his again, but the pictures won't stop. I try to push them away and focus on this profoundly beautiful moment in time, but my mind glitches and a barrage of glittering stills and moving scenes flood my consciousness.

"*Stop it.*"

He pulls back instantly.

"Not this!" I launch us back into the kiss. But there they are again, thousands of images crowding at once, in an overwhelming rush of remembering.

And now the pain.

Suddenly, my head is exploding with pressure. I stop kissing him and moan, my hand shooting to my temple.

"Evie, what is it?" He takes my face in both of his hands. And, as he looks at me, water churning around us, first light creeping above the horizon, I know it's finally safe to pull toward me all the knowledge I've been resisting.

"Why did I quit my doctorate?" I ask him.

"You want to discuss your doctorate? Now?"

He doesn't know I'm on the verge of some massive breakthrough. The neurologist I saw at the hospital said this is how it can happen. All these random flashes of memory can give way to it flooding back suddenly, and I'm sure I'm right on the brink.

"What was my thesis topic?" I ask.

He seems confused. "We didn't really know each other then. You weren't talking to me, remember? Sorry. I know you can't remember. I can barely think after that kiss."

"Drew, please! This is important."

He struggles to recall the information. "Something about linguistic fingerprinting? Idio-something? I'm not the linguist, Evie."

"Idiolect?" I say. "Someone's patterns of language use."

He leads me out of the water again and onto dryer sand, so we can have this conversation without being pounded by waves.

"Your father always got the order of adjectives wrong," I tell him.

"Yes, we've been over this. We have this wild suspicion he murdered my mother, but all we've got to go on is a wedding speech."

"Yeah, but in my nightmare last night, I received an anonymous letter someone sent to my office at the university."

The more I dwell on this, the clearer it's coming into focus. My office. Piles of paper with my research. The envelope. No stamp. No return address. It wasn't a nightmare. "'You're an interfering, young, conniving, dangerous woman . . .'" I say, all our previous suspicions refracting through this one crystal memory.

"Is that what it said?" Drew says, suddenly far more intrigued.

"The speech, the note, and now this letter. No wonder I'd written *Adjective order* in that notebook in my podcast studio."

"What else did the letter say?"

"'Pull your research. Pull your research, Evie, or . . .'"

My blood runs cold.

I look at Drew and know my face is an open book. Suddenly, *everything* crashes back in and I feel panicked and sick. "Oh my God," I cry.

I remember *every little thing*. It's just like that sense people talk about, before death, of seeing your life flash in front of your eyes.

But I'm not about to die. I'm waking up, and remembering every aspect of the arduous, horrendous story of the last thirteen years.

# 85

***Drew***

Finally, she's back. I can see every moment of our past reflecting across her face. She knows me. She remembers it all. This is Evie, with her full memory intact, reliving every moment that has brought us here.

"Drew!" She's shaking violently. It's like some sort of horrific, religious exorcism. But it's not about shaking things out or off. It's about things crowding in, swamping her.

"I remember it all," she says, wailing. "I'm so sorry!" She grabs both of my arms and holds on to me as if I'm going to flee. I'm not leaving. Not this time. I stand in front of her on the sand and stay with her while our entire history lands. While everything that happened to her reforms in her brain, settling into familiar neural pathways, bringing it all up and back and taking her through a life her mind has protected her from for days.

"Please stay?" she whispers. "I can explain."

Of course I'll stay. I wrap my arms tightly around her in an attempt to convince her she's not in this alone anymore.

"Oliver . . ."

Here it comes. The memories I've feared. The all-powerful sway. For thirteen years, no matter what he did, she always took him back. She was pulled toward him by some unseen magnetic force that forgave and forgave and forgave . . .

A sob rises from somewhere deep within her.

"He's dead," she cries. "Oliver is dead. The accident . . ." Visions of it seem to play across her face. It's like watching torture cross her mind.

And then she falls into uncontrolled emotion that seems to erupt from some place deeper inside her than I've ever known.

She looks into my face, ashen and distraught, and says, "Drew, it was all my fault!"

# 86

***Evie***

*Evie, if I can't have you . . .*

Oliver's last words crash in. You're meant to spread this horror out over *years*. It's even worse than squeezing a whole plot about someone's life into a movie—at least then you get two hours for it to play out. This is instant delivery of a huge chunk of my life, and I can't take it.

I'm standing on the beach, luminescent waves crashing beside us, but at the same time I'm back in the car on that cliff, hood crumpled against a tree, engine hissing, steam rising and swirling into the fog on the hillside, which seemed to have hushed around us—even the insects went into silent shock. Just the sound of our car, creaking and shuddering.

It was terrifying. I remember looking at Oliver and wondering who he was. Motionless. Blood oozing from his forehead. Eyes glassy, staring straight ahead. Only the very real pain shooting through my body told me this was real, and not some gruesome nightmare.

*That man is dead,* I thought. My eyes dropped to the wedding ring on his left hand, which had fallen into my lap.

Dead and *married.* Why was I in a car on the side of a mountain with a dead married man?

It's like I'm processing the memory of being confused now, while layering over it my intimate knowledge of the entire situation. Understanding exactly how we got there, and what led to him being so angry and losing control on that bend.

*No.*

"He didn't lose control," I say so softly Drew can't understand me. "Drew, he didn't lose control on that bend. He sped up!"

Now I'm flashing right back to high school and the first time we met. Oliver plunging into that pool with me. Drew dragging me out. Every tiny step we took that led us down a path I doubt either of us envisaged—a relationship born from jealousy and infatuation that burnt so brightly even as it went so catastrophically wrong.

The marriage empty, in the end, of everything except emotional violence. Him so angry. Me always so scared.

"I could have been stronger," I say softly. "I knew he was treating me badly . . ."

"Abusing you," Drew corrects.

"Shouldn't I have stood up to it, though? I'm an intelligent woman. Why didn't I just leave?"

He looks at me, straight on and serious. "Evie, he had you on a pedestal so high at the start and then pelted you with so many rocks, you couldn't find a way to clamber down. No move you made was safe. It doesn't matter how many letters there are after your name or how strong you are . . ."

Now I'm seeing the love-bombing at the start. The monitoring in the guise of supporting me. The hacking away of my self-esteem with every criticism along the way. I watched the life I longed for fall away from me. My plans. My higher degree.

He wanted to control the podcast I built, claiming he was "helping" me by producing the episodes. He was always making me dress in certain clothes and wear my hair a different way. Constantly editing, censoring. Not just the podcast, but every tiny aspect of my existence.

I glance at Drew and now everything floods in about him. All my feelings for him. The loss of the most important friend I ever had. *The day I missed his mother's funeral.* Standing on that cliff with Oliver, who wasn't ever going to really jump, and being forced to make the wrong choice, on the off chance that he wasn't bluffing. He knew I'd stay. He knew I couldn't bear to live with myself if it was my rejection that caused him to end it all, so he played that card, and Drew paid for it.

"I'm sorry," I whisper. "I'm so sorry, I'm so sorry . . ." It's all I can utter. He doesn't even know which bit I'm sorry for. It's all of it. "I wanted to be there for you at the funeral. I was on my way. And then Oliver . . ."

He shushes me and hugs me into his chest. I clutch his shirt and cry. More than a decade's worth of tears. So much grief smashing over me as the waves crash. So many dreams pixelated, fading into nothing. And I'm aware, suddenly, of the impact on my mind. The instability. The fear. The destruction of my confidence. How reluctant I have been to take any step, in any direction. Always potentially wrong, until that spiraled into mental illness—a dark whirlpool of anxiety and depression flaring at its height into fear for everyone I loved. Fear for my own life. Until my body couldn't take another second of the trauma and let go of even caring, flinging me into the safe haven of amnesia where I was protected from it all.

And then, right when I think I've remembered each tiny detail, I recall the trigger for everything.

# 87

***Drew***

I can't work out whether to let her ramble or call her parents or the ambulance. She's so distressed, she's all over the place. It must be horrific, being confronted with everything all at once. All her losses. Every complex emotion she's ever had, about every event, all mixed up. And she is gripping hold of me so hard it almost hurts.

"I pushed you away," she says, crying. "I pushed you all away."

I want to tell her it's okay. But it never was. She hurt us deeply, and now she's looking at me, her face a mess of understanding.

"Drew, it was all for you," she admits.

I don't understand.

"That letter . . ." she says.

"From Anderson?"

She starts pacing along the sand. "'Interfering, young, conniving, dangerous woman.' Of course it was him! Hear the pattern?" She stops. "I found his weird way of talking so fascinating. It's why I started studying author profiling in the first place . . ."

She's lit up like I haven't seen since we were at school and we'd get into a debate about something political or controversial. I used to provoke her sometimes—I'd fling a statement at her that I knew she'd want to argue with, because I wanted to see her this *alive*.

"When I read your mum's note," she says, pausing to place her hand on my arm empathetically, "I knew that was a strange way of constructing a sentence. But she was so sick, and on so many drugs—I didn't think much more of it."

I nod. I'd been too distressed to question it, either.

"Then I'd been so stressed out the day we got married. I was so worried I'd done the wrong thing. That Bree had been right, and I should have let her call it off. I wasn't properly listening to the speeches."

She sits on the sand, drawing her knees up close and hugging them. I get down beside her.

"It wasn't until Anderson started botching this in every conversation that I started paying closer attention. Because people typically don't speak like that. They simply get it right, all the time. Or wrong, in his case."

"That's when I started looking into similar cases. I came up with a research project for my doctorate that supported all the groundbreaking case studies that already enthralled me. To use linguistic evidence to crack cases where DNA or eyewitness evidence alone isn't enough . . . Think of it, Drew!"

I smile gently. "You get your memory back and it's all about the academics? Nothing's changed. But why did you drop the doctorate when it meant everything to you? You gave in to his demand?"

"He found out," she explains. "Oliver must have explained to Anderson what my thesis topic was, not realizing the link. His father sent me the threatening note, but I kept going. And then he turned up in my office one night, drunk. Terrifying. And demanded I pull out of the program. Destroy my research. I hadn't even been focusing on him—he'd just piqued my interest because it was such a good example of a clear linguistic anomaly. But then I wondered why he cared so much about what I was researching. And what he'd done . . ."

I can guess where this is heading. Part of me can't bear the confirmation.

"I knew I'd heard someone else speak like that but couldn't remember where. Until I finally remembered your mum's note. And when he suspected I was onto him, he was furious. I'm talking all-out, blood-boiling rage."

"Worried you'd pieced it together and would talk?"

"Worried I'd write a whole thesis about it! Or blather on my podcast, though there was little chance of that. The Roches drew up a nondisclosure agreement—I was banned from ever discussing family affairs—they were still so suspicious of my platform. That's why Oliver started producing my content. They couldn't let me have even that one thing just for myself. But then I confronted Anderson, Drew. About your mum. And I realized just how much he had to hide."

"About what? Her note?"

"Not about that, no."

"What, then? Him being my father? I mean, it's a bit scandalous, I guess, that he had another kid with someone else. But it's hardly earth-shattering. Even when the truth did come out when he was desperate about Harriet, it might have strained their marriage behind closed doors, but they're the type of family to push through it. It didn't cause a blip, professionally."

She looks wildly uncomfortable suddenly, even more than she did a minute ago. "It was more than that. While Anderson was throwing his weight around in my office, I felt physically threatened. And I had a flash of this time in Florence, with

Oliver. In bed. It wasn't just once, to be honest. It wasn't assault, exactly. But I suppose technically it wasn't *not* assault . . ."

She trips over her words as they struggle out of her mouth and I stare at her, horrified. Anger flaming right to the edges of my soul.

"It was borderline," she concludes, her upturned, injured face telling me a completely different truth.

"There is no such thing," I say, firmly. "No borderline. Evie, I'm so sorry."

"But Drew"—she looks at me, tears spilling down her cheeks now—"it wasn't borderline with Anderson and your mum. Not remotely."

A large wave crashes onto the beach and barrels toward us. Evie lurches to her feet away from it, but I can't move. It rushes at me. All of it. The white foam on the sand. The truth about who Anderson is. Who Oliver is.

*Who I am . . .*

The water recedes and she steps toward me again, holding out her hand to help pull me to my feet so we can stumble from the tide, where we fall again.

"By this stage I had almost given up," she admits.

"On what?"

"I'd already lost almost everything that mattered. It was late. I was the last one working in the faculty. Anderson was drunk and dangerous. Maybe I had a death wish? So I went for him. I confronted him. And maybe he really did intend to silence me that night because, Drew, he confessed everything. I think he meant to cleanse his soul by admitting it, finally, to someone, and then to erase me. But he must have lost his nerve."

I can barely breathe, with what she's telling me.

"I know exactly what happened that day with your mum."

# 88

***Evie***

Drew's hand holds firm on my knee. I'm about to tell him the hardest thing I've ever had to say to anyone, but he's looking at me, ready for it, while first light breaks on the horizon.

"Your mum knew she was dying," I begin. "She reached out to Anderson in a last-ditch attempt to help you."

The pain I'm inflicting, visible across his face, is almost too much to bear.

"Go on," he says.

"She knew the truth about him and what he'd done to her. All she wanted in her final days was to set you up for life. Have him give you the financial comfort you deserved as his son."

"She agreed not to ask him for more money. It was their arrangement," he argues.

"She was the one with all the power, though. She had maybe days left. She knew his secret violent past. So she demanded he do the right thing by you and change his will."

"He wouldn't do that," I scoff.

"No. So she threatened to file a report for a historic sexual assault offense if he didn't, and *that* would have destroyed him."

"He couldn't risk an arrest," Drew guesses. "And he couldn't risk blowing up his family. Mum could have brought down his entire life."

"Yes. And here he was, an experienced anesthetist with access to drugs that could have led to an overdose? And no one would be suspicious because of your mom's condition."

"Did he admit to that?"

"No."

I feel like I'm looking into the face of the younger boy I knew, in an adult body. I am shattering him on this shoreline.

Drew puts his head in his hands. I feel guilty for lobbing this at him, but I have to keep going—I'm scared if I don't say it as fast as it's coming back, I'll forget again.

"I figured it out myself," I explain. "I told him I knew he wrote your mum's note. An extra layer of protection in case it all fell through, and they did investigate further. I'm lucky he didn't kill me."

This makes him drop his hands and look at me again, weariness and concern evident across his dark features. "Why didn't he?"

"He was already on borrowed time. He'd got away with assault. With murder. I was thoroughly beaten down by Oliver at this point—and malleable. Anderson is a very astute man. He understood me, because he and Oliver and Gwendolyn had created this pliable version of me. They'd shaped me. He knew I'd bend to his will . . ."

"What did he make you do?" The anger is simmering in his tone. "Evie? Did he threaten you?"

I shake my head and look him square in the face. *Oh, God.* The truth is awful. I can barely utter it. "He made me promise never to say anything about this, and to disappear from all of your lives," I say, crying.

"Or what?"

I simply have to speak it. So I take a deep breath, and look beyond how mixed up it all is, and how confused I am, and how unwelcome this admission might be. "His exact words were that I had to cut all ties with all of you completely. Or something was going to happen to the man I love. His son."

He stares at me, surprised. "He threatened to hurt Oliver? Evie, that doesn't make any sense . . ."

I breathe deeply before making it perfectly clear: "No. Not Oliver."

*This* part I hadn't thought sufficiently through. The sacrifice I made, losing my relationship with my own parents, sentencing myself to a life of desperate loneliness—*it was all for Drew.*

Waves of memories break over me. Drew ambling into that classroom studio, looking so rough, because he was a teenage caretaker at the time, with a mum who was painfully unwell. Me, launching straight at him, demanding things of him. Him, rising to every demand, every time.

Right from the start, he stepped in behind me and pushed me forward into the life I wanted. He was never in front of me. Never in my way. He believed in me when I didn't believe in myself. And he's *still* here. Thirteen years later, even after I banished him from my life. Twice.

"'Pretend you don't know me . . .'" he says quietly.

"When I sent that text, it was because Oliver was threatening to jump off the cliff at The Gap if I didn't. He forced me to push you away, by threatening his own life. He said his death would be on me. Drew, I had to make the call. Not showing up to your mum's funeral is the worst thing I've ever done."

He is quiet, which unnerves me, but then a trace of compassion washes over his face. "I cut myself off from the very people who'd held me through everything," I say.

"You were prepared to stay isolated and alone and miserable in a terrible relationship for the rest of your life. You gave up your career. Everyone you needed . . ."

*That's how much I love you.*

"You've been here, all along," I tell him. "From the second you looked at me, with your feet up on that desk and your shoelaces undone, polishing that lens and asking me for my thoughts about the photo exhibit."

Within seconds, years seem to melt off him. Lines erase. The weight lifts.

Everything I feel for this man floods in, and I *lose* myself in the depths of it. Even with amnesia, I couldn't deny my intense attraction to him, and that he was a man I could love—maybe *had* loved. But this . . . this knowing that it was him all along, this is the truth I'd always kept from myself. Because acknowledging it while I was so deeply trapped would have razed me to the ground.

Just as quickly as my memory crashed back, fresh thoughts smash through all that hurt, past every wrong turn in the landscape I'd once been lost in, and storm to the surface. Visions of me and Drew and Harriet, older than she is now. Christmases in New York. Drew behind the camera, me in academic robes, speaking onstage . . .

It's every secret hope I'd never dared to picture until it was safe. *Until I was safe.*

Strangely, the only thing my mind is struggling to picture now is Oliver. When I try to, it's as though the amnesia left one last protective layer. All I imagine now is a blurred school uniform, leadership badges clinking—tiny emblems of empty promise for the "boy most likely to succeed."

I look at Drew.

"I need to get my life back. And my doctorate. And my podcast. I need *all the counseling* . . . and to rebuild everything with Mum and Dad. I want to meet Ivy and make it up to Bree. And I want us to go to the police and take down Anderson . . . I've got so much catching up to do." Even as the dreams are tumbling out of my mouth and I'm at risk of hyperventilating, I realize I don't have to do any of this alone anymore.

"It's Day One, Evie. We're not in any rush."

Drew tilts his head and tucks my hair behind my ear, his eyes taking a million years to travel slowly back to mine. Suddenly my heart thuds and my breath quickens, as if this is the start of a very inconvenient panic attack. But as he holds me in his steady gaze, I know this is something else entirely. It's excitement. It's delirious hope. It's me not wanting to wait, trusting him to stand with me now. And as I acclimatize to the sudden loss of gravity, I seem to breathe in every second of our history, from the moment he listened to my idea in that classroom and helped me make *Pictures of You* something special to his bringing me to the magic of this beach. All of it galvanizing me until our future catches alight.

"Drew, is there any chance you might want to take pictures of me forever?"

My suggestion seems to swirl through the air, an invisible

string holding a showcase of our best moments, mental images spinning gently in the silence as he contemplates the offer. This man is my safe place. He's my soft place to land. He's the ocean pontoon, from which I can dive as deeply as I want and always swim back to where it's secure and warm and protected.

"For all those years, it should have been you," I admit.

He reaches over and pushes me down onto the sand, leaning ove me so close I imagine I can feel his heart pounding through our clothes. "For all those years, Evie, it *was* you."

When we eventually break away and contemplate the distance we've traversed and the magnitude of the future we're planning, the sunrise has burst over the horizon, phosphorescence imperceptible again. It's still there, the neon magic. We just can't see it. And that feels like hope.

I raise my phone to take a selfie of our tearstained, sand-streaked faces. I know how it feels to lose every recollection, and I never want to forget this one.

"Smile, Kennedy," I say, and this time he doesn't hesitate. This time he's all in.

*This* time, it's luminescent.

# Author's Note

*Pictures of You* contains themes of domestic and family violence, sexual violence, gaslighting, coercive control, suicide ideation, parental death, and childhood illness. The novel was sewn together in response to schoolyard conversations I had in the 1980s and to messages from strong, brilliant women in their fifties, but it was my daughter Hannah Robertson's doctoral research that brought home for me the widespread and insidious nature of coercive control. It has been a beautiful privilege to work closely with my adult child on a fictional representation of the real-world problems she's tackling in the academic arena. Hannah, I'm enormously proud of you and your peers—young women who are working hard, like Evie did, to make the world safer for each other. This book is for you.

• • •

To Zibby Owens, Anne Messitte, Kathleen Harris, and to Diana, Sherri, Sam, Gabby, and the entire Zibby Media team, you are dream-makers who never rest in your drive to share our stories with the world. To the team at Penguin Random House Australia, particularly Ali Watts, Amanda Martin, Jessica Malpass, thank you for believing in my work. You have all changed my life.

To my agent, Anjanette Fennell—you are a tireless champion and dear friend. Together with Lou Johnson and Jeanne Ryckmans from Key People Literary Management, you give me every confidence in the future.

Katherine Berney has provided deep support and professional guidance. Thanks also to Brie for offering professional expertise.

Gaetane Burkolter has strengthened every fictional world I've created. Kate Solly, Kerryn Mayne, Sandie Docker, Nina Campbell, Rachael Morgan, Fionna Roberts, Vanessa Monaghan, Anna "Ruby" Rare, and all in the Canberra Romance Writers group have offered boundless support.

This book was written against a backdrop of extreme professional highs and opportunities (and pressure) and deep grief. While writing it, *The Last Love Note* became an international bestseller, and my beautiful mum slipped away from dementia. Thank you for pulling me through all of this and everything else, Lyndal, Ali, Al, Sal, Alison, Sarah, and Audrey and dear neighbours April, Mikey, Clair, and Harry.

Sarah, Abbey and Lucy, you continue to #KTF that I can do this and I feel your superhuman support. Victoria, Jake, Duncan, Meg, Rex, and Julian—I hit the family jackpot with you in my life.

Sophie and Sebastian, I always feel your incredible love, no matter where we all are. I don't know how I got so lucky as a mum.

Dad, you are my biggest cheerleader and forever our proud father and grandfather. We will never forget feeling this loved.

Jeff, the strength of your belief in my work pushes me

through the moments where I waver, even after all this time. I will love you and feel you around me forever.

Finally, to Mum. You didn't get to hold this one in your hands, but you always held me—even when you'd forgotten who I was. It was your hand that I felt on my shoulder minutes after you'd gone. Your pride, encouragement, and sweeping love shines on.

# About the Author

**EMMA GREY** is the author of six books, including two young adult novels, two non-fiction books on parenting, and her adult debut, the global breakout bestseller *The Last Love Note.* Grey lives in Canberra, Australia, where her world centers on her three children, loved stepchildren, and stepgrandchildren, writing, photography, and endlessly chasing the aurora australis.